The views faded to a shot of Earth's surface, by night, dated the day the Plague was announced. There were more as the plague progressed and the sparkling strands of light slowly began to turn off, portion by portion. Africa went before South America went before Asia went before North America went before Europe until the entire world was cloaked in preindustrial darkness. The last section that was lit was somewhere in the U.S., near Tennessee she thought.

The current night sky shot. Not a light to be seen.

The music ended. All there was was a scrolling night shot of the dead world from a satellite. It seemed like the movie had ended and Sophia almost got up, wondering why anyone would want to see this montage of horror. They'd all lived it.

Then there was the sound of the scratch of a match that touched a candle. The flame flickered for a moment, then puffed out to a background of childish laughter...

And came back as it faded back to her, Sophia, trying to light Mum's birthday cake and Faith blowing it out every time she tried. She *hated* that video. She'd been ten and Faith eight and she was sooo pissed at her. She'd been no help making the cake and then Da wouldn't make her stop. He thought it was funny. Had Da *kept* the damned thing?

Then back to the dark sky of a dead world. A satellite passing over India and North Africa. Shots of dead Mumbai, Cairo, Casablanca, scrolling fast...

Zooming in on a cluster of lights. The squadron center at sea. The only light in the blackness as the music crescendoed. Then a caption:

"Welcome to Wolf Squadron. The hell with the darkness. Light a Candle."

ISLANDS OF RAGE & HOPE

JOHN RINGO

Islands of Rage and Hope

Copyright © 2014 by John Ringo

A Baen Books Original

Baen Publishing Enterprises
P.O. Box 1403
Riverdale, NY 10471
www.baen.com

ISBN: 978-1-4767-8043-6

Cover art by Kurt Miller

First paperback printing, July 2015
Second paperback printing, January 2016

Library of Congress Catalog Number: 2014020007

Distributed by Simon & Schuster
1230 Avenue of the Americas
New York, NY 10020

Pages by Joy Freeman (www.pagesbyjoy.com)
Printed in the United States of America

As always
For Captain Tamara Long, USAF
Born: May 12, 1979
Died: March 23, 2003, Afghanistan
You fly with the angels now.

PROLOGUE

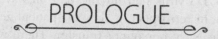

Mine eyes have seen the glory of the coming of the Lord:
He is trampling out the vintage where the grapes of wrath are stored;
He hath loosed the fateful lightning of His terrible swift sword:
His truth is marching on.

(CHORUS)
Glory, glory, hallelujah!
Glory, glory, hallelujah!
Glory, glory, hallelujah!
His truth is marching on.

—"The Battle Hymn of the Republic"

"Sergeant Hoag, pull your team out," Gunny Choy radioed.

"Never leave a Marine behind, Gunnery Sergeant," Sergeant Sheila Hoag replied.

The gunny's Humvee was high-sided on a pile of infected. More were piling on as he radioed. The team of Marines and some civilian and Navy refugees stuffed into the Humvee were safe. For now. On the other hand, they couldn't get out.

Hopkins was blazing through ammo on the 240 but the infected were swarming onto their Humvee, too. If she didn't watch it she was going to be in the same boat as the gunny.

1

"Gunnery Sergeant," Hoag radioed, backing around to try to keep some of the infected guessing. "I think if I can get in behind you I can push you off the pile."

The H7D3 virus had hit the base in waves. There had been, in retrospect, a slew of "patient zeros" in a large-scale Navy personnel transfer. There were only 7500 people on the sprawling base and when they were up to four hundred infected in "temporary care facilities" that made the worst gulags on Earth look like a picnic, and another four hundred dead from the virus itself, the base wasn't running so well.

Then the second wave hit. And all hell broke loose.

"If you don't get out of here, you're going to be in the same boat, Sergeant," the gunnery sergeant replied calmly. "We're clocked out on 240. You're about to be clocked out. We just had a civvy turn and bite one of the Navy guys. You are hereby ordered, Sergeant, to save your team and passengers. Make for the log buildings as previously ordered. Conserve your rounds. You're going to need them. Now, go. That's an order."

"Aye, aye, Gunnery Sergeant," Hoag said, putting the Humvee in reverse. She did, in fact, run over two or three infected but managed to keep from getting stuck. She spun out at one point, trying hard not to think about what she'd spun out on. Most of the infected were adults. Most.

"I swear to God if any of you turn on me I will fucking shoot you in the gut," Sergeant Hoag said, backing the Humvee up as fast as it would go. She hit a good place to turn around and practically spun the vehicle out.

They'd gotten the word that the fallback point was the logistics buildings around the piers on Corinaso

Cove. The problem being, they were on Corinaso *Point*. The piers were in sight. If they wanted to try to swim, then fight their way into the buildings through the infected, in hand-to-hand presumably, that would be totally golden. Right now they had to drive from point A to Point B around the cove while not hitting enough infected to get stuck.

She weaved around a couple of zombies and heard the breech click on the 240. They'd started off with three thousand rounds and gotten a resupply at one point. There were only 7500 people on the base. Where the *fuck* did the ammo go?

She wasn't even sure which log building to make for. There were several around the piers.

"Hopkins, you see any sign of resistance?" she yelled.

"Building Fourteen," Hopkins called. "Riflemen on the roof."

The problem being, there were infected swarming all around Building Fourteen like yellow jackets from a kicked hive. There was no way to get in there.

Two of the main doors slid open and a fire team started wasting infecteds at the opening while someone stood behind them, waving for the Humvee to enter.

She floored it, heading straight for the riflemen and the line of infected. She slammed infected to either side, plowing through them and hoping like hell she wasn't going to get high-sided. She practically jumped the last few as a Marine lance corporal dove to the side to avoid the oncoming vehicle.

Once through the doors she slammed on her brakes and skidded to a stop just short of hitting a pallet of water bottles.

"Everybody out," Hoag said. "Just get the fuck out."

There was a Navy lieutenant JG shoved in the back and that wasn't how a Marine was supposed to address an officer. The pogue could just put her on report for all she cared.

She sat there looking at those water bottles for a long time.

∽ ⊖ ∾

"We currently have an adequate stock of water. We'll see how long that lasts."

Lieutenant Colonel Craig "Kodiak" Hamilton was a WB: a waterboarder. Camp Delta most officially did *not* use waterboarding on the detainees. They did use various other methods, mostly psychological, to extract information from the detainees. Colonel Hamilton was one of the intelligence officers "involved" in such extraction. In his case, most figured that he just grinned at detainees and they gave him the locations of their blessed mother. He was 6'4" in his stocking feet and had won a silver medal in "all class" wrestling in the Olympics.

Right now, the whole issue of "perpetual detainment" and the IRCC and Human Rights Watch and all the rest was as relevant as... Well, right now Hoag couldn't really think of anything less irrelevant. Camp Delta had been reformatted, early, for "infected care," then it all went to hell. All Hoag knew was that none of the bastards were in the two facilities designated as fallback points.

The whole group was sitting in the meeting with their ankles tied. That had been practically the first order given. Get separated, tie your ankles. Request permission to untie. If you don't, don't be surprised if you get shot. The riflemen on the roof, still waiting, probably in vain, for more customers, were shackled. Chains allowed them to walk but they could barely run. And they had orders to shoot anyone who turned.

The only group not tied was the response team. And there was another team, tied, eying them. Everybody was eying each other. Too many times people had just turned out of the blue.

"There was a team out shutting off flow to other areas of the base," Colonel Hamilton said. "We're not sure how far they got and we've lost contact at this point. But we have free flow of water from the main tanks to these two buildings. As long as the water holds out, we'll be fine. It will, however, be rationed and we will fill every container we can find or make while it's running.

"Brigadier General Zick has the other building. The plan is to wait until the infected levels drop to the point we can make a breakout. If they do not drop, we will have to wait until someone comes along to break us out. There is a very adequate stock of food for the forty of us. Literally years worth. We will begin processes after this meeting to capture any rainwater we can. Are there any questions?"

"Any idea how long, sir?"

Ryan "Robot" Harris was the Navy lieutenant JG she'd carried in. He worked in base operations was all she knew about him.

"The last word we had was that everyone was in the same boat, Lieutenant," Hamilton said. "But I'm sure that as soon as they can restore order in the U.S., they'll send a team down to pull us out. Or, if we can, we'll self extract back to the U.S. There are boats here that we can do that with."

"Rations will be one ration per day for civilians, one and a half for Marine and Navy. The extra half is because we *shall* maintain physical fitness standards. We also shall maintain military customs and courtesy. This is a siege. Armies throughout history have withstood sieges with less adequate supplies and preparedness than..."

He paused as one of the Navy petty officers started to thrash.

"Get 'em off me!" the PO1 shouted, unbuckling his pants. "Get 'em off...!"

"No firing," Hamilton said. "Pin him down. Watch the teeth."

Hoag had already grabbed his wrist and was trying to wrestle him onto his face. The problem being, it was hard to wrestle with your feet tied. She and two other NCOs managed to get him pinned as Colonel Hamilton slid a confinement hood over his head. Then the colonel dropped a fast tie around the PO's neck and pulled it tight.

The howling was cut off abruptly but the PO continued to convulse for what felt like forever. Finally, he was still.

"We will need to create a containment area for bodies," Hamilton said, continuing the meeting as if nothing had happened. "That will need to be sealed away from the rest of us or there will be a significant health hazard. I will entertain suggestions on that in a moment...."

"Idle hands are the devil's handiwork," Colonel Hamilton said as Hoag rounded a corner of shelving. He was leaning up against the shelves, his arms crossed and one foot crossed across the other at the ankles.

The warehouse was big and filled from floor to ceiling with materials. Much of it was food. There were even quite a few pallets of water. It was a good place to ride out a siege.

But there were different kinds of sieges. Maybe back in the old days it was normal to be talking to a teammate and have him suddenly start screaming and clawing at his clothes. Maybe it was normal to have to strangle him to death to conserve rounds.

Maybe it was normal to leave your gunny behind.

She wasn't sure quite why she was wandering on the back side of the warehouse pretty much as far away from her squad as she could get. She also wasn't thinking, definitely wasn't thinking, about the .45 she had in her waistband.

What she did wonder was how Colonel Hamilton managed to always turn up at the wrong place at the wrong time. Only first sergeants were supposed to be able to do that.

"Yes, sir, they are, sir," Hoag said, coming to attention.

"Rest, Sergeant," Hamilton said, waving idly. "I'd start talking about how we need to find more activities for the men and solicit your advice, say that's why I'm here, play it off, but that wouldn't suffice. It wouldn't solve the problem of one of my NCOs slowly coming to the conclusion that if it's supposed to be 'death before dishonor' then maybe death will erase the stain."

"Not sure what you mean, sir," Hoag said.

"It's called 'counseling,' Sergeant Hoag," Hamilton said, straightening up. "Walk with me."

"Yes, sir," Hoag said.

"I was discussing the issue of choices with General Zick, before he turned and left me as senior officer," Hamilton said. "And before the batteries on the radios ran out. Choice, Sergeant, is a terrible thing, did you know that?"

"No, sir," Hoag said.

"It is," Hamilton said. "The French philosopher Jean-Paul Sartre said that all of life is choice. Since his general view of life was fairly nihilistic, that makes sense. Every choice requires decision. Every decision is a stress. Therefore, every choice is a stress. As you may have been told in leadership training, stress is not just cumulative, it is multiplicative. That is, each stress, small or large, multiplies the previous stress. Americans and Westerners in general, before the Plague, had a multitude of choices in their life. Decisions to be made every moment. Just stop or go on a yellow light was a stress, not to mention when to brake or accelerate. I read a 'weird news' report one time about a man who had killed his brother fighting over who shared the remote. To most, this looked like insanity. To me, it was a sign of the problems of choice and stress in American society. Do you get my meaning, Sergeant?"

"Sort of, sir," Hoag said. "But it still sounds insane."

"Clinically," Hamilton said. "At the point that the one brother killed the other, he was functionally insane. Due to stress. I don't know what other stressors were on him—did he not handle stress well?—but choice had brought him to making the choice to kill his brother. Over which show they were going to watch. If he was being forced to watch Oprah, I suppose it was less insane."

"Yes, sir," Hoag said, chuckling slightly.

"Being in the military under any circumstances involves tremendous stress," Hamilton said. "However, for the juniors, and you are fairly junior, Sergeant, that rarely involves stress related to choice. As a junior, certainly when you were a private, you were given orders and I'm sure you obeyed them. Now, as an NCO, you have more responsibilities, stress, and you have to use your experience and intelligence to expand upon orders. Stress. But you really, still, don't have the stress of choice. Of having to think beyond 'I've been given an order and must make sure my men comply.' The military does that to an extent deliberately. How well one handles stress is, functionally, one of the tests for promotion. Some have the innate ability to simply not feel it. Most have to learn how to manage it. So the military brings people, officers and enlisted, along slowly, teaching them by both classwork and daily operations, how to make good decisions rapidly and functionally and how to handle stress, including the stress involved in choice, wisely. Are you still with me, Sergeant?"

"Yes, sir," Hoag said.

"You may be thinking 'What the fuck is he talking about' but there is a point here," Hamilton said. "You have been very carefully not paying a lot of attention to the forty-five you picked up in the battle. But one of the choice stresses on you is whether you should use the forty-five, which is quick and clean but would waste a precious round, or strangle yourself as we did with your sole remaining squad member, PFC Hopkins. In that case, you're going to use parachute cord; you have it in your right cargo pocket. Tie it to one of the shelves, climb up, put a noose around your neck and do the dance.

"You have formed no strong bonds in the two weeks since we were besieged. None of these people are 'your' people. Some of them are Marines but they are not 'your' Marines. You have no ties to this group. You are fairly sure, as we all are, that most if not all of our families are dead back in the States. There is very little keeping you to this mortal coil. And you are struggling with the question of dishonor in leaving not just other Marines but your gunnery sergeant behind to be eaten by infected. About all you can reply at this point is 'Yes, sir.'"

"Yes, sir," Hoag said, her jaw locked.

"So, Sergeant, here is the question. Are you a Marine, Sergeant?"

"Yes, sir," Hoag said.

"The obvious answer," Hamilton said. "There you are, wearing the uniform, with your sergeant's rank and all. You, obviously, are a Marine. Do Marines obey orders, Sergeant?"

"Yes, sir," Hoag said.

"Then that was what you did," Hamilton said. "Lieutenant Harris confirmed that your orders from your gunnery sergeant were to leave him and his team, and their passengers, *behind.* If it had been the *president* and you were given that order, you should have obeyed it. If it was the *commandant*, you should have obeyed it. For one reason and one reason only: The honor would have been broken if you *disobeyed* the order. Not to mention we would have lost your team. And we are so very few. There was, in fact, *no* dishonor. There was great honor on both sides. On the gunny and his team for essentially holding the rear guard, permitting your team to escape, and on yours for obeying their solemn duty and their orders. Honor, Sergeant, is satisfied. I am not asking for agreement. I know that emotionally you do not agree. However, do you concur that I, your commanding officer and a Marine officer with *three* times as many years as you have in the Corps has stated 'Honor is satisfied'?"

"Yes, sir," Hoag said. "I understand what you are saying and concur that you said it."

"But you are still emotionally unsatisfied," Hamilton said. "Did you read science fiction before the Plague, Sergeant?"

"No, sir," Hoag said. "I really wasn't much of a reader before the Plague, sir."

"And, alas, we have few books in this wretched hellhole," Hamilton said. "I did. I read, but not science fiction, before becoming a Marine officer. However, one of the books that has been on the commandant's reading list for some time is a science fiction novel: *Starship Troopers*. That book started me on a quest for similar. It was hit and miss at first. Much of it is Sartre-inspired nihilistic dreck. But some is quite good and explores questions of the human condition you rarely find in common fiction or even nonfiction. An example comes to mind of the question of honor. The point that is made about dishonor is that in a situation of death before dishonor, eventually all you have are the dead and the dishonored. When you stand your post you can see the picked skeletons of the dead. We have far too many dead, Sergeant. We do not need more. Do you take my meaning?"

"Yes, sir," Hoag said.

"We are a lifeboat, Sergeant," Hamilton said. "A lifeboat of remaining sentient humanity. A large one but a lifeboat nonetheless. We've seen the infected feeding on each other, feeding on the rats that are feeding on the stores. Finding water. Walking all the way to the fresh water to drink and then apparently walking back to 'their' territories. We don't know how long they will remain. But as long as they remain, we remain. We shall outlast them if it takes weeks, months or years. Because we are so very few. And, Sergeant, when, not if, those doors open, we need, not want nor desire but *need*, every one of us to walk out of them. Is that need clear, Sergeant?"

"Clear, sir," Hoag said.

"All of us feel that stain of dishonor," Hamilton said. "Survivor's guilt. You just have a particularly specific form. Yet you, also, have a particular gift. You were given the gift of life, Sergeant. The gunnery sergeant did not, foolishly and selfishly, insist that you expend your life and your team's life trying to save him. You were given the gift of life by the gunnery sergeant. The true dishonor to the gunny's memory would be throwing that gift away.

"So I shall leave you to your forty-five and your parachute cord. But I would submit to you, for your consideration, that they are useful items in our future career of clearing the infected from our nation. A career we shall embark upon someday. And, Sergeant, I would very much like to have you with me when we do so. May God grant you wisdom in your choices. However, feel free to use the pistol if that is your choice. One forty-five round more or less won't matter. Just kindly lay out a tarp or something since you'll be leaving us to clear up your mess. Your choice, though."

CHAPTER 1

". . . says the Navy is still there and there's some group called
'Wolf Squadron' in the Atlantic. He's been catching fragmentary
back-scatter. That's all I've heard about it. You, over?"
"I don't have any of that but I could stand to see some Marines
coming down the road you know what I mean . . . ?"

From: *Collected Radio Transmissions of The Fall*
University of the South Press 2053

"We have a sierra, sir," the watch officer said.

It was four hours after dawn, local, and the third day of the Wolf Squadron float from the Canary Islands to Guantanamo Bay. So far, the sea had failed to give up its survivors in the *Alexandria*'s patch. There was an unofficial pool among the subs as to who could find the most sierras—normally ships but the squadron had picked up the sub crews' "Sierra," or "S" for sonar contact, and they now used it to refer to any floating vessel that warranted checking out.

"Finally," Vancel said. "Con, give me one third to target's bearing. Let's see what we've got. . . ."

"Division Seven, Division Seven, Alexandria, *over."*

"Division Seven, over," Sophia replied. With those sneaky ass sub bastards around, she was having to

13

get a suntan in a bikini. Olga had decided it was fair game to give the sub crews a show and was on the sundeck *en nu*. Sophia wasn't quite willing to give the last measure for sub morale.

"Sierra One: Life raft. Military. Item: Three. One Item appears emotionally disturbed. Recommend security team, over."

"Gimme the coordinates, over . . ."

"Here you go, sir," Staff Sergeant Alfred Joseph "AJ" Decker said, pinning the bound second lieutenant down and trying to avoid the snapping teeth. "It is lunch time, sir. Nice juicy fish eyeball, sir. You know how you like the fish eyeballs, sir. Full of tasty goodness and vitamins, sir. Private First Class Condrey, help me assist Lieutenant Klette with his midday meal."

"Aye, aye, Staff Sergeant," Private First Class Steve Condrey said, pinning the thrashing officer to the deck of the rubber lifeboat. He held him down with his remaining weight and helped the staff sergeant pry the lieutenant's jaws open.

They managed to get the fish eyeball into the officer's mouth and the lieutenant chewed and swallowed avidly, then let out a howl for more.

"I regret to say that that is all there is available, sir," Decker said, rolling off the officer. "You are aware, sir, that we are on short rations." He gagged the officer to avoid being bitten and then picked up a small slice of mahimahi. The flesh of the fish was actually considered, by long-term survivors, inferior to the eyeballs. "Good afternoon, Private First Class. How is your midday meal?"

"Excellent, Staff Sergeant," the PFC said, swallowing

the small sliver of fish like a guppy. "Finest sushi money can buy, Staff Sergeant."

"Every day is a holiday and every meal is a banquet in the Corps, PFC," Decker said, chewing the fish slowly.

"God Bless the Marine Corps, Staff Sergeant," the PFC said.

"God Bless the United States and her glorious Constitution, Private First Class," the staff sergeant replied. "Time to set the watch bill, Private First Class Condrey."

"Aye, aye, Staff Sergeant..."

"Staff Sergeant, permission to report!"

"Report, Private First Class!"

They were sitting in the boat back to back, as close to the position of attention as possible in a rubber raft, each of them intently scanning the horizon in their "zone." Lieutenant Klette had drifted into a zombie hibernation.

"Possible sighting of a boat under power on the horizon, Staff Sergeant!"

"Bearing?" Staff Sergeant Decker asked.

"My nine-thirty, Staff Sergeant!" Condrey replied.

"Acknowledged," Decker said without turning around. "Maintain watch on that contact as well as continuing visual sweep." He set his watch to alarm in five minutes.

"Aye, aye, Staff Sergeant!"

"Private First Class Condrey, status report on possible sighting?"

"Vessel continues to close our position, Staff Sergeant. Range approximately one mile. Vessel appears to be a motor yacht, Staff Sergeant. Personnel on the bridge are visible at this time, Staff Sergeant."

"Acknowledged, Private First Class," Decker said, turning around, still at attention. He shaded his eyes and nodded. "Vessel is confirmed. The private first class will assist the staff sergeant in dressing Lieutenant Klette."

"Aye, aye, Staff Sergeant!"

"Bleeding arseholes," Sophia said, looking through the binoculars. "That's a fucking *zombie*! They're dressing a fucking zombie."

The survivors were Marines from their uniforms. And they still had combat gear. And a live zombie. She had no clue what had possessed them to keep a live zombie onboard a fucking life raft but she was going to have to think about how to handle it. She had the funny feeling that shooting it as soon as it was in range would not be the right move.

What got her was that they were also close shaven and had nearly bald heads. Their uniforms were not even that bad.

She made an instant decision and slowed the boat.

"Walker," she said over the intercom. "Take the helm. I need to go below for a second."

"Roger, ma'am," Walker said, running up on the flying bridge. "Issues?"

"Those guys are... They've got a *live zombie* on a life raft. I'm going to go get into uniform."

"Can I look, ma'am?" Walker asked, holding his hand out for the binos.

"Go ahead," Sophia said. "Am I right that I'd better be in uniform, with all my doodads, when we pull these guys in?"

"Yes, ma'am," Walker said, looking through the

binos. "That would be for the best. And Olga as well. I don't know how or why they did this, but we're going to have to handle this very carefully, ma'am."

"Agreed," Sophia said, heading below. "Do not approach until I'm back up."

"Aye, aye, ma'am."

"Good afternoon, Marines," Sophia said, from the aft deck. She was in her best uniform with her new gold bars glittering in the sun.

"Good afternoon, ma'am!" the staff sergeant boomed, as close to attention as he could get in a rocking lifeboat and saluting with his M4. "Staff Sergeant Alfred Joseph Decker reporting with a party of one, Ensign. Our officer has suffered what appears to be heat stroke, ma'am. Permission to come aboard!"

"Permission granted, Staff Sergeant," Sophia said, returning the salute. "Evolution is as follows. You will toss us your line. My crew will assist you in bringing the lieutenant aboard. The PFC will board followed by yourself. You and the PFC will lock and clear all weapons before boarding. We will then do what we can for your lieutenant and his...heat stroke."

"Yes, ma'am," Decker said, his composure starting to crack. "Ma'am, permission to speak, ma'am."

"Granted," Sophia said.

"Ma'am, my last orders from my gunnery sergeant were 'Take care of the LT,' ma'am," Decker said. "I know the LT is...in bad shape, ma'am and I know you outrank a gunnery sergeant, ma'am. But I will remain in this lifeboat at my post before I will allow anyone to put my lieutenant down, ma'am."

"One moment, Staff Sergeant," Sophia said, turning

around. She put her hands over her eyes and tried as hard as hell not to cry. She wiped away the slight moisture and turned around.

"Staff Sergeant, I am an officer of the United States Navy," she said. "You have my statement that your officer can be boarded to this boat and absent orders to the contrary I will not terminate him for his current condition. However, Staff Sergeant Decker, you are now *back* in the United States Marine Corps. What orders are given by superior officers *I* cannot control and *you* cannot control. And *I* shall and *you* shall *obey* the orders of officers appointed over us. No matter how distasteful they may be. Nor may you *disregard* your oath to protect our nation and its Constitution to go floating around on a cruise on your lifeboat. Your life, your lieutenant's life, my life, are forfeit by the oath we swear. Do you understand me, Staff Sergeant!"

"Yes, *ma'am*," Decker said.

"For your information," Sophia said. "I may only be an ensign but I've been with this squadron since before it was a squadron, and my dad happens to be LantFleet. So what I will add to that earlier is...I'll do what I can for your officer, Staff Sergeant. But that's all I can promise. Now, lock and clear your weapons and prepare to board..."

The staff sergeant and his minion had been remarkably adept at feeding their lieutenant soup. They'd hardly spilled a drop as the zombie attempted to eat them. Afterwards the officer had been taken out to "relieve himself" off the aft deck, then secured below. She could hear him howling from the flybridge.

Then and only then had the two Marines accepted

the offered tomato soup. They drank it at attention. They did everything at attention.

She made sure their guns were secured in the safe in her cabin. They were out of rounds, anyway. She wasn't sure about their knives but they'd been persuaded to divest themselves of their combat gear.

"What happens in the compartment *never* stays in the compartment," she muttered, rubbing her face. "Just when I thought I'd seen it all..."

She picked up the radio. She knew when she was out of her depth.

"Flotilla, Division Seven. I need Flotilla Actual, over."

"I am aware of the SOP in this matter, Flotilla," Sophia said. "Break. However, these guys are so tightly wound you could use them to power the *Alex*. Request that Marines handle this as it is basically a Marine matter. If the gunny and the captain put this poor bastard down, that's one thing. I'm not sure what will happen if I try. Over."

"*Roger, Bella. Will pass this to Squadron. The one absolute condition is maintain the safety of your boat and your crew. Do you understand?*"

"Aye, aye, Flotilla. Will ensure the safety of my boat and my crew, over."

"*Flotilla out.*"

"Passing the buck are they?" Walker asked.

"Hell, I did," Sophia said as the zombie in the cabin howled. "Jesus, how did they stand it?"

"The most important factor in maintaining one's sanity, to an extent, in a survival situation is something to hold onto," Walker said. "Something to do and take care of and cherish. I had a knot record."

"Isn't that a contradiction in terms?" Sophia asked.

"Knot," Walker said. "K-N-O-T. It's a way of keeping track of events, days, using simple string. It was the Incan's only form of writing. Each type of string has a meaning, each type of knot. Very simple and infinitely complex. More complex than Chinese."

"What happened to it?" Sophia asked.

"I left it in the compartment," Walker said. "It was a way of surviving *there*. It was unnecessary in the outer world. But I have been found to be so aggressively sane it's a form of insanity. These Marines survived, in part, by caring for their officer. Which is a devotion so doglike it is virtually unheard of in the modern world. And by grasping so hard to their duty that it is nearly broken. Marines tend to be fairly OCD, anyway. The question is whether they can recover from their current mental state. Right now, they're having a hard time not following their 'Watch Bill.'"

"Any suggestions?" Sophia asked. "About what to do about the lieutenant?"

"Either keep him alive in a padded room," Walker said, shrugging. "Which will be interesting. Or have a formal ceremony where he's passed to the great beyond, preferably with a fast-acting poison. Play 'Taps.' Bury him with honors at sea. They took care of him until the decisions could be passed on to others. But it would have to be an honorable way to go out. Not you or I or Olga putting a bullet in his head and tossing him over the side. They would, I assure you, flip the fuck out if we did that."

"That's the first time I've ever heard you curse," Sophia said.

"Right now, ma'am, I want to revel in the glory and honor of the words: *Semper Fidelis*," the man said. "And burn the world down at the same time. I have seen a lot in my many years, ma'am, but this takes the cake. Truly wins the fucking lottery."

"I think I'm gonna have to get a little drunk to sleep tonight," Sophia said as the zombie Marine howled below.

"D . . . do . . . *What?*" Captain Smith snapped. "They kept him *alive? How? Why?*"

"The staff sergeant's last orders from his gunny were 'take care of the lieutenant,'" Isham said. "So they took care of him. Kept him alive. Kept him fed and watered, even at their own expense. Soph describes them as so tightly wound they could power a sub."

"Bloody hell," Steve said, picking up his phone. "Get me Gunny Sands. *Now!*"

"Lieutenant Klette, huh?" Gunnery Sergeant Sands said, shielding his face with his hand. "And Decker. That . . . I'd say it makes a certain amount of sense but it really doesn't, sir, I'm aware of that. Lieutenant Klette was the armor platoon leader. Newly arrived. Gunnery Sergeant Haughton was kind of a stickler about obedience to orders."

"Did I just hear a gunny say another gunny was a stickler?" Steve said. "This is hereby a Marine matter, Gunny. I've got enough on my plate. You and the captain have the authority and responsibility of figuring out what to do. I'll back whatever decision you make as long as it doesn't significantly affect overall operations. But that lieutenant needs to be off that boat. Fast. Take my boat, get out there. You at least, you and the captain if he has time. We're done."

"Aye, aye, sir," Sands said, standing up. "What's that word your girls use, sir? A zammie? This is a zammie for sure, sir."

Walker watched the radar screen, looking around occasionally on a visual sweep, then looked back at the screen. The *Bella Señorita* was cruising west under fair skies and a following sea, the most perfect conditions you can be in on a boat. And they were headed home, eventually. Back to the Land of the Big PX, sort of. It was one hell of a lot better than being in the compartment or, for that matter, any number of places he'd been in his life.

Even with the occasional howl from below. Besides, the zombie had mostly settled down after they put enough food in his stomach.

There was a blip on the radar screen and he noted it. Sometimes you got ghosts. But it was there again on the next sweep, and noticeably closer. Someone was in a hurry. And based on the next sweep, headed for the *Bella*.

"Bella Señorita, Bella Señorita, Achille Cono, *over.*"

"*Achille Cono, Bella Señorita,* over."

"*Approaching your position. Flag is not, repeat, not aboard. Here for pick-up on the Marines. Wake the semi-sane ones up if they're not. Out.*"

He went below and woke the skipper first. Knocking at her door.

"Enter," the skipper said. She was sitting up in bed when he opened the door, pistol in hand. "I was awake, anyway. I didn't think I wanted earplugs in with a live zombie on board."

"Your dad's fast boat is inbound," Walker said. "He's not aboard. They're here to pick up the Marines."

"Okay," Sophia said, getting out of bed. She was wearing PT shorts and a T-shirt. "I'll get my uniform on. How long?"

"Ten minutes or so," Walker said.

"I'll head up on deck in a minute," she said. "Get the staff sergeant up. Carefully."

"Yes, ma'am," Walker said.

"You need backup?" she asked.

"No, ma'am," Walker said. "I can handle it."

He knocked, hard, on the door of the cabin the Marines had been assigned.

"FIRST CALL, MARINES! ON YOUR FEET!"

"Status?" Decker said, yanking open the door.

"Inbound fast boat," Walker snapped. "Sounds like Gunnery Sergeant Sands. Five minutes. Uniform is MarPat and boots. No LBE, no weapons, no K-pot."

"Roger," Decker said. "You heard the man, Private First Class. Inspection in two minutes!" He slammed the door shut.

"Wow," Walker muttered, shaking his head. "Talk about wrapped like a string..."

He darted into his compartment and rummaged for a second, then came back out and stood by the door.

It snapped open and Decker nearly collided with him.

"Kiwi," Walker said, holding up the can. He slammed it onto the bigger Marine's chest.

"Roger," Decker said, taking the can. "Thank you, Mr. Walker."

"You are welcome, Staff Sergeant Decker."

~⊖~

"Your coffee, ma'am," Walker said, handing the ensign a cup. She was in uniform but still pretty bleary. "Status report, ma'am?"

"Please," Sophia said, taking a sip.

"I rousted out Olga, she has the conn," Walker said. "Fast boat is still few minutes out. The Marines are prepared for inspection. If I may make a recommendation. Have you ever performed an inspection, ma'am?"

"Of people in uniform?" Sophia said. "No."

"The way it works is the junior, usually an NCO, goes first and performs a preinspection. Then the inspector performs the inspection. There should be someone following to accept notes from the inspector. I would recommend, ma'am, that I take the first position and perform a preinspection. Then you inspect. You just have to seem to be looking at stuff. I'll make sure they're as ready as they're going to be."

"Any idea who was on the boat?" Sophia asked.

"I'm pretty sure it was the gunny on the radio, ma'am," Walker said. "Never met him but, met one gunny you've met them all. Marines are on the aft deck. If that idea meets with your approval, give me one minute and I'll be prepared."

"Sounds like a plan," Sophia said.

"Be right back."

Walker pulled out a piece of double-sided tape and taped down one corner of a pocket that was sticking out on PFC Condrey's uniform.

"Staff Sergeant Decker, ensure that both these uniforms are turned in for direct exchange as soon as possible," Walker said. "The LeafBrown pattern is sun-faded."

"Aye, aye, Mr. Walker," the staff sergeant said.

"Boots are clean and polished but unserviceable due to exigency of conditions," Walker said. "Again, DX item. Otherwise, good turnout, Marine."

"Thank you, sir," the PFC said.

"The PFC is ready for your inspection, ma'am," Walker said.

Sophia checked the PFC's uniform as if she knew what she was doing, then the staff sergeant's. She didn't find any fault.

"The order is 'Parade Rest' then 'Rest,' ma'am," Walker whispered in her ear.

"Marines. Parade rest. Rest," Sophia said, then looked at Walker. The man nodded as the Marines assumed the position of parade rest.

"Ol— Seaman Apprentice Zelenova! Status on the inbound."

"One mile out and still closing, ma'am."

"Radio to have them come up on the port side."

"Aye, aye, ma'am."

"Ma'am?" Walker said, taking her arm and drawing her lightly away from the Marines.

"Problem, Mr. Walker?" Sophia asked.

"They're facing to starboard," Walker said quietly. "They need to turn around."

"Okay, well . . ." Sophia said, starting to open her mouth.

"If I may," Walker said, pressing on her arm. "Wound tighter than a mainspring on an AK, ma'am?"

"So they can't turn around?" Sophia said.

"Start with 'Marine Detail, ten-hut!' Barked, ma'am."

"Marine Detail, ten-*hut*!" Sophia said.

"About face," Walker whispered.

"About face."

"And 'Parade Rest,' ma'am."

"Parade rest," Sophia said. "Was that right?"

"Do you *want* me to give you the class on command voice and drill commands?" Walker asked, smiling tightly.

"What I'd really like to know is how come *you* know so much about it, Mr. Walker," Sophia said quietly.

"I'm a man of many parts, ma'am," Walker replied. "And the boat is coming alongside."

"Celementina," Sophia said. "Mr. Walker. Get the lines."

"Permission to come aboard, ma'am!" Gunnery Sergeant Sands boomed.

"Granted, Gunnery Sergeant," Sophia said. "And this Marine detail is yours, Gunnery Sergeant."

"Detail, ten-shuh!" the gunny boomed as soon as his feet hit the deck. "Parade . . . Rest! Rest! Decker, Condrey, good to have you back!"

"Thank you, Gunnery Sergeant!" Staff Sergeant Decker boomed.

"What's the status on the LT, Staff Sergeant?"

"The lieutenant is below, Gunnery Sergeant," Decker replied. "The lieutenant is not in optimal condition, Gunnery Sergeant Sands. The lieutenant should have medical attention at the earliest possible instance, Gunnery Sergeant."

"The LT is a zombie, Decker," Sands said. "Which doesn't mean he's not a Marine. And Marines take care of their own. God knows I've killed enough Marine zombies and I and you and the PFC will keep *on* killing Marine zombies as long as we have to to secure our nation. But the decision has been made to keep the lieutenant as a psychiatric patient, barring needs of the service saying otherwise. If at some point we can avail ourselves of research facilities, the lieutenant may become a research subject. However, that research will be noninvasive. He will not be dissected, his head cut open or anything else along the lines. He is a Marine officer and will be treated with the most respect possible given his condition. That, Marine, is the final word of the current chain of command. Do you understand?"

"Yes, Gunnery Sergeant," Decker said.

"Do you have any questions, Staff Sergeant?"

"Gunnery Sergeant..." Decker said. "The private first class and I are...familiar with the officer's needs. Would it be possible for us to—"

"IS YOUR MOS PSYCHIATRIC CORPSMAN, STAFF SERGEANT?" the gunny screamed. "ARE YOU IN THE *NAVY*, STAFF SERGEANT?"

"NO, GUNNERY SERGEANT!" Decker replied.

"We need every Marine we can get, Staff Sergeant," Sands said, more gently. "Your mission, which you achieved against incredible odds, was to take care of your lieutenant. You did that. New mission. Kill every *other* fucking zombie on *Earth* until humanity is safe from that Scourge. Do you understand that mission, Staff Sergeant?"

"Yes, Gunnery Sergeant."

"*Marines*! Do you *understand* that *mission*? I can't heeear you!"

"YES, GUNNERY SERGEANT!"

"You *ARE* going to get your headspace and timing back, Marines!" the gunny barked, starting to circle the two. "You *are* going to drive on with the mission! You *are* going to remain eternally faithful to our *Nation*! You *are* Marines! And you *are* relieved of the duty of taking care of your lieutenant! Is that *understood*, Marines!"

"YES, GUNNERY SERGEANT!"

"Just so's we're clear," Gunny Sands said. "That was one hell of a job you did, Decker, Condrey. You're not going to get any medals for it, but I'll see if I can convince 'em you're not Section Eights. Because it was stupid and it was crazy. But we're United States Marines. Stupid and crazy is what we do. Oorah."

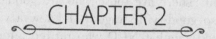

CHAPTER 2

"This is the voice of Free Texas, broadcasting from Hamlin. Primary assembly area is the silos on the southeast part of town. Bring all your guns and ammo, come peaceable and be prepared to work. We got a big job ahead of us, freeing our great state from the zombies. Stay away from the center of town, it's still crawlin' . . ."

From: *Collected Radio Transmissions of The Fall*
University of the South Press 2053

"This is a sad profession," Olga said, shutting the door to the cabin. From the looks of things, they were months too late for the occupant.

"If you pick up a weapon, you are embarking on a career of great sadness mixed with rare touches of glory," Walker said, stacking rolls of toilet paper in a cloth grocery bag. "It is one of the reasons not to pick up a weapon."

"Are you saying I shouldn't do this job?" Olga said. "That a woman's not good enough?"

The Ferretti 68 was well stocked. The owners had prepared for a long voyage away from resupply. Unfortunately, one of the things they had stocked without realizing it was the Plague.

"Far from it," Walker said. "You are good at it. You are a woman. Good, however, is a variable term in

29

the profession of arms. There are those who are very good with weapons, but not so good at killing. They are expert marksmen, but could not shoot so much as a rabbit. There are those who are good at killing, but not so good with tragedy. I knew a very good, experienced, combat NCO who retired after Rwanda because he was broken by the senselessness of it all. And this world is a mass of tragedy. Doing your job, you see that more than most. Being good at killing is not all that you must be good at to do your job."

"I suppose that makes sense," Olga said, pulling out a pile of sheets that were in a closet. "Faith really tries to avoid going in cabins that don't respond to a knock. She got that way after clearing the *Voyage*."

"The lieutenant is young," Walker said. "She may harden to the point she can withstand the sadness or someday simply walk away. In the meantime she is certainly good at killing infected and she acts as a strong motivator to her Marines. That is enough in a young officer."

"You seem to know a lot about the military for an English as a Second Language instructor," Olga said.

"As I told the ensign, I am a man of many parts," Walker said, grinning. "Celementina, let me help you with that," he added, picking up a case of oil jugs.

"Salamat, Tomas," the woman said. "I let you. Every time I squat and lift I'm afraid I will simply pop the bambina out. And then every time I *hope* I pop the bambina out! I am ready to have this child out of me!"

The engineer had already declared the engine a loss. The boat had been under power when an infected broke an oil line. Both engines had eventually seized. While the *Grace* could probably repair them, there was no real need for the boat and so they were stripping it rather than calling for a prize crew.

"We're going to have to do a supply drop pretty soon," Sophia said as Tom Walker tossed the case of oil onto the aft deck of the *Bella*. The two boats were lashed together in the light seas, the fenders keeping them from damaging their hulls.

"At least we're finding supplies," Tom said.

"Some more survivors would be nice," Sophia said. "And preferably nearly sane ones."

"Bella Señorita, Alexandria, *over.*"

"*Alex, Bella*, over," Sophia said, picking up the radio.

"*Prosecuting a sierra at this time. Lifeboat. Survivors. Over.*"

"Ask and ye shall receive," Tom said, grinning.

"Coordinates, over?" Sophia said. She looked at the coordinates and shrugged. "*Risky Business, Risky Business, Bella Señorita*, over."

"Bella, *this is the* Business, *over.*"

"Did you copy those coordinates from the *Alex*, over?"

"*No, over.*"

"Stand by for coordinates. Your pick up, over."

"*Roger*, Bella. Alex, *you got those coordinates, over?*"

"We're not getting it?" Olga asked, heaving a case of cans onto the aft deck.

"We're salvaging and it's not a clearance issue," Sophia said, shrugging. "Let them have it."

"Sir, we have a very light radar return at two-two-three," the tactical officer of the USS *Alexandria* said. "Could be a ghost but it's hanging in there. Probable sierra."

"Roger," Lieutenant Commander Vancel said. "Conn, come to two-two-three turns for one third to close contact."

"Come to two-two-three, aye. Turns for one third, aye."

Vancel looked at the periscope repeater and blew out.

"What happens in the compartment, huh?" he muttered. "COB."

"Sir?"

"These images do *not* get circulated. Not even to the nukes and tell them I'm serious."

"Not circulated, aye. May the chief of boat ask *why*, sir?"

"Oh, dear," Sophia said, looking through the binos. "What happens in the compartment, stays in the compartment. What happens in the ... Oh, screw *that*!"

"It's not his fault!"

Lee Ann McGregor was just turned twelve and an orphan. Also extremely pregnant. She was shivering under a blanket in the relative cool of the saloon, drinking tomato soup as if it was nectar and arguing to spare the life of the young man sitting next to her.

The hangdog young man in question, Kevin White, was seventeen. And currently surrounded by women who were looking at him like a zombie that was in their targeting reticle. Wisely, he was keeping his mouth shut.

"Miss McGregor," Sophia said calmly. "You're a little young to have this explained but it looks like the explanation is late ..."

"We never did anything!" Lee Ann said. "And, when,

you know, I started to show, Kevin sort of explained it. But we can't figure it out. We never did *anything*. Not *anything*!"

"If the only other male present could ask some questions without getting his head ripped off?" Walker asked.

"Go ahead," Sophia said.

"Kevin," Walker said. "It is nearly impossible for a man below a certain age to do 'nothing.' Pressures build, especially around a beautiful young lady. Pain occurs and, in fact, if 'nothing' is done actual damage can occur."

"Seriously?" Sophia said. "Hold it a second, you mean *actual damage*."

"Yes," Walker said. "Knew a guy who was very faithful to his wife, very disciplined and very religious. Also on a *very* long deployment. He eventually went to the medics because he was, well, leaking. The doctor explained to him that, no, whatever the Bible says, the system is designed to be used and is one way exit only. And if you don't occasionally let it out, it breaks. Pressure builds, valves become damaged and eventually if nothing is done you become, essentially, sterile. Also it is, long term, very bad for the prostate. Some yogis have managed to do that to themselves, intentionally, as a form of asceticism. However, I strongly doubt that young Mr. White was that disciplined. Mr. White? Nothing?"

"I couldn't do *nothing*!" Kevin finally snapped. "We had to pee, we had to poop! We'd turn our backs and, you know, do it. And sometimes I'd ask Lee Ann if she could maybe turn her back. But I was going that way," he said, pointing out to sea. "I wasn't . . . I didn't . . . I mean, if I was getting in trouble for what I *did*, that'd be one thing! But I'm getting in trouble and I didn't even get to . . . *I didn't do anything!*"

"Likely story," Olga said, her arms crossed.

"No, unlikely story," Walker said. "But that doesn't mean it's necessarily a lie. I mean, it's about as bad a lie as you could come up with. I'd have said there was another person in the raft when they first abandoned ship and that *he* knocked her up."

Kevin looked at him with his jaw down.

"Why didn't *we* think of that!" Lee Ann said. "Damn! But we still didn't do anything. Honest. Really, we didn't. I wanted to and..." She shut her mouth quickly.

"Okay, now, *that* is discipline," Tom said. "You, young man, are a credit to your parents. God bless them and keep them."

"I still don't buy it," Olga said, frowning. "This has only happened once in history and there was a donkey, not a lifeboat, in the story. And I don't see three wise men."

"Ah, but there *is* a rubber lifeboat in this one," Tom said. "And the romantic tropical currents. How *much* discipline, children? It is common, we have found, for people in lifeboats in southerly climes to remove much or all of their clothing from time to time. Especially during the daytime. Frequently all."

Both of them were intently studying the floor.

"Did you or did you not occasionally get naked?" Sophia asked. When there wasn't an answer she sighed. "Show of hands who has sunbathed nude while on this trip?" she said, raising her hand. Eventually the whole crew had their hands up.

"Seriously?" Lee Ann said, raising her hand tentatively.

"They tell me I have to wear clothes now that I'm an officer," Sophia said. "It's a pain."

"Okay, now I really don't believe 'nothing,'" Olga said. "You two could not have been nude in the life raft and him do 'nothing.'"

"He'd go over the side and I'd sort of turn my back," Lee Ann said. "All the time at first, then . . . I got curious. But he had his back turned. I'm still not sure what he was doing. Except it was a lot."

"Any storms?" Walker asked. "Rain and spray get into the raft?"

"Yes, sir," Kevin said.

"No way in hell," Olga said. "You're serious."

"Last extremely embarrassing question, Kevin," Walker asked. "You were in a boat with a beautiful, nubile, young lady you were trying very hard to be a gentleman with. No nocturnal, or rather sleeping, emissions?"

"Uh . . . once," Kevin said.

"The white stuff?" Lee Ann said. "That was kinda gross. And it was three times."

"Tada!" Walker said, holding up his hands.

"I'm not buying it," Olga said. "Were you spooning her?"

"You mean," Kevin said, leaning over and holding out his hands. "Nooo . . . Not . . . me to her. No way. That would . . . I couldn't have . . . Uh, uh. She'd curl up to *my* back. If I'd . . . No."

"Mr. Walker?" Sophia said.

"There was a previous case of noncontact conception," Walker said. "Potentially. A young woman near a Civil War battlefield, Shiloh if I recall correctly, was hit by a minié ball in the stomach. In the uterus to be precise. She survived. A few months later she was clearly pregnant. There was a bit of a scandal since ladies were not supposed to get pregnant unless married. She insisted she was a virgin and a doctor confirmed it."

"Seriously?" Olga said. "You're making this up."

"In the battle a young man had been hit in the right testicle by rifle fire," Walker continued. "Eventually the two were united and ever after people swore the child looked exactly like him. This was, admittedly, based upon the crude medical knowledge of the time and hoary folklore but she did give birth nine months to the day after the battle. And, yes, it was Shiloh—it was what they named the child. They later married and it turned out that one was sufficient as she had four more children by him. All of them looked much the same. Of course, I suppose she could have been banging the same neighbor the whole time.

"Sperm is funny stuff. Some men have sperm that can't swim straight. Others have, if you will, super sperm. Kryptonite won't stop the little tadpoles. Oh, here's another question. Lee Ann, do you like Kevin? Do you, occasionally, get sort of butterflies in your stomach?"

"I love him," Lee Ann said. "I know this is his baby and I *want* to have it. I love him. I know you're going to take him away but I'll keep looking for him *forever*. I'll cross the world and fight *zombies* to be with him."

"It should be noted that Romeo and Juliet were fourteen and thirteen respectively," Walker said. "Ah, true love. Which, among other things, causes the labia to open."

"The what?" Kevin asked.

"The lips of the vagina," Walker said. "I'm sure you've looked from time to time, you little pervert you. The labia is sort of the last line of defense. Salt water has the same chemical content as blood, semen or, for that matter, vaginal secretions. Which is why they taste salty. A little water in the bottom, a little nocturnal, or diurnal if napping during the day, emission, some sexual desire on the part of the young lady causing the labia to open and, voilà, one blessed event with noncontact conception. Or, if the baby has a white beard and a halo upon birth, I'm wrong."

"Or they did it like rabbits and are lying," Olga said.

"There speaks the true cynic," Walker said. "I'm promoting the vision of a medical miracle, something to be written up in studies if we ever are able to do something like that again, and you're being a cynic."

"I'm Ukrainian," Olga said. "It's genetic."

"There's a way to find out," Walker said. "However, despite some rather extensive medical background, under the circumstances, the only *male* in the crew declines to do the check."

"Extensive medical background?" Sophia asked. "More you have declined to mention?"

"I once took a course that included advanced midwifery, if you will," Walker said. "More advanced nursing. But I don't have a license. That's currently beside the point. Any of you ladies up for doing a little peering? Lee Ann, did you ever go to the private parts doctor before the Plague?"

"Yes," Lee Ann said. "Once. I sort of started early, and Mom . . ." She bit her lip, clearly trying not to cry.

"Okay, dear," Walker said, leaning forward and taking her hand. "The thing is, when you 'do it' as the young people say, there's a piece of tissue that tears. It's why the first time sort of hurts."

"Kevin told me that," Lee Ann said.

"I only know 'cause, you know, you *know*," Kevin

said, incoherently. "I've never done it with, you know. I mean, I've never even *done* it, okay? There, I admitted it. I've *never* done it, okay?"

"You seriously think these two could lie about this?" Walker said to Olga.

"Getting to the point of saying no," Olga said. "That spastic series of sentences could only come from a virgin."

"The point is, there are other ways it could tear," Walker said. "Did you use tampons or pads?"

"That's pretty private, don't you think?" Lee Ann said.

"I think we're way past that point of privacy about your twat, Lee Ann," Walker said. "Tampons or pads?"

"Pads," Lee Ann said, pouting.

"Okay, now, Miss Olga is going to go with you into the cabin and she's going to ask you to get like with the private parts doctor. And she's going to have to fiddle about in your private area."

"Why me?" Olga said.

"Because if there's a woman on this boat more familiar with that view than you, I'd be much surprised," Walker said.

"Is that a problem?" Olga said.

"No," Walker said. "But if it comes up again, I'd like to watch."

"Okay, you two, time out," Sophia said. "So you want Olga to do an inspection? Down there?"

"Yes," Walker said. "If she is virgo intacta there's no way that he intentionally knocked her up. No seventeen-year-old heterosexual male can stop at 'I'll just put in the tip.' Cannot. We don't have a speculum but for something this simple you can use your fingers. Use gloves."

"Miss McGregor," Sophia said. "Are you okay with

this? I'm saying, as the captain, that if everything is . . . there, then it's not Kevin's fault. . . ."

"And I'll get the spare room ready for three wise men," Olga said.

"Hell, I'm calling the CDC," Walker said.

"Ahem," Olga said, coming out the lower decks. She was drying her hands off.

"Well?" Sophia asked.

"Well . . ." Olga said, frowning furiously. "Ahem . . . The smarmy bastard appears to be right."

"Smarmy?" Walker said.

"Seriously?" Sophia said.

"Seriously," Olga said. "It's there. Fully intact. Shouldn't *it* have stopped them?"

"Super sperm," Walker said, shrugging. "And, Ensign, we really should call the CDC on this one. It's not their field but it's truly fascinating, medically."

"I really didn't do anything!" Kevin said. "Honest."

"Except, you know, *go* all over a lifeboat," Olga said.

"That is really not something that can be prevented," Walker said.

"I know," Olga said. "It's just . . . Jesus she's young, Tom!"

"Mary was thirteen," Walker said, shrugging. "She's not even the youngest in the squadron. Although the rest were pretty straightforward 'what happens in the compartment' and, no, we don't want your help, thank you. We're going to be looking for a desert island . . ."

"So what happens now?" Kevin asked.

"What happens now is that when Lee Ann gets her composure again, I get to piss all the women off again."

⊷⊖⊷

"You're serious?" Olga said, furiously. "You want them to do it? What is it with you men?"

"You want the full lecture?" Walker asked, seriously. "Or just the medical one? Here's the medical one. Lee Ann is small. Very small. She's not fully developed as a woman. She needed about a year to be really ready to be a prima gravitura..."

"What?" Sophia asked.

"First-time mother," Walker snapped. "She is going to need all the help she can get with the delivery if it's not going to be a C-section. Rate of survival on nonanesthetized, no antilabor drugs C-sections is essentially zero. C-section is out. Theoretically, somebody, not me, could perform a late-term abortion."

"No," Lee Ann said, clutching her stomach. "This is my baby."

"I said theoretically," Walker said. "We don't really have the tools. Back at the squadron with some help from the CDC and the shop on the *Grace*, maybe. Maybe Lieutenant Fallon could do it without botching it. But Lee Ann says no, anyway. So the only functional alternative is natural delivery."

"Get to the part where Kevin *has* to boff his twelve-year-old girlfriend," Olga said.

"Could be any male at this point but Kevin is the best choice," Walker said. "Vaginal sex during late pregnancy thins the cervical walls and makes for an easier delivery. No matter what, Lee Ann's delivery is unlikely to be anything like easy. But it makes for an *easier* delivery. It's the difference between likely to be deadly and maybe possible. With some actual medical assistance and something resembling an infirmary, which means she needs to be back on the *Boadicea*.

ASAP. But, yes, Kevin needs to begin having sex with Lee Ann. Soon. And frequently. At least once a day."

"I'm in favor," Lee Ann said, raising her hand. But she looked a little frightened.

"We need to call this in to Squadron, anyway," Sophia said. "And we'll get a medical read on it from CDC. If they know anything about pregnancy."

"There are books," Walker said. "I'm sure they've got more than epidemiology on their servers."

"You know what?" Sophia said, rubbing her face. "I know the whole thing about not jumping the chain of command. But this isn't really military. And I really need to talk to my da right now . . ."

"So he's right?" Sophia said.

"From what I've read, yes. That was known back when you were . . . Never mind . . . Just . . . Technically he is right. Over."

"Ick," Sophia said. "I just . . . Maybe calling you *wasn't* the best choice, Da. Over."

"I'm glad you did. We never get to talk. But, I've got to get this straight. This Walker guy thinks she got pregnant from involuntary emissions on the damp bottom of a lifeboat? Over."

"Yes," Sophia said. "She's . . . virgo intacta. And they're both . . . Like Olga said, only virgins could be that incoherent about it. Over."

"You're not particularly incoherent about it, over."

"You've been talking to us about it since we were kids in one way or another," Sophia said. "And let's just say this cruise has been a real eye-opener."

"I'd say sorry but I didn't start the Plague. Okay, Walker. What's his medical background, over?"

"I'm not sure," Sophia said. "He said he took a course once that included advanced midwifery. I'm not even sure what that means except it has to do with delivering babies."

"God knows we're going to need it. Okay, I'm going to get the CDC to call you and see if they can confirm what you've said. I'm also going to pass this around in the official news bulletin. Over."

"Uh, isn't this a little private, Da?" Sophia asked.

"Well, it's that or every little old lady on the Boadicea *will be beating him with their canes. Squadron, out."*

"Permission to speak, sir?" the chief of boat of the *Alexandria* said.

"When do you ask, COB?" Vancel replied. "Sure."

"Hate the situation that we're in, sir," the COB said. "Really getting to hate fish. Don't want to think about what's happened ashore, sir. But this Wolf Squadron thing is like the best soap opera *ever*."

"And turns out she got knocked up by sitting where the guy had spewed in his sleep!"

"No fuckin' way!"

"That has got to be the *lamest* excuse *ever!* 'No, seriously, Mom, I got pregnant from a life raft deck!'"

∽⊖∾

"Can you describe these involuntary emissions in more detail?" Dr. Chang said, leaning into the screen. Arnold Chang was an internist as well as an epidemiologist at the CDC whom Dodson had brought in for the consult. "What were the conditions on the interior of the life raft?"

Sophia had seen boiled lobsters less red than Kevin.

Lee Ann was just looking pissed. But in a second she'd start crying.

"Doctors..." Sophia said.

"Doctors," Walker said. "Any of us could describe common conditions in life rafts. The interiors are frequently wet from salt spray. When there is rain, it is usually admixed with spray. The salt content is always high, generally higher than salt water. The clothes also tend to develop high salt content, one of the reasons persons tend to disrobe in the tropics besides heat. It would be useful to keep in mind that you are dealing with two victims of extreme trauma. They are still suffering from dehydration, exposure and malnutrition. They are, in addition, quite young. A degree of care needs to be used in your approach, with all due respect."

"Preliminarily, I concur with your hypothesis, Mr. Walker," Dr. Dobson said. "As I concur with your sentiment. Among other things, well, one of the reasons to get into research is we don't tend to *have* much in the way of bedside manner. Having reviewed what we have on pregnancy, not enough given your conditions, I also, reluctantly, concur with your advice to begin and maintain sexual congress. That would probably get me de-licensed, given the young lady's age, were there still a Medical Licensing Board. However, it is the correct medical advice and given that the two are ... already in the current condition ... I concur. And, yes, this is one for the record books...."

"One last," Dr. Chang said. He'd been leafing through a book as they were speaking and now looked up. "Found a coincidental item. Medical report on an accidental pregnancy in Miami, 2007. Persons were in a group that was engaging in sexual activity. They were, in their minds, protected by condoms. However, they did not understand how to properly use them and were sharing. When one male would get done, the other would flip it inside out. Three young ladies became pregnant due to incidental contact. The young ladies were monogamous to single partners but were all pregnant by partners who had shared the condom rather than their primary partners. So something similar has been documented, although a condom being passed around is not the bottom of a rubber lifeboat."

"Close enough," Dobson said. "I would say that is a fair confirmation. Tell the young lady and gentlemen we're sorry for the indelicacy of the questioning. But we're researchers who have nothing to research. We're sort of starved for something new. CDC out."

Dobson looked across the lab at Barry Martin, his lab assistant.

"You know," he said, leaning back and interlacing his fingers on his shrinking belly. "When you get into this profession, you think about what you're going to be doing in the event of a really bad plague. I always saw myself, out there, in the ruins of civilization, wearing a moon suit and searching for survivors. Never in my wildest dreams did I picture being on Skype with a yacht in the middle of the Atlantic trying to figure out how a twelve-year-old girl got pregnant. Just was *not* on my bucket list . . ."

"Hey, I just figured something out," Olga said.

"What?" Sophia asked wearily. She felt like she'd just fought her way through a typhoon.

"Walker, Dobson and Chang," Olga said.

"Your point?" Sophia asked. "Other than it sounds like a law firm?"

"Three Wise Men! Okay, two wise men and a wise guy..."

Zero Three Hundred local. The definition of Oh Dark Thirty. Everyone should be asleep. And the Hole should be up.

Walker opened up the cabinet that contained one of the Navy hand-helds. They were generally kept off unless there was an away team. None of the boats in the division had away teams operating at the moment.

He turned it to a random frequency and keyed it.

"*Alexandria, Alexandria*, Marigold, over."

He waited.

"*Calling station unidentified. Identify for verification, over.*"

"Verification is call sign. Following eyes only, FDO-SAC. Code is Marigold, repeat, Marigold. Verification: Four-One-Three-Six. Will contact same time, same frequency, tomorrow. End message. Repeat: Eyes only, FDO. Do not, repeat, *not* contact Squadron. Over."

"*If you are screwing around on this frequency, we will find you and have your ass.*"

"Contact only the FDO," Walker said. "Or I shall have yours. Marigold, out."

"Skipper, sorry," the duty officer said. "We just got a weird, really weird, call. Voice only."

"Go ahead," Commander Vancel said, rubbing his eyes. He wasn't getting out of the rack unless it was important.

"Where'd it come from?" Vancel asked, replaying the recording on the handheld.

"Somewhere in Division Seven," the OOD said. "I can't tell if this guy is fucking around or...Well..."

"It's for General Brice," Vancel said, rolling out of his rack. "She was the flag duty officer at SAC when it went down. I'll send it on as a personal e-mail attachment. Log it, though."

"Marigold?" Brice said, looking at the e-mail. She really wasn't terribly busy most of the time and today was one of those days. She was good at her job, which involved getting other people to do theirs and then just keeping that going. Unfortunately, since most of the people she had working for her were über-competent, that meant she had lots of time on her hands. In the middle of an apocalypse. Not a good thing.

So her curiosity was piqued.

She typed in the word as a search in the intelligence database. It wasn't by any means a complete database. The "complete" database had been the whole of SIPRNET, the DoD's secure version of the internet. But The Hole was designed as a backup in the event of, well, an apocalypse, and it had at least extracts of a lot of stuff.

There were various references. Several operations had included "Marigold" in their operations name. Most of them were black ops but not all.

However, there was also a flag officer code name listed.

Upon retirement, all flag officers as well as "select" others were given a code name and a contact method. The reason was that flag officers held a lot of secrets in their heads. Even after retirement, they were potential targets for espionage or terrorist assassination. If they happened to be travelling in a country where a revolution kicked off, they could call a number and response would materialize. Even if the USA had to send Rangers in quietly—as it had on numerous occasions.

She clicked the link and blanched.

"Oh . . ." she said, panting. She felt slightly faint. "Ooof-dah. Oh, it *can't* be . . ."

She listened to the voice recording again and compared the information. The four digit code was the last four of the Social. The voice even sounded the same.

Then she pulled up the manifest for the squadron and started hunting, checking names against the file. The basic name wasn't anywhere on there but she knew it wouldn't be. But the handle . . .

"Thomas Walker," she said, putting her hand over her mouth and trying not to cry. "Son of a bitch. *Night Walker*. He's alive. There *is* a God in heaven."

"Bella Señorita, Alexandria, *over.*"

"*Bella* here," Sophia said, wondering if she should put up the bimini top. The tan was getting pretty deep.

The guys on Columbus's ships had probably been about ready to mutiny at this point. But that was because they didn't know where they were going, where they were or when they were going to get there. If you did, the South Atlantic Equatorial Current cruise was a real beauty. Not much to see but ocean, but in winter it was just lovely rolling combers heading in your general direction, clear skies, seabirds, whales, flying fish and the occasional bit of debris from the death of human civilization.

"Bella, Alex. *Prosecuting sierra. Geared freighter. Approx six hundred feet length. Approx twenty-eight kay gross tons. Containerized and noncontainerized deck cargo. Visible infected. Zulu count five visible. Over.*"

"Roger, *Alex*. Send coordinates, over."

She thought about it for a second, then picked up the other radio.

"Flotilla, Division Seven, over."

"*Division Seven, Flotilla, over.*"

"Got a geared handysize with some infected," Sophia said. "What's the status on Marines, over?"

"*Sort of tapped out working a liner, Division. Recommend give it a pass, over.*"

"Flotilla, be advised. Geared and has noncontainerized deck cargo, break. Looks like really nice salvage. Break. Without getting off the boat myself I am confident my people can handle this without Marine assistance. We're talking walk in the park here. Over."

"Is she really that laid-back about taking on a freighter with zombies on it?" Petty Officer Third Class Kevin Drum said. "I mean, she sounds *bored*."

"The last time Seawolf took a walk in a park it was Washington Square when the zombies overran the last concert in New York," Lieutenant Gregory Spears said. The flotilla commander was a former stock broker and weekend yachtsman. He hadn't realized the difference between telling people how to do their jobs and potentially sending them to their deaths until he'd taken the job. He wasn't enjoying that part of it. "Her definition of walk in the park is not a normal definition." He thought about it and keyed the radio.

∞ ⊖ ∞

"Washington Square walk in the park or a walk in the park walk in the park, over."

Sophia giggled and keyed the radio.

"The 'we've got this' kind, Flotilla. Take your pick."

"Do not endanger your vessel. Minimize risk to your personnel. Do not go directly alongside."

"Do not endanger vessel, aye," Sophia said. "Minimize personnel risk, aye. Do not go directly alongside, aye."

"Seriously, don't get yourselves in a scrum. That's what Marines are for."

"Will not get in a scrum, Flotilla. Over."

"Approved. Flotilla out."

"Hoist the black flag," Sophia said over the intercom. "Man the grapnels. We have a ship to take me hearties! Arrrh!"

"So, Thomas," Sophia said. "As an English as a Second Language teacher with 'some civilian shooting experience,' how good a shot are you?"

The freighter was pretty big compared to the *Bella Señorita* but ships like the *Iwo Jima* and liners like the *Voyage* had given Sophia a new appreciation for the word "big." And if any of the gear was running, it was a real catch. The noncontainerized deck cargo wasn't much—some boat hulls, mostly—but one of the containers had been opened and apparently contained food, based on the well-fed zombies on the deck and the seabirds flying in and out. Probably fresh water as well. Zombies could occasionally figure out how to tear into cases of bottled water.

"I would say fair to good," Walker said. "But that is on my scale of judging such things. I will also say that catenary is going to be a bitch."

The freighter was not rocking much in the relatively smooth seas. The *Bella*, on the other hand, was bouncing quite a bit. And they were not rocking in time.

"Always is," Sophia said. "Okay, shooting challenge. You, me and Olga. As skipper I'm going to have the edge on both experience and weapon so I'll spot myself one zombie."

"Are you sure about that, Skipper?" Walker said. "My definition of good would be most people's definition of excellent."

"Choose your weapon, Mr. Walker," Sophia said.

"Is this a duel?" Olga asked. "Don't you need seconds?"

"A pistol?" Sophia said. "Okay…"

She'd turned out with her personalized M4 with Leupold scope. Olga had her M4. Walker had a 1911.

"I am capable enough with a rifle, ma'am, but pistol or submachine gun are usually my preference," Walker said turning his right shoulder towards the zombies clustered by the rail. "Whenever you're ready, ma'am."

"I think I'll spot," Olga said, setting her weapon down and getting on her stomach.

"Works for me," Sophia said, getting in the prone and wrapping the sling around her arm. "The one item I will note on this is always miss high if you're going to miss. The one thing you don't want is rounds coming back at the ship."

"Understood, ma'am," Walker said. "Thank you for that tip."

"Why do I think you knew it already?" Sophia said, lining up a target.

"I did not, actually," Walker said. "Makes sense. But this is, in fact, a new experience for me, ma'am."

"I'll work forward to aft, you work aft to forward. Engage at will."

Walker missed his first shot, high, and was less angered than pleased. He knew that he would not be doing any better with a rifle at this range. And he had missed because of the catenary. Which meant he had something new to learn about shooting and that was becoming increasingly rare in his experience.

Sophia missed her first two shots but she was used to that. Catenary was, as Walker had noted, a bitch. The U.S. Navy SEALs had managed to shoot three pirates in similar if reversed conditions, each with one shot apiece, at night, without hitting a hostage. How, she was still wanting to learn. But so far although the Marines were somewhat trained in catenary shooting, no real "expert" had turned up.

Her third shot scored, high and center, on one of the infected and he dropped out of sight.

"Excellent shot, Ensign," Walker said.

"Thanks," Sophia said, keeping her eye in the scope.

∽⊖∾

Walker was firing one-handed, arm extended, his left hand on his hip. It was not a normal firing position but it gave the added advantage of being very flexible. That flexibility had him, at first, chasing the targets. When he realized that wasn't the best choice, he waited until they came into his target zone, then adjusted minutely.

Head shot.

Now he was getting in the groove....

There were originally seven infected on deck. Sophia and Walker fired nearly simultaneously and the last target dropped.

"Okay," Olga said. "That was definitely a head shot. But I can't tell which of you got him. And you were neck and neck up to that point."

"Walker," Sophia said.

"Skipper's," Walker said.

"From the way the head came apart I think it was both," Olga said.

"Since the Hole is so interested in 'Marigold,' whoever he is, upload this to General Brice's attention," Lieutenant Commander Vancel said, watching the screen. "And let's go find some more prospects."

"That's gotta be a both," Olga said. "Yuck."

"It was," Walker said, chuckling. "This is the forty-five going in here on the cheek. The skipper's five-five-six went into the right eye. I'd say either one was a kill shot. The interesting question is what is in the container."

The answer was fruit juice in cardboard containers. The infected had managed to rip their way into the pallets and get both liquid and some nourishment. The bodies of a few crew as well as feathers of seabirds indicated there had been other sources of protein.

"I'm glad I've got a respirator on," Walker said. He'd armed up with a 1911 and a pump shotgun and changed into his blue coveralls. But other than that he was just wearing a respirator. Olga was in full combat gear with a balaclava against bites to the neck. "Let's check out the rest. You lead."

"You're such a gentleman," Olga said.

"I'm a firm believer in female equality," Thomas said. "After you."

"I really don't like this," Olga said. Belowdecks was dark as a tomb. Also silent as one except for a rattling and banging of metal as the freighter slowly rocked in the swells. Each bang, though, was startling. They were too irregular to predict.

"Does get the blood pumping, don't it?" Thomas said as they swept through the crew quarters. The area was a mess and the reason was apparent in a naked body, past bloat and long dead. "Don't think we're waking him up, no matter how much noise we make. But the body hasn't been mauled. That would tend to indicate this area is clear."

"So we can go back, right?" Olga said.

"Mechanical spaces still to go I would think. But you're in charge."

"I think the engine room was closed up," Olga said, sweeping around one of the massive generators. "No crap, no dried blood."

"And no body," Walker said. "I would say this is legal salvage and in decent condition."

"Flotilla, Division Seven," Sophia said, then looked down to the aft deck at the clearance crew. "You two, get out of your gear and grab a drink. I know how nerve-wracking that can be. Flotilla, Division Seven."

"Division Seven, Flotilla."

"Ship is clear. Seven live infected now KIA. One previous KIA in the interior. Mechanical and working spaces in good shape. Diesel engines and onboard fuel. Recommend this one for a salvage team. Geared and loaded with cargo."

"Will pass that on to Squadron, Division. Any problems?"

"Walk in the park, Flotilla."

"Okay, let me make this *real clear*," the salvage crew boss said. "This one had better actually be *cleared.*"

Adam David Saddler had been a master mariner, driving ships like this one, for thirty-five years before the Plague. What he had not been, had no desire to be, was a cop, a soldier or, for that matter, a zombie hunter. He thought anyone who did it for kicks or for pay was an idiot. He'd had to kill one of his crewmates when the poor guy turned on their lifeboat. He was not interested in meeting more.

"Had that problem before?" Sophia asked.

Two off-shore inflatables were filled with a crew from the *Grace Tan*, ready to, if possible, get the ship underway to join the squadron.

"Yes, we have had that problem before," the captain said. "And we don't find it funny. Did you clear the engineering spaces?"

"Yes, we cleared the engineering spaces," Olga said. "They were closed. We only found one infected belowdecks. It was dead and it hadn't been chewed on."

"Don't suppose you cleared out the bodies," one of the crew asked.

"No, we didn't," Olga said. "That's what you big... strong... men are for. We just killed them."

"Need your clearance people to accompany," the salvage boss said.

"That's why they've got their guns."

"What are you going to do with the container?" Walker asked.

"If we can get everything running, probably hose it out and close it." Suzanne Grazier had been a full rate deck hand on a freighter that had been infected. She'd jumped ship with three of her shipmates. One other had survived and they had both been quite happy to see a boat like Sophia's come along. Especially given the pregnancy. She'd liked both of the guys who had turned but the upside was, she knew who her baby's daddy was. "It's not worth trying to undog it and winch it over the side. And I don't think the stuff's going to be good anymore."

There was a slight rumble under their feet and Suzanne grinned.

"Well, that's one thing working," he said.

"And we're away," Sophia said. The salvage boss had grumpily declared the clearance of the M/V *Paul Østed* "good enough" and taken over the ship. "Now we just have to catch back up to my division. Full power, helmsman!"

"Full power, aye," Olga said, pushing the throttles forward.

"But that way," Sophia said, pointing to starboard. "You're headed for, well, Antarctica right now."

"Details, details . . ." Olga said.

CHAPTER 3

*"... KING OF MIAMI AND THE KINGDOM OF FLORCUBATAMP!
ALL SHALL BOW BEFORE MY MAGNIFICENCE ...!"*

From: *Collected Radio Transmissions of The Fall*
University of the South Press 2053

"Bella, Bella, Bella, *this is the* Finally Friday, *over.*"

"*Friday,* Bella, over," Olga said in a bored tone.

"*Fuel state, three hundred fifty gallons. Water, twenty gallons. Our ROWPU is acting up and the oiler can't get it fixed so far. Lots of food, lots of booze, not so much on the water and fuel thing. Captain McCartney asked me to add that this is an official 'we need fuel' call. Over.*"

"Roger," Olga said. "Will pass that on to the division commander. *Bella,* out."

"Anything new?" Sophia said, coming up on the fly bridge.

Azure and silver. She'd been reading quite a bit and on Walker's suggestion had dug into Hornblower. Part of her gift from Mr. Lawton had been a slew of e-books and they included all of the Horatio Hornblower series. She now knew what a "cutting out expedition" was supposed to be like. And the description of southern seas was accurate as all hell. Perfect blue, perfect silver, perfect days of peace and quiet and not a damned problem in the world except an almost complete lack of people to save and Olga going slowly stir crazy.

Next up: Aubrey and Maturin. Which Walker said was more historically accurate. That should be interesting.

"*Friday* is low on fuel," Olga said. "They're *officially* declaring they need fuel."

"How low?" Sophia asked.

"Three hundred and fifty gallons," Olga said. "I figured it out. That's about a day's worth the way we're going. Assuming they don't have to make a speed run."

"LeEllen should have called that in sooner," Sophia said, frowning. "Okay, I'll call it in to Flotilla. If needs be we'll cross-load; we're nearly topped up."

When Olga had gone below, Sophia picked up the radio.

"Flotilla, Division Seven, over."

"*Seven, Flotilla, over.*"

"One of our boats is nearly out of fuel. The other two are in good state but it's been luck of the draw on finding boats with fuel and *Friday* drew the short straw. We can cross-load but we also are about topped up on supplies and have some passengers. Request permission to do a drop-off and tank run. Over."

"*Roger, Seven, I'll pass that to the flotilla commander. Anything else, over?*"

"Be advised, *Friday* is one day from dry and also low on water," Sophia said. "Can cross-load to keep her running, but would like a reply as soon as possible. That's it. Division out."

∽ ⊖ ⌒

"Division Seven, Flotilla Commander. Need to speak to your division commander, over."

"Division Actual, aye," Sophia replied.

"Cross-load fuel, then return main squadron for supply and passenger drop and tanking. Do you copy, over?"

"Return main squadron, aye. Cross-load for run, aye."

"Take crew rest aboard larger vessels, then return to sweep. Flotilla out."

"Woot," Sophia said. "Back to civilization, such as it is."

The first thing that was evident was the cruise ship M/V *Boadicea* on the horizon. In a sea of darkness it was the sole bright spot. As they closed with the squadron center, more ships became apparent. The *Grace Tan*. The diesel tanker *Ho Yun*. The *Paul Østed*. Other, smaller, support ships. Motor yachts in a ragged formation following along like attention deficit baby ducks. Zodiacs zipping between the ships even at this late hour. A Zodiac filled with a Marine clearance team passed a few miles to port, headed out for some heavy clearance.

"Squadron, Division Seven, over," Sophia radioed when they were about five miles from the formation.

"Division Seven, Squadron. Switch to Forty-Six for Squadron Traffic Control, copy?"

"Switch Four-Six for Traffic Control, aye," Sophia said, switching frequencies. "Squadron Traffic Control, Division Seven, three motor yachts, requesting orders. Be advised, one of us needs to tank, over."

"Division Seven, TraffCon. Unrep not authorized

at night absent emergency. Are you declaring an emergency, over?"

"Negative, Squadron. They can probably hang in there till morning. Request early tanking, over."

"Roger, I'll make a note. Come to One-one-four. Move to rear of formation. Join motor yacht contingent to the rear. Do not approach within one hundred yards of other motor yachts. Do not approach within two hundred yards of ships. Copy?"

"One one four, aye," Sophia said. "Rear of formation, aye. Motor yacht contingent rear, aye. Do not approach within one hundred yards other yachts, do not approach within two hundred yards ships, aye."

"We'll try to get you tanked after dawn. I've made a note to unrep ops. Keep somebody on radio watch that's actually on the radio. TraffCon, out."

"Friday, Business, Bella, over."

"Finally Friday, over."

"Risky Business."

"Follow me," Sophia said, slowing down. "We're to get behind the rest of the motor yachts. I've put in a request for tanking at dawn. No unrep at night. *Friday*, can you hang in there?"

"Should be fine, Bella, over."

"They also don't want us to be closer than a hundred yards to other yachts and two hundred from ships," Sophia radioed. "Let's try to actually look like we know what we're doing. I'm going to come to One-one-four. Try to turn on the same spot I do and get right in line. Copy that, over?"

"Friday. We can do that, over."

"Business. *Let's make a show even though nobody's probably up at this time of night."*

"Try to maintain a line with regular interval even after we join the formation," Sophia said. "Turning to one-one-four now."

"Holy crap," Ryan Reppe said, looking through binos at the approaching division. The master mariner was the midwatch officer of the deck of the *Grace Tan* and monitored TraffCon since it was where most mistakes started to show up first. He'd wondered when the division was going to turn but as they tracked like beads on a string, instead of heading to the rear like a gaggle of idiots, he was mildly impressed. "That division may know what it's doing. Will wonders never cease?"

"Seawolf's division," Katie Phillips said. Phillips had been a deckhand before the Plague with some experience as a watch stander on large vessels. Ships like the *Grace Tan* and modern freighters were largely self-driving when at sea. They followed preprogrammed courses that only needed a human staying awake to watch for emergencies. She'd been with the squadron for two months, unlike Reppe and was now studying for her master's ticket.

"Seawolf," Reppe said. "Oh, the admiral's daughter?"

"Commodore, sort of, but, yeah. She's pretty good."

"Hopefully they can figure out how to unrep without sinking their boat," Reppe said.

"Seawolf could unrep at night," Phillips said, shrugging. "And her captains could probably do the same..."

"Glad we're not unrepping at night," Sophia said, yawning. "Your conn, Mr. Walker. Try not to hit anybody."

"Will do, ma'am," Walker said. "Little breezy this morning. Mind if I take the mid-deck helm?"

"Not at all," Sophia said. "I think I'm going to just hang out for a bit before I head below. It's nice to see signs of civilization for a change. It's going to annoy the hell out of everybody, but I want you to do radio checks on the thirty and hour with both the other boats. Nobody is going to go to sleep on this watch. And keep a check on *Friday*'s fuel. We should have cross-loaded more. If there's an emergency, wake me up."

"Yes, ma'am," Walker said.

Walker did three checks on the other boats, then set the autopilot and made a quick trip to the galley for a cup of coffee. He checked their position and it was still tracking to the *Grace Tan*. Knowing what he'd find, he went up to the flying bridge.

The fifteen-year-old ensign was curled up at the helm of the boat, shivering slightly, sound asleep. He pulled a blanket out of a drybox and tucked it around her before heading below.

"Ma'am," Walker said, shaking the ensign's shoulder.

"Left, left, left!" Sophia said, sitting up. She rubbed her eyes and shook her head. "Fuck, I hate those..."

"Yes, ma'am," Walker said, handing her a cup of coffee. "They are a bitch and a half."

"Know any tricks to handling them?" Sophia said, sipping the coffee. She was gray in the predawn light.

"A few," Walker said. "They don't make them go away, just make them less horrible. If they work at all for you."

"Later, maybe," Sophia said. "What's up?"

"Starting unrep ops in thirty minutes," Walker said. "Most of the boats waiting are dry. We're actually not scheduled until eleven hundred if, as they said, we get in then. The *Friday* thinks it has enough to make it to this afternoon. They asked if we had inventories, I said yes. They didn't seem to believe me. Our first operation is passenger drop-off but we're to use the offshores and take them to the *Boadicea*. Boat is working fine, Batari is making breakfast."

"I swear to God, Walker, I can get Da to make you an instant chief petty officer, at the least," Sophia said.

"Oh, I'm not qualified to be a chief, ma'am," Walker said, grinning. "I don't have a coffee cup welded to my hand."

"Okay," Sophia said, looking around. "I'll get everybody to get their packs ready. Since we've got time until unrep, we'll get them fed first. That will take some of the strain off the rest of the squadron."

"Yes, ma'am," Walker said.

"Get some sleep, Tom," Sophia said. "You've earned it."

"I can keep going for quite a while, ma'am," Walker said. "And you're probably going to need help today."

"Sunk Investment, Sunk Investment... *What is it about 'come up to our port side' you don't understand? We have guns and we will use them. Over.*"

"Dry" turned out to be an understatement of the state of most of the boats in the ragged formation. During the night four had fallen out of formation when they had to shut their engines down and go to generator only to make it to morning. A smaller resupply ship, designed to support megayachts, had been running around behind the formation since dawn tracking them down and getting them fueled back up.

Two more were under tow having had "mechanicals" overnight. They were awaiting engineering survey crews from the *Grace* to determine if they could be repaired or would have to be abandoned.

And the resupply was not going quickly. The skippers and crews of the boats were rarely experienced and the little experience they did have was tooling around the ocean looking for survivors. Coming alongside a large ship for underway replenishment, not so much.

One thing that was holding things up was that there were some supplies to come off and some supplies to come on. Everyone was supposed to have an inventory of what was to come off and what was a critical resupply item. So far, few of the boats had had that. So as each came alongside there was an argument with the resupply crews about what needed to be onloaded and offloaded. The crews were particularly protective of their gathered liquor stores and virtually all of them wanted toilet paper and parts.

"Uh, Grace, our starboard side hull is sort of weak. We really need to come up to your starboard, over."

"Define 'weak,' Investment, over."

"We sort of have a leak there. The hull cracked when we were clearing another boat. We've got it glued with Aquaseal but it's still leaking. Bilge pump is handling it but I'd rather not come up to port if that's okay. Over."

"You're floating around on a cracked hull?" TraffCon screamed. *"Stand by for lifting operations. We'll take you aboard and check your hull. And you had better be serious or you're not going to be a skipper anymore. Switch to fifteen for lifting instructions. Jesus, people. Tell us stuff like this first, okay? Finally Friday, Finally Friday, over."*

"Finally Friday, *over.*"

"*Come alongside the* Grace, *our port, our* port, *do you copy, over?*"

"*Come alongside,* Grace *port, aye.*"

"*No cracked hull,* Friday, *over?*"

"*No, TraffCon, over.*"

"Mr. Walker," Sophia said. "Take the conn. I'm going to change into uniform, then get over to the *Friday* for their unrep."

"Roger, ma'am," Walker said, taking the helm.

"I'll try to get back aboard before we come alongside," Sophia said.

After a quick change and washing her face she jumped in the Zodiac and zipped up to the *Friday* as it was cautiously maneuvering up to the much larger ship.

She tossed the mooring line to one of the crew assembled on deck and boarded without asking permission. She was pleased to see that there were stores piled on the boat's aft deck, ready for offload. Including liquor. If it wasn't *all* the liquor, that was beside the point. They'd included liquor. No toilet paper, though.

"You taking over?" LeEllen asked as Sophia came up on the bridge. She was creeping up to the larger boat.

"Your boat," Sophia said. "I'm here to smooth out any problems. That's all."

The crew already had every fender on the boat tied off on the starboard side of the motor yacht and there were more tied off on the *Grace Tan.* Port was the lee side, the downwind side, of the massive supply ship. If they were in a harbor, they could just have tied up to the bigger ship. The problem being at sea there were waves. The two ships could not actually tie up to each other. Unrep required that the smaller boat first tie off at a slight distance from the larger ship, then hold that position as the two ships moved along, side by side. The fenders were there to keep the smaller ship from being cracked like an egg if they did touch.

There were three yachts on the deck of the supply ship on cradles. From the looks of them, they were being refurbished to be added to the squadron. Sophia sometimes wondered if her da was doing this just to "own" more motor yachts than anyone else in the world. There were no open cradles so she wasn't sure what the *Grace* intended to do with the *Sunk Investment*. From her experience with Skipper Buckley, sink it and fire him was the correct answer.

A dinghy came alongside and a team led by a man in his fifties clambered aboard.

"Who's the skipper?" the man yelled.

"Here," LeEllen said as the man came up on the flying bridge.

"I'm the away unrep boss," he said. "Blake Parker at your service. I'll take the helm. You run your crew. From now on, making sure you don't sink is my responsibility."

"Your conn," LeEllen said, lifting her hands from the wheel.

"Any chance you've got an inventory?" the man asked as he expertly came up to the bigger ship. "On and off?"

"Here," LeEllen said, pulling out a printed out sheet.

"Barry!" the man yelled. "Inventory!"

"Seriously?" the younger man said, coming up on the flying bridge and taking the sheet. "Roger, I'll call this in."

"They're about dry," Parker said, looking at the gauges. "Get the fuel hose over here first."

He conned the boat up to the supply ship which threw

a line attached to a rubber covered grapnel onto the sundeck. The unrep crew quickly got the line onto the boat, then used it to haul a heavier line onto the yacht. With that they got four lines aboard so that the yacht was essentially moored, at a distance, from the supply ship. By the time the fourth line was in place, the fuel hose was already being lowered from the supply ship.

"*That* is a well trained crew," Sophia said wistfully.

"They should be," Parker said. "We've been doing this enough. Who are you, Ensign?" he said, looking at Sophia, quizzically.

"Division commander," Sophia said.

"Here to tell us what we're doing wrong?" the unrep boss asked.

"Here to make sure *my* crews are doing it *right*," Sophia said.

"So far so good," Parker said. "You've actually got an inventory. That's a big help. We used to tell the boats to bring it over when they joined so we could have stuff ready. Nobody ever had one so we gave up. We just do it on the fly, now. Pain in the ass."

"All three of my boats have their inventories prepared," Sophia said. "Would it help to get them over to your people?"

"A lot," the unrep boss said, looking over his shoulder at her. He keyed the radio on his shoulder. "Charlie, Blake. This division's actually got its inventories and stores requests. Want to send somebody around collecting them?"

"*On it.*"

"We do have some toilet paper," Blake said. "One of the boats found a container that we could get to. But don't ask for feminine hygiene products."

"We've got some," LeEllen said. "And the boats have been sharing around."

"This boat's got a problem with its ROWPU," Sophia said. "We think it's the filters but we haven't found any that fit in our clearance. Any chance you've got some of those?"

"Depends on the make," Parker said.

"HRO," LeEllen said. "Seafari mini. We think it's the sea strainer rather than the osmo membrane. But we don't have any parts for either."

"Charlie," the unrep boss radioed. "Got somebody can check out this boat's ROWPU?"

"Not right now. I'll put it on the list. What's the make?"

"HRO Mini," Parker said.

"Stand by."

The unrep crew had brought over a set of cargo nets on a zip-line and were working with the *Friday* crew to move the material on the aft deck into it. As soon as one net was loaded, it was sent back aboard the ship on the same line.

"We don't have any parts for a Mini onboard. I've got a couple that are in good shape and would probably fit. I'll send Mellan over as soon as he gets freed up."

"Okay," Parker said. "You heard the man."

"Thought that might be the case," LeEllen said.

"You're not asking for *anything*?" the unrep boss said, looking at a copy of the inventory.

"We've been salvaging a lot," Sophia said. "And sharing around. And I told my people not to ask for stuff you're not going to have. About the only thing this boat needed was fuel."

"You, young lady, are a delight," Parker said. "People

are asking for fresh vegetables. Right. Like we've got those. We're about done here. That your Zod tied up, Ensign?"

"Yes," Sophia said.

"If you don't mind, I'll catch a ride to the next boat with you. We're sort of overloaded."

"Not an issue," Sophia said.

The untie was done more or less in reverse with one line after another going back aboard the supply ship until the yacht was free. Parker maneuvered it away from the *Grace* until it was a hundred meters out, then lifted his hands from the controls.

"Your boat, ma'am," the unrep boss said. "And I thank you for being prepared."

"Thank you for a professional job," LeEllen said.

"Call in to TraffCom for parking instructions," Parker said. "Ensign, after you."

"Roger," Sophia said, heading down to her Zodiac.

"Barry, I'm riding with the ensign," Parker said. "Which is the next boat?"

"The *Negocio Arriesgado*," Sophia said, pointing. "It translates as *Risky Business*."

"Risky business this is indeed," Parker said. "Let's cast off. Time's a-wastin'."

"You're Seawolf, huh?" Parker asked as Sophia pulled away from the boat.

"Yep," Sophia said. "Is that an issue?"

"No," Parker replied. "People talk. 'She's only a skipper 'cause of her dad.' Captain Gilbert said you're a skipper 'cause you have your shit together. I wasn't sure. Glad to have a confirmation. You guys really fight your way out of Central Park? Just the four of you?"

"No," Sophia said.

"Thought so."

"There was a team of National Guardsmen we hooked up with," Sophia said. "And my uncle and a security guy. And it was Washington Square."

"So that's no shit?" Parker said. "Seriously?"

"Seriously," Sophia said. "And it wasn't fun. Well, Faith had fun. Me, not so much. I'd only brought along a forty-five and I just about ran out of rounds. When the lights went out, every fucking zombie in New York descended on the concert. It... Yeah, it wasn't fun."

"Sorry," Parker said, nodding. "I thought that was bullshit. But... wow."

"Estrella," Sophia yelled, cruising down the side of the *Risky Business*. "Coming aboard with the unrep team. Tell Lillie."

"I was sweating having to figure this out," Rainey said, watching the unrep crew handle the lines. "Glad there's somebody else to do it."

"Every one of those people could be doing something else," Sophia said. "Running boats, some of them even running ships..."

"Like me," Parker said, watching the unrep to make sure nothing was going wrong. "I'd much rather be running a freighter or a supply ship. Or even one of these. Instead of dealing with mostly moronic or bitchy captains. You're an exception, ma'am, let me make that clear."

"Oh, I can be a bitch," Lillie said, laughing. "But I'm so grateful I don't have to do this I'd discuss having your babies if I didn't already have a bun in the oven."

"When are you due?" Parker asked.

"February, March," Rainey said. "Like most of the squadron."

"And that's gonna be a time for any man in his right mind to be at sea..."

"And, we're away," Parker said as the unrep of the *Bella Señorita* was completed. "Jesus, three tons of stores from you guys. Might I officially say thank you for that and for the way your people were prepared."

"Put it in your report," Sophia said, smiling. "And thank you for your professional help. Hope you get that boat someday soon."

"Eh, I'm doing good work," Parker said, shrugging. "Any time I wonder why I'm bothering, I watch the night sky video."

"Night sky video?" Sophia asked.

"They run it in the theater on the *Boadicea* on a regular schedule," Parker said. "It's sort of mandatory for freshies but a lot of people attend. You should see it. It's... Yeah. Anyway, I've got to get going. Light a candle and all that. Thank you, again."

"And thank you," Sophia said. As the unrep boss boarded his boat she keyed the radio for TraffCon.

"TraffCon, Division Seven. Unrep complete. Marching orders. Over."

"Move to rear of small boat flotilla, north side. Switch to channel twenty-three for orders."

"Rear of flotilla, north side, aye. Switch twenty-three, aye," she radioed. She picked up the mike for division ops and keyed it. "Okay, ladies, follow me. And let's give them a show..."

CHAPTER 4

*"We've got the grain silos cleared in south Vicksburg and as long
as we don't show any lights at night the zombies don't cluster.
Bring ammo if you're coming in. Even any reloading material you
find. We've got the equipment if you've got the primers..."*

From: *Collected Radio Transmissions of The Fall*
University of the South Press 2053

". . . Understood. Division out." Sophia switched back
to division frequency.

"*Business, Friday, Bella,* over."

"Risky *Business.*"

"Finally Friday, *over.*"

"Here's the orders. We have until day after tomorrow, oh-eight-hundred, for rear area activities, whatever
those are. So we've got the rest of the afternoon and
all day tomorrow. Rotate your crews as you see fit.
Crews and skippers can visit *Boadicea* or *Tan. Tan* is
for supply issues. *Boadicea* is for downtime. Either the
skipper or *two* crew members must be onboard. I'm
hereby amending that to two crew, period. So figure
out your rotation schedule and then send them off
to the *Bo. Friday,* clear, over?"

"Bella, Friday. *Two aboard, day and a half off. Over.*"

"*Business,* clear, over?"

71

"*Got it*, Bella. *Will do.*"

"Okay," Sophia said, turning around. She'd taken the belowdecks helm for the short conference and the crew were in the saloon directly behind. "You all get that?"

"Got it, Skipper," Walker said.

"Tom, you probably want to get your head down?"

"I could use some sleep, yes," Walker said.

"I'll take first watch on the boat," Sophia said. "You can be the second onboard. Rest of you can head out if you want. I need at least one of you back by midnight. Any questions?"

"There's a market on the *Bo*, ma'am," Batari said. "I could use some spices and condiments. Can I take some stuff to trade?"

"Go and look, first," Celementina said. "I would like to go over to the *Tan*, too. For the same. Look and see what they have t'ey're not giving up. We might still have some stuff t'ey want to trade. I can' believe you gave up all my spares."

"They don't fit our boat," Sophia pointed out.

"I could have used them to trade with t'ese other boats, Skip," Celementina said. "I bet I find parts for t'e *Friday*."

"Just don't lose the offshore," Walker said. "I guarantee that people are just taking off in those. If I may suggest, Skipper, one of us stay on the offshore. I can stay up, run people around. Then go back and get them at midnight. That's plenty of sleep. Probably they can cadge rides around. Then tomorrow, if they've made any deals, we can close them. But that would leave just you onboard."

"*Friday, Business, Bella*, over," Sophia said, keying the radio.

"Business."

"Friday."

"Have the second crewman take your people where they want to go. Pick-up will be at the *Bo* at midnight. If they want to go someplace else, they can catch a ride. Do not leave your dinghies or offshores tied up and unattended. Copy?"

"Business. *Why, over?*"

"They go missing," Sophia radioed.

"*Got it.*"

"Friday, *aye.*"

"Okay," Sophia said. "Any more questions or comments?"

"When are you going to the *Bo*, ma'am?" Walker asked.

"Not sure I am," Sophia said, shrugging. "I'm good onboard. You can either head over on midwatch or you can head over tomorrow."

"Do we *have* to be back by midnight?" Olga asked, pouting. "There may be interesting things going on afterwards. Parties don't usually get really going until around eleven. And there might be handsome Marines aboard."

"No," Sophia said. "That's when the boat's coming to pick people up. If you stay overnight, we'll run another boat over at oh-eight hundred. And I'm sure you can convince somebody to give you a ride."

"I'm *sure* of that," Olga said, brightening. "Oh, you meant on a *Zodiac?* That could be fun."

"Bella Señorita, *Squadron, looking for* Bella *Actual if aboard, over.*"

The sun was slowly setting in the west and Sophia was thinking about getting some more clothes on.

She'd been in her usual bikini. But the temperature hadn't really dropped, yet.

"*Bella* Actual," Sophia replied. "Hi, Da."

"*You coming to the* Bo, *over?*"

"Not today," Sophia said. "Gave my crew some time off. Over."

"*Roger. Squadron out.*"

"Well," Sophia said. "That was abrupt. Love you, too, Da."

Sophia had slipped into a track suit when the sun went down. She only had one Navy uniform and she saved that for when she needed it.

There were Zodiacs moving around from boat to boat all the time but one was headed her way. Since theirs was alongside it was either crew coming back early or somebody coming for a courtesy call.

"*Bella Señorita, Squadron Actual, over.*"

"*Bella* Actual, over," Sophia replied.

"*Mind if your mom and I come aboard?*"

"Glad to have you," Sophia said. "Sorry about not coming over to the *Bo*. I wanted to give my crew the time off."

"*Which is why you're an ensign. We're approaching in a Zod. Be there in a jiff.*"

"I was planning on coming over tomorrow," Sophia said, hugging her mother.

"You don't want us on your boat?" Stacey teased. "Not keeping your room clean?"

"My boat is ready for inspection," Sophia said. "My rack, not so much. And Batari is over on the *Bo*. So I'm going to have to cook."

"I think I can remember how to find my way around a galley," Stacey said.

"I need to head to the helm," Sophia said. "I'd wake Thomas up but he's been running since mid-watch last night."

"I'll join you if you don't mind," Steve said.

"We see each other plenty," Stacey said. "I think I see him more doing this than when we were home."

Walker woke up at the sound of voices and slid his hand under the pillow. Then he heard the skipper laugh and went instantly back to sleep.

"How are things going?" Sophia asked, sitting down at the interior helm. The boat was on autopilot so all she had to do was be there for emergencies and to monitor the radio.

"As well as could be expected," Steve said. "Better even. The night sky video has helped immensely with some building pressures from the Euro block."

"That's the second time I've heard about that video," Sophia said. "Description?"

"Watch it," Stacey said, laying out some sushi rolls. "It's better if it's not described. Then you'll come back and watch it again."

"We'd gotten a video from The Hole to show to our people," Steve said. "It was powerful but I ran it past Zumwald as a cross check. He said let him have it and he'd get back to me. Came back a week later with a new one. And it was, yeah, better. But you do need to see it. I think it's over the top. Most people don't agree."

"I suspect you'll hate it," Stacey said. "And not be

able to keep from crying. Your cook left these in the fridge. What is the fish? It's good."

"Something we found under a raft," Sophia said. "It looked like a triple tail but it wasn't. I was sort of afraid of eating it but Batari just chopped it up."

"Putting cooks on the small boats is making more sense," Steve said. "But there's a bunch of work to do on the large ships, too. And you really can't have people trying to cook for themselves, there."

"So what's the problem with the Eurotrash?" Sophia asked, taking a sushi roll. The fish was still fresh and richer even than tuna.

"The Euros are, understandably, interested in when the squadron is going to put some ships over clearing Europe," Steve said, shrugging. "I'm sure that when I do, Americans will ask why we're not putting all our resources to the U.S. And China has officially requested aid."

"Hell, we don't even have a Pacific squadron clearing the West Coast," Sophia said. "We're not even clearing the *East* Coast."

"We're getting there," Steve said. "Now that the tropical season is over we can work our way in. I'm looking at various concepts. We'll do it. And Europe and, yeah, Asia. Somebody has to..." he added, rubbing his face.

"Da, it's not all on you, you know," Sophia said softly.

"No, it's not," Steve said. "It's on all of us. But we'll get it done. Well, we'll get it more done. I want lights on. I want cities lit. Small cities, mind you. There's not going to be many left of us on the land. But we'll get it done. How is the clearance going?"

"We find boats, we clear boats," Sophia said,

shrugging. "Same old same old. Occasional odd items. No biggie."

"Having any problems with your skippers?" Steve asked.

"No," Sophia said. "They're good and they're getting better. Teaching them to teach their crews is the tough part. They're learning. Thomas has been a damned blessing, I'll tell you that."

"The ESL teacher?" Steve said, taking a bite of sushi.

"He's more than an ESL teacher," Sophia said. "I don't know what, but he's a damned good shot. He's *covered* in scars. Not like Olga; I know combat scars at this point and he's been blown up and shot so many times he must be held together with stitching like Frankenstein's monster. And he's like a walking dictionary, not to mention a walking translator bot. He says he's a man of many parts. I'm wondering *how* many."

"That sounds like an issue," Steve said, frowning. "If he's been less than forthcoming, that's a trust issue."

"He's been less than forthcoming," Sophia said. "But I trust him. Totally. I don't know *why* I do. Yes, I do know. He's former military. U.S. He *feels* like Fontana, you know? He says he was a truck driver but his records got lost. Bull. He was an NCO or something. A senior one. He sort of has that feel. Not like a gunny. Army. But he doesn't, too. Like, he has a quote for everything, like you, Da. But, I dunno. There's more. All I know is I trust him and he's one hell of an asset."

"Should I look into it?" Steve asked.

"I'd prefer you didn't," Sophia said. "You're the boss and it's up to you. I don't know why he doesn't come out and say what he really was, but I'd hate to lose him."

"I ever talk about the French Foreign Legion?" Steve asked.

"Not really, no," Sophia said. "I sort of know what it is."

"More like was," Steve said. "Formed by Louis the Fourteenth to build up his forces. It only takes non-French volunteers as enlisted men. All the officers are French. The 'enlisted' over the years have included generals from other armies, usually ones that were on the run for some reason. They're given new names and new identities and as long as they do their full term of service, with honor, they can live under them for the rest of their lives as full French citizens. After World War Two it was filled with former SS, many of them under death sentences for their actions in World War Two. You practically had to speak German to be in a French unit."

"That's screwy," Sophia said.

"It worked for centuries with one notable exception," Steve said. "A mutiny in the 1960s that was an attempted coup. Point being, I'm sure there are all sorts of people in the squadron who have taken the opportunity to become someone else. To forget what they were. As long as they don't screw up badly, I'll take that. The problem being, leopards don't usually change their spots."

"I'd say his spots are red, white and blue," Sophia said.

"I'll take that."

"You missed me mum and da," Sophia said as Walker came up from the cabins. He was showered, shaved and his iron gray hair neatly styled. Not bad for four hour's sleep after a nearly twenty-four-hour run.

"Heard them, could tell they were friends, went back to sleep," Walker said. "Any food left?"

"We made more," Sophia said. "When I heard you getting up I made fish tacos."

"You, Skipper, are a drunkard's dream," Walker said, uncovering the dish and spooning some of the meat onto a pita.

"Da was curious about you," Sophia said. "And a touch paranoid."

"Why?" Walker asked.

"Because I know a fraud when I see one," Sophia said. "Which isn't quite right. You're not a fraud in the classic sense. You're just not saying everything."

"True," Walker said, shrugging. "If that's an issue I will, reluctantly, ask for a transfer."

"I told him you were former military," Sophia said. "Certainly more than four years. Probably a retired senior NCO although you've been an officer. Probably an instructor in something technical with combat experience. From the languages and combat experience, that says Special Forces. And you're not really like a gunny or a sergeant major. And that I didn't consider you a threat or I wouldn't have given you a weapon. Also that I'd pitch a tantrum if he tried to pull you off my boat being a 'good da.'"

"You, young lady, live up to your name," Walker said, smiling. "Correct on virtually all particulars. Is it an issue?"

"Nope," Sophia said. "As long as it's not an issue. Da said most people who change their background can't change their spots. I said yours were red, white and blue. If that's not the case, then there's probably an issue."

"I wouldn't put it quite so patriotically," Walker said, shrugging. "I've never been one to wrap myself in the flag. Probably because many who do didn't really accept all that it represented, good and bad, and others did so for personal gain rather than true patriotism. But what I do wrap myself in is what this squadron represents. Soldiers do not, by and large, create. They destroy. The question always is whether what they are destroying promotes the value of civilization and the advancement of man and specifically Western concepts and philosophies or degrades them. If it degrades them, valid target. If it promotes them, invalid target. Terrorists? Valid targets. Infected? Valid targets."

"That makes sense," Sophia said. "One question, pure curiosity between the skipper and her crewman. Senior NCO or senior officer?"

"If it's truly between you and me," Walker said. "Both. Serially. NCO then officer then senior officer. And this *may* be a trust issue for you. I've been in contact with General Brice. I knew her before the Plague. On a purely personal note, I was pleased to know Shelley survived.

"Shelley and Under Secretary Galloway are onboard with me just cruising for now. There are many reasons. Your father has things under control. As much as it is possible given the conditions. He has the, the term is 'social capital,' to pull this off. The majority of this squadron is not made up of professionals, and long-term social bonding items are in disarray. Your father and your family act as a social bond for this squadron, which is much more post-apocalyptic gypsy tribe than a professional military force.

"I could probably take more useful roles than being a deckhand on a boat. However, the addition of my expertise would be relatively minimal and I'm enjoying what we do. I also enjoy training bright young officers. A point of which General Brice is fully aware. So absent objections from yourself or Squadron, or your da, here I remain. Unless things change and my former position becomes necessary."

"Now I'm going to have a hard time not calling you 'sir,'" Sophia said, her brow furrowing.

"You've always been polite, Ensign," Walker said. "Mr. Walker more than suffices. Tom is fine. Neither is my real name. Calling me 'Walker' works best. It was part of my handle."

"What was your handle?" Sophia asked. "If I may ask."

"Skaeling, actually," Walker said. "It means Night Walker."

"More like 'Boogie man,'" Sophia said pointedly. "Those who walk in the dark. Things that go bump in the night. The Native American tribe that drove out the Vikings from Newfoundland."

"And in Dari it turned out to translate as prostitute or street walker," Walker said, grinning. "Caused a bit of an issue at one point."

"Dari?" Sophia said.

"One of two dialects of Persian used in Afghanistan," Walker said. "The other being Tajik which has the same translation. General Kamal of the Northern Alliance found it quite amusing to call me by my handle. I should probably go see if anyone wants to come back to the boat, ma'am."

∞ ⊖ ∞

Steve tapped his fingers on his desk in thought, then hit the connection to The Hole.

"Duty officer," Lieutenant Colonel Justin Pierre said. "Good . . . evening your time, Captain."

"Good evening, Colonel," Steve said. "I have an unusual request."

"Glad to be of service if I can, Captain," Colonel Pierre said.

"The service record extracts you have," Steve said. "Do they include aliases or handles?"

"In some cases, Captain," Colonel Pierre said, his brow furrowing. "Do you need me to run a name?"

"Yes," Steve said. "Thomas Walker."

The colonel had leaned forward into his keyboard, hands set to type and now leaned back, raising his hands and folding them.

"Could I get back to you on that, Captain?" the colonel said. "Something's come up."

"Certainly," Steve said blandly. "Hope things are okay."

"Fine, just . . . something's come up. Be back if not tonight then tomorrow early."

"All right," Steve said. "Have a good rest of your shift."

He tapped his fingers on his desk again, then sighed.

"Something is fishy in Omaha. . . ."

Steve was just out of the shower, drying his hair and contemplating the fact that Stacey had been rummaging in her lingerie drawer when the phone in his quarters rang. Since that invariably meant some sort of emergency had occurred, he was not in the best of moods when Stacey, wearing not much more than a lacey bra and panties, handed him the phone.

"General Brice," she said, her hand over the mike.

"General," Steve said. "You rang?"

"Sorry to call you so late, Steve," Brice said. "But I didn't want to leave you hanging on the call you made to us. Thomas Walker."

"I'd wondered, when the colonel so abruptly changed the subject, ma'am," Steve said. "I don't mind having the pros back-channel, ma'am. Considering everything, it's necessary. But putting someone on my daughter's boat was sort of..."

"*That* I didn't do," Brice said. "It was more happy coincidence. Happy because you couldn't get a better guy to *be* on your daughter's boat. At least not alive and in contact. I'll give you two statements about Walker and that is all you're going to get. Along with an order. Just leave him be is the order. He's fine where he is at the moment. That's my decision and the under secretary's. Are we clear?"

"Yes, ma'am," Steve said thoughtfully.

"So here are the two facts. Fact one: he's former Special Forces. Fact two: He's retired. That's all you have the need to know.

"He likes what he's doing, he's earned what is effectively downtime and there's no better hand at training a young officer. Personally, you want him right where he is. Professionally, while he'd be an asset in your shop, he'd more or less automatically boot you out if he returned at rank. And *he* made the point that for social politics reasons, that wouldn't work. When you create a splinter cell to go bootstrap the Pacific, the under secretary and I have already pegged him, notionally, as CINCPAC. He doesn't know that and he doesn't need to. It's late your time. Do you have any salient questions?"

"No, ma'am," Steve said. "That pretty much covers it."

"Steve, seriously, he's not a threat, quite the opposite, and I know him personally, not just professionally. He's a great guy. You're lucky to have him where he's at."

"Sort of got that, ma'am," Steve said. "I can even see him wanting to play deckhand. I miss those days myself."

"If you need someone that's 'next level,' he's there," Brice said. "But, notionally, we're looking at next stage. Get some sleep and don't worry about Night Walker."

"Walker?" Stacey said worriedly.

"Turns out I can now chase you around the cabin with my mind focused on that," Steve said. "Super-secret squirrel. As trustworthy as black ops gets I suppose."

"I was a little worried," Stacey said, nodding. "That's good to hear."

"Hmmm..." Steve said. "Now, you have exactly one second's head start, then I'm going to tickle the life out of you."

"I'm just glad you think pregnant women are sexy..."

"So, how was your away time?" Sophia asked, yawning. It was past midnight and she was ready for the rack. "And I see Olga didn't make it back. No surprise."

"What they want for parts is crazy," Celementina said. "I found a new water pump for the engine but they want a case of good booze."

"We kept back some cases," Sophia said, shrugging. "I wonder where it came from, though."

"Like I say," Celementina said. "Nobody turn in all their stuff they find. They trade it. They only turn in the stuff they can't trade."

"We still have the cases," Sophia said. "And we'll know better next time. Batari?"

"Plenty of spices and condiments," Batari said. "Good stuff, too. Prices, not so bad. I can probably get all I need with some of the jewelry and a couple of bottles."

"Works," Sophia said. "Okay, tomorrow, we'll go in shifts, get all the stuff we need we didn't get from Squadron. Walker, you want to go over tonight?"

"I'll take the watch, ma'am," Walker said. "You get some sleep. I can run over tomorrow evening if I want to. Any other stuff we need to know or should know?"

"We can sleep aboard?" Celementina said. "The *Boadicea*. There's cabins for us if we want them. Like a hotel. Might be where Olga is."

"There's an internet, sort of," Batari said. "Really more like Spacebook. You can check on people in the squadron. Everybody has an account already set up. Oh, and you've got to see the night sky movie."

"Blackness, I would think," Walker said. "At least if it's current imagery."

"You need to see it," Celementina said, looking at Sophia with an odd expression. "I'm so glad we're doing this. All we see is the boat. I didn't really understand, you know? Just see it."

"Okay," Sophia said. "On the agenda for tomorrow. We'll see if we get Olga back so some of us can go get some...I was going to say shore leave..."

"Big boat leave?" Walker said. "Get some sleep, Skipper. I'll take the watch."

CHAPTER 5

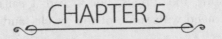

"... we ain't gonna give in to these fuckin' zombies..."

From: *Collected Radio Transmissions of The Fall*
University of the South Press 2053

"Ensign, welcome aboard," the red-headed man said, offering his hand.

The *Boadicea* was in movement, cruising very slowly eastward. Most floating docks were designed to be used in ports and stationary, not at sea and in movement. This "floating dock" was actually the bottom of a lifeboat that had been reconfigured and was held away from the ship's hull by two davits usually used to raise and lower lifeboats.

"Thanks," Sophia said, stepping off the Zodiac. She didn't really need the help but she sort of touched his hand getting onto the floating dock. Most people probably needed *a lot* of help.

She'd worn her uniform. It wasn't mandatory but she'd worn it anyway. She'd debated then rejected the Master Savior Badge. The nonsubdued version, cast gold from salvaged jewelry, was authorized for wear with NavCam. She had decided to wear her Small Boats Badge. The badge was unauthorized but most of the small boat people wore one. It was a Viking longboat tossed in a storm. That she could get her head around. The Master Savior Badge was just a touch too gaudy.

"I guess this is old hat for you, Seawolf," the man said, grinning. He was vaguely familiar but a lot of people were.

"I know we've met..." Sophia said.

"I guess I was just another face," the man said. "Spring Keyzers. You picked me up about a month ago. Until I saw the movie I hadn't really realized how *many* people you must have picked up."

"Sailboat," she said, shaking his hand. "Out of commission. What are you doing working guest relations? I'd have pegged you for small boat ops."

"I'd had enough sailing for a while?" Keyzers said, smiling tightly. "Maybe later. I guess I'm sort of lighting a candle keeping freshies from going in the drink."

"Understandable," Sophia said. "Hope you're doing better."

"Much," the man said.

"I'll get out of your way," Sophia said. "You take care."

"You, too, miss."

"That was you, wasn't it?" a woman said, coming out of the theater. She was crying, as were most of the people with her. "The girl lighting the candle? Thank you."

"For what?" Sophia said. She knew she'd never seen the woman in her life. But she was getting that a lot. Random strangers walking up and saying "thank you." She wasn't sure why. Some of them even hugged her and she wasn't the huggy type. "And the what?"

Sophia had decided that since everyone was talking about the "night sky" movie she should probably see it. So she was waiting for the next showing. Most of the people with her were "boaties," people fresh off a lifeboat. You could tell by the way they were slightly swaying on the relatively stable *Boadicea*. Not to mention being thin, extremely tan, wearing slops that didn't fit well and shivering slightly in the air conditioning. They had a "sponsor" with them, whom she vaguely recognized. She was pretty sure she'd picked her up.

"Everything," the woman said, hugging her. "Just... everything. Thank you so much for what you've done. It must have been so hard..."

"We need to get going so these people can see the movie..." her sponsor said, gently prying the woman loose.

"The theater is clear," the next group's sponsor said. "If we could start moving in...?"

"I've never seen this before," Sophia whispered to the sponsor. The lady was probably in her seventies. "Anything I should know? Like, what *that* was all about?"

"Really, miss?" the lady said.

"I've been out on ops since we left the Canaries," Sophia said.

"Then, yes," the sponsor said. "I think you are going to *really* need these."

She handed Sophia a handful of tissues.

The video started with a montage of videos and stills that most people knew and remembered, to the background of Billy Joel's "Miami 2017." No sound on the videos, just the music. The President announcing the Plague. National Guardsmen in MOPP4 at check points. Riots. Video of reporters in "Infected Care Centers," vast warehouses with "afflicted" tied to cots and even mattresses on the floor, writhing and snarling, covered in feces and sores. Flashes from the CDC briefings. The fairly famous scene of the Fox anchor going nuts on camera. A skyscraper on fire in some foreign city. Quite a few of the shots were from NYC. Fires, riots, fighting in the streets in what looked like Queens. A carrier being evacuated by helicopter with the caption "USS *John C. Stennis* evacuated due to rampant H7D3 infection." It had been more screwed up than she realized even before the Fall. She'd been head down in the lab most of the time. A scrolling tally of the living was across the bottom of the screen, dropping like a stone, six and a half billion, then six, then five, then four... The body count of civilization ending.

The views faded to a shot of Earth's surface, by night, dated the day the Plague was announced. There were more as the plague progressed and the sparkling strands of light slowly began to turn off, portion by portion, Africa went before South America went before Asia went before North America went before Europe until the entire world was cloaked in preindustrial darkness. The last section that was lit was somewhere in the U.S., near Tennessee she thought.

Then the shots zoomed down, pre-Plague satellite and file images of New York, Beijing, Moscow, Tokyo, Seoul, Hong Kong, filled with people and life and laughter, the cities bright by day and night with a trillion incandescent and fluorescent and neon and LED lights proclaiming to the heavens that Here Was Man.

And then the same cities, in current satellite shots,

with avenues choked with decaying vehicles, and raven-picked bodies, and naked infected roaming the deserted streets.

The current night sky shot. Not a light to be seen. A world cloaked in preindustrial darkness.

The music ended. All there was was a scrolling night shot of the dead world from a satellite. It seemed like the movie had ended and Sophia almost got up, wondering why anyone would want to see this montage of horror. They'd all lived it.

Then there was the sound of the scratch of a match that touched a candle. The flame flickered for a moment, then puffed out to a background of childish laughter . . .

And came back as it faded back to her, Sophia, trying to light Mum's birthday cake and Faith blowing it out every time she tried. She *hated* that video. She'd been ten and Faith eight and she was sooo pissed at her. She'd been no help making the cake and then Da wouldn't make her stop. He thought it was funny. Had Da *kept* the damned thing?

"Quit it, Faith," she heard herself say. "It's Mummy's birthday . . . birthday . . . birthday . . ."

Upbeat instrumental music she didn't recognize, the screen said "Call to Arms" by Angels and Airwaves. *Mile Seven*, the forty-five-foot Hunter sailboat they'd started on. New York burning as they sailed out. The first light storms. Trying to figure out *how* to run a sailboat. Catching fish for dinner. Faith grinning and holding up that big albacore she'd caught. The tropical storm that had caught them off Bermuda. Another video, this one taken by Faith as they were being tossed about like a leaf in the middle of the storm.

"Having fun, Sis?"

"I blame Da for this, you know," she heard herself say.

"Funny, I blame *you*."

At the bottom there was a notation: Wolf Squadron: Squadron manning: 4. Steven John Smith, 45. Stacey Lynn Smith, 38. Sophia Ann Smith, 15. Faith Marie Smith, 13. With shots of each of them from New York and the Hunter days. A couple of those were from the paparazzi who had caught them leaving the BotA building.

Then a shot of the *Tina's Toy* as they were approaching the first boat they'd "rescued." Crüxshadow's "Sophia" started.

A shot of Tina, looking small and sad with her name captioned. Pictures of Mum and Da and Faith and herself, pulling out the remains of Tina's family. Ripping up carpet. Scrubbing the decks. Mum in the engine room covered in oil from a burst line. Sophia hadn't seen Tina in forever, didn't even know where she was. Last she'd heard the girl was on the *Boadicea*. She made a note to look her up.

The manning was now "5." Although, honestly, Tina was never a lot of help. At the bottom the names of the members of the squadron were scrolling continuously. The scroll kept getting longer and longer as more and more people joined the "squadron."

A picture of them bringing aboard the survivors from their first lifeboat. Chris and Paula and all the rest. She'd taken that shot. Paula was in the South Wing, Flotilla Four, now, still skippering the *Linea Caliente*. She and Chris had just gotten engaged, last Sophia heard.

The pic Da had them take of the group off Bermuda. "We few, we happy few" as he'd put it. There were twenty-five people in two boats and she knew all their names. She'd held most of their hands coming over the transom. Just like the guy on the floating dock had held hers to get onboard.

Then more boats, the first squadron in Bermuda Harbor with captions of the boats. The *Grace Tan*. The *Tina's Toy*. The *His Sea Fit*. The disabled oceanic tow boat *Victoria's Boss* which as far as she knew was still anchored in Bermuda. People she knew were around, somewhere, but she hadn't seen in months. The USCGC *Campbell*. She and Faith throwing grapnels onto the boarding platform at the rear and the survivors of the crew being picked up by the squadron boats. Chris Phillips pulling a survivor aboard his boat at sea. A shot of the machine shop Mike Braito had set up on the *Victoria* with Mike sweating over a piece of metal he was grinding down. Another person she hadn't seen in forever. The number at the bottom kept clicking up. More and more names scrolling across until the family's was lost in the welter.

Two dozen survivors became three, then four. Then a hundred. More boats working at sea. People who had been seen clambering aboard rescue boats now manning them or working in the *Victoria*. Fishing and cleaning fish. Faith reloading Saiga magazines. Sophia at the helm of her first boat. More survivors coming aboard, wearing sunglasses and shielding their eyes or reveling in being on a boat that was under power.

The *Voyage Under Stars*. A video taken of the death camp emaciated survivors in cabins and the man jumping overboard to the sharks. The *His Sea Fit* cruising past the massive liner, the Bertram 35 looking like an ant next to the supermax ship.

Then a shot of all the infected gathered on the landing deck as the music died. And Faith's voice came up on the radio. Sophia knew what was coming. For those who weren't catching the words, they were flashed on the screen.

Faith Marie Smith (13): "Da, the Dallas cleared off a deck and put in a ladder. If we wait, the zombies are going to come around again. You know how they are. Permission to, I dunno . . . Get a foothold is what Soph just said."

Steven John Smith: "Do you have a backup plan?"

Faith Smith: "No, but I've got lots of guns and knives and a machete. I'm still looking for a chainsaw."

Disturb's "Warrior" started as the voice-over was ending. The vocals came in as Faith went over the side. They'd cut the resulting scrum so it looked as if she was kicking ass not getting it kicked.

Videos of Da and Faith and Falcon and Hooch being washed down by the Coasties, the wash water red with blood. Shots taken from a gun camera of the scrums on the interior. It must have been from Fontana's weapon, the tracking was too smooth for anybody else. The *Charlotte* towing in the *Campbell*, an attack sub being used as a towboat. Boats shuttling back and forth, some shots of her, Captain Sherill who was a flotilla commander now, Chris and Lloyd and Steven, Tina feeding an emaciated survivor soup. Sophia was pretty sure it was Rusty Bennett, now one of the gunners on a gunboat. She'd seen him when he was skinny, not the "robust" guy he was now, but she'd never realized he was *that* bad off. He looked dead.

Video of the interior of the *Voyage* with *masses* of infected bodies piled up by the foursome. Survivors having to pick their footing to get through the passages. All of it in the light of taclights and flashlights. Crews pulling cases of ammo and medicine off the *Campbell* and then loading the ammo onto the liner. Survivors going through decon showers.

The liner, black and dead as the squadron was sailing away.

Atreyu's "Honor" as they approached the USS *Iwo Jima* interspersed with more shots of people coming off of life rafts and boats. The fight when the four boarders entered the cavernous interior of the assault carrier. Marines and sailors coming off the *Iwo*. A good shot of Staff Sergeant Januscheitis stumbling off the *Iwo* into a boat, then another, obviously right after, turning around and going back in again, just putting on his gas mask and this time rigged up for some *serious* zombie hunting. A video someone had gotten of a "scrum" with the infected in the interior and Faith doing her usual job of grandstanding with a Halligan tool. Pallets of ammo, medicine and supplies being lowered over the side into waiting boats. She was there, getting one loaded on the back deck. Wash-down again, with a dozen Marines standing under powerful water sprays, the blood pouring over the side. Faith was in there but she was hard to spot. Shots of the interior by taclight, showing the corridors choked with recent and old dead. A clear shot of a chewed corpse wearing MarPat with a clocked-out .45 by its side. Gunny Sands, thin as a rail, on the leading edge of the flight deck saluting Da as he walked up. The gunny carrying the flag off the ship in the closing and the hatches being welded shut. The *Iwo* was still there and still plenty full of ammo and supplies if they needed them.

The Canary Islands. Nightwish's "Last of the Wilds." Pure instrumental. The first use of gunboats. A shot of Anarchy laying waste to infected on a beach. She'd have to check her log to figure out where. The landings in small towns. Clearing the *Boadicea*. People stumbling onto boats in marinas. The crews enjoying a lunch and beverages in San Sebastian de la Gomera. The "Israeli Beach" scene, as she mentally tagged it, with everybody having guns leaning up against their chairs just in case some infected showed up. The whole group posing in front of "The Corner Café at the Marina" with their guns and bottles of wine. She hadn't realized how many people were videotaping.

She hadn't realized how often *she* was being videoed. Or how many group photos she'd been tagged in.

The manning numbers kept going up.

Faith's premature landing on the cruise liner pier at Santa Cruz de Tenerife when the infected had poured out of the interior of the supermax liner and the four Marines had had to call for close fire support from the gunboats. Clearance in Santa Cruz harbor. More liners to clear and survivors in shorts and sunglasses fumbling their way onto boats. Climbing the cliffs at El Chorillo to pull the survivors out of condos. That had been a nightmare. Especially for Faith who *hated* heights. Clearing small towns and picking up refugees. A shot of her with her sniper rifle, picking off some infecteds. Sergeant Major Barney dressing down Seaman Recruit Steinholtz on a breakwater. Again. Shots of Anarchy. Lots of shots of Anarchy.

A short shot of Cody's funeral at sea as the song died with the caption "Specialist Cody 'Anarchy' Smith, U.S. Army, KIA, Canary Islands Operating Area."

She wasn't sure if "eaten by sharks" was technically Killed in Action but she wasn't going to bitch. She still missed him.

Then the song she'd been wondering if they'd use: Nightwish's "Last Ride of the Day" as the "Manning number" kept clicking up and up.

Machine shops and unrepping and people cleaning out the *Boadicea*. Ripping up carpet, just like she and Da and Faith had done so many months ago. Clearing out the skeletons "Da's Little Helpers" left of the bodies. Vacuuming those up. Scrubbing bulkheads and floors. Cleaner mattresses coming aboard from salvage. People working in galleys and engine rooms and the main saloon filled with people. People boarding the *Social Alpha* off a Zodiac. Squadron ops with civilians and military manning radios and computers. Tracers at night. Dinner in one of the mess halls. A swarm of Marines going up a boarding ladder into a ship. A shot of a full flotilla heading to sea, the boats nose up and crashing through the waves. Nurses helping survivors that were on death's door. Loading the battle boxes on a gunboat, case after case of .50 caliber ammo coming out of the hold of the converted fishing boat. More chewed infected on a beach with the video focusing on the cloud of brass pouring out of the new water-cooled dual .50s. Coiling down ropes. Grapnels going over to a derelict boat. A group of Marines holding a line against a mass of infected somewhere in the Canaries. Faith was standing behind them apparently buffing her nails. A team working on a stripped-down engine in an engine room. A sewing shop she didn't even know they had. More survivors over transoms. The market in "Downtown" on the *Boadicea*. A shot of her, Sophia, in the pass in review, saluting Da. A Zodiac sporting a tiny Irish flag crewed by what looked like a child outbound into the setting sun. Gunboats chewing up infected in a marina with Zodiacs inbound for the beach. Faith in combat rig, striding past a group of rigged up Marines, the girl's face like an axe, returning their salutes as if she'd done it a thousand times. The pass in review, making it look much more professional than it had actually been. The full squadron heading out to sea with Mount Teide glowing red in the background.

Then back to the dark sky of a dead world. A satellite passing over India and North Africa. Shots of dead Mumbai, Cairo, Casablanca, scrolling fast...

Zooming in on a cluster of lights. The squadron center at sea. The only light in the blackness as the music crescendoed. Then a caption:

"Welcome to Wolf Squadron. The hell with the darkness. Light a Candle."

At the bottom was "Manning: 3,201."

Sophia realized she'd used up all the tissues. And all she wanted to do was go back to the boat and head back out to sea.

"Mr. Walker," Steve said, gesturing to the chairs in his office. "Sophia."

"Captain," Sophia said, sitting down.

Sophia had gotten the word that she had to "meet with the squadron commander" before the division headed back out for operations.

"This is more of a 'Sophia' and 'Da' conversation," Steve said.

"Have I done something wrong?" Sophia asked.

"If you had, it would be a captain and ensign conversation," Steve said. "And, frankly, I think the real answer is that people will be . . . conflicted about that. It's time we talked about vaccine production with the powers-that-be."

"Fuck," Sophia said quietly, lowering her head.

"I am somewhat out of my depth, sir," Walker said, looking back and forth. He thought for a moment, then looked at Sophia. "Seriously?"

"I was told you were quick on the uptake," Steve said.

"Somebody had to do it," Sophia said, shrugging. "Better me than Faith."

"I'm still unsure that it needed to be or should have been my fifteen-year-old daughter," Steve said. "But you are the only thing we have close to an expert. We haven't even picked up any biology laboratory technicians."

"I barely counted as one of those, Da," Sophia said. "And I'm really hoping that I'm not going to be stuck in a lab making vaccine until who knows when."

"You won't be," Steve said. "We've found people with . . . well about the same background as you had when you started working for Doctor . . . Damn, what was his . . . ?"

"Curry," Sophia said. "Doctor David 'What is it about Mad Scientist you don't understand?' Curry."

"Do I have a purpose here, sir?" Walker asked.

"I suppose that is up to you, Mr. Walker," Steve said. "I have some people who are generally capable of managing a lab. I don't, sorry, consider one of those people to be Sophia. On the other hand, I've been given the impression that you have some abilities over and above tying knots. And, frankly, the ensign is going to need someone . . ."

"As emotional support when it becomes common knowledge that Seawolf the Hero started out working in a clandestine human chop shop?" Walker said.

"That. Yes. Although for now that will continue to remain confidential."

"I'll be okay, Da," Sophia said. She didn't look okay.

"You will be eventually," Steve said. "Because this will eventually become sort of 'well, that's how it works.' And, note, we're going to have to vaccinate all the *babies* we're about to have. They won't automatically be immune to H7D3."

"I hope somebody has some clue about that because I'm totally clueless and I don't want to kill a baby," Sophia said.

"Mr. Walker, will you admit to some knowledge of this field?" Steve said.

"Honestly?" Walker said. "I passed the Special Forces Medical course, if that's what you're asking. I haven't been in anything resembling a biology lab in thirty years. And even then it was a very brief course on analyzing medical complaints under field conditions."

"So I was right," Sophia said, brightening. "You *were* Special Forces!"

"Yes, I was," Walker said. "Am, for certain values. You're never ex-Special Forces unless you get thrown out. In fact, technically, I'm still a member of the U.S. Armed Forces."

"Whatever you're willing to admit to, that brings up an entirely separate issue," Steve said. "We are about to have a baby boom. Lieutenant Fontana is a graduate of the same course. You and he are, in fact, our *best trained* people at, well, *everything* medical. Our one trained nurse worked her whole career in a doc-in-a-box. And even then she was mostly a triage and taking blood pressure type."

"Special Forces medics are not doctors, sir," Walker said. "We're very clear about that."

"There *are* no doctors, Mr. Walker," Steve replied. "The only known MDs in the world are in a hole at the CDC. When in the fullness of time we retake the Atlanta area they will be mobile. In the meantime, we have no doctors nor nurses nor any of the rest."

"Checked the islands, sir?" Walker said.

"Which ones?" Steve asked.

"Most of them," Walker said. "There were little medical schools all over the Caribbean, sir. I'd be surprised if some of the instructors didn't survive. Even the advanced students would be useful."

"That is . . . interesting," Steve said. "And something no one else had brought up. But it is not germane to the current discussion. I'm aware that I cannot order you to do anything, Mr. Walker. Both because you insist you are a civilian and, from what I can surmise, if you did 'blow your cover' I'd be outranked."

"Really?" Sophia said.

"That is not to be discussed, Ensign," Steve said. "But we need medical personnel desperately. Both for the vaccine program and for the approaching baby boom. Would you be willing to temporarily suspend your cruise to assist?"

"You don't need to sweat it, Captain," Walker said. "I was planning on bringing it up. Just wasn't sure *when* was appropriate. I am at your service in this matter. Both to help set up the lab and as a baby doctor."

"Thank you," Steve said. "You are hereby the lab manager for the initial vaccine production. Sophia is in charge of the lab, you manage it. Does that work?"

"Absolutely," Walker said. "And as soon as we get it up and running, and someone else to manage it and run it, I'll segue over to baby doctor. I'd appreciate a brush up with the doctors at the CDC."

"You can feel free to schedule that for yourself and Fontana," Steve said. "You'll both be talking with them extensively. I'm going to pull Fontana off of running Marines and put him in charge of setting up the facilities for pregnancies involving medical emergencies. Nurse Fallon is already getting swamped with late-term complications. So... Sophia, are you ready to break cover? At least with the Powers-That-Be?"

"What's that thing that Lee said at Appomattox? I would rather die a thousand deaths. Ready."

Steve clicked something with his mouse and nodded at the screen on his computer.

"Sorry to keep you waiting, Dr. Dobson," Steve said. "As has been discussed, one of my original crew had experience working in a professional if clandestine laboratory that produced attenuated vaccine prior to the breakdown in civil order. NCCC Galloway, we have assurances that there will be no legal repercussions from your office."

"None," Galloway said. The National Constitutional Continuity Coordinator, functionally the Acting President, was formerly the Under Secretary for Under Deputy Secretary of Defense for Nuclear Arms Proliferation Control. He was one of many civilian appointees rotated through secure points in the event of a disaster like, laughably, a zombie apocalypse. The point was to have a civilian, preferably someone elected or approved by Congress in charge of the military and nuclear release codes. He was number one hundred and twenty-six on the very long list. "You have the documents as well as my personal assurances."

"Very well," Steve said, touching another control. The conference came up on the large plasma behind his desk. "Ladies and gentlemen, my daughter Ensign Sophia Smith."

"Sophia?" General Brice said, startled. "*Seawolf?*"

"Somebody had to do it, ma'am," Sophia said, her face tight. "I won't say I'm glad or anything, but if we hadn't we'd have been in the same boat as the Lawtons and the subs. Even if we *didn't* get the Plague."

"And the other gentlemen is . . . ?" Dr. Dobson said.

"Thomas Walker," Steve said. "He is a former SF medic who has management experience as well as some slight lab experience. He knows a Bunsen burner from a test tube anyway. He will be managing the lab."

"Sophia," Dr. Dobson said. "Since there is a blanket pardon in place for all persons involved in the vaccine production you were involved in, could you give us a few more details, please?"

"The lab was for Bank of the Americas," Sophia said. "It was run by Dr. David Curry . . ."

"I could see Dave doing that," Dobson said, grinning mirthlessly.

"I . . . saw many of the CDC teleconferences when the Plague was spreading," Sophia said. "Dr. Curry kept it running in both the hot and cold zones. So I recognize you, sir. My job was most of the processing. Dr. Curry would . . . do initial preparation of the materials. It was the one bit I wasn't willing to do."

"Initial preparation?" General Brice said. "Sorry but we're going to have to approve this for use by the sub crews. We need to have some idea of what exactly is going on."

"Grinding up the spinal cords," Sophia said tightly. "They would be brought in by..." She stopped and looked at her dad.

"My brother Thomas Smith was General Manager for Security and Emergency Response for Bank of the Americas," Steve said. "Tom's teams, covering as one of the standard contract Biological Emergency Response Teams, would find infected, secure and terminate, strip the spines and deliver them to the lab."

"I see," General Brice said. "Go on, Ensign."

"Dr. Curry would do that part of the preparation. It isn't tough except emotionally. Drop the spinal cords in a blender and hit blend."

"Okay," Secretary Galloway said, twitching slightly.

"Then he would give me the materials for processing. Centrifuge until the layers are separated. Remove the liquid containing the virus bodies using a pipette. Separate using a medium, which is the most time intensive part. Also... 'tedious' doesn't begin to describe it. It's like watching paint dry except you have to actually pay attention to it. Measure an exact volume of virus bodies into containers. You can use glass test tubes for that but we used disposable ones. Calculate the X-ray charge for that volume depending on whether it was primer or booster. X-ray with the specified output and time. Remove the irradiated virus bodies and place precise quantities in vaccine containers. Mix with specific levels of deionized water. Then there's quality control. When we started, Dr. Curry would test it with reagents, I'm not even sure what kind, then double check with the SEM..."

"Sem?" Galloway asked.

"Scanning electron microscope," Dr. Dobson said. "According to your records, there's one at the immunology lab at Guantanamo. May or may not be working. On the other hand, there's a way to make one that's not too hard. According to Commander Freeman, a nuclear engineering specialist would find it child's play. Ditto the mass spectrometer they're going to need. And we know what the reagents were. That's different from them being available. What about a vaccine test kit?"

"They had those in New York," Sophia said uncomfortably. "That's what he switched to when they came out."

"Vaccine test kit?" Galloway said. "Again, what?"

"When vaccines suddenly hit the street, there was only one source," Dobson said, just as uncomfortably as Sophia. "Which at the time was classified as first degree murder with bells and whistles. What we are now planning on doing in job lots."

"Agreed and understood," the NCCC said. "On the other hand, we're already killing the infected in job lots. Might as well put them to some use. Callous? Yes. Necessary, also yes. We've had the discussion."

"The point is, sir, if I may," Sophia said, gulping, "street dealers were offering vaccine. Sometimes it was just distilled water. Say one of them gets busted. What is he actually carrying? Remains of a person who was murdered or just water? One is a con, the other is conspiracy to murder. So they came out with small test kits for 'street vaccine.' Cop busts a guy with what looks like vials of water, tests it, it's vaccine, he busts him for possession plus they start capital murder charges."

"Ah," Galloway said, nodding. "Makes sense."

"I was sort of there on the sharp end, sir," Sophia said. "I spent a good part of the time in New York terrified somebody would burn us and I'd end up in prison. I knew the Fall was coming. I did *not* want to be in prison when it hit. Thing is, the tests were cheap, mass produced, and they actually were accurate enough to tell if the vaccine was good or not. Not only could they tell if it was good, they could determine if it was good primer or booster and even whether it was from a human or another 'higher order primate.' Just inject a few drops into the plastic thingy and it gave you a response in a few seconds. So then the dealers and people who wanted to buy vaccine on the street started buying them. They were selling over the counter in New York before the Fall. We're going to need more than the X-ray generator. We've found those. What we really could use, for quality control, is some vaccine test kits. Not to mention graduated pipettes, tips, syringes... And separation medium. That's going to be hard to find. There's a lot of material besides an X-ray generator."

"According to our records Gitmo should have all of it," Commander Freeman said.

"Then I guess we need to take Guantanamo Bay, sirs, ma'am," Sophia said, shrugging. "If it's as well stocked as indicated, I can get the lab up and running in a day or so. And then we can start taking poor deranged Marines, sailors and civilians and turning them into vaccine," she ended, a tad bitterly.

"Ensign Smith," the NCCC said. "I want you to know that whatever your feelings in this matter, this will not be held against you legally in any way. And for myself, personally, thank God you did do what you did, didn't get caught and are going to do again. It is, literally, the salvation of humanity. Hole is out."

"Anything we can provide on this end at this time, Ensign?" Dr. Dobson said.

"Prayer?" Sophia said. "I'll get back to you when we're getting the lab set up."

CHAPTER 6

". . . got into Powderhorn on my sled and picked up some supplies from the Meijers yesterday. Any closer to downtown and the zombies are still crawlin'. Lots of them, by golly. How in tarnation are they survivin'? It's been a little cold don'tcha know . . ."

From: *Collected Radio Transmissions of The Fall*
University of the South Press 2053

"Another fine day at Guantanamo Bay, Sergeant!" Hoag said as she popped her head up through the roof hatch.

It was dawn and changing of the guard at Building Fourteen Survival Center, Gitmo. A constant watch was maintained on the rooftop. Nobody was, at this point, absolutely sure why. While the infected level had dropped, it hadn't dropped enough for them to get out. Not nearly enough ammo. And there was, so far, no sign of any relief.

"Another glorious day in the Corps, Sergeant!" Sergeant Andy Weisskopf replied.

"Any change in the infected status, Sergeant?" Hoag asked.

"Infected count for the night was sixty-seven, Sergeant," Weisskopf said. "All but three were known infected. Al Hoodat managed to run down a previously

107

unidentified and unknown female and have his way with her. He also killed her in the process and a great feast was had by all. Other than that, no major incidents."

"Ah, zombie snuff porn," Hoag said. "The highlight of any watch. I relieve you, Sergeant."

"I stand relieved, Sergeant," Sergeant Weisskopf said.

"Flag party coming through," Staff Sergeant Cindy Barnard said, coming through the hatch. "You two yardbirds want to get out of the way?"

"Aye, aye, Staff Sergeant," Hoag said, stepping aside as the flag party came up on the roof.

When General Zick had "turned," overall command had devolved to Colonel Hamilton. As far as anyone could tell, the colonel was the commander of Gitmo. A such, the flag was raised on Building Fourteen instead of on Eighteen. Eighteen was in sight and still holding out as well. They were mounting their guards. Mostly Navy but they were there at least. When the radios ran out they'd resorted to flag signaling and writing reports or orders on a white board and holding it up to be read. The flag signaling was tough at first—they had to get the instructions via white board—but there was a signals ET over in Eighteen who knew it. They'd learned. They'd also learned international light signaling since using a mirror was generally quicker than flags and you could use lights at night. There was, in fact, a fairly regular conversation going on between the two buildings.

Eighteen had about the same losses as Fourteen and were in slightly worse shape water wise but maintaining rationing and catching what few rains came the way of Gitmo. They estimated based on water use they could hold out for two years. Six if there were some tropical storms. One of the petty officers was a logistics geek and had crunched the numbers.

What they didn't have was a bugle. One of the Navy seaman had, in all seriousness, suggested he could make up a kazoo and do Reveille on the kazoo. That had been turned down after some discussion of the relative merits. It had become custom to hum the Marine Corps Hymn as the flag was raised on its unfortunately short pole.

Hoag dropped her salute as the flag reached the top of the pole and was tied off.

"Sergeant Hoag, have you accepted the watch?" Staff Sergeant Barnard asked her.

"Yes, Staff Sergeant!" Hoag replied.

"Then perhaps you or Private Capedon should turn around and check the entrance to the bay, Sergeant," Barnard said. "And use your issued binoculars to check out the small, civilian yacht that has just entered the port..."

"Mr. Walker," Sophia said, looking through her binoculars.

She knew that Da had used "special privilege" to let her boat be the first into Guantanamo Bay. She wasn't going to complain. When she saw the American flag, and the Marine flag party, on the distant warehouse she was just trying not to cry.

"Yes, ma'am," Walker said.

"Green flare, please," she said, not looking away. "Then mount the flag on its staff."

"Staff Sergeant, reply with green flare," Hamilton snapped, looking through the binos. There was more than the one yacht at this point. The first yacht had been followed by two more, then two fishing trawlers that had apparently been converted to gunboats. All of them sported the American flag. But while he was willing to accept that sign of being friendlies, notionally, at face value, whether to trust the group would be a longer term decision.

"Yes, sir," Barnard said. "Sergeant Hoag. The signal is green flare."

"Aye, aye, Staff Sergeant," Hoag said. They kept a ready box of pyro on the roof just for the occasion. She pulled out a green flare and uncapped it. "Fire in the hole. Flare, flare, flare."

The group of boats spread out and slowed, two of them deploying RHIBs. The group started coursing back forth across the entrance to the bay.

"Sir?" Barnard said. "Question . . ."

"They're checking the soundings for larger boats or ships, Staff Sergeant," Hamilton said. "Probably looking for wrecks or obstructions. General order, personnel who want to make the climb can come up on the roof. Designate an area for viewing. Send the same order to Eighteen."

"Don't think we have to, sir," Barnard said. "They're all up."

"Send the order nonetheless, Staff Sergeant," Hamilton said.

"Aye, aye, sir," Barnard said.

After about an hour of sounding the main channel, the first group headed farther into the anchorage. It was followed by a line of vessels, most of them yachts or the converted gunboats. There were sixty of those.

Those were followed by larger vessels, two megayachts, supply ships, tankers and a small cruise liner. There were even some oceanic tugboats and trawlers that weren't converted to gunboats.

"That is a sight for God-damned sore eyes, sir," Staff Sergeant Barnard said.

"Yes, it is, Staff Sergeant," Hamilton said. "Yes it is."

The anchorages were sounded and apparently some of the upper ones were found lacking. All the ships anchored in the lower area, opposite Point Corinaso.

At the same time, the smaller yachts and gunboats were deploying all over the anchorage. It looked like chaos and some of it clearly was. There were a few near collisions. However, in another hour or so the gunboats were arrayed by points on the windward and leeward sides, their guns pointing landward.

"There's a light, sir," Barnard said, pointing to the liner.

There was, indeed, a signal light flashing on the liner. Just dots and dashes.

"Signal mirror, Staff Sergeant," Hamilton said.

"Sergeant Hoag, signal readiness to accept communication," Barnard said.

Sheila took the signaling mirror and signaled "GA" "Go ahead."

"Captain Steven Smith, commander Wolf Squadron, Task Force One, USN, to senior survivor, Gitmo, over," Sheila said as the signal came in.

"Signal Lieutenant Colonel Craig Hamilton, USMC, acting commander, Gitmo, over."

"Wolf Squadron?" Lieutenant Harris asked.

"Send list of surviving personnel civilian and military. Include service and rank for military. Note any

*medical conditions including pregnancy with note on
known complications. Stand by for assault and clearance
at dawn. Have personnel prepared for evacuation not
later than zero seven thirty. Do not repeat not attempt
break-out until ordered. Semper Fi. Stay put. Wolf out.*"

"Wolf Squadron?" Harris repeated.

"I have no more idea than you, Lieutenant," Hamilton said. "But I am unwilling to look a gift horse in
the mouth. Even a colorfully named one."

"These jokers *can't* be Navy," Hoag said, shielding
her eyes. "Even Navy's got better discipline than this."

When her watch was relieved she'd gone down into
the warehouse and dumped her battle rattle but went
back up on the roof. After months of monotony and
"zombie porn" being about the only entertainment,
watching real live people doing stuff was a relief.

Once it was anchored, the squadron didn't seem to
be doing much. Most of the "on watch" if that was what
they were, were catching a tan. Some were washing
down the decks. People were up in the promenade
of the liner and on the megayachts, looking back
at the Marines and looking around the harbor like
they'd never seen one. There were about a hundred
ocean-capable Zodiacs zipping around, most of them
driven by what looked like kids. There were even some
people out just zipping around on wave-runners. There
were only a few uniforms visible. Even the guys, and
some women, working on the machine guns were in
shorts and mostly shirtless. Most of the women were
wearing bathing suits. People were fishing.

A lot of the women in view were pregnant. That
was no great surprise. She, Cindy and a civilian who

was "elderly" were the only women in the building not carrying a bun. Idle hands weren't the *only* devil's handiwork. Colonel Hamilton's only comment was "never give an order that's not going to be obeyed." Despite regular PT and even training classes there wasn't much to do in the Survival Centers.

A couple of the Zodiacs had zipped into the main pier area and waved to the groups on the roofs of the building. But there hadn't been another major communication. They'd sent the list of survivors and gotten an acknowledgement.

"I think it's mostly civilian," Cindy said. "I've seen two Marines on the liner and some Navy uniforms. But not many."

"Same here," Sheila said. "I'm wondering what they meant by 'assault at dawn.' And why dawn?"

"And I know how much more than you do, Sheila?" Staff Sergeant Barnard said. Hoag was off duty and they were close enough in rank for her to use first names. "We've waited seven months. We can wait one more night to find out."

"Nice Christmas present, though," Sheila said.

It was a *lot* like waiting for Christmas morning. The sun set with the quick finality of the tropics and then it seemed like the real party started. All the gunboats and accompanying yachts had their lights cranked up to full and were booming music. It could be heard all the way to their position when it was to windward. Every group seemed to have a different playlist. People were dancing on the deck and drinking. Oddly enough, all the ships and boats anchored away from the land were nearly blacked out.

"I so need to be on *that* side of the zombie wall," Sheila said.

Staff Sergeant Barnard was off duty by that time as well and was leaning on the edge of the roof, watching the party.

"Same here," Barnard said. "With any luck, tomorrow night. I'm hoping we get some time off."

"That would be nice," Sheila said. "This has been downtime and it hasn't. I could use some real downtime."

"Staff Sergeant," Colonel Hamilton said. "A moment of your time?"

"Yes, sir," Barnard said, coming to the position of attention.

"Please, Staff Sergeant," Hamilton said. "Rest. Tomorrow morning I want the flag raised at the moment of dawn. Oh Seven Zero Three. When we evacuate, we'll leave it up and ensure at least a small team of Americans maintain it. I'm aware that the communicator was, ostensibly, a Navy captain. However, he may or may not be aware that if everyone evacuates Guantanamo Bay, even for a moment, it automatically reverts to Cuban hands."

"Yes, sir," Barnard said.

"The main point is that the flag go up precisely at dawn," Hamilton said. "I am not sure if we and the squadron have the same interpretation of 'dawn' but I would like to ensure that if so the flag goes up as the assault manifests."

"Yes, sir," Barnard said. "I'll ensure the flag goes up at dawn, sir."

"Sir," Hoag said. "Permission to speak."

"Of course, Sergeant," Hamilton said.

"Sir, I know that Captain Smith ordered no break-out before ordered, sir," Sheila said. "But the infected are clustering towards those boat lights and the music, sir. I think we probably could make it to the docks right now. If we signaled for pick up . . ."

"You've seen Marine uniforms aboard, Sergeant?" Hamilton said. "I think they are there for a reason. And, yes, the infected are clustering towards those boats, Sergeant. Those boats with fifty-caliber machine guns apparently converted to water-cooled, meaning they can fire continuously as long as they have ammunition, Sergeant. The average trawler that size is capable of carrying about one hundred thousand pounds of cargo. That translates to *three* hundred thousand rounds of fifty-caliber BMG, Sergeant. I rather think that Captain Smith has the infected *exactly* where he wants them. And if they detected us breaking out, they would no longer *be* where the captain wants them. I have no desire to offend a Navy captain. So *we* shall stay where the captain wants *us*, Sergeant."

"First call, Lieutenant," Staff Sergeant Januscheitis said, shaking Faith's shoulder.

"Finally," Faith said. She'd barely managed to get to sleep last night. Her cabin was fairly sound proofed but the party had been in full swing until late and she had an early first call. Then there was the fact that today they were going to take and *hold* a position. Gitmo *was* going to be taken and it *wasn't* going to be handed back to the infected when they left.

"Apple juice, ma'am," Januscheitis said, handing her a cup.

"Above and beyond, Staff Sergeant," Faith said,

taking a big gulp. It was about the only way for her to wake up in the morning and actually worked a bit better than coffee. "Time to go kill us some infected. It's a glorious day to be in the United States Marine Corps, Staff Sergeant."

"Glorious indeed, ma'am," Januscheitis said.

Sheila had pulled her battle rattle back up to the roof and slept there. And she did get some sleep. The distant music didn't affect that. It was better than the zombies howling.

She woke immediately when her shoulder was shaken, though, and started pulling on her battle rattle.

She was up and observing the squadron before the first touch of light. There were people moving around the gunboats and some out on the decks of the bigger boats. And she was seeing more uniforms, now. Not everybody was in them but the gunners and some of the people at helms were in NavCam.

There had been various songs playing in the different groups but then they all shut off, some of them in mid tune. There was a moment of silence, then a piano started playing, apparently from all of them.

She could barely catch the tune but she knew it. "Homeward Bound" done by the U.S. Navy Sea Chanter's Choir.

"Marine Staff Sergeants are not supposed to cry," Staff Sergeant Barnard said. "Flag party, TEN-HUT!"

"In the quiet misty morning," Faith sang in a high perfect soprano, counting off the Marines boarding the Zodiac. *"When the moon has gone to bed . . ."*

∽⊖∾

"Look at the liner," Petty Officer Granson said, pointing.

Sheila stopped waiting for the gunboats to open fire and looked at the liner. In the predawn light it was apparent that Marines in battle rattle were boarding Zodiacs off the cruise liner.

"I'll be homeward bound again . . ." she sang as the music died.

"God, I'm glad we're in a harbor this time, staff sergeant," Faith said, taking her seat and not even bothering to strap in for once. "Coxswain, we're in."

"Okay," the coxswain said.

"That's a way of saying 'let's roll,'" Faith said, sighing. "Navy!"

The song died on the last ping of piano and was replaced by a bouncy J-Pop sounding tune Sheila didn't recognize.

"Oh," Granson said, laughing. *"Somebody* has a sense of humor."

"You know it, PO?" Sheila said.

"Andrew W. Kay," Granson said. "'Ready to Die.'"

"This is your time to pay," Faith sang. *"This is your judgment day. We made a sacrifice, and now we get to take your life . . .* Lock and load!"

"All boats, prepare to open fire," Sophia said, over the freq that was *not* being used to carry the combined broadcast.

Her division had been "augmented" by the *Golden Guppy* and the *Wet Debt* and assigned "Radio Point" just off the main piers area. Into which the infected had clustered nicely. And it was almost time to send them beyond the veil.

But Da wanted every gunboat to open fire at once. She knew the words to the song...

"... *it's just a thing we like to do* ... FIRE!"

"*YOU BETTER GET READY TO DIE!*" Faith caroled as just about every Ma Deuce in the bay opened fire simultaneously. "*You better get ready to kill! You better get ready to run 'cause here we commme....*"

The bouncy J-Pop sounding tune had shifted to thrash metal. Sheila couldn't quite catch the words but she did hear intercoms all over the bay suddenly boom "FIRE!" It seemed like the back of every gunboat exploded as the .50 caliber rounds started shredding the crowded infected. Zombies were being blown in half by the concentrated fire and she found herself screaming "OOORAH" at the top of her lungs. But she was drowned out by the rest of the Marines. Sheila looked over her shoulder from the beautiful sight of a dozen gunboats hammering the infected into so much meat and the flag had *just* reached the apex of the pole. It was officially the dawn of a new day.

That was beautiful timing.

So was the timing of the Zodiacs inbound full of Marines. They hit the pier seconds after the fire started. There were still a few infected who hadn't managed to figure out the party was over on Corinaso and Radio Point. The first Marine ashore jumped from the Zodiac onto the wharf and promptly blew that zombie rapist motherfucker Al Hoodat into mush with what looked a hell of a lot like a Saiga shotgun. Then he used the Saiga to wave for the rest of the Marines scrambling up onto the dock to pass him by. Some of them saluted as they passed and the officer would just tip his helmet with the smoking barrel of the Saiga.

"Okay, that dude's got *style*," she said, pointing.

"Chick," Sergeant Weisskopf said, looking through the binoculars. "Pardon me, that would be *lady*. Second Lieutenant. And, Jesus, she *had* to be just out of OBC when the Plague hit."

"Weisskopf," Staff Sergeant Barnard said. "Your watch is extended. Everyone else, downstairs and prepare for evac!"

"Roger, Staff Sergeant," Sheila said. "You heard the staff sergeant. Move it, people!"

"Sir," Faith barked. "Second Lieutenant Faith Marie Smith, U-S-M-C."

Faith had been practicing under Gunny Sands' tutelage and gave the lieutenant colonel a parade-ground salute worthy of the Marine Guards.

"Pleasure to make your acquaintance, Lieutenant," Hamilton said, returning the salute just as formally. "What's the game plan?"

"We'll evac your people on foot to the boats, sir," Faith replied. "Any who have movement difficulties we've got stretchers. The squadron Marine team will remain to hold the base, sir, and begin clearance operations. Your personnel will have three days off on the *Boadicea* to get their headspace and timing back, sir."

"You *do* intend to hold the base?" Hamilton asked.

"We're holding Gitmo for the indefinite future,

sir," Faith said. "It's the first land base we've done that. The primary purpose is to assure the security of materials, sir."

"Would the captain permit leaving some of my people in place temporarily?" Hamilton asked.

"The captain anticipated that question, sir," Faith said, grinning suddenly. "The answer is by all means, sir. He would like to meet with you, sir, so that you can be relieved of any anxiety regarding controlling legal authority, sir. There *is* an NCCC and a chain of command, sir."

"So something survived," Hamilton said, nodding. "Good. Good to hear. No land bases, not so good. Some remnant, good."

"If you would care to accompany the sergeant to the boats, sir," Faith said, gesturing, "we can begin the evacuation whenever you're ready, sir. Stand by..." she said, holding her ear. "Just wax 'em, Janu. We don't collect till we have the facility up and running. Roger. Sir?"

"We're moving out, then," Hamilton said. "Staff Sergeant, one team to remain here, the rest move to the boats."

"Aye, aye, sir," Barnard said. "Hoag, your watch. You just drew the short straw. Go relieve Weisskopf."

"Aye, aye, Staff Sergeant," Hoag said, trying not to curse.

CHAPTER 7

*"... IS THE WRATH OF GOD UPON THE WORLD
FOR ITS SINS! THOSE WHO HAVE BEEN
TAKEN ARE THE SINNERS OF THE WORLD
AND THE RIGHTEOUS HAVE BEEN SPARED ..."*

From: *Collected Radio Transmissions of The Fall*
University of the South Press 2053

"Well, this is convenient," the lieutenant said, her hands on her hips, looking at the Humvee. "Anybody know if this thing still runs?"

Hoag had, at the orders of the "Lieutenant," sent Capedon up to tell Weisskopf he was relieved and to head to the boats. But she had to "stay on site" until relieved. And the lieutenant had "hey-you'd" her to "show them around."

She wasn't sure about the lieutenant. Not 'cause she was a female, obviously, but because Sheila was wondering just how old she was. She didn't look old enough to have gone to college.

"We used it for charging the radios until the fuel ran out, ma'am," Hoag said.

"No fuel, less convenient," the lieutenant said. "Staff Sergeant Januscheitis!"

"Ma'am," Staff Sergeant Januscheitis said.

"Wheels."

"Yes, ma'am," the staff sergeant said.

Hamilton accepted the hand of the Navy crewman on the Zodiac, who looked as if he was a teenager, and boarded the boat gingerly. He was the last on of the personnel who were evacuating the base. And he still wasn't sure it was the right choice.

"Sergeant," Hamilton said to the Marine who had led them to the craft. "I have a few quick questions."

"Yes, sir," the sergeant said.

"Were you a Marine prior to the Plague?" Hamilton asked.

"Yes, sir," the sergeant replied. "I was on the *Iwo* when we got hit, sir. I was a thirty-three eighty-one, sir. Corporal, sir."

"Where's the *Iwo*?" Hamilton asked. "Other operations?"

"Not enough trained people to man her, sir," the sergeant said. "It's floating in the Sargasso Sea with the hatches welded shut, sir. Our total manning is only three thousand and change, sir. That includes sick, lame, lazy, old and children, sir. Mostly civvies."

"So...this is an actual *Navy* operation, Sergeant? Or not?"

"It's...it's Wolf Squadron, sir," the sergeant said. "The captain's a real captain, sir. Gunny and the captain both agree he's just like any Navy captain, sir. But he was a high school teacher before the Plague, sir. It's civilians who've never been in the military who are trying to figure it out and civilians who didn't want to be military who are bosses. Hell, sir, She-wolf, Lieutenant Smith, sir? She's thirteen and there is not one damned person who works with her, or is under her command, sir, who minds. Not after you see her in action, sir. The lieutenant is one badass zombie killer, sir.

"Sir, I'm a *cook*. But Captain Wolf's approach is that every Marine is a rifleman, sir. Navy and civilians can do chow. Marines are for killing zombies, sir. Period. The last few months I've blown more rounds than most guys did in Fallujah, sir. Clearing *ships* which is a *bitch*, sir. Clearing a God-damned supermax liner, sir, is a stone-cold, black-as-pitch *ungodly* bitch, sir. And, sir, I'm losing count of how many we've cleared.

"It's just . . . I don't know how to explain it, sir. It's Wolf Squadron, sir. I mean, sir, just trying to explain Staff Sergeant Decker is hard enough, sir."

"And who is Staff Sergeant Decker, Sergeant . . . ?"

"Coming up!"

The person emerging from the roof hatch was a staff sergeant with the nametag "Decker." He climbed up, then marched, as if he was on parade, to the edge of the roof and looked around. Then he did an about face and marched back to the hatch.

"Begin evolution!" he boomed into the hole. He had bent at the waist to shout and then straightened to the position of attention and did an about face. After that, he marched back to the edge of the roof, did another about face and assumed the position of parade rest.

"May the sergeant inquire what the evolution is, Staff Sergeant?" Hoag asked. She'd never seen a guy wound this tight who wasn't straight out of Boot Camp. She'd seen some Staffs who were pretty wound, but this was ridiculous.

"Two-forty, Sergeant," the staff sergeant replied, looking into the distance. "My team is to emplace and maintain a fire-support position against infiltration of additional infected to this zone, pending clearance operations."

"Are there any additional orders for my team, Staff Sergeant?" Hoag asked.

"Your team's orders are to maintain a presence on this facility until ordered relieved by your colonel, Sergeant. Does your team have sufficient materials to do so?"

"Yes, Staff Sergeant."

A lance corporal had climbed up the ladder and dropped a rope down, then hauled up a machine gun while they were talking. He then started hauling up box after box of ammo. His movements were almost as robotic as Decker's.

"Do your watch personnel all remain by the hatch, Sergeant?" Decker asked. "I am unfamiliar with your standard operating procedures."

"Private Capedon is the roving patrol, Staff Sergeant," Hoag said, taking the hint. "Who should, in fact, be roving, not watching other people work."

"Roving, aye, Sergeant," Capedon said, walking down the roof.

"We did determine, early on, that the rover had to move to different paths, Staff Sergeant," Hoag said. "Otherwise the roof tar gets worn down and causes leaks."

"Understood," Decker said as the sweating lance corporal finished hauling up a ton of ammo.

"Two thousand rounds, Staff Sergeant," the lance corporal reported, standing at attention.

"Where is the rest of the team, Lance Corporal?" Decker said.

The lance corporal bent over, at the waist, and looked down.

"Climbing the ladder, Staff Sergeant."

"Pending their arrival, emplace the weapon on the south wall, oriented to the southeast, Lance Corporal," Decker said.

"I do not have a compass, Staff Sergeant," the lance corporal replied as a corporal climbed out of the hatch. He hoisted a PRC over the coaming and dropped it practically on the lance corporal's feet.

"I'm going to shove one up your ass if you don't get out of my way, Lance Corporal," the corporal said.

"Aye, aye, Corporal," the lance corporal said.

"Lance Corporal Condrey," Decker snapped. "Two steps back, march!"

"Permission to emplace and prepare the weapon, Staff Sergeant?" the corporal said. His tone was a mixture of bored and pissed.

"Emplace the weapon, Corporal Douglas," the staff sergeant said. "Weapon shall be emplaced on the south wall, oriented to the southeast."

"South wall, aye," Douglas said. "Southeast orientation, aye. Pag, grab the ammo."

"Grab the ammo, aye, Corporal!" the new lance corporal said, snappily. "Grabbing ammo, Corporal!"

The weapon was emplaced and loaded, then the corporal tapped the assistant gunner "Pag" on the shoulder.

"Maintain the watch, Lance Corporal," Douglas said. "Staff Sergeant, permission to engage the local expert in intelligence transfer?"

"Permission granted," Decker said.

"Sergeant, a moment of your time?" Douglas said.

"Granted," Hoag answered, waving him towards the center of the flat roof.

"Corporal, a question?" Hoag said. "Is there an issue with the staff sergeant?"

"Staff Sergeant Decker's okay, once you get to know him, Sergeant," Douglas said. "For being flat fucking nuts, that is. He's up here mostly to give him something to do that doesn't take a lot of flexibility. He's in charge as long as he doesn't tell me I have to march everywhere with a fricking two-forty."

"So . . . that's wound pretty tight, Corporal," Hoag said, making a slight gesture with her head.

"Oh, you should have seen the staff sergeant when he *boarded*, Sergeant," Douglas said. "This is him being *laid-back*. Short story, the last order his gunny gave him when they evacced the *Iwo* was 'Take care of the LT.' So when the LT went zombie, instead of, you know, quote taking care of him unquote—strangle or shoot him, have a short ceremony, toss him over the side—as any *rational* human being would do, they kept him *alive*. As a zombie. *On a life raft. For six months.*"

"Holy shit," Hoag said, trying not to look over at the staff sergeant.

"So, I really asked you over here to fill you in, Sergeant," Douglas said. "Because with Staff Sergeant Decker around, do everything as if you were doing guard mount at the White House and he's happy. When you don't do everything precise and by the book, he starts to get . . . fidgety. You don't want Decker the Deranged getting fidgety. It's not pretty."

"I *so* need some time off," Hoag said.

∞ ⊖ ⌒

"Welcome aboard the *Boadicea*, Lieutenant Colonel," the officer of the deck said as Hamilton reached the top of the floating dock's stairs.

He'd already been informed it was a "Navy Auxiliary" vessel so Hamilton saluted the OOD, then turned and saluted the flag.

"Permission to come aboard," Hamilton said.

"Granted," the officer wearing NavCam and silver chicken wings said. "Captain Steven Smith, Colonel. Glad you made it."

"Thank you, sir," Hamilton said, shaking the captain's hand.

"Let's get out of the way so my people can get your people settled," Captain Smith said, taking his elbow. "If the people coming aboard have been severely deprived we generally offer them tomato or chicken soup. In your case, might I offer you a small belt..."

"America," Smith said, raising his glass. There was a finger's thickness of scotch.

"The Corps," Hamilton said, raising his and tossing back the drink. "That's good."

"Lots of good hooch to be had on yachts at sea," Smith said. "Shortest possible in-brief. Then you can go get a shower and a real rack or food someone has cooked or whatever. You are hereby relieved of your duty of holding Gitmo. I'm not sure who we're going to leave behind when the majority of the squadron sails out, but it's unlikely to be you. One thing we'll do before food, shower, et cetera is get you on the horn with the Hole, which is the only remaining headquarters, so you can relieve your suspicions about this outfit. But here's the in-brief.

"There are no significant land areas not held by infected. There are a few self-sustaining, for the time, one family basically islands that show light. We haven't contacted any of them; we know they're there by satellites. Other than that, it's infected on every continent and major island. This squadron was bootstrapped. There's a video that's part of the larger in-brief.

"There are thirty-six submarines still at sea, and nine crews who are on desert islands, which are uninfected. We have to produce vaccine for them. We cannot produce quote modern vaccines, unquote. The only choice is attenuated virus vaccines. That requires spines of infected and a radiation generator. The primary purpose of taking Gitmo was to access the base hospital and get its X-ray machine and various other equipment working as well as raid it for supplies. With that, and the spines of poor dead Marines, sailors and civilians, we can make vaccine. Then we can get the subs replenished and in many cases put their people to work on surface jobs. We are critically short of technical personnel. With the sub crews and the shops here and elsewhere, we can really get going. We're going to give your people three days off here on the *Boadicea* or in some cases on one of the megayachts. That's standard. After that, it's back to work. God knows I can use a professional officer.

"For your information, I'm Australian born, a naturalized American citizen and an 'instant captain' by grace of the NCCC, Under Secretary of Defense Frank Galloway, and the acting Joint Chiefs who are a collection of one Air Force brigadier and some colonels and equivalent in the Hole. There's more, much more. But that's the short and skinny. Any questions more important than talking to the Hole or getting a shower?"

"Just that you do intend to hold Gitmo, sir," Hamilton said. "There's a treaty that states that if we ever leave the base unattended, it automatically reverts to Cuban ownership."

"I'm aware of the Treaty," Smith said, smiling grimly. "That is the least of our concerns, Colonel. There *is* no Cuba. Nor shall be any time soon. The main concern is that from time to time when there were people who did not care for our culture, they were put to sea in sailboats and told to make their own way. Some coasted along behind the squadron and we make sure they get fuel and food. Others have more or less disappeared. Some of them are known semi-hostiles. I don't want any of the latter availing themselves of the material generously paid for by the U.S. taxpayers. So we will maintain a significant presence here until the stores are exhausted or we relocate them. At that point, we'll probably pull out. If anyone wants it, they can have it. This is not truly American soil and if I'm going to put our energies to anything, it is clearing our nation. There continues to be some minor interest in it from a SLOC perspective but that may have to be ignored due to manning constraints. Which will be up to the JCS and the NCCC and not on your plate. Understood, Colonel?"

"Yes, sir," Hamilton said. "Still trying to adjust to the new conditions."

"Which is why you get three days off," Smith said. "One aspect that is more or less mandatory is a short orientation film. I hope you enjoy it."

"Yes, sir," Hamilton said. "Sure I will. With due respect, though, sir, I would like to speak with the Hole, sir."

"Why am I not surprised?" Steve said, smiling.

"So, is there a purpose to this machine gun mount, Corporal?" Hoag said. She was mildly afraid to try to ask the staff sergeant. Or turn her back on him. He was standing at attention, staring into the distance as if zombies would start coming over the ridges at any second. The lance corporal wasn't much better. He'd been assigned to the radio and was holding the mike in his hand, instantly ready to answer any call.

"If the clearance teams run into trouble they can't handle, they bring the trouble back here," Douglas said. "Or to one of the gunboats. Amazing how far an infected will follow a vehicle that's moving slow enough. Also in case any of them show up to interfere with the landing areas."

After getting the Hummer going, the lieutenant and her crew had used it to get some of the five-tons running. The five-tons had fifty mounts. They'd been loaded up, taken to the docks, had Brownings mounted in them, then headed out to go clean up any remaining infected.

"That I'm familiar with," Hoag said. She'd really wanted to go with them. She wasn't even sure what she was doing on this rooftop and wondered when they'd be relieved. It wasn't a Marine thought but they'd patrolled this same damned roof for so *long*.

"*Alpha One Four, Alpha One Four, Squadron, over.*"

"Squadron, Alpha One Four, Papa, over," Condrey replied.

"Original Gitmo Team to evac to Boadicea *for crew rest. Code is Honor, over."*

"Oh, thank God," Hoag said.

"Original team to evac to *Boadicea*, aye," Condrey replied. "Code is Honor, aye."

"Squadron out."

"Sergeant," Staff Sergeant Decker barked. "Secure your roving patrol. You are relieved of guard duty. Proceed to Pier Three for pickup by fast boat. Copy?"

"Secure roving patrol, aye," Hoag replied. "Relieved of duty, aye. Proceed to Pier Three for pickup, aye. Permission to speak, Staff Sergeant?"

"Permission granted, Sergeant!"

"The pick-up point is three hundred meters from this location, Staff Sergeant," Hoag said. "Request cover fire."

The staff sergeant seemed to freeze. He was barely breathing.

"I think you overclocked him," Douglas whispered.

"Corporal Douglas!" Decker barked. "Redeploy machine gun to cover evaccing team."

"Redeploy to cover evac, aye," Douglas said.

"Sergeant Hoag," Decker barked. "Move out!"

"Oorah!"

"Oorah!" Faith shouted, laying down fire with the .50 BMG. "I LOVE these things!"

There weren't really that many infected to engage. But she *was*, by God, going to lead the convoy doing "initial clearance" and she *wasn't* going to let some PFC have all the fun.

"With due respect, ma'am," Januscheitis radioed. *"Short controlled bursts."*

"Staff Sergeant there *shall* be a vehicle-mounted water-cooled version," Faith radioed back. "Make it so."

The "initial clearance" process was simple. Drive around in "medium lift" five-ton trucks looking for infected and kill them. The infected were drawn to the sound of the heavy diesels, not to mention the firing. As they came in sight the machine gunners and Marines in the back of the trucks took them under fire. If anyone ran into anything heavy, they could fall back on the support point or the gunboats.

So far that hadn't been an issue. The base, while complex, was easily enough laid out that the majority of the infected had come down to the points to be killed. The clearance teams had gotten into the dependent housing and so far there hadn't been anything they couldn't handle. The very few infected that had made it all the way to the five-tons were instant road kill and the occasional small piles made by the lieutenant or the other gunners were easy enough to negotiate.

"*Yes, ma'am,*" Januscheitis replied.

"Seriously, Staff Sergeant, a water-cooled vehicle-mounted version should not be an impossibility and the additional firepower would be a useful addition. I think this is a very good idea. Of course, it is *my* idea so of course it's a good idea."

"*To do that properly we'd need to write a staff study, ma'am.*"

"Agh!" Faith said. "Not a *staff study*! Now I'm conflicted, Staff Sergeant. Is it worth a staff study? Yes, I do believe it is. I can combine it with my regular course work as an ISS. Kill two birds with one paper."

"*That is being intelligently lazy, ma'am,*" Januscheitis said.

"I take that as a compliment, Staff Sergeant," Faith replied. "Now find me more infected to kill."

"Team Two, Clearance Ops. Status."

Faith switched frequencies without looking.

"Serious lack of resistance, Ops," Faith replied. "Estimate less than two hundred infected found and eliminated. No serious concentrations. Clearance path ninety percent complete. No survivors found."

"Green flare observed from direction of Base Housing Area Six. Location southeast of Grenadillo Point. Clear housing area, search for survivors."

"Survivors would be nice," Faith said. "Roger, Ops." She switched freqs again. "Objective: base housing area Six, southeast of Grenadillo Point. Janu, you got any clue where that is?"

"Back to the main base road, hang a right, couple of miles up on the right."

"Kirby, find us a place to turn around..."

"Team Two, Clearance Ops."

The sun was sinking in the west and Faith had been half wondering when they'd get the call. Clearance on boats was a day or night proposition. Didn't really matter when you were in the bowels of a ship. Clearing on land, zombies could come at you from any direction. The plan had been to suspend at sunset.

"Team Two," Faith replied. They'd found fifteen survivors in addition to the "survival centers." Most of them were dependents, a couple of civilian workers and two Navy storesmen. They'd found one Marine, the only survivor of a team sent out to shut down and redirect some of the water mains. He'd holed up in the base club with a group of dependents that hadn't made it to the survival center. Fortunately, they'd left the water on to the base club.

"*Suspend clearance,*" Ops radioed. "*Return to piers for evac.*"

"Roger, Ops," Faith said and switched frequencies. "Janu, we're done for the day. Turning around and heading for the pier."

"Roger," Staff Sergeant Januscheitis replied.

What they hadn't seen in the last two hours was infected. The combination of the gunboats and their own sweeps appeared to have run them out of town.

"This job is getting boring," Faith said, dropping into the seat in the five-ton. "I'm ready for a serious scrum."

"Ma'am, with due respect, knowing your father there's all sorts of scrums we're going to get into in the future," PFC Kirby said.

"There's that," Faith said, crossing her arms. "But I'm named *Faith* not *Patience*. At least I'm not doing paperwork...."

"...proceeded...through...base...housing... area...four..." Faith typed, laboriously, with two fingers, her tongue sticking out of the side of her mouth. "Re...covered...four...survivors... God, I *hate* reports!"

"Oh, nummy, nummy," Sophia said as she pulled up to the dock. "Nummy nummy Navy preprepared rations. What a treat!"

"I can do many things with these, ma'am," Batari said.

"Getting them loaded is going to be the interesting

part," Sophia said. She had two pregnant crewmen. Very pregnant at this point. "We'll have to..." She paused as the radio squawked.

"Bella Señorita, *Flotilla.*"

"*Bella Señorita,*" Sophia said, handling the radio as she pulled up to the dock.

"*Change of orders. Stop replenishment ops and proceed to the* Boadicea. *Master to meet with Squadron Commander.*"

"Frack," Sophia said, backing the boat. "Cancel replenishment, aye. Report Squadron Commander, aye. You hear that everybody?" She keyed the loudhailer. "We just had a change of mission. See you guys later!"

"Check-in time with Dad?" Walker asked.

"I have no clue," Sophia said. But she had a sinking feeling she did.

"Bella Señorita, *Flotilla.*"

"*Bella Señorita.*"

"*Additional orders: Crewman Thomas Walker, report Squadron Commander.*"

"Have you been *bad*, Thomas?" Sophia asked.

"I was *born* bad, miss."

CHAPTER 8

*"... WAS THE WRATH OF ALLAH UPON THE UNHOLY
INFIDELS AND THE APOSTATE WHO CALLED
THEMSELVES THE CHILDREN OF ALLAH ..."*

From: *Collected Radio Transmissions of The Fall*
University of the South Press 2053

"Ensign Smith reporting as ordered with party of one," Sophia said, saluting.

"Have a seat Ensign," Steve said, waving to the chair. "And Mr. Walker of course."

"Bit of déjà vu," Walker said, grinning.

"We have Gitmo," Steve said. "Marines reported essentially no resistance by fifteen hundred hours. So now we've got to see if the main hospital is as good as promised. You two will be part of the 'special survey' team entering the hospital tomorrow morning to look for vaccine production materials. Right now I'm holding off on your identity as the vaccine production expert. But you're going to have to partially break cover tomorrow. CDC has sent a list of materials they think you'll need based on needs, wants and desires. You know what most of it is at least; I can't make heads or tails of it." He slid a sheet across the table.

"Better than I'd have written," Sophia said, looking at the list. "Some of the stuff I wasn't sure what you called it. The filter stuff is going to be critical."

"Dr. Dobson will be up on a satellite video link through a laptop courtesy of some of the Navy people and Mr. Lawton," Steve said. "If you can't figure out whether something is useable or what it is, he can advise."

"Yes, sir," Sophia said.

"Mr. Walker, I'd appreciate your support in this as well," Steve said.

"Captain, when I signed on I put myself under your de jure command," Walker said. "If you were asking me to do something clearly illegal, then I'd have to think about it. Absent that, you're the commander, Captain. You don't have to tap dance about giving me orders."

"I appreciate that," Steve said drily. "We're also going to be stripping the hospital of general medical supplies, equipment and medicine. That will be your area, primarily. Although everything is potentially useful, items related to obstetrics are high on my personal list of priorities."

"Understood," Walker said.

"You'll be working with Dr. Chang through the same sort of link," Steve said. "Brief is at zero five thirty tomorrow morning in Conference Room One. Just bring your entry gear with you. Do either of you have body armor?"

"I think I'll skip it, sir," Sophia said. "It's only of use against bouncers. I'd rather wear Tyvek if that's permitted."

"Up to you," Steve said. "The Marines are going

to be providing security and clearance so you should be able to do this in short sleeves."

"What's your status, Sergeant?" Staff Sergeant Barnard asked, sticking her head in the door of the cabin.

The Marines had been assigned cabins in "Marine Country" on the cruise liner. Sheila was sharing a room with Sergeant Cutter from Building Eighteen but this was the lap of luxury compared to the "Survival Centers."

Hoag was enjoying sybaritic pleasures like a working flush toilet, a shower with currently no water restriction and a real, honest-to-goodness comfortable rack. She knew as a Marine she should be all about Spartan but it would be damned nice to be able to lay her head down in an almost private room and snore the snore of the just. She wasn't sure what to do with the rest of her three day pass but she'd heard there was a spa. She was seriously thinking massage.

"I just had my first shower in six months, Staff Sergeant," Hoag said, grinning. "My status is *glorious*, thank you. I was just trying to decide whether to hit the gym or grab some chow."

"Unfortunately, we just caught a mission," Barnard said.

"Oh come..." Hoag started to say, then stopped. She was a Marine and there was only one thing to say. "Aye, aye, Staff Sergeant."

"Sorry, Sheila," Barnard said. "I know we were supposed to get three days off but just about everybody is getting tasked. At least Marines. Too many jobs."

"No issues, Staff Sergeant," Hoag said, drying her hair. "Be ready in five."

"Not that much of snap kick," Barnard said. "Round up your team. Uniform is still PT gear. First order of business is turn in your uniforms and other issue clothing for DX or wash. They have a washing service aboard, glory be. Draw new. After that you're off till tomorrow at first call. Brief is at zero six thirty. Fastrep, going ashore at dawn to provide security for salvage teams looking at the haji hospital. *Iwo* Marines will handle clearance."

"Roger," Hoag said. "So just uniform issue tonight."

"Roger and be ready to roll early tomorrow," Barnard said.

"So much for getting hammered."

"Operation Echo Bird," Captain Wilkes said, bringing up a PowerPoint slide with an overhead view of the hospital. "Background. The Clayton Beauchamp Critical Care Center was constructed in 2010 to give full-function medical support to detainees at Camp Delta as well as support for displaced persons with critical medical needs during disaster relief missions. The hospital is a Class One facility equivalent to a Navy hospital ship or a primary military medical center such as Bethesda Naval Hospital or Walter Reed Army Hospital.

"Mission purpose: Primary. Recover vaccine production materials, both fixed and consumable. Secondary. Recover general medical materials, fixed and consumable, for the squadron . . .

"The objective is a six-story-high, two-wing building constructed primarily of reductive precast concrete . . ."

"Query," Captain Smith said. "Reductive?"

"A type of concrete formulation discovered, or rather rediscovered, about ten years ago," Dr. Dobson said. "It absorbs airborne and contact trace materials, including biologicals, and chemically reduces them. It was starting to be used in all hospital construction just before the Fall because it wipes out bacteria on any of the exposed concrete surfaces. This bunker we're in was made from it. Rediscovered because there's a Victorian era lion statue in London that has the same properties."

"Continue," Smith said.

"Primary objective is the west wing," Wilkes said, bringing up a tighter shot. "West wing has patient rooms including the ICU and epidemiological quarantine rooms on the upper floors. Lower three floors are administration and labs including epidemiology and radiology. The primary supply stores for both are also in that wing. One of the survivors in Building Eighteen was a corpsman. He worked in the primary base hospital, rather than the 'haji hospital' as it's called but he had been there several times. The following is a 'best remembrance' schematic of the location of all the primary objectives..."

"An *hour* briefing?" Faith said as they loaded the trucks. It was still predawn but the sun was going to be coming up any minute. "We're just taking a fricking building. It's not even the size of a *small* liner. Go in, kill any zombies, get the stuff. It's not a big deal."

"Ma'am, I've sat through longer briefings than that on how to do a parade mount," Staff Sergeant Januscheitis said. "It's part of being in the Corps. You're going to be *doing* briefings like that pretty soon, ma'am."

"I'm not using PowerPoint," Faith said. "I'm not."

"With due respect, ma'am," Januscheitis said. "You're in the Humvee. And *not* as gunner."

"I liked the *old* Corps," Faith said, frowning. "Board the boat, kill the zombies, get chow."

"Did we have our apple juice this morning, ma'am?"

"Yes, we did, Staff Sergeant," Faith said, taking a deep breath. "And it's not even the twenty-sixth unless you were wondering. Looks like the lame and lazy are loaded. Let's get this wagon train a-rollin'."

The "haji hospital" was on the far side of a line of ridges south of the main base. As they crested the ridges, the hospital and "Camp Delta" came into view. Team one, led by Lieutenant Commander Volpe, had cleared the exterior zones of the Camp Delta area yesterday and found a few zombies and no survivors.

Nice view, though. Camp Delta was laid out on the shores of the Caribbean and it was a fairly peaceful day at sea. It basically looked like a sprawling cross between a prison and a Sandals resort. The hospital was on a hill west of the command complex for the Camp.

"This was not exactly the worst place in the world to be in prison," Faith said.

"No, ma'am," Kirby said.

"Except in a zombie apocalypse," Faith said. "In which case, there was nowhere good to be in prison."

Faith's Humvee was not leading the parade. The convoy was led by two armed five-tons, then Lieutenant Commander Volpe's Humvee, then Faith's team, two more five-tons with gunners up in the cupolas, the command unit led by Captain Wilkes and finally the "Gitmo Marines" led by their surviving lieutenant who were "escorting" the "special salvage teams." The "escorts" were in five-tons with the team members, including Sophia, in Humvees. If they had more Marine enlisted they'd nearly have a company. As it was, it was more like a reinforced platoon. There was even a corpsman along although he was with the salvage teams as a guide.

"All this parade needs is an elephant," Faith said.

"Anything you want to talk about, ma'am?" Kirby asked diffidently. "You don't seem to be your usual sunny self. With due respect."

"I hate having to work with my sister," Faith said. "Especially when, whatever Captain Wilkes thinks, she's in charge. I don't like being bossed around by Sophia. Pretty much covers it, PFC."

"I . . . had an older sister, ma'am," Kirby said. "I know the feeling."

"I guess the fact that I can actually talk to mine should be a good reason for me to be happy," Faith said, sighing again. "Message received, PFC."

"That . . . I didn't mean . . ."

"No. All good, PFC," Faith said. "I need to adjust my attitude and get the mission done. Gung ho and all that. All good."

Faith's team had the job of doing entry from the rear of the hospital, which was the support and maintenance area. There was a fairly standard loading dock and roll doors with a personnel door to the west side. There were a couple of dead bodies on the loading dock and in the immediate area, all picked down to skeletons by seabirds and insects.

As soon as the Humvee rolled to a stop Faith unassed and waited as the rest of the team got out of their vehicles.

"Command, Team Two," Faith radioed as soon as everyone was arrayed. "Personnel door is open. No apparent threats. Prepared for entry. Staff Sergeant, let's get ready to roll."

"Weapons on safe, lights on," Januscheitis said. "Lance Corporal Pagliaro, point."

"Aye, aye, Staff Sergeant," Pag said.

"*Roger team two,*" Wilkes radioed. "*Begin entry. Careful on blue on blue.*"

"Careful on blue on blue, aye," Faith replied. "Which I'll repeat. We've got Volpe's team coming in from the front. Do not shoot Hooch, however much you might want to. Let's roll."

"Begin entry."

"One-hour briefing," Faith said, stepping over a rat-chewed corpse. "Nearly a division of Marines..."

"Reinforced platoon at most, ma'am," Janu said, trying not to chuckle.

"And there is, like, nada," Faith said. She stopped and looked in a room. More corpses. Some of them were kids. The hospital was packed with them. What there weren't were any living infected. No water. "Which is the worst kind of clearance, Staff Sergeant. Trixie doesn't like this kind of clearance."

"Sort of have to agree with Trixie, ma'am," Januscheitis said.

"Wizard, Shewolf," Faith radioed. "This position was clear six months ago, over."

"*Concur,*" Captain Wilkes replied. "*Position clear. Survey and Salvage team, begin ops.*"

"I'm an electrician, not a radiological specialist, ma'am..."

PO3 Jared Osburn had spent most of his time since

exiting the USS *Dallas* fixing the myriad electrical problems of the squadron. But this was the first time that he'd even seen the power set-up for a cesium X-ray machine. And he knew diddly about what it was actually putting out.

"We're getting the right output readings, ma'am," PO1 Shawn Hougo said. The "nuke" machinist mate *did* know diddly about radiological systems. Quite a bit more than "diddly" in fact. What might be tough for a radiological technician was basically day one of Nuke School. "It appears to be fully operational. This ward was not significantly affected by the results of the Plague."

"The rest of the hospital sure was," Faith said, shaking her head. "Can you pick it up and move it?"

"Carefully," Hougo said. "Yes, ma'am. We'll have to do it the same way that they got it in here: Take out a wall."

"Be better if the hallways were clear, ma'am," Osburn pointed out. "We're going to have to take it out on a dolly. Really have to have the hallways clear."

"And we can't wait for Daddy's Little Helpers to do their trick," Faith said with a grimace. "Okay, we'll call it in. X-ray machine works. Probably should be pulled out. And we gotta clear the halls."

"Ma'am?" Januscheitis said. "They need the techs upstairs. They found a centrifuge."

"Oooo," Sophia said, her arms wrapped around the centrifuge. "Nice..."

"You're weird, Sis," Faith said, looking at the device. It just looked like a waist-high white box.

"Six-liter capacity," Sophia said. "One hundred

thousand rpm. This one is better than ... Anything I've ever used."

"So we're good?" Faith asked.

"As soon as we find out if it works," Sophia said. "Ozman! Need power ... !"

"How many air maintenance personnel do we have?" Steve asked, looking around the hangar. For once the helos—two CH-53s, three Coastguard Seahawk variants and a CH-46—were not riddled with holes or left out in the elements for months. They'd finally pitched the Lynx off the back of the *Social Alpha* to reduce weight. "Can we get at least one of these running?"

"Yes, sir," Lieutenant Bryan Szafranski said. The Coastguardsman was the sole surviving airframe maintenance officer on the base they'd found. "None of my people ... made it ..."

"I'm sorry for your loss never covers it," Steve said. "But ... ?"

"There are several airframe mechanics among the surviving Marines, mostly from the *Iwo Jima*," Szafranski said. "I don't have specific service records but they should have some familiarity with the CH-46 at the least and probably the Seahawks. And the birds are in good condition given the time they've been sitting. They'll need a thorough inspection, though, before I can certify them to fly."

"Understood," Steve said. "Parts?"

"Sufficient for now, sir," Szafranski said. "If you're intending extended operations, we'll need more."

"Eventually, then, yes, we will," Steve said with a note of satisfaction. "Now if we can just make vaccine ..."

∾ ⊖ ∾

"Nope," Sophia said, shaking her head as she entered her father's office. "Or, rather, sir, there are insufficient consumables, notably separation gel, to make any significant quantity of vaccine. And by 'any significant quantity' I mean so much as ten units of booster or primer. There's maybe a cup left."

"Damnit," Steve said as the rest of the hospital survey leadership filed in.

"We've got everything else," Sophia said, slumping into a chair without asking. "And we turned the hospital upside down looking for more. But it's a hospital, not a research center. There probably wasn't much there to start with. It's not used in treatment at all. There's some indication that some was used. The one box we found was open and mostly empty. Maybe someone in the hospital was making vaccine on the side. But that appears to be it in inventory and that's gone."

"What about the rest?" Steve asked.

"For making vaccine?" Captain Wilkes asked.

"Vaccine first," Steve said.

"Functional X-ray machine, functional, excellent even, centrifuge," Sophia said, looking at her list. "General lab equipment, although not as much as I'd like. Bunch of glassware got trashed. Syringes and pipettes. Not as much of those as I'd like but you can make work-arounds. Basically everything we need except gel. And, Captain, Da? The more I think about it, the more I realize what a problem we're going to have with that."

"Short explanation?"

"She covered it on the ride back, sir," Walker said. "The gel is basically the same gel you use in DNA electrophoresis, if you're more familiar with that."

"Pretend I'm not," Steve said, grinning mirthlessly.

"Okay," Walker said. "It's a gel that allows molecules to slip through. The smaller molecules slip through faster, the larger slower. Make sense?"

"Yes," Steve said.

"After you separate the virus bodies you want just certain proteins," Walker said. "Which are a certain size and thus pass through the gel at a certain rate. To make the vaccine you have to dump the centrifuged material into the gel and then wait a specified time."

"Which is effing tedious," Sophia said. "You remember when we'd get bored on the boat and I'd say 'Better than waiting on a gel'?"

"That's what you were talking about," Steve said, nodding.

"You have to have this stuff to make the vaccine, Da," Sophia said, sighing. "Sorry, sir . . ."

"Not the big issue," Steve said. "So where do we get it?"

"That's the problem," Sophia said. "We . . . the powers that be? They weren't making infected into vaccine as a regular program, you know? But there were a lot of people who *were* doing it. By the time we finished with . . . the Program, finding gel was nearly impossible. Everybody was out. And even Dr. Curry said making it was pretty much out of the question. I mean, could somebody make it? Sure. Dr. Dobson may know how. But I guarantee it takes stuff we don't have. One kind is made from some kind of algae. We need more. And we're going to need a lot, at least two hundred pounds or so, to make enough vaccine for all the sub crews. And it was already in short supply at the Fall. I'm not sure we're screwed but . . . I think we're screwed."

"Table that for now," Steve said. "General supplies."

"Essentially it comes down to anything nonconsumable, plenty, sir," Walker said. "There were even plenty of OB materials. At least, plenty in any normal situation. Anything consumable except Viagra was shot. Antibiotics, antivirals, disinfectants, pain medications, all the pharmaceuticals, were if not used up, then essentially used up. There wasn't even a single full bottle of Betadyne in the whole place. The exception is things like anesthetics used in surgery. That we've got. Morphine and codeine, not so much. I think they were either stealing the opiates at the end or using them to tranq the infected."

"So," Steve said, looking out the window. There was a sub surfaced in the distance. The *Boise* had suffered a critical failure in their air handling system and was out of action for the foreseeable future. They were keeping well away from any wind-blown source of infection but they *had* to open up their hatches. "We have to find a source of consumable materials. I'll toss that to Dobson. Captain Wilkes."

"Sir," Wilkes said.

"Thank you for handling what I'm sure was another nightmare," Steve said.

"Probably the worst part was there *wasn't* any resistance, sir," Wilkes said.

"But we have a Marine colonel now," Steve said. "And in case you haven't heard the news, functional helos over at the air base."

"I get a stick back, sir?" Wilkes said, his eyes lighting.

"You get a stick back," Steve said, smiling. "That's the good news. I'm not sure whether to inform certain parties of the bad news personally or let the chain of command handle it. I think the latter. It will be a learning experience."

"I'm not following, sir," Wilkes said.

"What MOS is Staff Sergeant Januscheitis, Captain?" Steve said.

"They're WHAT?" Faith screamed.

"It's my MOS, LT," Janu said, continuing to pack his seabag. "It has been...a real pleasure and honor having you as a skipper, Skipper."

"Oh, hell no!" Faith said. "They are *not* taking my platoon sergeant!"

"Ma'am," the staff sergeant said, straightening from his packing. "I've kind of shown you the ropes on some stuff along the way, haven't I?"

"Janu, without you..." Faith said, shaking her head. "I mean, I'd never have been able to do this. You do it, really. I'm still trying to figure out how to write reports. And...stuff. I've still got no clue about operational planning!"

"Well, then, ma'am, let this be my last class, for the time being, on how to be a Marine," Janu said, going back to packing. "I've got a job to do. It's actually my job, which infantry stuff isn't, and it's important. We've been needing helos. I fix helos, ma'am. Now, unless you want to try to convince somebody to rebranch a thirteen-year-old without so much as a high-school degree as an aviation maintenance officer, and do nothing for the rest of your Marine career *but* paperwork, you need to realize, ma'am, that this is how the Marine Corps works. It's not just that you have to go where they tell you to go and do what they tell you to do. You have to watch other people go and do what they're told to do. I'll be around. If you want to get together, on or off the books, if you need me to explain something, ma'am, I will always be there. I'll always be your first NCOIC and, hell, generals go hunting for them for their sergeant majors and, ma'am, I look forward to being your sergeant major one day. But it's time to cut the apron strings. For me to go do the job I'm supposed to do and you to go be the crazed zombie-massacring warrior bitch you are, ma'am. And remember no dangling participles."

"I could talk to..."

"Don't even, Lieutenant," Januscheitis said, shaking a finger at her. "You're either a Marine or you're not. If you're a Marine, there should only be two words going through your head right now or you're not really a Marine, LT."

"*Semper Fidelis*?" Faith said, tearing up.

"Oh, stop that, Faith," Januscheitis said, kissing her on the top of her head. "There's still less than four thousand of us. It's not like we're going to lose track of each other. And it's unbecoming of the fine young officer you've become. Now take a deep breath, say 'Oorah' and carry on with whatever crazy ass mission your daddy assigns next. Understood, Marine?"

"Understood, Staff Sergeant," Faith said, sniffing and wiping her eyes. "Gung ho? Sorry, but I cannot quite get an oorah out, yet."

"Staff Sergeant?" Pagliaro said, tapping on the hatch.

"Come," Januscheitis said.

"Orders for the LT," Pag said. "Report to the colonel at earliest opportunity."

"Which means, Lieutenant?" Januscheitis said.

"Right damned now since I don't actually have

anything more important going on," Faith said, giving him a hug.

Januscheitis stepped back, came to attention and gave her a salute worthy of a parade ground.

Faith carefully returned it with all due form.

"Carry on, Staff Sergeant," Faith barked.

"Aye, aye, ma'am," Januscheitis replied.

Faith then turned and left the compartment.

"Have a seat Faith," Hamilton said, gesturing to a chair.

The office on the *Boadicea* had been one of the Staff Side officer's offices and had a nice view of the base, if a burned-out post-apocalyptic Navy base was your idea of a nice view.

"By now you have heard that Staff Sergeant Januscheitis and some of the other *Iwo* Marines are being transferred to aviation support?" Hamilton said.

"Yes, sir," Faith replied.

"Just 'yes, sir'?" Hamilton asked.

"Marines go where they're told to go and do what they're told to do, sir," Faith said.

Hamilton leaned on one hand and regarded her levelly.

"But you're not happy about it," he said after a moment.

"No, sir," Faith said. "Not going to bitch about it, sir. Stuff happens, sir."

"Do you know what my job was here at Gitmo, Lieutenant?" Hamilton asked.

"I heard it was interrogator, sir," Faith said. "I don't have a problem with that. What with everything that's gone on . . . I was a kid when 9/11 happened, sir. I'm one of the ones who wondered why we were keeping them alive after we'd gotten all the intel we could from 'em, sir. I'd have thrown them to the sharks like Anarchy, sir."

"The reason that I was an interrogator was, at least in part, my Ph.D. in psychology, Lieutenant," Hamilton said. "And, no, I'm not going to psychoanalyze you. We've far too much to do. I will compliment you, though. I had fully expected, in fact just lost some money, that you were going to go storming to your father, insisting that you keep the staff sergeant."

"We'll keep in touch, sir," Faith said. "And if things change I *will* pull strings to get him back, sir, you can be sure of that. But he has a mission to perform. The question, sir, is do I? I mean . . . You've *got* Marine officers, now."

"Including you, Lieutenant," Hamilton said. "Are you asking to be relieved of your oath over this?"

"No, sir," Faith said. "Subject of the transfer is closed for me, sir. I'm just saying, you've got fully qualified and trained Marine officers. I'm not sure I've got a role anymore."

"I have *four*, including you, Lieutenant Smith," Hamilton said drily. "Five with Lieutenant Fontana and he's about to be pulled off for medical support. As to 'fully qualified,' your job remains what it has been. Leading your men, and now women, into battle to kick the shit out of infected. The technical term is 'duty with troops.' Is that an issue?"

"No, sir," Faith said.

"The roster is going to change but not entirely," Hamilton said, looking at his computer screen. "Your new platoon sergeant will be Staff Sergeant Barnard.

Squad leaders will be Sergeant Smith, whom I think you know, and Sergeant Hoag, with whom you are probably barely acquainted. Exact mission, for now, is open. Infected are cleared from the base areas. There is a meeting at 0900 tomorrow, which I understand is a brainstorming session."

"Yes, sir," Faith said.

"Was that, 'yes, sir, I heard about it' or 'Yes, sir,' to fill in my pause?" Hamilton asked.

"Fill in the pause, sir," Faith said. "And I'd heard about it. Wasn't sure whether I was attending or not."

Hamilton just nodded.

"Know what a brainstorming session means?" Hamilton asked.

"People sit around and throw out ideas, sir," Faith said. "I take it it's about the lack of supplies in the hospital, sir."

"Correct," Hamilton said. "I'm not going to order you to keep your mouth shut. If you have a really good input, input. I am going to order you to *listen*. Pay attention not only to what people are saying but what they are not saying and *how* they are saying it or not saying it."

"I don't quite get you, sir," Faith said, frowning.

"An unfortunately large percentage of an officer's job is meetings, Lieutenant," Hamilton said. "They tend to be very damned boring and very damned important at the same time. I don't have the qualms that many do about you being a Marine officer. In fact, I think the only qualms are among the civilians. Everyone has seen you do your job, as a troop leader, and seen you do it well. From what I have picked up, you even are good at thinking ahead and anticipating problems. You let your NCOs handle what's happening and look to the future while being, obviously, very badass in the present. All very good things in any young officer much less a my-god thirteen-year-old. I'm sort of flummoxed for what I have to teach you about *combat*, at least against infected. My job, therefore, is to teach you the rest of being a Marine officer. And one part of that is how to work a meeting. Which we'll be doing tomorrow. Do you have any reports left to turn in?"

"Yes, sir," Faith said. "I'm about halfway through my AAR on the hospital operation."

"Issues?" Hamilton asked.

"I'm still getting used to military report-writing procedure, sir," Faith said. "And the report really boils down to 'There was nobody home.' I'm not sure how much more there is to write. I mean, I do know there is more to it than that, sir, but there's not much. I can't seem to find enough words to fill out a full DF."

"Then don't," Hamilton said. "Write it up as you would and turn it in. You're right. There wasn't much more to it."

"Yes, sir," Faith said.

"Captain Wilkes wanted at least a thousand words?" Hamilton asked.

"Yes, sir," Faith said.

"I come out of a slightly different culture," Hamilton said. "The more information and less verbiage the better. I don't care if it is only three lines, if it has all the information needed and avoids buzzwords. If it doesn't, then we'll talk."

"Yes, sir," Faith said.

"I'll see you tomorrow at the officers' call, Lieutenant," Hamilton said. "Type it up, put it on the server.

If there are any issues we'll cover them tomorrow. Oh, and this time don't run it past Staff Sergeant Januscheitis first."

"Yes, sir," Faith said, gulping.

"Zero nine hundred," Hamilton said, waving at his forehead. "Be there."

"Congratulations on your clearance of Guantanamo, Captain," General Brice said.

"Thank you, ma'am," Steve said in a puzzled tone. "I think the congratulations should go to Captain Wilkes, however. It was his plan and execution, General. And we're still a bit up in the air over where to get materials for the vaccine. We're considering a sweep of the Leeward Islands."

"Which is critical," Brice said. "But they're going to need to hold in place rather than start the sweep. Or perhaps start it but not for that primary reason."

"Ma'am?" Steve said, cautiously. "Something you haven't been telling me?"

"Many things, Steve," Brice said, sighing. "Many things. But not 'keeping secrets' from you. You said, 'don't joggle my elbow.' By the same token...Captain, I'm looking at the *world* here. And there is nothing you can do for most of the world. We know where five of our supercarriers are that were at sea. Four are aground, one is sunk. Because it would be idiotic, I don't say 'Captain, would you mind going to the Seychelles and clearing the *Carl Vinson*?' You don't need the stress of knowing. Sorry to bring that up."

"I understand, ma'am," Steve said, nodding. "I would if it was even vaguely conceivable. What does that have to do with Gitmo?"

"Nothing," Brice said. "In the same way, I decided not to say 'clearing hell out of a small island is really important and really time critical because...' Let me just say that there is good news and better news. The good news is that we've found you an MD *and* a world-class microbiologist."

"Where, General?" Steve asked curiously. "Walker?"

"No," Brice said, chuckling. "His expertise is more in taking lives. The better news is that you've now created a condition in which she and her colleagues might be able to land."

"Okay," Steve said. "I'm going to admit to total confusion, ma'am."

"Those current videos we sent of the night sky," Brice said. "They didn't *all* come from satellites..."

CHAPTER 9

"... on Abatiku atoll. If there is anyone listening.
Please, we're barely holding on ..."

From: *Collected Radio Transmissions of The Fall*
University of the South Press 2053

"Change of agenda for the meeting," Steve said, pulling up a satellite shot of an island. All of the officers as well as Walker, Gunny Sands, Sergeant Major Barney and Chief Schmidt were present. General Brice and Dr. Dobson were attending via satellite video. "Marines and some presently unspecified Naval forces will head down to the Leeward Islands. Part of that will be to sweep for any remaining medical supplies, textbooks and so on. Part of it will be other missions. Which is the primary focus of this meeting. First, the good news. We now have a *possibility* of getting not only a microbiologist but several mechanical engineers, a former SEAL and, will wonders never cease, an MD."

"Where?" Walker asked.

"Well, that is in part up to Colonel Hamilton," Steve said. "General Brice?"

"We've been looking at this mission for some time," General Brice said. "Mission is to thoroughly clear a small island—our suggestion on that is Anguilla in the British Leeward Islands—and then secure a golf course on that island."

"General," Walker said, "with the forces that we have, securing a golf course would be functionally impossible."

"It's not a suggestion, sir," Brice said. "It's more of a desperation move. And it's not exactly 'secure the golf-course.' It's 'secure the *island* with *focus* on the golf course.' We're just hoping that the Dragon can hit an *island*."

"Dragon?" Faith said excitedly. "They're real?"

"The ISS resupply vessel?" Sophia asked. "I didn't think they were personnel rated."

"Oh," Faith said. "Rats, I was hoping . . . Oooh, astronauts?"

"The ISS," Colonel Hamilton said, shaking his head.

"Oh, bloody hell," Sergeant Major Barney said.

"I thought it was evacuated, ma'am," Faith said. "That was what we'd been told, ma'am."

"Which was true for values of true, Lieutenant," Brice said. "When it was impossible to return the full crew, we were holding off on mentioning that there were still five on the station. Just before the Fall, a prototype Dragon crew vehicle was shot up to the station with, well, as much in the way of supplies and parts as they could fit. But the decision was made for the crew to remain in space. The crews have reduced immune systems, along with dozens of other physical problems. Dropping them into the middle of a plague was not a good idea. Everyone hoped that . . . we'd be able to keep things under control. Get a handle on the Plague. *Three* returned on a Soyuz. What happened to them, and one of them was an American mission specialist, we don't know. But five are still trapped on the station. The Dragon has never been tested for human reentry. It has been *refitted* for it, but... They're out of time, materials, air and their last heat exchanger is about to fail. When it does, the ISS will turn into an oven. A really, really hot one.

"The problem has been, well, obvious..."

"A sufficiently large area sufficiently clear of infected," Colonel Hamilton said.

"Which has people there to help them and people with *vaccine*," General Brice said. "There's an ironic aspect to this. The initial Dragon was similar to the early U.S. space missions: it was designed to land at sea and be picked up by boats. The one that was sent up as an emergency resupply and rescue vehicle was their *ground* landing prototype. Even if things got bad, they envisioned that someone, somewhere, would hold the land and, of course, there was no way that they could get help in an apocalypse at *sea*."

"Oh, God," Sophia said, holding her hand over her mouth and trying not to laugh.

"Yes, Ensign," Brice said drily. "They've been up there for *months* watching the squadron build and cursing their luck. Some of those night sky videos, they provided."

"How accurately can they land?" Walker asked.

"Much more than Soyuz, apparently," Brice said. "They say they think they can hit the driving range on the golf course. Assuming that an untested prototype works. I'm saying secure the whole thing and set a perimeter to stay out from under—well, an untested prototype space-to-ground landing vehicle that has some pretty serious rockets it uses to land."

"Shelley," Walker said, shaking his head. "You're overthinking it."

"Oh?" Brice said. "Sorry; oh, sir?"

"Quit that," Walker said, smiling. "There is exactly zero we can do to support the landing. It's going to land just fine or it's not. And if it's off a bit, we'll have troops under very powerful rockets. Last, sorry, General, there is no way that this number of personnel can secure that large a perimeter. So we back off. We stay onboard the ships. We let her land. Then we go back ashore and get them out."

"Oh, *please* let it land safely," Sophia said, holding her hands in prayer. "I so don't want to run the vaccine program."

"Thought you'd like to hear that, Seawolf," Brice said.

"Does it matter if they hit, well, scrub on the way down?" Walker asked. He was looking at the island on a laptop.

"I'd have to ask them," Brice said. "I'm sure a tree or large rock would ruin their day, and the slope of the LZ is obviously important. Why?"

"The golf course is on the narrow part of the island," Walker said. "If they land in the water, I assume that's pretty much all she wrote. If they can handle scrub, the eastern end of the island is much broader, has a relatively low area that is mostly scrub with several large fields. Why not there? For that matter, there's an airfield."

"I was thinking in terms of securing a perimeter, sir," Brice admitted. "If we're not going to . . . I'll get with them. We have a very limited remaining link—dit/dash code, believe it or not—or I'd have them in on this conversation."

"Then the order to them is shoot for *anywhere* on Anguilla," Walker said. "And we'll come get them. Or, rather, two charming young ladies will come get them while Marines and Navy landing personnel hold the perimeter. Do not open the hatch until they get 'shave and a haircut.' Infected are attracted to light and sound signatures and whoa is this going to be a *doozy* ... If that meets with your approval, Colonel, Captain, General."

The colonel, captain and general looked at each other for a moment.

"Looks like a good outline," Captain Smith said after a moment. "Questions, comments, concerns."

"Fire, sirs, ma'am," Faith said. "The whole area's already burned but it's grown back." She'd been looking at the satellite images as well.

"Good point," Colonel Hamilton said. "The area is very dry. The rocket motor is going to cause a fire. Possibly a large one. The area has already been swept by them several times."

"Question, ma'am," Sophia said, raising her hand.

"Go, Ensign," Brice said.

"Why not Gitmo?" Sophia asked. "It has a golf course."

"Not as flat," Brice said. "Gitmo is surrounded by rather steep hills in case you haven't noticed. Anguilla is not *flat* but it is flatter. Essentially it's an atoll. It appears to be the best island which is closest and also has a medical school so you can do two missions with one clearance. Also do we really want to drop a prototype rocket on our only land base? We've been gaming this for a while, Ensign. The decision was made in favor of not possibly destroying Gitmo even if we lost the ISS crew. There are no good choices in this world these days only less bad ones. Fire."

"Look for a fire truck?" Sophia said, shrugging. "There should be one somewhere on the island."

"Assuming we can get to it," Walker said. "We'll have to have the truck near the landing point for the roll out. But, honestly, most of this is going to have to be done on the fly."

"How long until they are completely gone, ma'am?" Hamilton asked.

"Depends on the heat exchanger," Brice said. "They have air for another two weeks, water for about a month. They're out of food and have been for a week and on very short rations before then. But they are down to one heat exchanger which means they hit nearly a hundred and fifty degrees on the interior every time they fly through the sun zone. That goes out and they bake to death on their next pass. In the meantime, it's bake, freeze, bake, freeze . . ."

"So as soon as possible it is," Hamilton said. "Point of order . . . Mr. Walker's exact position is somewhat ambiguous . . ."

"And it will remain that way for the time being," Brice said. "Absent Mr. Walker wanting to take over this mission?"

"Pass," Walker said. "Accompany, yes. Help? Absolutely. Among other things, we will be unable to perform the operation without the support of some of the pregnant women and at least one baby doctor along is going to be necessary. I *recommend* putting it under Colonel Hamilton. We don't have an equivalent Naval officer of rank other than Captain Smith. I suppose we could put Lieutenant Commander Isham in charge."

"Oh, hell, no," Isham said, laughing. "I just make sure the paperwork is straight."

"Which was my plan," Steve said. "Very well. Mission of the task force is to begin clearance and sweep operations of the Leeward Islands beginning with the island of Anguilla with first mission being recovery of the astronauts. Details of clearance of that island to be determined when you get there. We're pretty good at snap-kicking but I think we'll need to look at how you're going to be supported and supplied before you leave. So, despite the time issues and the problems of the ISS crew, plan for leaving in three or four days. Any questions?"

"Is it an opportune time to discuss the wider mission, sir?" Hamilton asked.

"How difficult do you think it will be to sweep the minor islands, Colonel?" Steve asked.

"Seriously, Da?" Faith said with a snort, then clapped her hand over her mouth.

"My subordinate seems to think it would be a walk to just clear them all," Colonel Hamilton said drily. "Lieutenant Smith?"

"Looking at the maps, these are going to be as easy to clear as the Canaries or easier," Faith said, shrugging. "These are small islands, small towns. Smaller than the Canary towns in most cases. Some of the *islands* are the size of Corillo. With the additional Marines, even without the ones that have been drawn off for helo work, we can blow through these like Michael Moore eating a bag of Oreos..."

Colonel Hamilton did a facepalm as most of the rest of the conference clearly tried not to laugh. The exception was Dr. Dobson who looked momentarily offended, realized the group he was dealing with and composed his features. Faith didn't seem to notice as she scrolled around on her screen.

"Some of them are just too big," Faith said, still ignoring the meeting. "I'm not sure, right now, which are possible and which aren't..."

"Which task I'll assign you," Hamilton said. "Determining which are doable and which aren't. To answer the captain's question."

"Here's the real bitch, sir," Faith said, still poking at the computer. "How recent are these shots?"

"Post-Plague," General Brice said.

"Any way I can bring *this* up on the plasma, ma'am?" Faith asked.

"You're locked in," a voice said. What Faith was looking at came up on the plasma.

"Oh...damnit!" Steve snarled.

"Every big harbor I was looking at had cruise ships," Faith said, looking up. "Those we *can't* blow through. And they're all, or mostly, big islands. Do we ignore them?"

"Primary mission is rescue the ISS crew," General Brice said tightly. "Secondary mission is find materials to produce vaccine. The survivors are going to have enough supplies to hold out until we have time to clear them, or...they are not."

"Input?" Sophia said.

"Go ahead, Ensign," General Brice said.

"Once hard clearance is complete on most of these towns, my...Navy crews can generally sweep for the materials, ma'am," Sophia said. "Marines could then potentially do what they can about cruise liners? While we're doing that?"

"Can they clear *hospitals*, Lieutenant Commander Chen?" General Brice asked.

"Getting there, ma'am," Chen replied. "If they're in the same condition as the one here . . . yes."

"Take that on a case by case basis," General Brice said. "Priorities are as stated. The sub and ISS crews are *not* going to last forever. And, sorry, they have more critical skills than the average cruisegoer. You do *not* clear liners, which takes forever, at the expense of the mission. Captain Smith?"

"Are you looking for my concurrence, General?" Steve said. "I concur. And we can roll the light boat flotillas at any time. Marines have been rearmed and while the Gitmo Marines haven't had much down time, I'm sure they can roll at any time."

"Mission is to secure vaccine materials and other medical supplies from small islands in the Caribbean, focusing on the Leeward Islands," General Brice said. "Supplemental but priority mission to clear an island, Anguilla is our suggestion, to recover the ISS capsule and the personnel. Which will require a quarantine facility as well. Force structure and commander shall be designated by squadron commander. Mission may engage in rescue, including hard clearance rescue, so long as it does not interfere or degrade primary mission. Mission commander can use discretion on target size. Wolf?"

"Light boat Wings," Steve said. "All five. Supported by the *Grace Tan* and *Money for Nothing*. Marine force can use the bunks on the *Grace Tan*. Overall Command, Colonel Hamilton. Critical personnel, Mr. Walker, who is already in the light boat flotilla, and Ensign Smith, ditto. Lieutenant Fontana will remain with the squadron to begin establishing conditions for the coming baby wave, which we need to keep in mind. Try to leave refugees either in place or centralized on one island. We've spare weapons from one place or another and mission commander can arm refugees with said weapons and ammo for defense against the infected as he sees fit. Questions?"

"Operation name," Isham said, looking at his notes. He looked up and shrugged. "It's a military thing, right?"

"It's a military thing, yes," General Brice said, smiling slightly.

"Operation Leeward Sweep," Steve said, shrugging. "Not like we need to keep it secret or anything. Although..." He paused in thought. "We do need to keep the ISS thing secure."

"Sir?" Hamilton said, frowning.

"General Brice withheld the information about the ISS due to morale concerns," Steve said. "Given that six plus billion people just died, that we lost the people on the ISS is just a blip. Knowing that they could get back was what was withheld with the cover of 'they already came back.' That morale issue remains. We'll have to do all the preparations without explaining why. Give orders. Do not inform your personnel, until the last possible moment, of the purpose. They should get a chance to see it inbound. But there's a good possibility that some aspect of this, besides the final landing, may fail. If it fails before it comes into sight, call it a drill and carry on. Understood?"

"We'll get it done, sir," Colonel Hamilton said.

"However, time is awasting and we need to get started."

"At this point I think the better is the enemy of the good," Steve said. "General?"

"Concur," Brice said. "Good luck. SAC is out."

"I'm not sure what I'm going to tell my people," Sophia said. "Going to get a lot of questions."

"Leave that up to me, ma'am," the sergeant major growled. "Of course, you may have to sit on Seaman Apprentice Zelenova."

"Olga I can manage," Sophia said.

"Any issues, Lieutenant Smith?" Steve asked.

"No, sir," Faith barked. "We will proceed in a gung ho manner, Captain. Or my Marines will regret the day they were born, sir. Personally looking forward to a stroll in the dark."

"Oorah," Walker said, stifling a chuckle.

"Remember that the better is the enemy of the good in this," Smith said, standing up. "Meeting adjourned."

"St. Croix... maybe," Faith muttered, looking at the screen. "St. Martin, no God-damned way..."

"Busy, Sis?" Sophia asked, tapping on the open office hatch.

"Colonel Hamilton has me figuring out which islands we're going to conquer," Faith said, snarling. "Since they're on the way, he had me add in Puerto Rico and the Virgin Islands. First of all I have to figure out where all these damn medical schools *are*, then figure out, by eyeball, if I think they're clearable. *Then* I've got to figure out how much ammo and supplies we're going to need!"

"Which is what I've got to do," Sophia said. "Figure out how much fifty we're going to need. My suggestion of 'why not just fill the gunboats with double that on the *Grace'* was not taken well. Anyway, *I* need to know what the targets are so I can submit a requisition for ammo that, coincidentally, is 'fill up the gunboats with double that on the *Grace.*'"

"So hurry up?" Faith snapped.

"No," Sophia said, sighing. "This is called 'coordination.' We're supposed to work together."

"Oh, joy," Faith said.

"Can I suggest a shortcut?" Sophia said.

"Think you're smarter than I am, as usual?" Faith said, then winced. "Sorry, Soph. I *know* you're smarter than I am. I just hate this paperwork crap. I agree with you. Just take all the ammo and food we can load and figure out the rest later. But if you think you know which islands to clear...?"

"It's not that," Sophia said. "Just... You think Nevis *is* clearable?"

"Yes," Faith said. "The towns aren't all that big. I'm sort of worried about Zylons infiltrating behind us, but...yeah. Not even tough."

"Bring up a spreadsheet," Sophia said, pulling up a chair. "Now, you said St. Croix, maybe. St. Martin?"

"No damned way," Faith said. "Or...it looks like it would just take a hell of a long time and ammo..."

"Right, you got population and area of those islands...?"

"I hate you, Sis," Faith said about thirty minutes later. "I really do."

The answer lay in the combination of population density and area. Even with an intensely populated island, which none of them were, it was possible to clear one if the area of the island wasn't too great and the building structures weren't overlarge. Really it was just a matter of finding the population density and maximum population. Which boiled down to "Nevis, yes, St. Martin, no." Various other islands fell into similar categories with a few in the "maybe" column.

"I hate you, too, Faith," Sophia said, smiling. "Want the really bad part?"

"What?" Faith asked.

"Hang on..." Sophia said, going to the main menu. A couple of seconds later a video screen came up. "Hi, COB!"

"Hello, Ensign Smith," the COB of the *Alexandria* replied. "Am I finally getting a chance to meet your sister?"

"That you are, COB," Sophia said. "Lieutenant Faith Smith, Chief Petty Officer James LeRoy, Chief of Boat of the *Alexandria*."

"Pleasure to meet with you, Chief," Faith said, nodding at the video screen.

"Same to you, Lieutenant," the troll-like chief said, his face creaking into what might have been a smile. "You and your sister have been real morale boosters when we needed it. So to what do I owe the pleasure, ma'ams?"

"Your guys got some time on their hands?" Sophia asked.

"Too much," LeRoy replied.

"Faith has been assigned to determine better and worse targets for possible clearance in Eastern Caribbean. We've come up with a matrix of size and population density with known max/mins. Think your guys could refine it down a bit for us?"

"Cheating on your homework, again, Ensign?" LeRoy said, smiling.

"*Cross-check*, Chief," Sophia said. "And something for your guys to do. Besides, we're officers. We're supposed to buff our nails while enlisted do all the work."

"Shoot the rough over," the chief said, clearly trying not to break his expression. "I'll make sure you're on the right track, ma'am."

"Thanks, Chief," Sophia said, closing the connection.

"You *cheat*?" Faith asked.

"If you ain't cheatin', you ain't tryin'," Sophia said. "The point, Sis, is first let computers do as much of the work for you as you can get them to do, and don't hesitate to reach out to people who a.) have time on their hands and b.) are going to be much better than either of us at doing this. You need to know *how* to do it, don't get me wrong. But wasting your time crunching numbers that the sub crews can crunch isn't, in fact, what an officer is supposed to be doing with her time. You figured out, basically, what is and is not doable. The model. Nevis is doable, St. Martin isn't. That's what you know and they don't and you put it in a form that gives them an outline. Now let them work inside those parameters to pick out possible targets and you refine that down. Because the next step is figuring out how much ammo and materials we're going to need."

"Aaagh," Faith said, clutching her head. "I *hate* logistics! No, I take it back. If you've got enough ammo, you're good. You just steal the rest."

"Oh, good God, Sis," Sophia said. "It's not that hard."

"Sophia," Faith said carefully. "Seriously. First of all, you've always been the brain. I admit that, okay. Just like you'd admit I can kick your ass, right?"

"You've done it enough times," Sophia said, frowning.

"Second, you were in *high school*. I was barely working with fractions and they *still* give me a headache."

"You want to be an officer or not?" Sophia asked. "Serious question."

Faith thought about it for a long few seconds.

"Yes," Faith said. "I'd sort of like to be a grunt and there's... Yes. So I guess you're saying I've got to get smarter?"

"Just willing to learn, Faith," Sophia said. "I know you get headaches with this stuff. Pain is..."

"Weakness leaving the body," Faith said. "So how do we figure out how much stuff we need?"

"Fortunately, we have the Canaries to draw on as an example," Sophia said, going into the server and hunting through files. "This is it. This is all the ammo and material we used in the Canaries by operation. Okay, I'm not going to do this for you. How do we use this stuff to figure out how much we're going to need?"

Faith just looked at her for a second. Sophia hated that look.

"Is this a *word* problem?" Faith said. "I *hate* word problems."

"Yes, this is a word problem," Sophia said, trying not to sigh. "*Life* is a word problem. Okay, okay, hint. How big is Charlestown?"

"You mean in Nevis?" Faith said, starting to look it up then pausing. "Oh, Walker knew that. Fifteen hundred or so. How did he know that, you know?"

"Just... Let's skip the subject of Walker for right now," Sophia said uncomfortably. "Okay, fifteen hundred. What was the population of, say, San Sebastian de la Gomera?"

"I have no idea," Faith said.

"Faith, I'm not going to hold your hand the whole time," Sophia said. "Try to think."

"I don't remember ever seeing it," Faith said.

"So..."

"I don't have an internet to look it up, Sophia!" Faith snapped. "You know where I can get an atlas that would have it?"

"Oh, good God, Faith!" Sophia said. "Do you mean you haven't been accessing the Hole?"

"We can access the *Hole*?" Faith asked.

"They've got a massive database which is accessible to all military personnel," Sophia said, shaking her head. "I mean, a bunch of it's classified of course... Okay, type in your network password...."

"Don't look," Faith said, shifting her shoulder. She slowly typed in a long password.

"Maybe you *should* go for enlisted," Sophia said, shaking her head.

"What's that supposed to mean?" Faith snapped.

"'I love Gregory Januscheitis' is not what you call the most secure password," Sophia said. "Not to mention kind of being an issue since you're an officer and he's enlisted."

"Hah, if that's all you know!" Faith said. "It's got a 1 for the I and two dashes."

"How in the hell did we come from the same parents?" Sophia asked. "I swear you have to be adopted. Okay, click on the link that says... What?"

"What?" Faith said, looking at a series of named buttons.

"What are we looking for?" Sophia asked.

"I don't... Wait... Population of... Gomera."

"Pre-Plague, mind you, although . . . I wonder if the secure areas might have infected populations, that would be useful . . . So, what is population data in terms of those icons?"

Faith searched through the buttons.

"Oh," Faith said, clicking one. "Human geography."

"Got it," Sophia said.

"I don't see Canary Islands . . ."

"Try Spain," Sophia said, trying not to sigh.

"Oh, yeah," Faith said. "Spain . . . Canary Islands . . . Gomera . . . San Sebastian de la Gomera . . . about eight thousand."

"How much ammo did we use?" Sophia asked.

She got the look again but Faith flipped over and checked the other sheet.

"Holy cow," Faith said. "We used thirty-five *thousand* rounds of fifty-cal in *Gomera*?"

"And you guys used another nine thousand rounds of seven-six-two and six thousand of five-five-six," Sophia pointed out. "For about eight thousand residents before the Plague."

"I start to get Gunny's whole thing about one shot, one kill," Faith said, poking around the data. "I thought so. We only use an average of *ten* rounds to the population of a liner . . . Some of that, not much, was on the *Bo.* . . ."

"Most of the 'inhabitants' of a liner are, sorry, dead," Sophia pointed out. "And it's real short range. But you're on the right track. To figure out how many rounds we're going to need for the operation . . ."

"How many rounds of each caliber per kill?" Faith said.

"Per population of the town before the Plague which

is the only hard data we've got," Sophia corrected. "And it's different, like you said. Liners are different but the towns are different, too."

"So . . . averages," Faith said. "Figure out how many rounds we used per pre-plague citizen of the towns at each town and then figure it out for the towns and islands we're going to take. Agh. Spreadsheets and spreadsheets . . ."

"But you've figured out what we need in terms of data, right?" Sophia said.

"Yeah," Faith said.

"Can you write it out as an equation?" Sophia asked.

"I think so," Faith said. "I'm not sure about the right, you know, notification or whatever. But it's like rounds used by type versus the pre-Plague populations and then get an average?"

"Okay, what we do is we write that up and we get the subs to do it," Sophia said.

"Again with the subs," Faith said.

"One, they're nukes," Sophia said. "They're serious math guys. This is actually *too* easy for them. Two, they're bored. Three, they feel like they're not really contributing. This *does* help. But you figured out what we needed in terms of information. Which is what *officers* are for. Okay, other supplies."

"Seriously, we can probably scavenge for most of it," Faith said. "We're going to need ammo and if we're going to do the liners, probably batteries. Food, water, fuel . . . there's boats and stores."

"Not as much fuel stores as you might think," Sophia said. "We were having a hard time finding those in the Canaries. The tanks at the marinas were mostly dry 'cause people tanked up and ran."

"Fuel...we just load up the *Grace Tan*? What's its max tankage?"

"Which is pretty much the answer we're going to have to give," Sophia said. "Fortunately, we do have fuel here at the base. The tanks are almost topped up. Water? These islands don't have much."

"They reconfigured Gitmo as a disaster support base," Faith said, grinning and diving into the server for another file. "I was talking about it with Smitty. There are diesel powered water filtration systems, big ones, big enough to supply a small town. We'll take some of those along with us on the *Grace*. That gives us water. There are...five of them in a warehouse over by Grenadillo."

"Put in a requisition for them," Sophia said. "Okay, food, yeah, we can probably scavenge. But we need a base supply. Enough for the unit for, say, thirty days..."

CHAPTER 10

*"...atoll is zombie free, mates. We're setting up best we can.
Got the gennies running anyway and we've got a functioning
loo! What a blessing it is to sit on porcelain again!
Any bloody ammo is appreciated so we can start clearing..."*

From: *Collected Radio Transmissions of The Fall*
University of the South Press 2053

"I need to admit something, sir," Faith said as Colonel Hamilton perused the operations and logistics report.

"You got help?" Hamilton asked.

"Sophia was working on some of the same stuff, sir," Faith said. "So we put our heads together on it. And some of the number crunching, I...delegated. I *could* do it, sir, with a computer at least, but I was trying to figure out *what* numbers had to be crunched, sir. But I figured out *most* of it myself, sir. And the rest was mostly Sophia asking questions. But I did get help, yes, sir."

"That's a lot of 'buts,' Lieutenant," Hamilton said. "Which is understandable. If you'd tried to figure this out yourself from first cause it would have taken you a month, I'm sure. It would have taken any second lieutenant a month. Well, most. I agree on your three initial targets. I'd even say the 'maybes' like St. Croix

176

are doable if we're given enough time. You want to take five-tons?"

"I hadn't worked with them until we got here, sir," Faith said. "They really are the thing for land clearance. We can probably do it with scrounged transport. But the five-tons are way better, sir. They've got the gun mount and ground clearance. I've gotten stuck on bodies more than once in the Canaries, sir. It's not just that you're stuck with a wave of infected coming at you. It's . . . There's a lot of really raunchy stuff about this job, sir, but spinning out on bodies is high on the list, sir."

"Duly noted," Hamilton said. "I'll put it in consideration. Did you happen to give consideration to how to transport them, Lieutenant?"

"All of these islands have ferry docks, sir," Faith said. "Some of them are smaller than others. We'd have to find, survey and man a small ferry. But even a small truck ferry could carry at least two five-tons, sir."

"I'll take that up with Commander Chen," Hamilton said. "It has merit. Your estimate for ammunition consumption is, I think, low. What's it based on?"

"The Canaries, sir," Faith said. "We compared the population, pre-Plague, of the towns to our ammo usage and then carried it over to the pre-Plague populations of the local towns. That's the ground combat rounds. Soph and I both worked on that as well. I took all the ammo and batteries and Soph took the other consumables."

"The point is, we used *six* times as much ammo in terms of similar conditions in Iraq," Colonel Hamilton said, looking up. "Are you saying our current forces, undertrained as they are, are that much *better*?"

"Uh . . ." Faith said, thinking about it. "Zombies don't duck, sir?"

Colonel Hamilton regarded her evenly for a moment, looked at the spreadsheet, looked back.

"Point again taken, Lieutenant," Hamilton said. "The ROWPUs?"

"We always need more water, sir," Faith said. "And I think that's on the Navy side anyway, sir."

"I am in the unusual position of being a Marine officer in charge of a Naval expedition," Hamilton said. "So I have a similar report from, as you put, the Navy side. Did Sophia conceive the idea?"

"I . . . I sort of said we should take them, sir," Faith said nervously. "I mean, they're just sitting there, sir. Sophia asked about water 'cause it's always a problem for the boats. I don't really think about it since the boats supply it but she had a point."

"And again I'll take it under consideration," Hamilton said. "It's not a bad report. I'm going to tweak some of the numbers based on gut, red-line it and compile it with the Navy side for requisitioning. As I said, I agree with your assessment of the best objectives. Next: the captain wishes us to be able to arm the residents of the islands against the potential of, well, pirates as well as any remaining infected."

"Yes, sir," Faith said.

"There are apparently remaining weapons on the *Iwo* but it's not worth our time going back to get them," Hamilton said. "Especially since there's a source closer to hand, if a bit . . . unpleasant. So we're going to scavenge."

"The weapons of the . . . fallen on the base, sir?" Faith said.

"Yes," Hamilton said. "Wellington once said the only thing that could be worse than a battle won must be a battle lost. The truth, I think, is the opposite. The losers don't see the results whereas we *do*. I'm not sure it's the best conditions for you to get to know your new platoon, short as it is. But that is your next mission. Round up your platoon and go scavenge all the weapons and magazines you can find on the base."

"Yes, sir," Faith said.

"As you're doing so, see which are still functional, clean them up and when we clear an island issue them to what seem to be trustworthy locals," Hamilton said. "Any questions?"

"Just one, sir," Faith said. "It's ... um ... fourteen hundred. Should we start today, continue at night or start in the morning, sir?"

"Start this afternoon, at the very least figuring out how," Hamilton said. "Staff Sergeant Barnard is familiar with the base and it's always a good idea to listen to input from your NCOs. But I'd like you to at least get started today. Main op tomorrow."

"Yes, sir," Faith said.

"Very well, Lieutenant," Hamilton said. "Dismissed."

He waited until the door had closed to chuckle.

"'Zombies don't duck,'" Hamilton said. "Write that on your damn hand, Craig."

"'Tention on deck!" Smitty boomed as Faith walked into the squad bay. The NCOs were in the bay checking the gear, new and old.

"Whoa, whoa," Faith said, somewhat nervously, waving both hands. "At ease and all that. Staff Sergeant ... Barnard?"

"Yes, ma'am," Cindy said, still standing at parade rest.

"Rest, Staff Sergeant," Faith said, sticking out her hand. "Lieutenant Smith."

"Yes, ma'am," Barnard said, shaking her hand. "Good afternoon, ma'am."

"We caught a mission," Faith said. "We need to... chat about how we're going to detail it out."

"Roger, ma'am," Barnard said.

"Let's talk about it in my broom closet," Faith said, waving at the hatch. "Staff Sergeant Decker."

"Ma'am," the staff sergeant boomed. He was still at rigid parade rest.

"You're in charge while we're gone," Faith said. "You will recall our discussion about the importance of reestablishing flexibility."

"Aye, aye, ma'am," Decker boomed.

"Oorah, Staff Sergeant," Faith said, gesturing at the hatch. "Staff Sergeant Barnard."

"I looked at a regular TOE," Faith said as they walked down the corridor. "We've got too many NCOs, don't we?"

"By TOE, ma'am," Barnard said. "But I don't think there's such a thing as too many NCOs."

"Not about the mission—but what would you think about trying to set up a mini boot camp?" Faith said. "We need more Marines and unless we find another LHA or take one of the big bases, I'm not sure we're going to find many more."

"I think we're short on hands to do that, ma'am," Barnard said. "And I think it would be up to Colonel Hamilton and the gunnery sergeant."

"Agreed," Faith said, opening the door of her

office. "I'm just thinking about the fact that we've got three staff sergeants and less than a platoon's worth of grunts. Besides, I think Decker would be better off as a drill instructor than on active ops."

Barnard boggled for just a moment at the thought of Decker as a drill instructor.

"With due respect, ma'am," Barnard said. "I think drills need a *bit* more flexibility."

"They need less than is required in field ops," Faith said, sitting down. "Grab a chair, please, Staff Sergeant. That's the point. It would be nice if we had some drills with more flexibility but the area where you need the least would seem to be drills. Or maybe *just* that. That Monty Python sketch, sergeant major marching up and down the square. Decker and Condrey, that's the *only* thing they really can do, drills. If it's not right in a manual they'd read before being castaways, they're pretty much stuck. When we had a little down time, I've had Decker drilling me on marching and commands. He's as perfect as you can find on all that stuff. Figuring out how to get wheels, how to find power and ammo and food in the ruins, how to interact with the survivors, not so much. And have you ever inspected their gear? I mean, that's what the basic portion really is, drilling, how to be a Marine and getting your gear shipshape. That Decker and Condrey *can* teach. And Christ knows we need more Marines."

"That . . . does makes some sense, ma'am," Barnard said.

"If we ever turn up a former Marine who's too old to run with the young pups, maybe," Faith said. "Team him up with those two. Let them run the recruits around and drill the hell out of them, have the old guy to keep them from totally flipping out on the recruits. Which is a thought for another time. We've actually got two missions, one coming up and one that's a 'now' thing. You've probably heard we're doing a float."

"Yes, ma'am," Barnard said. "Medical supplies."

"We don't know where to get them," Faith said. "There's no one place that we know there's a big stockpile of what we need. The critical item is a gel to make the vaccine. But that's generally where there are other medical supplies. So we're going to go on a Caribbean cruise. You know, travel to exotic foreign lands, meet interesting zombies and kill them?"

"Yes, ma'am," Barnard said.

"This time the plan is to do a rough clear on the towns and even islands we hit and probably leave the inhabitants to their own devices," Faith said. "We did something similar in the Canaries but it was mostly the Navy doing it. Thing is, there are still going to be infected roaming around even after we blast through. So the locals need some guns since they're generally in short supply on those islands. We've still got spares but it makes more sense to clear up the ones here on base. Which is our first mission. We're supposed to collect up all the weapons, ammo and mags of the 'fallen,' check 'em out, decide which are still useable and which aren't, clean 'em up and rack 'em for issue to local 'militias' after we've cleared the islands."

"Roger, ma'am," Barnard said tightly.

"Yeah, great detail," Faith said. "But somebody's gotta do it. Thinking about it, I'd put Staff Sergeant Decker and PFC Condrey on inspecting and cleaning detail. That way they're bound to be perfect."

"Roger, ma'am," Barnard said.

"About the only thing I know about being a Marine and being an officer is what I've picked up in books and what I've learned in the last few months," Faith said. "I wasn't one of those kids who grew up wanting to be a Marine and watching *Sands of Iwo Jima* or something. The way I ran things with Staff Sergeant Januscheitis was something I got in a book. We get missions. We get missions all the freaking time. All I really need is the platoon to be ready to perform the missions. All their gear straight, able to shoot without hitting each other, able to handle the commo and find their way around. We've got no time for training and nobody really knows each other now. But this job ain't actually all that hard. Like I told the colonel, zombies don't duck. But all that's on you. Okay?"

"Aye, aye, ma'am," Barnard said.

"When we get out on missions, I'll dump the simple stuff on you," Faith said, shrugging. "Sorry, best way I can put it. I'm not big on words. I tell you we need wheels, you find the wheels and get 'em running. I say we need a house cleared, you handle it. I'll be figuring out where we're going next and which house to clear. You get it done. Okay?"

"Aye, aye, ma'am," Barnard said.

"I'm still a green lieutenant," Faith said. "Killing zombies I got down pat. Running a platoon, that I'm still learning. So I'm going to be asking your opinion on stuff. And hopefully most of the time we'll agree and I'll say 'Yep, sounds good, go for it.' But if I say we're doing it another way, we're doing it my way, okay?"

"Yes, ma'am," Barnard said.

"Bottom line is if something fucks up, people may get pissed at you," Faith said. "But it's really on me.

"So, we got a mission," Faith said. "We gotta pick up all the weapons on the base, get 'em sorted out and get 'em fixed up and cleaned. How do you think we should detail that out, Staff Sergeant?"

"I see they kept the last bullet for themselves," Sergeant Douglas said, pulling open the back door of the Humvee. A desiccated and bug-chewed female corpse in NavCam tumbled out at his feet. The skull cracked away from the body and rolled onto his boots. A half-dozen rats followed it and skittered under the Humvee. "I do so *love* my job."

"You hear anything about what we're going to do with the bodies, Sergeant?" Lance Corporal Ken Ferguson asked. "That's our gunnery sergeant in there."

"We dumped Captain Carrion's little helpers on the bodies on the points," Douglas said. There was a .45 on the floor in the rear compartment and an M4. From the looks of things, they'd all shared the .45 at the end. The M4 was out of rounds. "But other than that, I really don't know. We haven't been doing much cleanup, but we hadn't planned on holding any of the places we hit. Maybe they'll get the civilians to collect 'em up. But don't figure on a lot of ceremony. There's not enough of us left to bury the dead and we've got more important missions. And we're done here... Building seven next..."

"How long to sweep the base?" Steve asked, looking at the operations plan.

"About five days, sir," Colonel Hamilton. "To fully sweep it."

"Two," Steve said. "Get as many weapons picked

up as you can in two. Detail some areas for the Navy ground people to sweep as well. Day three you need to be rolling. Clean them up on the way to Anguilla."

"Yes, sir," Hamilton said. "The question has been raised about the dead, sir."

"Which has already been considered," Steve said. "Lieutenant Commander Isham is getting teams together to gather them up and get them buried. Mass grave, mind you. We'll be working on that while you're on the op. As noted, we're going to hold this base for the time being and it's a public health issue. As are the legions of rats and flies. We'll be getting it cleaned up and habitable while you're on float, Colonel. So, good news, not your problem. Bad news: ground clearance ops have their own unpleasantries. Two days, Colonel. Any questions?"

"No, sir," Colonel Hamilton said.

"Base this size I can't believe they don't have AT-ATs," Isham grumped.

The handysized freighter M/V *Paul Østed* was unloading its cargo onto Pier L. All of it. A team had gone through its computerized manifest and triaged the containers based on "this is definitely useful, this is possibly useful, this is not useful right now." The plan was to unload all the containers, sort them out, reload the "useful"—pretty much *anything* in terms of "consumables"—while checking the "possibly useful." The "this isn't useful" were going to be stacked and stored.

"AT-ATs?" Steve said. "Like the elephant tank things in *Star Wars*?"

"Those big gantry cranes," Isham said. "Like they had, you know, in Tenerife?"

Fortunately, the ship had its own cranes. Unfortunately, as usual, the people using them had limited experience. The answer was "don't hurry." On the other hand...

"Well, we couldn't exactly use the ones in Tenerife, Jack," Steve said. "Bit of an infected problem. How long?"

"Two weeks, minimum," Isham said. "You have no clue how much stuff is in there."

"Alas, most of it useless," Steve said.

"There are two, count 'em, two containers listed as 'medical supplies,'" Isham pointed out. "Don't know what kind until we get to the detailed manifest. But the codes indicated pharmaceuticals and equipment. That should be good."

The ship had been out of Rotterdam headed to a series of small African ports when the Plague had been announced and it was "stranded" at sea. Shortly after the crew, which had naturally already picked up the virus, had gone zombie. The captain had left a quite detailed log up to a point.

"Anything like that is useful," Steve said. "The truth is that everything we critically need is sitting on some ship, somewhere. If we had, say, the internet we could probably even figure out which and where."

"Wouldn't that be nice," Isham said. "I know what business I'm getting into when I'm done with this Navy shit."

"I think it's the only business there's *going* to be for the foreseeable future," Steve said. "I just hope we can keep civilization functioning in that environment."

"You worry too much, Steve," Isham said, turning away from the unloading ship.

"Clearance of the bodies on the base?" Steve asked. The pier had been cleared but he could see the seagulls squawking over the bodies on Radio Point.

"Not a lot of takers," Isham said. "I've got some guys with civilian construction experience digging a pit for a mass grave. You know how big a mass grave you need for about seven thousand bodies?"

"Big is about the best I can do," Steve said.

"The same guys are willing to go around with front-end loaders to pick them up," Isham said. "Problem being, you got to have people on the ground, too. And between being afraid of the infected and, well, not being into moving bodies…"

"We're keeping back some Navy masters-at-arms," Steve said. "Have them roust out the 'lazy' among the SLLs. At gunpoint if necessary. The carrot will be we're going to be rough clearing some Caribbean islands. If they help out on this, and they will even if we've got to break out whips, we'll put them on a nice Caribbean island with some weapons in case of infected and they can just scavenge and beachcomb the rest of their lives."

"We might have to get whips," Isham said. "They're pretty comfortable with a bed, water and sushi."

"There was a study done post-Katrina," Steve said as they walked down the pier. "About how refugees respond. About ten percent have to have *something* to do to help out and they tend to be the first to jump ship and get out of whatever refugee camp they're in. At the other end, ten percent will do anything they *can* to avoid leaving food and a place to sleep. They used cruise ships for some of the refugees and that bottom ten percent had to be physically removed from them. So round up that bottom ten percent and tell them they can either pick up bodies or we will drop them off on the Cuban side, where the infected *haven't* been cleared, and they can try to fend for themselves. I am that serious."

"That's kind of like murder," Isham pointed out.

"I'm kind of past caring, Jack," Steve said. "I'm going to send my daughters out on another ugly mission to help save the world, and I really don't give two shits about people too lazy to help."

"You warmed up enough, Lieutenant?" Fontana asked as Faith pounded the bag.

"Warmed up enough to kick *your* ass, Lieutenant," she said to the hulking former SF NCO.

"So the student shall defeat the master?" Fontana asked, humorously, putting in a mouth guard.

"What student?" Faith said, directing a light snapkick in his direction. "You think I'm *your* student?"

"How's the new platoon?" Falcon asked.

"Honestly, I can't really tell," Faith said, blocking his punch and going for a wrist bar, which he evaded. She feinted a punch and tried another snap-kick. You had to be careful with Fontana; he'd put you on your ass if he caught your kick. "I know I have to let the new staff sergeant handle shaking them down. I know that. And I need to just let her do her job clearing the base. But I want to get out there picking up weapons and stuff. Hell, I want to go beyond the cleared zones and do some zombie hunting."

"You at least are *going* zombie hunting," Fontana said. "I am stuck here playing catch-up on being a baby doctor. I have dealt with more insane women and looked at more vaginas in the last week than I ever wanted to see in my life."

"TMI, Falcon," Faith said. She attacked with a blurring combination of kicks and punches, then backed off. As usual, she couldn't break through his defenses. She'd taken a couple of different styles of martial arts since she was a kid, but Fontana had been a hand-to-hand instructor in the Special Forces. It had been noted almost from 9/12 that occasionally soldiers, especially people like SF who were out on or beyond the front lines, had to actually, you know, fight for their lives and occasionally that got down to hand-to-hand. Which was why, eventually, SF had gotten serious about hand-to-hand training. It was Fontana's training as much as anything that Faith had used when it got down to "scrums." Not that it had in a while.

"Two thousand four hundred and eighty-three women in current manning in the squadron," Fontana said. "More women survived than men. No clue why. Of those, eighteen *hundred* are pregnant. With most coming to term within a month of each other. And when one woman in a confined group goes into labor, it tends to cause a ripple effect. We've already had twenty-six premature births. *One* looks like he might survive. We're going to have more and more. God help us if we have a storm or something. Any sort of global stress, even a big weather change, can trigger premature labor."

"Well, I've made up my mind," Faith said. "Sex, maybe. Babies, never."

"One does tend to follow from the other, Faith," Fontana pointed out.

"Every time we do a sweep, I've been picking up birth control pills and stashing them," Faith said. "So there."

"I wouldn't place my...trust in birth control pills that are probably out of date and for sure have been overheated," Fontana said. He managed to get a punch through that rocked her back on her heels.

"Better than the alternative," Faith said, dropping back. "I'm considering losing my virginity. You up?"

She attacked like lightning as he froze for a second and managed to get in a hard blow on his head that stunned him for a brief moment. One roundhouse kick and he was down.

"Hah," Faith said, holding up her hands in victory. "Treachery wins again! And, sorry, I wasn't actually serious. I'm looking for somebody a bit closer to my own age." She held out her hand to help him up.

"Well, just be careful, okay?" Fontana said, rubbing his jaw. "You realize if you *do* get pregnant I'm probably going to end up looking at your twat and that would just *ruin* our relationship. Now prepare to have your ass kicked..."

CHAPTER 11

"...if anybody has a doctor, we sure could use some advice..."

From: *Collected Radio Transmissions of The Fall*
University of the South Press 2053

Thomas Fontana entered the curtained alcove and picked up the chart.

"How's it going, Tina?" he asked.

"Fine, Lieutenant," Tina replied, moving the ultrasound wand around.

They were still in the process of stripping both base hospitals. High on the list was anything obstetrics related.

"Hi, Missy," Fontana said, looking at the chart and the ultrasound. "How've you been feeling?"

"Ready to get done," the girl said. She was nineteen and had been on a cruise with her parents when the plague hit and the captain ordered abandon ship. The inevitable had occurred on the lifeboat which, fortunately, had also managed to contain no infected.

"How's the morning sickness?" Fontana asked, pulling out a stethoscope.

"Morning, noon and night," Missy said, dimpling. "But at least I'm not throwing up sushi all the time. It tastes better going down."

191

"Lemme listen in on junior," he added, putting his stethoscope in his ears. He straightened up after a moment. "Nobody, including the doctors in the CDC, have any clue if there's going to be effects from things like being castaway, okay?"

"Okay," Missy said unhappily. It wasn't like she hadn't heard it before.

"That being said, looking at the ultrasound, listening to the heart, this appears to be a nice normal, healthy, active baby," Fontana said, sort of smiling. His face wasn't really made for it.

"I hope so," Missy said. "I just want him ... her to be okay, you know?"

"I know," Fontana said, scribbling in the chart. "We all do. We are so few. Keep up the prenatal vitamins, try to keep them down for that matter, but it's all looking good ..."

"Lieutenant," one of the nurses said, sticking her head in the cubicle. "We need you in exam six."

"It's going to be fine," Thomas said, smiling and waving as he walked out.

"What's up?" he asked the nurse.

"Patient is presenting with abdominal pain," the girl said carefully. She was obviously trying to remember the lingo since "nurse" was a stretch. "She has a fever of one oh one and her BP is lower than her last visit."

"Okay," Thomas said, taking the chart and entering the cabin. "Hello ... Cathy."

"I'm sorry to take up your time, Lieutenant," the woman said unhappily. "I wasn't supposed to be in until next week. But I think something's wrong."

The woman's pregnancy hadn't been as easy as Missy's. She'd had bouts of high blood pressure and the fetus had never been terribly robust. He would have put her on daily checks if he had the time and people.

"Let me do a quick check," Thomas said, pulling out his stethoscope. He listened for a moment, then said: "I'll be right back."

He stepped out into the hallway and down to the nurse's station.

"Start prepping the OR," he said.

"Problem?" Lieutenant Fallon said.

"Pretty sure that fetus is dead. Please tell me we have some Keflex left. 'Cause I'm also pretty sure it's necrotic."

"You guys look like you could use a drink," Steve said, waving his tray at the table. "Mind if I?"

"Please," Walker said.

They'd eventually set up an "officers" area in the dining room. Walker, as one of the "doctors" was automatically included. Steve didn't always use it; he preferred to strike up conversations with random people to get a feel for what was going on. But tonight it looked as if it was the right place to be.

"Bad day?" Steve asked, taking a bite of fish.

"Two premature deliveries," Fontana said. "In the U.S., pre-Plague, they'd be in intensive neonatal care. As it is, I just wrote 'stillborn.' Which they weren't, exactly, but they didn't last long. And one that died in the womb."

"Ouch," Steve said.

"I'm not going to ruin your dinner describing taking it out," Walker said. "We're now pumping the mother full of some of our precious remaining antibiotics and we're not sure it's going to work."

"I just gave orders to have the ablebodied, by *our* estimation, among the sick, lame and lazy start clearing the bodies on the base," Steve said, continuing to eat. He'd told himself at the beginning that he had to eat regular meals no matter what. "At gunpoint if necessary. When I hear things like this, those decisions come easier."

"The instructors in Q Course stressed over and over again, 'You are not an MD,'" Fontana said. "I mean, I've got no real clue about toxicology, histology, rheumatology . . ."

"So if I recall correctly," Steve said to fill in the pause, "we're anticipating three to four hundred serious complications?"

"When we actually started doing exams and crunching the number, we got it to three hundred forty," Fontana said. "Probably. Statistically. We're getting up to about forty that have lost them one way or another. Three late-term abortions based on serious complications. Four if you count today. We don't have the original studies so we don't know if early to mid-term miscarriages count. Anyway, at this rate only three hundred to go. Yay."

"The way things are going, if we could materially and socially, I'd say pull the babies on at least two hundred of the mothers," Walker said, munching placidly on a tuna roll. "Which we can't because there's not enough trained hands and there's no way you can get them all to agree. Not to mention it would be horrible for morale."

"Losing all two hundred mothers is going to be just as bad," Fontana said.

"Are we going to?" Steve asked quietly.

"Yes," Walker replied. "We are. Not necessarily the two hundred I'd pick but we are going to lose two supplies for various small ports in Africa. A lot of the stuff is useless to us, of course. But there were, in fact, several containers containing baby 'stuff.' At least according to the manifest. Notably dried formula and vitamins. And, glory be, there were even two containers of condensed milk. If all else fails, there's always wet nurses. Diapers. That's going to have to be the old-fashioned way. Cloth we have. Pins we have. Rubber pants, not so much. The sewing shop is cutting up a bunch of rain-gear we found to make some. Probably not enough. The big problem is that we have to send out the small boat squadron on this sweep. Which will probably push them up into 'we're dropping babies' time. And a third of the crews are pregnant women."

"I noticed," Walker said. "We've pulled most of the ones that have been showing signs of at-risk pregnancy off of deployable status. That doesn't mean we won't have problems."

"Understood," Steve said. "One of the reasons to send you with the sweep."

"Unfortunately, that means I'll be working off the *Grace Tan*," Walker said. "So I won't have the pleasure of your daughter's company."

"You're not going to be spread out this time," Steve said. "Have all your serious kit in the *Grace Tan*'s sick bay and use the *Bella* as your moving boat for checking up on the ladies of the float. Think of it as housecalls. Boat calls at least. Did you know that was one of Sophia's potential careers?"

"Pregnant?" Fontana said.

"She wanted to be a doctor," Steve said. "I'd gotten quite comfortable teaching school. One of the points, between us, to this whole program is that I hundred or so to pregnancy related complications. We've already lost ten. Lot more to go. Possibly less if we have enough equipment or find some MDs or anyone with enough surgical training to emergency C-section."

"On the other hand, that means sixteen hundred new children," Steve said.

"More," Fontana said. "We have an unusually high number of multiples. Should be two percent, it's more like five percent. No clue why. Admittedly, more of those mothers are in the 'at risk' group. But we'll have more than one child per mother on average."

"All to the good," Steve said. "The truth is, no children, no future. Not for a civilization enshrining the notion of the Rights of Man and all the rest. In which case there is no damned point to *any* of this."

"I hate to stick my nose in," Walker said.

"Mr. 'Walker,'" Steve said drily, "you can and should any time you'd like. I've yet to hear anything come out of your mouth that wasn't on point."

"Has any thought been given to the aftermath?" Walker asked, smiling slightly. "Babies require various support materials if they are going to grow properly. Among other things, not all mothers provide adequate milk. And post weaning, they'll need adequate food and vitamins. Study I read somewhere indicated that high survival rates in the toddler years didn't really start until we developed lactose tolerance and started milking cows. Then there's the whole 'diapers' issue."

"The answer is 'Thought had been given,'" Steve said. "There also was little in the way of answers until you and my daughter saved the day."

"How did *we* save the day?" Walker asked.

"The *Paul Østed*," Steve said. "It was loaded with

sincerely doubt that the bastard who did this died in the Plague. He was going to have a vaccine. He's probably holed up somewhere laughing at the mess he's created. Someday, someone will find him."

"Oh, let it be me," Fontana said. "Please."

"I really can't think of anything that is worth doing to him that is also worth violating the Constitution," Walker said. "There is literally no sufficient torture ever invented by man on Earth. If we do find him, I'd just put a bullet in his head and go on with trying to repair the damage. Hope there is a hell."

"More or less my thought as well," Steve said.

"Lieutenant?" a lady in a nurse's uniform said, walking up. More like waddling. "Mr. Walker... we've got another emergency patient."

"And I need to get back to work as well," Steve said. "Good luck."

"How's it going, Sergeant Smith?" Faith said, stepping out of the Humvee.

She'd made it a habit to check on the progress of the sweep at least once each day. Colonel Hamilton had counseled her that it was primarily an NCO job and had her working her butt off on plans for the island hopping operation. But they were her people and the colonel agreed that she had to show her face from time to time.

"Just fine, ma'am," Smitty said, saluting. Faith returned it and he continued setting an M4 in the bed of a civilian pickup truck. It was the best vehicle for their purposes. He tossed the spent magazine that had been in the well into a five gallon bucket. There were others for any remaining ammo.

So far there hadn't been any complications at all. The gunboats and their sweeps had apparently killed the vast majority of the remaining infected. Occasionally one would turn up but the sweep teams were armed.

Not so much the body recovery teams. There was one of those in the distance walking next to a front-end loader. They were accompanied by a Navy master-at-arms who *was* armed. Also keeping them in front of him. As she watched, they stopped and picked up the pieces of what had once been a member of the base, tossing them into the bucket of the front-end loader.

"Every day's a holiday and every meal's a banquet," Faith responded.

"Every day I'm not trapped in a compartment is a good day, ma'am," Smitty said, grinning. "And at least it ain't August. I hear it gets a bit hot here then. How've you been, if I may ask, ma'am?"

"I hear there are people who adore paperwork," Faith said. "Sophia kind of likes it. Me, not so much. And apparently that's what officers are for; doing paperwork. Nobody told me that when I took the oath. I'm sort of feeling screwed." She grinned to show it was a joke.

"We've got a float coming up, ma'am," Sergeant Smith said. "That should take care of some of it."

"Yep," Faith said. "Islands to clear, zombies to kill, people to save. My kind of party. You seen Staff Sergeant Barnard?"

"She's up by Corinaso Point, ma'am," Smitty said.

"Well, I guess I need to go to Corinaso Point, then," Faith said. "Take care, Smitty."

"Will do, ma'am," Smitty said.

∽⊖∾

"So that's the LT?" Lance Corporal Robert "Bubba" Freeman said.

"That is Shewolf," Smitty said. "I think she got the word she was supposed to act more like an officer or something. Or she'd be down here pitching weapons with the rest of us."

"No disrespect intended, Sergeant," LCP Freeman said. "I just have a hard time with . . . I mean you and the rest of the *Iwo* Marines have talked about her, but . . ."

"Do not let Shewolf fool you," PFC Kirby said. "She is one absolute badass. Forget the video. You gotta see her in action for it to make any sense."

"She's not all that hot at long-range," Smith said. "Zombie gets within fifty meters of her and zap it's gone. We're all good. With Shewolf it's like breathing. None of which matters. She is, yeah, our platoon leader and a Marine officer and you show her that respect. Trust me, when you've worked with her for a while you won't just show her respect. You'll want to have her babies."

"Staff Sergeant," Faith said, getting out of the Humvee. She kept wondering when she was going to get driving lessons. But officers got drivers so, so far, it was all good.

"Ma'am," Barnard said, saluting.

"We need to get this operation terminated by thirteen hundred," Faith said, returning the salute. "Which means all vehicles back at the pier? The stuff that hasn't been sorted and prepped we're now going to do on the boats. So all that has to be prepped this evening for loading. And I want a one hundred percent inspection of all gear before lights out. Most of our load-out is being handled by Navy: ammo and suchlike, okay? But the teams need to get their gear prepped for the float. If there's anything that needs to be DXed, better we do it here which means tonight, okay? Load-out starts at zero five tomorrow morning which means first call at zero three. I convinced the colonel we could use the extra couple hours. If it takes all night, well, it's a sixteen-hour float to Anguilla and we don't have anything to do the first night, okay?"

"Yes, ma'am," Staff Sergeant Barnard said.

"Anything you want to bring up?" Faith said.

"No, ma'am," Staff Sergeant Barnard said. "Back to the piers by thirteen hundred. Evening ops will be prep for float. Is that all, ma'am?"

"Yep," Faith said. "I guess I'll see you back at the boat."

That evening Staff Sergeant Barnard stopped by the colonel's office.

"Busy as we are, sir," Barnard said uncomfortably, "moment of your time?"

"Of course, Cindy," Hamilton said, waving her in. "As long as it's not a long moment. Issues?"

"I need some counseling on something, sir," Barnard said, closing the hatch. "It has to do with Lieutenant Smith..."

"Booyah!" Faith said as the *Grace Tan* cleared the harbor mouth.

She was sooo glad to be back to doing what she knew: Killing zombies. The whole prep thing had been nothing but a nightmare of not knowing what to do and knowing that she was getting it all wrong. *This* she knew.

"Happy, ma'am?" Corporal Douglas said, grinning.

They were standing by the side rail watching the land slide by since at the moment there was nothing else to do. Everything was stowed and locked down and the preoperations meeting wasn't for another two hours.

"I can't believe I was getting sick of the land," Faith replied, a tad dishonestly.

"Well, we're going to be on land soon enough, ma'am," Douglas said.

"It's different, Derk," Faith said. "Another zombie killing smash-and-grab. That's not the same as being stuck on land, or for that matter on the *Bo*, doing paperwork."

"Lieutenant Smith to the Colonel's office," the tannoy boomed. *"Lieutenant Smith to the Colonel's office."*

Faith started to open her mouth to say something like *"What now?"* and then checked it.

"Gotta go, Derk," Faith said.

"Yes, ma'am," Douglas said, smiling. "Your master's voice."

CHAPTER 12

From the Halls of Montezuma
To the shores of Tripoli
We fight our country's battles
In the air, on land, and sea;

—Marine Corps Hymn

"Morning, Faith," Hamilton said, waving to a chair. "Glad to be headed out?"

"Yes, sir," Faith said, sitting down. She quirked an eyebrow at Staff Sergeant Barnard who didn't respond at all. Uh, oh.

"Faith," Hamilton said. "Staff Sergeant Barnard brought something up with me that I hadn't really noticed . . . for various reasons. A habit that you've developed. It's both a minor issue and a major issue, which will make sense in a moment. The habit is a minor issue that's easily corrected. The reason for the habit is what's the major issue and we'll try to resolve that as well. First things first. This is a counseling session. There are various types in the Marines, verbal, written, etc. They're generally thought of as punitive. In this case, it's a counseling session in the same way as a psychological counseling session. Despite my promise not to psychoanalyze you, we're going to delve into some of that at a certain point. However, this is not proscriptive. It is not punitive. We've got an issue and we're going to resolve it. Do you understand?"

"Not really, sir," Faith said, trying not to look at Barnard. She felt as if she'd been stabbed in the kidneys. "I'm not sure what the problem is, sir."

"Staff Sergeant?"

"Ma'am," Barnard said. "With due respect, are you aware that you end practically every sentence with a question?"

"No?" Faith said after a moment's thought. "I do?"

"Yes, ma'am," Barnard said. "You just did. And, no offense intended, but it makes you sound . . ." She paused and looked at the colonel.

"What the staff sergeant is trying not to say is that a Marine officer should appear and sound confident," Hamilton said. "After the issue was brought up I discussed it with Captain Wilkes and Lieutenant Volpe, both of whom expressed surprise at the question. They had never noticed it. They found you exceptionally confident, especially given your age and lack of experience. Which leads me to believe that the lack of confidence, if that is what this manifests, is recent. Any thoughts?"

"No, sir," Faith said.

"Staff Sergeant," Hamilton said, nodding. "You've expressed your issues, and quite tactfully I might add. I'll take it from here."

"Yes, sir," Barnard said, getting up and leaving.

"She really was tactful," Hamilton said, leaning back and steepling his fingers. "She is also, understandably, worried."

"Yes, sir," Faith said.

"That was a 'yes, sir' to fill in the pause, wasn't it?" Hamilton asked.

Faith thought about it for a moment.

"Yes, sir."

"Faith, you have two of the absolute requirements for being a Marine officer," Hamilton said, grinning. "You have a font of physical courage and enormous stubbornness. Let's try to see if we can get past the latter, shall we? What's your problem with Staff Sergeant Barnard?"

"I don't have a problem, sir," Faith said.

"Not even since she dropped the dime on you?" Hamilton asked. "Not feeling stabbed in the back?"

"Sir..." Faith said, frowning. "I'm not sure if it was what a staff sergeant is supposed to do. I think Janu would have just pulled me aside and said 'Hey, LT, you're saying everything with a question.' I don't think he would have gone running to..." She paused and shrugged.

"His buddy the colonel?" Colonel Hamilton said mildly.

"I didn't say that, sir," Faith said.

"But it was what you were thinking," Hamilton said. "You know I frequently call her 'Cindy.' Not, by the way, the way that most Marine colonels referred to their subordinates. Perhaps I've spent too much time on joint ops. Or perhaps it's, you know, being a research psychologist at heart. But let's discuss the issue that Staff Sergeant Barnard brought up. Ending a sentence that is supposed to be declarative with a querying tone indicates lack of confidence. This is both well understood psychology and something that is consciously or unconsciously noted by those around you. Especially political enemies and subordinates. Again, there is evidence to suggest that that lack of confidence is recent. And it is an issue for the upcoming operations. Your Marines have to trust your orders. They will follow them anyway, the staff sergeant will ensure that. But they *should* trust them especially since you are, in fact, *the* expert in what we're going to be doing. So let's start with the 'okay' thing since there is a simple remedy."

"Yes, sir," Faith said.

"That would be 'Oh, Colonel, great and wise leader, what is the remedy?'" Hamilton said.

Faith frowned for a moment.

"'Oh, Colonel, great and...'"

She frowned again.

"Great and wise leader," Hamilton said, smiling. "But that's good enough. Faith, say 'Oorah.'"

"Oorah?" Faith said.

"Now without the querying tone," Hamilton said.

"Oorah, sir," Faith said.

"Now, when you are speaking from now on, when you're not quite sure where to go next and want to say 'Um' or 'Okay,' insert 'Oorah,'" Hamilton said mildly. "It can be taken to extremes. I knew a Ranger officer who was *horrible* at public speaking and unfortunately in a position where he had to give multiple briefings who would give briefings which were seventy-five percent 'hoowah?' It got to where you wanted to strangle him. For that matter, my first first sergeant inserted the word 'fuck' when he didn't know what to say. As an officer and a lady I'm sure we both prefer if you said 'Oorah' instead, oorah?"

"Oorah, sir," Faith said, smiling slightly.

"You're afraid you're not going to live up to the standards of a Marine officer," Hamilton said. "You think the local Marines think you're just a mascot or a joke. Because your daddy gave you the job, which is true, and that you can't really do it, which is not true. Do you not trust them?"

"I . . ." Faith said, her face working. "I don't know how to answer the question, sir."

"In your own time, as many oorahs as it takes," Hamilton said.

"Then, yeah, sir," Faith said. "I . . . Sir, sometimes I get parade rest and at ease mixed up. I don't know how to march and I don't know marching commands, sir. Not really solid, sir. I've mixed that stuff up around the Gitmo Marines, and I know they're laughing at me. What kind of a Marine doesn't know how to march? The kind that's never been to Parris Island or Marine Officer Basic Course. They think I'm not a real Marine, sir, and maybe I'm not. It's not that I don't trust *them*, sir, sort of. It's that they don't trust me. They think I'm a joke, sir. I know they do. And . . . that's a real problem, sir."

"If it were true, and it may be, it would be a problem," Hamilton said. "To an extent. But . . . let's start with why it's not, okay?"

"Okay," Faith said tightly. "Yes, sir."

"Did you get into a lot of military jokes . . . pre-Plague?" Hamilton asked.

"Not really, sir," Faith said. "I was on some boards and had some friends who were military but . . . not a lot."

"There's a list, been around a long time," Hamilton

said. "It's a list of 'Things you don't want to hear an officer say.' Basically, when they say certain phrases, bad things tend to happen. Got it?"

"Yes, sir," Faith said. "Is it second lieutenants saying 'Okay?'"

"No," Hamilton said with a chuckle. "But a few examples. If you ever hear a first lieutenant say 'I have an idea,' it's best to run."

"Yes, sir," Faith said, smiling.

"A captain saying 'I've been thinking . . .' same thing," Hamilton said.

"Yes, sir."

"In the case of second lieutenants, the phrase you should *generally* fear is 'In my experience,'" Hamilton said, smiling.

"But . . ." Faith said, holding up a finger.

"But that's a very important *point*, Lieutenant," Hamilton said. "Nobody in the military, not the Air Force or the Army or the Marines or Navy, where it's 'ensign,' *nobody* trusts a second lieutenant."

"But . . . sir . . ." Faith said worriedly.

"Yes, there is a but," Hamilton said. "And we'll discuss that in a moment. This comes first, Lieutenant. You don't *have* to be panicked by the fact that your NCOs, some of them, do not fully trust you. That is *normal and standard*, Faith. It *is*. You Are A Second Lieutenant. The fact that you're also thirteen, unable to drive, have a tracing case of acne and have never *seen* Parris Island are simple cherries on the cake. The jokes about second lieutenants are innumerable and as old as the military. Jokes about junior officers go back to the earliest armies. You can find them in cuneiform and scribbled on the walls of Roman toilets.

'Tribune Marcus Aurelius could not find Gaul if he was in Alesia.' Which was a city in Gaul, by the way. Normal, standard and customary. It is *not* directed at one Faith Marie Smith particularly. It's a function of that gold bar you bear, often referred to as the 'baby shit bar' in the Army for a reason. So chill *out*. It's not about *you*. Okay?"

"O...kay?" Faith said. "But, sir..."

"Faith, there are no 'buts' on the chill out part," Hamilton said. "That's a requirement. Deep breaths. In through the nose, out through the mouth. In through the nose, out through the mouth. You are *not* trying to clear a super-liner with no help. The world does *not* rest on your shoulders. There are others to *help*, Faith. You're among *friends*. Okay?"

"Yes, sir," Faith said. "Okay. And now you're doing it, sir."

"I've done it for a long time in similar circumstances," Hamilton said. "You might have caught it from me. But *I* know when it's appropriate. So I want you to really try to internalize that, Faith. Absent significant experience to the contrary, as in getting things right when it matters, troops *don't trust second lieutenants*. They mostly act as not particularly bright messengers from higher, that being me, and impediments to getting the job done. Good ones, smart ones, follow their NCOs around like baby ducks and try to only whisper *possible* orders to *them* lest their ideas be awful. They're not stupid. Most of them anyway. But they are inexperienced and suddenly dealing on a day-to-day basis with a Brave New World called the Marines or Army or Air Force which are filled with in-jokes, institutional knowledge and arcane terminology, most of which they have no clue about since you can't cover it all in any reasonable training course, even West Point or Annapolis. And acronyms. My God, the acronyms. So they are, by and large, extremely *useless*. They exist solely as sort of larva of officers-that-may-be. Some day they may be of use. Some day they may be very good indeed. But not, generally, as second lieutenants. I'm aware that you have a similar lack of experience with the military. Do you get that is how the military views your rank?"

"Yes, sir," Faith said. "Sort of."

"There is one sort of second lieutenant that is somewhat more trusted by the troops," Hamilton said. "That is a mustang. You know what I mean by that?"

"An officer with prior service, sir," Faith said.

"In that case, the troops tend to trust them more," Hamilton said. "Oddly, many officers are less enthusiastic even in this day and age. Or were in the pre-Plague military. So we get to your earlier 'but.' You are, in a way, a mustang. But your prior experience is not military. It is quite simply surviving and fighting in this environment and doing so *splendidly*. The problems with this being that you are, yes, thirteen, not prior military much less Marines, and last but not least, even in this age, you are a girl. It was only recently that women were approved for front line combat and none had made it through any of the Marine combat officers' courses. Very few women have significant combat experience. If there was a woman in the pre-Plague military with as many combat hours as you already have amassed I would be very surprised. So while Marines may be aware of, and often admire, female Marines who have some combat experience, even those women's experience tends to be limited. And thus they are not thought of as 'real *infantry* fighters.' So all of this causes... Sorry, Faith, get ready..."

"Sir?" Faith said.

"I'm about to pull out a psychobabble phrase," Hamilton said, grinning. "The term is 'cognitive dissonance.' Can you say 'cognitive dissonance,' Lieutenant?"

"Cognitive dissonance?" Faith said. "Which means what, sir?"

"Let's imagine for a moment that you grow up and the sky is always blue," Hamilton said. "Then one day you're taking a class in college and the professor quite seriously intones: 'The sky is *not* blue.' Which for certain values is true, by the way. It's not blue. It's clear."

"Okay... sir?" Faith said, frowning. "Really?"

"Really," Hamilton said, smiling. "That feeling you have, that sort of pulling in your brain, is cognitive dissonance. It's when your knowledge set is suddenly challenged by new information. It can actually cause some slight discomfort. 'Thinking about that gives me a headache.' It's because your brain is having to open up new areas to additional resources and the disused arteries swell causing a slight headache."

"So *that's* what causes it," Faith said happily.

"I take it I've been giving you headaches," Hamilton said, grinning. "Good. Proves you're doing your job. Some people learn to shunt it aside into a sort of box. 'I don't like that thought so I'm not going to think about it.' Those are the people that they joke about a new thought and a cold drink of water which has some truth..."

"Sorry, sir, lost me," Faith said.

"You've never heard the expression 'You could kill her with a new thought and a cold drink of water'?" Hamilton said, frowning.

"No, sir," Faith said.

"Skip it then," Hamilton said after a moment. "The point being that your Marines, the Gitmo ones at least, are dealing with cognitive dissonance. Our job is to get them past it as simply and rapidly as possible. Because the truth is that you really *are* the right person for this job. If you weren't, you'd be doing something else in a jiff. I really don't care who your daddy is."

"Yes, sir," Faith said.

"A lot of it will wash out when we get to the action phase," Hamilton said. "That is where you are preeminent. Staff Sergeant Barnard *will* obey your orders. She's not the sort of NCO to undermine her officer. And she will intelligently expand upon them. Just tell her what needs doing and she'll get it done. Oorah?"

"Oorah, sir," Faith said.

"Going to cover a few things I haven't had time for before we get to the skill training," Hamilton said. "Faith, have you ever really thought about what you're planning in terms of career?"

"Not really, sir," Faith said. "I sort of . . . I guess I sort of thought I'd found what I was going to do if I grow up."

"If?" Hamilton said.

"No disrespect, sir, but have you taken a look around?" Faith said. "It's not about being a Marine and getting in scrums, sir. It's the *world*. I mean, Cody bought it by falling in a harbor and getting eaten by sharks, sir. If," she concluded, shrugging.

"Well, let's go with 'when' for the time being," Hamilton said thoughtfully. "The promotion ladder for junior Marine officers since World War II has been fairly fixed. You spend six months as a second lieutenant, and absent truly screwing up, like getting caught dealing drugs, you get promoted to first lieutenant. And about two years later to captain if you've done an even reasonably decent job. But that was then. Right now, we've got, well, a zombie apocalypse. We're actually rank heavy. For less than a company of 'other ranks' we have a colonel in charge. We have two other Marine officers and an overabundance of sergeants and staff sergeants. So even under normal circumstances, I don't see you making captain any time soon. There's not really any slot likely. It's not you, it's . . . reality?"

"Yes, sir," Faith said. "Sir, I'm not sure I'm qualified to be a lieutenant. I'm sure I'm not qualified to be a captain."

"And so am I," Hamilton said. "And that would be the case even if we had a crying need for one. That's the second part. *I* think you're qualified to be a lieutenant and you've shown that you can be a good one. You even do paperwork fairly well," he added, smiling.

"Not . . . what's that thing like an asteroid? Not my best thing, sir?" Faith said.

"Métier?" Hamilton said after a long thoughtful pause.

"Sorry, sir, words," Faith said. "Not me."

"Got that," Hamilton said. "But you know, if I had a choice between some glib and glittering staff officer and 'not words, me kill zombies,' guess which I'd choose, Faith? Unfair question, that would be 'me kill zombies good.' Because, in case you haven't noticed the world, Lieutenant..."

"Heh," Faith said, grinning slightly.

"Back to the hallowed promotion ladder," Hamilton said. "I agree with your assessment that you'd make a horrible captain. Now. You're going to be a very good one. Some day. But absent strenuous objections, as long as I'm your commander, I'm going to keep you at your current rank for a looong time. You understand why?"

"I'm thirteen, sir?" Faith said, shrugging. "It really doesn't bother me, sir."

"That's part of it," Hamilton said. "Big part. But more than that, it will give you time. Time to get that confidence not just fake it. Time to do the jobs over and over again. Including, yes, paperwork. Probably some staff time. Which is, by the way, nothing but paper pushing."

"Yes, sir," Faith said unhappily.

"Don't look so grumpy," Hamilton said. "If you do anything enough you get better at it. I never expect you to be a perfect glittering staffer. Or, maybe you will be. But if you do nothing but for a year or so you will get better."

"Yes, sir," Faith said.

"So to recap," Hamilton said. "Nobody trusts a thirteen-year-old girl. Nobody trusts a second lieutenant. So none of it is personal. It's just cognitive dissonance. And when you hit the beach a bunch of it will just go away. The Marines who have worked with you before trust you and that will be infectious. Especially since you're not really at home unless you're killing infected, correct?"

"Yes, sir," Faith said.

"In the meantime, we're going to teach you how to fake it until you make it," Hamilton said. "You've had the class from the gunnery sergeant in command voice. Correct?"

"Yes, sir," Faith said.

"Why don't you use it?" Hamilton said. "Skip the question. From now on, use it. Always."

"Yes, sir," Faith said.

"You must look up the definition of 'always' some time, Lieutenant," Hamilton said. "When I say always, I mean All The Time, Lieutenant! When you're talking to the staff sergeant! When you order dinner! When you're talking to your mother! Every single word that comes out of your mouth from now until I tell you you can quit *will be* command voice! Do you *understand*, Lieutenant?"

"Yes, sir," Faith said. "I mean, Yes! Sir!"

"There you go," Hamilton said. "Now you sound like a Marine lieutenant! Oorah?"

"Oorah, sir," Faith said.

"That was laid-back oorah," Hamilton said. "I sort of like laid-back oorah, but Lieutenant Faith Smith is not *permitted* laid-back oorah. Try it again, oorah."

"Oo-Rah!" Faith barked.

"If you're not sure what to say, what do you say, Lieutenant?" Hamilton said.

"Oorah, sir!" Faith barked.

"You're still unconfident about marching and drill commands," Hamilton said. "You sort of like Staff Sergeant Decker, don't you?"

"Yes, sir," Faith said, then frowned. "Sorry. Yes, sir!"

"Before we continue, words to eliminate from your

vocabulary," Hamilton said. "Sorry and okay. Possibly others but those are a start. Understood?"

"Aye, aye, sir!" Faith barked. "S . . . s. . . . Aye, aye, sir!"

"Marines are *respectful*," Hamilton said. "They're not exactly *polite*. They don't apologize. Ever. They don't say 'Excuse me could you pass the pepper, please?' 'Pass the pepper, please!' You should also try to eschew contractions. 'It is,' not 'it's.' 'Do not' as opposed to 'don't.' Short, declarative sentences. Whenever possible, less than ten words. To the drill thing. Where there are no more pressing details, you will continue to drill PFC Condrey to Staff Sergeant Decker's direction. Since you'll be doing the training schedule on the float you'll find the time. Decker—though, in my professional opinion, bat-shit insane—has all the Marine aspects that you lack. You can learn from his example. Roger?"

"Roger, sir!" Faith snapped.

"Onboard, you will march, ramrod straight, absolutely everywhere," Hamilton said. "Eyes front and on parade."

"Aye, aye, sir!" Faith said.

"When you hit the beach, it's up to you," Hamilton said. "I don't want anything interfering with your combat ability. However, I strongly suggest that you bark every order. Forget you're thirteen, forget you think they don't trust you. You are the mistress of this mission. Own it. You do this for a year, and that's the minimum I'm going to require, and you're never going to be able to do anything else. And then you will truly be the epitome of a Marine officer. Oorah? Now we both have a briefing to prepare for."

∽ ⊖ ⌒

"'Tention on deck!" Sergeant Smith snapped.

The Marines had berths but the ship had not been designed to carry Marines. So most of their combat gear was stored separately. It was also where the weapons were being sorted and cleaned for issue to "local militias" if they found survivors.

"Staff Sergeant!" Faith said without calling "at ease."

"Ma'am?" Staff Sergeant Barnard said.

"Inspection in combat gear, quarter deck, ten minutes. All Marine landing personnel. Carry on."

Faith spun in place and exited the compartment.

"What...the...hell...?" Smitty said.

"All of you fall in on your gear," Staff Sergeant Barnard said, shaking her head. "You *will* be on the quarterdeck in five minutes."

CHAPTER 13

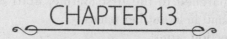

First to fight for right and freedom
And to keep our honor clean;
We are proud to claim the title
Of United States Marine.

—Marine Corps Hymn

When the Marines fell in on the quarterdeck, in this case an open area on the fantail of the forward-stack vessel, Faith was leaned up against one of the cargo containers, buffing her nails. She was, however, in full ground combat gear with her own addition of spare knives.

She let Staff Sergeant Barnard fall the Marines in and do a preinspection. When the staff sergeant was done she strode to her assigned spot at the front of the formation and saluted.

"The unit is prepared for inspection, ma'am," Barnard said.

Faith looked at her watch and nodded.

"You have one minute and thirty seconds left, Staff Sergeant," Faith said, without barking, returning the salute or straightening up. "You *sure* you want me to take it?"

"The unit is prepared for inspection, ma'am," Barnard repeated.

217

Faith straightened up, returned the salute, then marched over.

"Follow me," Faith barked.

She marched to the first Marine, Staff Sergeant Decker, and held out her hands.

"Inspection, arms!"

Decker unclipped his M4 then threw it at her, which she caught and inspected. She tossed it back and then began a meticulous inspection of his gear. Starting at the top she inspected his helmet, pulling on all the straps, looking under it, yanked at every loose bit of equipment, checked every button. She pulled out his magazines and inspected them. She handed one to Barnard.

"Spring is weak, get that DXed," she snapped.

"Yes, ma'am," Barnard said.

"A weak spring can cause jamming in combat, Staff Sergeant," Faith stated. "My Marines do not go into combat with bad mags. Other than that, good turn-out, Decker."

"Thank you, ma'am," Decker snapped.

She pivoted right, stepped to the next Marine, Corporal Douglas, and pivoted left to face him.

"Inspection . . . arms!"

"This Ka-Bar is not sharpened." A fast-clip on an M4 sling snapped when she yanked on it. "Dirty gas tube." A helmet strap weakened from wear. Faith didn't appear to check a single item that was cosmetic. All she checked was what they were going to need in combat.

It took nearly two hours while the Marines stood at parade rest or attention sweating in the sun. They were sweating not so much from the heat as from the reality that a thirteen-year-old was making some of them look like dumb recruits. And Barnard was slowly acquiring a pile of equipment that did not meet her lieutenant's satisfaction.

Finally it was done and Faith marched back to the front of the formation followed by Barnard. Faith paused for a moment looking at the Marines balefully.

"Sergeant Smith, front and center!" Faith barked.

When Smitty was in place, at attention, Faith gestured from the staff sergeant to the sergeant.

"Staff Sergeant, transfer that pile to Sergeant Smith." Once the transfer was complete she gestured back to the formation with her chin. "Resume your position, Marine."

"Aye, aye, ma'am," Smitty snapped, double timing back to his place.

"When I say 'fall out,' fall in on the gear locker and carry on with your previous mission," Faith boomed. "Fall OUT. Staff Sergeant, a moment of your time," she finished. It was very nearly a whisper.

When the Marines were gone, Faith gestured to the rail.

"Staff Sergeant, the colonel gave me an order," Faith said mildly. "That order was to 'command voice' every word that came out of my mouth. I think he'll forgive me for not command voicing this. If I start in on command voice, by the time I'm done they'll hear me belowdecks and I think this should be between us, don't you?"

"Yes, ma'am," Barnard said.

"Staff Sergeant, how many tours did you do in combat zones, pre-Plague?" Faith asked. "I assume you were in the Sandbox."

"Yes, ma'am," Barnard said. "Six, ma'am."

"Your MOS is . . . administrative, isn't it?"

"Yes, ma'am," Barnard said. "Oh, One-Eleven."

"Was the Fall your first taste of combat?" Faith asked.

"I was in a couple of ambushes in Afghanistan, ma'am," Barnard said. "I wasn't just a fobbit on my last tour. I had to go outside the wire as part of my duties. Outside the wire there wasn't much that was safe, ma'am. And we took a good bit of mortar and rocket fire."

"So, total, maybe, what, ten hours?" Faith asked.

"Yes, ma'am," Barnard said.

"And in the Fall, when did you go to free-fire?" Faith asked. "I get that it was pretty much the last day."

"Yes, ma'am," Barnard said.

"So maybe ten more there?" Faith asked. "Because, sorry, standing on a rooftop does not count."

"About that, ma'am," Barnard said.

"When people ask me 'how many times have you done this' I generally say 'I'd have to check the log,'" Faith said. She pulled out her H&K, slid back the slide with her thumb, checked for a round, dropped the mag and pressed down to make sure it was full all without looking and without a break in speaking. "So after I got done talking with the colonel and the preplanning meeting, I decided to actually *check* the log. I am technically credited with a *thousand* hours of direct infantry combat against infected." She reinserted the mag and holstered the weapon, again without looking, and just kept staring out to sea.

"Thousand, ma'am?" Barnard said, her mouth dropping open.

"Thousand, Staff Sergeant," Faith said. "Kind of surprised me. And that is in the last six God-damn months. The point to that is not that I'm a billy bad-ass. It's that every *single* item I checked was something that fucked up on *me*, Sergeant. *In combat*. Because, yeah, I've *seen* that much combat. I've got that much experience of fighting for my life, generally at short ranges when seconds count. I've had guns jam, straps break, knives not be sharp enough to cut a throat. And, Staff Sergeant, *don't* ask me how many throats I've cut because there's no log for that. My point is that thing about assumptions. I assumed that a Marine staff sergeant would understand what her boss meant by 'make sure all the gear is straight and get anything that needs it DXed.' That's on me. I should have made sure you understood what I was saying. And now we got to get it fixed on the float instead of back at Gitmo where there was a bunch of spare shit. Oorah?"

"No excuse, ma'am," Barnard said, stone-faced.

"The point to this stuff we just did was not to make you look or feel like a fool, Staff Sergeant," Faith said, still not looking at her. "I know I don't work real good when people make me feel stupid. I figure most people are like that. I just realized a couple of things after the colonel was done 'counseling' me. Since you didn't trust me you didn't trust that I knew what I was talking about. You didn't trust my experience 'cause I was a kid and a second lieutenant. You were, Staff Sergeant, assuming. And you didn't understand what I meant. Not with this. I don't mean to cut you down in any way, Staff Sergeant. But you're a clerk. You're not infantry. I don't know if you wanted to be infantry but you couldn't 'cause you were a girl. But you're not, and you're not real experienced at it.

"You don't know how shit fucks up at the best of

times in combat. Forget that 'fog of war' crap. I'm talking about an M4 jams with a bunch of infected running at us and the guy has to remember how to clear it and ends up ADing his buddy in the ass. And our M4s are *gonna* jam. 'Cause we have to cover them in oil to keep the salt from fucking them up but as soon as we hit the fucking beach that fine sand is gonna stick to them and jam them like a son of a bitch. That kind of 'shit fucks up in combat.'

"Now, I realize that you probably didn't understand that and you so you didn't understand the *order*. Again, my bad. That doesn't mean I think I know everything, Staff Sergeant. I'm not ... what's that word? I'm not salty. I don't know *shit* about the Marine Corps. You've got me in spades on that. I can find Parris Island on a map, now, but all I know is that Quantico is in Virginia someplace. And what the fuck is that thing about a Tavern?

"And you can probably score high expert on a rifle range and I'd maybe score marksman. Hell, if you hadn't been getting the platoon in tune, I'd have brought you in to explain all the paperwork crap the colonel's been throwing at me 'cause I spend most of my time trying not to cry I'm so fucking clueless. And I hate feeling stupid. I'm getting so fucking *frustrated* with all this paperwork and planning *crap* ...

"But day after tomorrow we're going ashore on what is sure to be a really *great* little island, the overheads are awesome, to go do the only thing I *do* know, which is killing the fuck out of infected. And Staff Sergeant, for God's sake, if you don't understand one of my orders, please, Cindy, *ask*. Because if you don't, you're going to get some of my Marines killed.

And that will *really* piss me off. And, Cindy, you *don't* want somebody like me pissed off."

She turned and looked the staff sergeant in the eye.

"Because I don't do words real good, Staff Sergeant, and I don't know how to do that crap where you write an evaluation report that sounds good but makes people look like shit. I can't do that stuff good. When I say I'm gonna kill somebody, Staff Sergeant, I ain't talkin' about their *career*. Oorah?"

"So this is Anguilla," Ensign Joseph Buckley said, conning his way into Road Salt Pond Bay. "Not much to look at."

The island was low and sandy with a few small hills. The shore of the bay was a nearly perfect crescent-moon-shaped beach with bright white coral sand and waving palm trees while the waters of the bay were a gorgeous mixture of turquoise and cerulean. There were low, one- and two-story, block buildings scattered among the trees. There were two piers, one to the east and one to the west, located at about the one third position on the beach. The westerly pier was their primary target, a medium sized "cargo" pier which, unfortunately, did not have cargo cranes but appeared to be intact and unblocked. The easterly pier was a small pier for small boats. A large "deep water" outboard was still attached by one line but it was sunk to the gunnels.

The picturesque beach was littered with the debris of a destroyed civilization—trash, bits and pieces of clothing, grounded boats and picked clean skeletons, their bones as white as the sands. Many of the buildings had been scorched by fire as had many of the trees. In fact, it looked as if a fire had swept across the entire island.

There was a small ship, an island support ship like the *Erik Shivak*, grounded at the tip of the eastern cape.

"Christ," Ray Hoover said, shaking his head. "This place is a mess."

The first mate of the *Bad Juju* was in his thirties and covered up male pattern baldness by shaving his head. A former "rent-a-slave" in the IT business, he'd volunteered for small boats after being stuck in a liner compartment for months. However, he'd long before regretted his actual posting. The name was bad enough but the captain...

"Yeah," Buckley said, trying to figure out where to anchor. "Even the Canaries weren't this..."

What, exactly, they weren't would have to wait as the, fortunately slowly moving, boat ground to a halt with a rather nasty crunching sound from below.

"Aw, crap," Buckley said, tossing his captain's cap over the side.

"Hey, Skipper?" Kevin Schlossberg yelled from below. "We're taking on water!"

"Not *again*!"

"All divisions," Lieutenant Commander Chen radioed, shaking his head. "All divisions. Be on the lookout for submerged wrecks..." He set the microphone down and shook his head again. "Including the *Bad Juju*... In retrospect..."

"No gunboats on Forest Bay?" Colonel Hamilton asked, looking at the operations map. "It would seem closer to the anticipated high infected density around the Quarter than Sandy Hill."

The final touches were being placed on the landing

operation. The island was the first assault designated for "Operation Leeward Sweep" so they were trying to get each item as set as possible to develop SOPs. The entire command team was present but most of them were keeping their mouths shut.

"Overheads and charts indicate that Forest Bay has some significant reefs, sir," Lieutenant Commander Chen replied. He was the senior Navy officer for the operation. "Sandy Hill is more safely approachable and the cape provides wind and wave protection, making for a more stable gun platform. We have no detailed information on how far our nightly... activities will bring the infected but indicators in the Canaries were from as much as five miles away. We believe that this lay-out will draw something like ninety percent of the infected. The question, of course, is if they can all make it to the target beaches before dawn."

"Out of pure curiosity," Colonel Hamilton said. "Who came up with this technique?"

"Captain Wol—Smith, sir," Lieutenant Commander Chen said.

"Simple, brutal and effective seems to be his call sign," Colonel Hamilton said. "Lieutenant, the scuttlebutt is that there tends to be a bit of a party when you're drawing in the infected."

"That has, occasionally, been an aspect of this procedure, sir," Chen said carefully. "It is necessary to make noise and rather than, say, continuous air-horn blasts we generally play music. And... there is some drinking. And I will admit, sir, that that has occasionally, notably at Las Galletas, gotten out of hand. I've been dialing down on it, sir."

"Pass the word," Hamilton said. "Not this time. With

a reason. In this case, we're dealing with a *very* small island and we're more or less *surrounding* it. Fifty-caliber rounds go quite a ways. To be exact, they are lethal at up to seven miles. If we get too free with fire, we're going to end up shooting one of the other boats that's not even in *sight*. We need to ensure that the gunners stay strictly within their fire limits. Alcohol and such assurances simply do not match. I'm aware that you should not give an order that won't be obeyed and that keeping liquor off the boats is impossible. So pass the word the party is *after* we clear the damn island and all the guns are put away. Roger?"

"Aye, aye, sir," Chen said, making a note.

"Senior and experienced personnel, such as we have, are to ensure that each gun has traverse limiters in place," Hamilton said. "And ensure that the gunners understand those fire limits and why we have them. I do not want to have fifty-cal rounds dropping around my ears. Are we clear?"

"Clear, sir," Chen said. "With your approval, I'll distribute my senior people to the outlying forces to ensure that. I'd appreciate some assistance from Ma Deuce-experienced Marines for the main landing force. That way I can distribute out the chief and the sergeant major."

"Agreed," Hamilton said. "And the plan is approved with one slight modification."

"Sir?" Chen said.

"*I'm* picking the playlist," Hamilton said.

"Staff Sergeant," Faith stated, as they were leaving the final planning meeting. "Moment of your time in my office."

"Yes, ma'am," Barnard said.

Faith marched to her office, entered and sat down.

"The general plan, as briefed, is that the Marines, oorah, are to quarter here on the *Grace Tan*, oorah, until first call at 0400," Faith said, her jaw clenched. "Thereafter we chow, assemble, final brief and perform landing after clearance by Navy heavy fire at dawn, oorah?"

"Yes, ma'am," Barnard said, standing at parade rest.

"As you may have noticed there is a four-hour preinspection this afternoon on the prep schedule, oorah," Faith said. "I inserted that preinspection in the op-plan. During that preinspection I will instruct you on my task, conditions and standards for combat preinspection. After that you and I will perform an after-inspection review and determine if this is a procedure, oorah, you find conforms to your views, oorah? Do you have any questions?"

"No, ma'am," Barnard said.

"Inspection begins at fifteen hundred," Faith said. "We will not form the personnel. We shall, oorah, take each Marine one by one into the gear locker. This technique, oorah, is currently..." Faith paused and frowned. "There is no SOP, oorah. There should be an SOP. We will establish that SOP, oorah?"

"Roger, ma'am," Barnard said.

"Dismissed."

"I've got a target," Seaman Apprentice Rusty Bennett said nervously.

Rusty was used to shooting up zombies with the .50 caliber BMG affectionately referred to as the Ma Deuce. He'd even gotten pretty damned good, in his opinion, with the monstrous machine gun. He wasn't worried about whether he could hit anything. What was making him nervous was all the Mickey Mouse. The new Marine colonel who was in charge was being a prick. He'd never even heard of a range limiter before and had to dig through all the parts and crap that had come with the gun to find it. And then he'd had to get the sergeant major, before he left, to show him how to hook it up.

"Sorry," Rusty added. "I've got a target, sirs."

"So I see," Colonel Hamilton said as an infected trotted down the beach. It was hunched over as if it was sniffing for something. It was a young black male, nude as all the infected were, his lanky, twisted hair dangling down into his face so Hamilton wondered how he could even see. "Is the SOP to engage any target at will, Lieutenant?"

Lieutenant Commander Chen was nearly as nervous as Rusty. But he was better at hiding it.

"Infected are drawn to any sign of carrion, such as flocks of seagulls, sir," Chen said. "Our SOP is to engage any infected that are in the target zone early and often. That begins the attraction process. And infected don't seem to avoid the target zones. They cannot make the connection between loud gun noises and other infected dying. So, yes, sir, we engage if they are in the target basket, sir."

"One last check," Hamilton said.

"Uh, sir," Rusty said, swinging his barrel towards the target. Just past it the barrel bumped up against the limiter. "It's about to get off to the side."

The infected was heading north on the beach and approaching the edge of the fire-limit zone.

"Then we shall wait for a better target," Hamilton said. "For that matter . . . Do we know the current location of Division Five?"

The other four gunboat divisions had already left the rendezvous for their respective fire points. Division Five was going to be crossing the fire zone of Division One at some point. Admittedly, it was going to be nearly four miles away and on the other side of the island. On the other hand, .50 BMG had a "general area of effect" range of . . . about four miles. Meaning if you had, say, a dozen .50 calibers firing at the right angle to drop their rounds into an area, they could, in fact, hole a boat at four miles. And probably sink it.

"No, sir," Lieutenant Commander Chen said. "I can find out pretty quick."

"Let's hold off firing until everyone is in their proper place," Colonel Hamilton said. "Something to add to the SOP for this. In fact, in the future, we probably just need to have all the boats on one side of the island."

"Some of the islands I wonder if it would be an issue, sir," Lieutenant Commander Chen said. "Islands like Saba, the interior topography is going to make it nearly impossible for us to have rounds go over."

"Point," Hamilton said, looking at the low-lying atoll. "Anguilla, however, is not such a case. Wait until all the divisions are in place, do a final check on the guns for their angles, then we can go to free-fire. In the meantime, have your gun crews unload and stand down. I can see that Rusty here, at least, is itching to kill him some infected. Right, Seaman Apprentice?"

"Yes, sir," Rusty said.

"Call that in to all the divisions. They are not free-fire until all boats are in place, all limits are set and all guns have been checked by senior personnel for limits."

"Aye, aye, sir."

"Bloody hell," Sergeant Major Raymond Barney said, looking through the binoculars.

They were cruising east in the Anguilla Channel—which runs between the relatively low and small island of Anguilla and the much larger and more prominent St. Martin. The two islands more or less defined the juncture between the Caribbean Sea and the Atlantic in the area and the boat was rolling on waves coming in from the open Atlantic. Which was what had caused the oath on the part of the sergeant major. Not the waves, the mass of wrecked ships, carried in by the Great Southern Current and piled up on the jagged rocks of St. Martin. It looked like some sort of twisted regatta from Dante's *Inferno*. There were freighters, tankers, yachts, sailboats, megayachts, lifeboats and life rafts, ships that didn't quite meet any description he could come up with. There was even what looked to be a section of an oil platform.

"We came through this sort of stuff at night on the way in," Lieutenant Matthew Bowman said. The skipper of the *Golden Guppy* and commander of Division Five was a thirty-five-year-old who had made his money early in tech and set out to sail around the world just in time for a zombie apocalypse. "But you could still see the outlines."

"I mean, there's usually wrecks," Barney said, lowering the binos and shaking his head. "They were all over the Canaries. But that is bloody *insane*."

The sergeant major was sixty-two, a retired British Army light scouts NCO and NCOIC of the Naval Landing Parties. His position was technically slightly ambiguous. As a British citizen and former soldier he could not, actually, "command" American forces. On the other hand, nobody really questioned who was in charge when Navy parties hit the beach. He'd been detailed to "accompany" Division Five, which was not hitting the beach, to "ensure safe practices" of the Navy gunners. After which he was going to have to take a fucking Zodiac all the way back around the island to link up with Division One. He'd flipped a coin with his nemesis, Chief Petty Officer Kent Schmidt, USN, as to who got the furthest out division and lost.

"Div Five, Flotilla."

"Division Five, over," Bowman replied.

"Status check."

"Passing Forest Harbor at this time, Flotilla," Bowman replied.

"Roger. Supplementary orders. Do not load weapons until all vessels report in position and ready to fire, over."

"Do not load weapons until all boats in position, aye," Bowman replied.

"Flotilla out."

"Wonder what that was about?" Bowman said.

"Fifty-caliber Singer has a maximum range of seven miles, sir," Barney said. "This island is three miles wide at its widest. Those bloody Singer rounds are going to be bouncing off these block houses and going all the way across the bloody island, sir. Our path takes us through *three* possible impact zones. And one of those rounds *will* go all the way through these cockleshells, sir. I'd rather wondered about whether we'd get shot up heading to the anchorage, sir."

"You didn't bring that up in the meeting," Bowman said.

"I was leaving it up to the Yank colonel, Lieutenant," Barney said. "But I'll tell you I've been keeping a bit of an eye out for bits of ocean churned up by descending Singer rounds, sir. You might want to do the same in case others haven't gotten the word, sir."

"And what would that look like, exactly?" Bowman said nervously. He was now scanning the surface of the water intently.

"Bit like flying fish jumping, sir," Barney said.

"Those are all over the place!" Bowman snapped.

"Really, sir?" the sergeant major said, smiling slightly and still looking through the binoculars.

"Oh, now you're just yanking my chain!"

"Am I, sir?" Barney said, grinning. "What gave you that impression? In seriousness, the answer was honest and, of course, useless. The rounds can and will cross the island, spotting them incoming is hard to impossible since the tracers will have burned out and even then only one in five is a tracer. If it happens, by the time we know we'll have a half-inch hole through ourselves, and that is not what you call a survivable wound. So we'd better bloody well hope that everyone's got the word, sir."

"How screwed up can one sailing cruise get?" Bowman said, shaking his head.

CHAPTER 14

Our flag's unfurled to every breeze
From dawn to setting sun;
We have fought in every clime and place
Where we could take a gun.

—Marine Corps Hymn

"This technique, oorah, was developed with Lieutenant Fontana's help, oorah?" Faith said, standing in front of Decker. She was in full ground combat gear with her face shield up. She even had her Barbie gun strapped across her chest but no magazine in the well. Added to the ensemble, and not normal, was a bulging messenger bag slung over her shoulder. She'd dropped that before starting the inspection. "It is based upon the way that you . . . oorah . . . do the preinspection for somebody who's doing a jump, oorah? Questions?"

"Like a parachutist, ma'am?" Staff Sergeant Barnard said.

"Lieutenant Fontana is a Green Beret, oorah?" Faith said. "They call it something different, oorah? Airport or something, oorah? But it's how they inspect a jumper. Da used to inspect me and Sophia the same way. Da used to be a para. So, we start at the helmet and face shield, oorah? Grab the face

233

shield and flex it in with the base of your palms on the bottom of the face shield, oorah? It should flex a bit but not crack or be too solid, oorah? And it can't be so scratched you can't see through it. Then push up on the bottom while holding your other hand on top of the helmet. All of the shields are supposed to be attached to the helmet. It can't be loose, oorah? Or an infected'll pull it right off in a scrum, oorah? Watch your hand there, you can cut yourself. Been there, done that, oorah...? Decker, you need to pay attention to this. You're going to be doing it, too."

"Aye, aye, ma'am," Decker barked.

It took thirty minutes just to walk the staff sergeants through what was essentially a PJMC, pre-jump manifest check, used in "airborne," not "airport," operations.

"You really got to watch the magazines, oorah?" Faith said. "Bunch of 'em ended up sitting for months with multiple rounds or full loads. That really fu... messes up the springs, oorah? If the spring feels weak, it's probably bad."

"Oorah, ma'am," Barnard said.

"Oorah," Faith replied. "Don't know how to say this. Doesn't matter if they need a shave, their boots ain't shined or there's bloodstains on their uniform. All that matters is their gear is right, oorah? Now you and Decker start doing checks on all the rest of the platoon. I'll watch and critique, oorah?"

"Aye, aye, ma'am," Barnard said.

"Decker, check Sergeant Hoag," Faith said. "You check Derk, Staff Sergeant. Derk's been through this and knows the drill. I'm going to go prepare them," she added, hefting the bag. "I'll send them up when it's time."

"Aye, aye, ma'am,"

"Derk," Faith said. "Barbie gun."

"Aye, aye, ma'am," Corporal Douglas said, unclipping his M4 and handing it over.

"Nobody saw this," Faith barked. She opened the gun, slid out the bolt, closed it up, latched the dust cover and handed it back. Then she pocketed the bolt. "I should remember to get that back to you. But if I don't, for God's sake don't hit the beach that way, oorah?"

"Aye, aye, ma'am," the corporal said.

"Fumitaka," she said, dipping into the messenger bag then holding out a Ka-Bar to the lance corporal, butt first. "Switch Ka-Bars. Don't go ashore with this one."

"Aye, aye, ma'am," Fumitaka said, switching blades. He fingered the edge and shook his head. "You couldn't cut butter with this, ma'am."

"That's the point, Lance Corporal," Faith said, making a note in her notebook. She adjusted one of Filipowicz's sling clips so it was barely hooked, switched out one of PFC Summers's magazines for one with a bad spring and generally spent ten minutes making sure that there were various minor faults scattered through the platoon. She also wrote down each "fault" so her Marines wouldn't actually go into combat with messed-up gear.

"Now it's a *real* test, oorah?" Faith said, walking back to the gear locker.

"Okay," Fumitaka said. "I guess maybe she does know what she's doing."

"O ye of little faith," Corporal Douglas said. "Semper Fi, boys and girls. And keep your mouths shut."

"Douglas!" Faith yelled from the next compartment. "You're up!"

"Inspection complete, ma'am," Barnard said, stepping back from Corporal Douglas.

Faith was standing between and slightly behind the two staff sergeants. At Barnard's words she dropped her head, reached into her pocket and wordlessly handed Douglas his bolt. Barnard's face went white and she winced but didn't say anything.

"As I mentioned, Staff Sergeant, I have made just about every mistake possible when it comes to combat," Faith barked, pulling out her little green notebook and scribbling a note. "Next! I screwed that one up on the *Voyage*. The miracle is that I am alive. Staff Sergeant Decker, while I appreciate and often admire your *intense* attention to detail, we have thirty Marines to go through. You *will* learn to be both fast *and* accurate. Oorah?"

"Aye, aye, ma'am," Decker said. He was barely halfway through his check on Sergeant Hoag's gear.

"Begin again, Staff Sergeant Barnard," Faith said.

"Attention on deck!" PFC Randolph bellowed. Since he and Fumitaka were facing the hatch they were the only ones that saw the colonel enter the compartment.

"Carry on," Colonel Hamilton said. "Good afternoon, Lieutenant."

"Good afternoon, sir!" Faith barked.

"I was mildly curious about a four-hour inspection period on the plans," Hamilton said.

"Checking that all combat gear is shipshape, sir," Faith responded. "Lieutenant Fontana and I developed an evolution to ensure that during the early days of the squadron, sir. Instructing the staff sergeants on that evolution, sir."

"And how is it going?" Hamilton asked.

Barnard had drawn Fumitaka's Ka-Bar and fingered the edge. She glanced at the lieutenant who switched it out with the original. The dull one went back in the messenger bag.

"Better and better, sir," Faith replied as Randolph's loosened clip popped free under a tug from Decker. Decker reclipped it and tugged again so hard the PFC, who was standing at parade rest, nearly went on his face. "Once we have this evolution down it will take less time, sir."

"I see," Hamilton said, standing at parade rest. He didn't seem in a mood to leave.

Faith wasn't going to let that get to her; she just continued with the evolution.

"Hold it," Faith snapped about ten minutes later. She dipped into her pocket and pulled out a firing pin, then handed it to Lance Corporal Saul. "Make sure that gets back in its right place, Lance Corporal. Carry on."

"May the Staff Sergeant inquire when the Lieutenant forgot to put in her firing pin, ma'am?" Staff Sergeant Barnard asked through gritted teeth.

"I did not make that error," Faith replied, making another note in her book. "It was someone else. But I've come close more than once."

"Carry on," Colonel Hamilton said, turning around and leaving the compartment.

"As the colonel said, Staff Sergeant," Faith said, checking her notes. "Carry on."

"And evolution is almost complete," Faith said, checking her notes. She nodded a few times, then pulled the now refilled messenger bag off her shoulder. "Staff Sergeant Barnard, go ahead and take this into the next bay and switch out anything you'd like on your gear. Just keep a list in case I miss anything. I'll inspect Staff Sergeant Decker while you do that. Bring the rest of the platoon into the bay when you come back."

"Aye, aye, ma'am," Barnard said.

"Staff Sergeant Decker," Faith barked, pointing in front of her. "Front and center."

"Aye, aye, ma'am," Decker replied.

"You can do this both quickly *and* accurately, Decker," Faith said, starting at the top. What had taken Decker, repeatedly, at least seven minutes took Faith less than two as she sped through the check from top to bottom. "You *will* get to the point you can do this in under three minutes, Staff Sergeant. That is the standard that I set and you *will* make that standard."

"Aye, aye, ma'am," Decker said.

"Admittedly," Faith said, dropping out of command voice, "a big part of it is practice, practice, practice. You'll get plenty on the float. You're doing well, Staff Sergeant," she added, looking him in the eye. "You're doing *well*, Decker. You're a credit to the Corps."

"Thank you, ma'am," Decker said.

"The colonel wants you to instruct me on drill commands, Staff Sergeant," Faith said, resuming command voice. "When we have time on the float I am supposed to drill some of the enlisted with you instructing me. I know I have got a lot to learn in that regard and I also know that you know the manual back and forth. You oo—gung ho with that?"

"Yes, ma'am," Decker said, his face working. "Gung ho."

"Hang in there, Staff Sergeant," Faith said quietly. "We've all got our problems. And Trixie really likes you," she added in a whisper.

"Thank you, ma'am," Decker said, then frowned. "Permission to ask a question, ma'am?"

"Speak, Staff Sergeant," Faith said.

"I am unaware of a member of the squadron named Trixie, ma'am," Decker said.

"That's right," Faith said. "You haven't met Trixie, yet. I'm sure you will at some point. Probably at some point when we clear the island. Or you can ask Sergeant Hocieniec. But I would appreciate it if you would ask him in private. Trixie *doesn't* like Staff Sergeant Barnard..."

To get everyone into the compartment meant crowding around the lieutenant and Staff Sergeant Barnard in a huddle. The Marines behind Faith quickly learned another use for their helmets and face shields. Packed in the way they were there was no room to dodge when Faith found something she didn't like and it went flying over her shoulder...

"Did I miss anything, Staff Sergeant?" Faith asked, handing back the staff sergeant's pinless bolt.

"Not that I caught, ma'am," Staff Sergeant Barnard said.

"There's still items that were not planted that did not meet my standards," Faith stated. "Deal with that this evening. There will be another inspection, with all weapons and ammo, at zero five thirty. Dawn is at zero six forty-seven. We are scheduled to go ashore at zero seven hundred. To make sure that everyone is aware of the plan, we will go ashore and form a perimeter for the off-load, by Navy and civilian personnel, of the five-tons. Once we have secured the five-tons, Naval ground landing personnel will take over the security position while we will sweep the island looking for additional infected and survivors, oorah? Survey and salvage personnel, oriented on the hospital and medical school, are scheduled to land at eleven hundred hours. We will accompany them to the target facilities, clear them if necessary and provide security for the extraction of any high value materials. Back to the docks to reverse it all by sixteen thirty. We are to be off the island by sunset, oorah? Anchors are to be aweigh by nineteen hundred and we are away to sunny Saint Barthélemy to lather, rinse and repeat. Everybody but the staff sergeants rack your gear and fall in on the troop bay. Fall out.

"Staff Sergeants. We were going to do an after action review on this but the inspection's run late, oorah? Don't focus on this tonight, we've got the action tomorrow which is more important. But start thinking about how to draft this as an SOP, oorah? Other than that, make sure the troops are fed, watered and bedded down by twenty one hundred, oorah? We have an early first call, chow and ammo draw before the inspection. Tomorrow morning, concentrate on ammo quality and proper mag loading, oorah? Only NCOs will carry grenades. Ensure that all shipping clips are *off* the grenades. Keep the shipping clips handy since we're probably not going to use up all our grenades. Questions, comments, concerns?"

"Fuck a freaking duck," Sergeant Weisskopf said, racking his gear. "I know you want to have her babies but I am getting sick and tired of Barbie telling me how to be a Marine. I mean, she went from 'Hi, I'm Faith!' to Hitler. What the fuck is up with that?"

"I will say that *something's* crawled up her ass," Sergeant Smith said, checking again to make sure he'd put his bolt back. "But the way I'm looking at it, we've got two senior NCOs, one of which is a clerk and the other's a tanker with . . . flexibility issues. I think the skipper's just trying to make sure every fuck-up she can prevent is prevented."

"What?" Weisskopf said, sarcastically. "Like somebody's going to leave their firing pin out of their weapon?"

"One little mistake," Smith said.

"Seriously?" Weisskopf said, snorting. "You really did that?"

"We were supposed to have the crossing as an easy cruise," Smitty said, shrugging. "After clearing liners in Tenerife we needed the fucking break. Kick back and relax for whatever horrors awaited us in the sunny Caribbean. Instead we spent practically every damned day in fucking Zodiacs going a hundred miles an hour across the middle of the fucking Atlantic. Clear a boat, either head back to the *Bo* or sometimes doss on one of the small boats. And we'd have to get all our gear cleaned up whenever we had the chance and the time.

Which wasn't much of either. We got to where we were clearing in our sleep, okay? We cleared four *liners* on the crossing. We'd end up covered in blood. I had to pull my weapon all the way down I don't know how many times. And I mean *all* the way. Washing out my fucking action was a daily thing. Sorry, Sergeant, but you know you're a post-Fall Marine when rinsing down your magazines to get the blood and hair and brain matter out of them after an op doesn't make you puke.

"So, yeah, I forgot to put in my pin one time and didn't find out till I'd opened up a hatch with about two bazillion screaming infected on the other side. And do you know who saved that from turning into a scrum? The fucking lieutenant, okay? 'Cause while I'm cycling my weapon over and over and forgetting that I'm in everybody else's way, not to mention I've got a backup, the LT's firing *past* me and nailing fucking infected. Tomorrow is probably going to be easy as shit. Clearing an island like this is a walk in the park. This cruise is a fucking vacation so far. It's clearing liners that's a nightmare."

"Hopefully we won't have to," Weisskopf said, shrugging.

"You want to think about that?" Smitty said. "*You* were in a warehouse. *You* could see the sun. You had plenty of air. You knew how long your water was going to hold out. Try being in a pitch-black compartment thinking 'Hey, the Coast Guard or somebody is going to rescue me any day' and any day turns into 'any week' or 'any month.' Before long, for the few who're still alive, it's going to be 'any year.' And we're going to be driving right past them 'cause that's the mission, right? I still gotta wear sunglasses on a cloudy day. There are people *dying* in those liners. There's women going to give birth in those compartments. And we're going to drive right past."

"Rack your stuff," Staff Sergeant Barnard said. "And get the lead out. We're supposed to observe the initial engagement against infected this evening, then catch chow. Then rectify the remaining items on gear. Lights out at twenty one hundred. First call is zero four thirty. You will be fully prepared for the lieutenant's inspection at zero five thirty. Then the op. So fall out on the quarter deck to observe Navy operations against the infected."

"Permission to just get chow now, Staff Sergeant?" Sergeant Smith said. "Been there, done that. Seen one slaughter on the beach, you've seen 'em all."

"Was not a question, Sergeant," Staff Sergeant Barnard said. "It was an order."

"Aye, aye, Staff Sergeant," Smitty said.

"Holy crap," Sophia said as a slow thundering, bass guitar riff echoed across the darkened bay. "Your colonel listens to *Sentenced*?"

"I was unaware of the colonel's taste in music, Ensign," Faith stated. She'd caught a Zodiac over to the *Bella Señorita* for supper since despite her usual and standard problems with her sister she was sick and tired of dealing with Barnard for the day. Sophia's shit was kind of relaxing. And Batari was a *really* good cook. "As he is my superior officer, oorah, I will neither approve nor disapprove, oorah?"

"Sis, I get why the colonel told you to talk like that," Sophia said. "But it is just fucking weird."

"An officer and a lady should maintain proper

military decorum at all times, oorah?" Faith said. "Which includes, oorah, use of...oorah...crap, not good...improper, oorah? Which includes use of... improper language, oorah?"

"Were you trying for 'indecent' there, Sis?" Sophia said, laughing. "Does 'crap' count?"

"Oh, hell, I don't know!" Faith snapped. "I'm just making this up as I fucking go, ok—Oorah?"

Faith pulled on one last strap, stepped back, tapped PFC Robert Lee Edwards on the shoulder, then marched back to her position at the front of the formation.

In this inspection she'd concentrated on ammo and other consumables. And she'd found a few things that still didn't satisfy her. The Marines all had all their ammo and it was in good condition. But some of the batteries she'd checked were bad and a few of the NCOs had missed a shipping clip on their grenades. She'd wordlessly handed off all the "stuff" she found to Staff Sergeant Barnard. Who had already done a preinspection and missed them.

The Marines were back on the quarter deck for this formation, facing forward. The *Grace Tan* had massive sodium arc lights that gave more than enough light in the predawn for Faith to perform the precombat inspection.

When Staff Sergeant Barnard approached, Faith simply checked her watch and said: "Post."

When the staff sergeant was at the rear of the formation in her position, Faith looked around at the Marines.

"In about ten minutes the sun will rise on the

island of Anguilla," Faith boomed. "At that point, the Navy gunboats will lay waste to every living infected in view, oorah. We shall observe this operation until we get orders to board Zodiacs, junior personnel first, by teams. At the colonel's command, we shall then take those Zodiacs to this fine and beautiful beach to begin clearance of the island, oorah? When you exit the Zodiacs, spread out just up from the water and take a knee, oorah? You have free fire authority to engage any remaining hostiles in view. Once we are sure the area is secure we shall secure the pier and begin off load of the five-tons. We will then take the five-tons to sweep the island, oorah?

"This is a really simple operation, oorah? There's light infected. Should be a walk in the park. Just remember you can get mugged on a walk in the park, oorah? Don't let your guard down, pay attention to your sectors, obey your orders and we'll all get home in one piece, oorah? At my command, fall out on the aft rail to observe Naval gunnery engagement."

"This is *light* infected presence?" Sergeant Hoag said.

Dawn comes swiftly in the tropics. In northern climes there is a long period of gradually lightening darkness, the "blue time" of Before Morning Nautical Twilight. The Caribbean had the same but instead of twenty or thirty minutes it seemed to pass in seconds, going from nearly pitch black to bright. And as it brightened it revealed a scene from a Dürer engraving.

It seemed like there were hundreds of infected on the beach, most of them feeding on the bodies hit by previous fire. During the night there had been occasional shots from the dual water-cooled .50s on the gunboats.

They would wait until a group of infected found one of the bodies, then add to the piles. Eventually, there was enough infected food in scattered groups along the beach that between the available resource, the lights and the music, zombies from throughout the island came for the party and stayed for the banquet.

"Yes," Sergeant Smith said. "If you think about it, there were a lot more at Gitmo. Worst I ever saw was Tenerife. At least on the ground."

"I guess that makes sense," Hoag said.

"And this time we've got multiple divisions firing from multiple points," Smitty said. "That spread 'em out."

The music, which had been a really eclectic mix of death metal, thrash metal, operatic rock, '70s rock and roll—the colonel was apparently a big Doors fan—and even classical, paused. There was a brief moment of silence on the bay as the light brightened, then it started up again with "Anchors Aweigh."

"Really, Colonel?" Hoag said. "The *Navy* anthem?"

The guns opened fire as the introductory flourish ended.

She'd previously watched the slaughter of infected they'd grown to know and loathe from a rather distant warehouse. The *Grace Tan* was anchored a bare two hundred meters off the beach. It was different from this angle.

"Oh, yeah!" "OORAH!" "Go, Navy!"

The big dual, water-cooled fifty-calibers were shredding the infected. Bodies were being blown in half. Some of the brighter ones started to run. The Navy gunners were having none of that. The sound track had segued to another metal piece after the Navy anthem, then into the Marine Corps Hymn.

"At ease!" the lieutenant bellowed. "That's our cue. Board the boats, by teams, junior first. Time to go take that beach, Marines!"

The Navy gunners had been careful to keep the "bait" away from the cargo pier which was the center of the landing operation. The Zodiacs drove their bows ashore and the Marines clambered over to . . . silence. The tropical wind was blowing, there was a bit of a smell of carrion, there were some long burnt out buildings and, that was it. That and the wrack and ruin.

"Force Ops," Faith called, looking around. "Marine Team is calling this zone clear for off-load."

"Roger, Marine Team. Stand by."

"Already there," Faith muttered. She was slightly back from the line of Marines, standing a bit over ankle deep in green tropical water and watching a coconut palm waving in the trade winds. "Why is it that we keep ending up in such *great* looking places and never seem to get any shore leave?"

She didn't seem to notice that there was a skull right by her left foot.

"Aren't there remaining infected on the island, ma'am?" Lance Corporal Saul asked.

"Oh, yeah, that," Faith said, shrugging. "One of these days, Lance Corporal, we are going to clear something thoroughly enough we can have some damned shore leave. I may even be forced to drink something with an umbrella in it."

She leaned down and picked up the skull.

"But maybe we'll do a police call first, mon," she said, holding the skull up to her mouth and using a bad Caribbean accent. "Otherwise it might be . . . grim."

CHAPTER 15

*In the snow of far-off Northern lands
And in sunny tropic scenes;
You will find us always on the job—
The United States Marines.*

—Marine Corps Hymn

"Marine Team, clear perimeter buildings and establish security perimeter at base of dock, over."

"Roger, Ops," Faith said. "Staff Sergeant Barnard, you hear the order?"

"Yes, ma'am," Barnard said. She was standing more or less at the same position as Faith a bit farther down the beach.

"You establish the perimeter at the pier with Squad One," Faith said. "I'll accompany Squad Two on sweeping the buildings. Ensure that your squad's weapons are on safe. I don't want any friendly fire 'cause there are human shapes moving around the buildings. Oorah?"

"Aye, aye, ma'am," Barnard said.

"Hooch!" Faith yelled. "Move out."

"Aye, aye, ma'am," Sergeant Hocieniec replied.

"You know," Faith said. "A little paint, some curtains . . ."

The Bayside Bar and Grill had obviously been a pretty popular island beach bar. Now it was a fire-scorched shell. They only knew the name by figuring it out from the half burned sign. There was a burned skeleton behind the bar along with shattered bottles and glassware. It was apparent whoever it was had been dead before the fire. There were scraps of clothing so it probably wasn't an infected.

"Possibly a roof, ma'am," Sergeant Hocieniec said, pointing up. There was a partial roof but through most of it you could see the sky and palm trees.

"Fiddly bits, Sergeant," Faith said. "That is what NCOs are for."

"Yes, ma'am," Hocieniec said, smiling.

"Leave alpha team here," Faith said. "Oriented thataway," she continued, knife-handing southeast. "Staff Sergeant Barnard," she said, keying her radio.

"Here, ma'am," Barnard said.

"Leaving one team in the building as a security team," Faith said. "Preparing to sweep west. Check fire, check fire, check fire."

"Check fire, aye," Barnard said.

Hocieniec started to step out the door and Faith held out her arm blocking him.

"Let the word spread," Faith said. After a moment she keyed her radio. "Check fire check, Staff Sergeant."

"Check fire, aye, ma'am," Barnard replied.

"Now we go," Faith said.

The westerly buildings were support buildings for the pier. There was an abandoned storage container, a medium sized warehouse and support building, two large above ground fuel tanks and a parking area. There was the usual scatter of abandoned cars in the parking area as well as a large boat or cargo container forklift. It could be either one; they looked pretty much the same.

The main doors to the warehouse were open—any infected inside should have been drawn out—but they approached cautiously nonetheless.

The interior was mostly filled with boat support material including a small machine shop. There were some small outboards up on racks.

"Check and clear the office," Faith said.

"Aye, aye, ma'am," Hooch replied. "Bravo team."

"Aye, aye," Hoag replied.

The door to the offices had been forced and there was another long-dead skeleton in it. Other than that it was clear.

"Clear," Sergeant Hoag said, before walking back into the equipment building.

"Can't really use this as a security position," Faith said. "Sergeant Hocieniec, get the team up on top of the storage container. That will give us a better look around."

"Aye, aye, ma'am," Hocieniec said.

Sergeant Hoag waved for her team to leave the warehouse. As Faith started to open her mouth, Lance Corporal Robert "Bubba" Freeman cleared the entrance and immediately took fire.

"Back!" Faith shouted as rounds began to zing through the equipment shed. It sounded like half the beach group was firing at their position. She dove behind a drill press. "God-damnit, check fire! Check fire!"

Faith's call was being stepped on by calls of "Movement!" But after a minute or so, and waaaay too many rounds, the firing stopped as did the radio calls.

"Anybody hit?" Faith asked.

"I caught a graze, Shewolf," Hooch said.

"Bad graze?" Faith asked.

"No, ma'am. Think it was a chunk of concrete or something."

"Staff Sergeant?" Faith called after a moment.

"Here, ma'am," Barnard said.

"We're about to exit this equipment building and do some stuff in the parking lot," Faith said. "Could you *clarify* that fact with whoever just tried to kill Lance Corporal Freeman and, by the way, *missed*. And could you once again ensure that all of your Marines' weapons are *unloaded* and on *safe*? Because that shot was too fast for the weapon to *not* have been locked, loaded and off safe? Pretty please with honey and *fucking sugar on top*?"

"Marine Team, Force Ops."

"Marine Team," Faith replied laconically.

"Any casualties?"

"One graze," Faith said. "Fortunately or unfortunately, the marksmanship quality was poor. Continuing the mission. Staff Sergeant?"

"Here."

"Check fire, check fire, check fire."

"Check fire, aye," Barnard replied.

"You can get mugged on a walk in the fucking park," Faith said, standing up. "Freeman, this time, remove your helmet, stick it on the end of your rifle and wave it out the door before exiting..."

∽ ⊖ ∾

"Time to regroup," Faith said as she reached the pier. The Navy personnel were starting to unload onto the cargo pier and the *Grace Tan* was carefully backing up to the end, being tended by two tug boats. "Organization will be as follows. Send one of your teams into the bar to take over from alpha second. Other team between the bar and the road to the left. Alpha second to take the right side of the road in contact with alpha first which will remain on the top of the container. That leaves the beach itself open. I'll get with Navy security and make sure they have that covered. Understood?"

"Aye, aye, ma'am," Staff Sergeant Barnard said.

"With one exception. Who was it opened fire *first*?"

"PFC Funk, ma'am," Barnard said. "I have counseled him on fire discipline."

"And he's about to be counseled again," Faith said. "PFC FUNK, FRONT AND CENTER!"

"Aye, aye, ma'am," the Marine said, trotting over. He took the position of attention, looking off into the distance.

"Go down to the beach, put your feet in the water and assume the front-leaning rest position, oriented landwards," Faith said.

"Aye, aye, ma'am," Funk said, trotting back down to the water.

"Ma'am," Barnard said. "Marine Corps regulation states that physical training may not be used as corrective punishment."

Faith just stood there for a moment. She was partially faced away from the staff sergeant so it wasn't apparent that the young lieutenant's face had gone white with anger.

"Staff Sergeant, I gave you an order to redeploy the squads," Faith growled, very quietly. "I do not recall asking your opinion. You have exactly five seconds to follow my order."

"Aye, aye, ma'am," Barnard said, her face tight.

"Force Ops, Marine Team," Faith said after a few deep breaths.

"Force Ops."

"Request a couple of Navy ground teams to anchor the beach," Faith said. "We've got from the equipment building to the bar."

"Roger, stand by."

"Standing by."

"Hi, Sis," Sophia said, walking down the pier.

"Good morning, Ensign!" Faith boomed.

"Oh, do not start with the whole command voice thing," Sophia said.

"I do not know what you are referring to, Ensign," Faith barked.

"It's 'that to which you refer' technically," Sophia said. "How's it going? Saw your Marines try to kill each other."

"Frankly, it's going too well," Faith said. "'Cause I'm wondering when it's going to fuck up and it's giving the Gitmo Marines the idea that this is all easy."

"How long you going to have that guy do push-ups?" Sophia asked curiously.

"Since he tried to *kill* me, probably a while," Faith said. "And I'm not having him do— FUNK, WHY ISN'T YOUR BACK STRAIGHT? WHAT ARE YOU, *NAVY?*"

"You know he's carrying like a hundred pounds of gear," Sophia said.

"That's the point," Faith said. "The more he sweats the less *I* might bleed. RECOVER! JUMPING JACKS! BEGIN! ONE, TWO, THREE, FOUR...YOU COUNT! STOP WHEN *I* GET TIRED!"

"Hey, I got a call..." Sophia said. "Roger, Force Ops, can do. Roger. Will coordinate with Marine commander. You want *us* to cover *you*?"

"One team on each end of the beach," Faith said, gesturing both ways. "That way if the gunners get twitchy trigger fingers, they kill Navy not Marines."

"Oh, thank you very much," Sophia said. "But a point. Force Ops, Navy Landing Party..."

"CEASE EXERCISE!" Faith yelled. "MARINE, YOU HAVE FAILED ON *TWO* COUNTS, BAD FIRE DISCIPLINE *AND* POOR AIM! YOU ARE A *DOUBLE* DISGRACE TO OUR BELOVED CORPS! ON YOUR BACK, MARINE! FLUTTER KICKS! BEGIN! ONE, TWO..."

"Hold up," Faith said, looking through the printed out sheets. The five-tons had been unloaded and the Marines were now in the process of sweeping the island. For a change she was sitting in the front seat instead of on the gun. For one reason, their "map" was printouts of the overheads. They were at a round-about, which had a post in the middle with some weird triangle thing, and she was trying to figure out the way to the hospital. She looked over at the airport, then down at the map and put two of the sheets together side by side. "I'm pretty sure it's that way," she said, pointing right. "But hang on. Staff Sergeant, I'm pretty sure we take the right fork thingy. You concur?"

"Concur," the staff sergeant replied after a moment. She was riding in the trail five-ton.

There was a burst of fire from the gunner overhead and Faith looked up in time to see a dog come apart.

"Seriously, Quade?" Faith yelled. "It was the size of a collie! Save your rounds for infecteds!"

"Aye, aye, ma'am," Lance Corporal Quade said.

She looked over at Sergeant Smith, who was driving, and rolled her eyes upwards. He just shrugged.

"Take the right fork thingy, Sergeant," Faith said, going back to shuffling papers. "We'll find it eventually..."

"Son of a *bitch*," Faith muttered as they approached a beach on the south side of the island. "Staff Sergeant, turn around. How in the hell can we keep getting *lost* on an island this *small*?"

"Found the fire station, ma'am," Sergeant Smith said.

"And a fire truck," Faith said. "Which isn't specified on this map. But I think we're in *this* area..."

"Stop at this gas station," Faith said.

"We've still got nearly a full tank, ma'am," Sergeant Smith said.

"I'm getting a fucking *map*, Smitty..."

"Shit, she *is* crazy," Barnard muttered, shaking her head as the lieutenant bailed out of the five-ton and headed into the interior of the gas station. They hadn't encountered many infected but they were random. They seemed to appear out of nowhere. "Lieutenant, we should deploy a security team."

"*You gotta be joking me,*" Faith replied. "*Negative. I'm just looking for a—*"

"Lieutenant?" Barnard said. The call had cut off mid sentence.

"*Skipper is looking for a better map,*" Sergeant Smith radioed.

The lieutenant appeared out of the block building a moment later holding a map over her head and headed to Barnard's truck. She had another stuffed in her cargo pocket.

As she did an infected burst out of the bushes and charged her from her right. The direction her rifle was *not* pointing.

"*Too close,*" Barnard shouted to the machine gunner, scrabbling at her rifle. There was no way to get fire on the infected before it got to the lieutenant. And the Marines were not wearing "close contact" gear. If it got a bite in on the girl...

The lieutenant looked over her shoulder, drew her pistol, fired one round one-handed into the infected's chest then another into its head. She decocked her pistol, dropped it back in its holster and went back to reading the map. The entire event had been one continuous motion. She didn't even seem to notice.

"Oh..." Faith said, climbing up on the running board of the five-ton. "Oorah. I think I've figured out where we are...."

"Staff Sergeant," Faith barked, standing at parade rest.

"Ma'am," Barnard said.

They were standing outside the Princess Alexandria Hospital as the Marine teams swept the building. The hospital was a two-story construction, not much larger than a McMansion, with large windows and airy arch construction.

Like most of the island it had been swept by fire. Faith was pretty sure they weren't going to find much in the way of supplies.

"We need to get some training in on the float," Faith said. "I'm seeing a lot of sweeping going on on this clearance. And then there's the fire discipline issue coupled with the accuracy issue. We can only really train on shooting on land. Not sure how to handle that. Maybe take a day on a desert island; lots of those around here. The lack of basic marksmanship worked in our favor in this instance but it's not generally a good thing. The sweeping issue and general CQB we can do in the *Grace Tan*. Oorah?"

"Yes, ma'am," Barnard said.

"Left wing is clear of all infected," Hocieniec radioed.

"Roger," Faith said.

"Right wing is cleared," Sergeant Weisskopf called a moment later.

"Roger," Faith said, changing frequencies. "Force Ops, Marine Team."

"Go, Marine Team."

"Hospital is clear," Faith said. "No way to secure it. Cannot guarantee security for Navy sweep personnel. Be advised, been on fire. Probably a bust."

"Roger," Force Ops replied. *"Stand by."*

"Don't we always," Faith said. "Call in the dogs, Staff Sergeant. Odds we go on to the medical school."

"Marine Team, Force Commander. What's the security situation on the ground?"

"Complicated," Faith replied. "There is a higher

infected presence than I would have guessed. Most of them didn't make it to the beach. Constant minor leakers. Stand by. Quade, is there something wrong with your eyes?"

"Ma'am?" Quade called.

"Hello!" she yelled, knife-handing. "Target in your sector, Marine!"

"Aye, aye, ma'am," LCP Quade called, targeting the infected with a three-round burst.

"But we haven't been hit by a large force," Faith continued. "I'd say that Navy ground team can handle this, over."

"Sweep the medical school, then return to the pier," Hamilton radioed.

"Sweep the medical school, then return to the pier, aye," Faith replied. "Marine Team out. Okay, let's load up and roll out." She sighed, drew her pistol and pointed it at Funk. "Duck."

Funk hit the ground and she shot the infected crossing the courtyard in the head.

"They're coming from fucking *everywhere!*" Faith snarled, decocking and holstering the pistol. "This is why I prefer clearing ships."

The two-story tile-roofed medical school had not caught fire. The fires had seemed to miss that part of the island. It also had a fair number of infected.

"Oh, that explains it," Faith said, looking to the east.

"Explains what, ma'am?" Barnard asked as there were more shots from the interior.

"Look over there," Faith said, pointing to the east. There was a large pond that was tinged a bright green.

"I'm not sure what I'm looking at, ma'am," Barnard said.

"Zombies can survive anywhere there's water, Staff Sergeant," Faith said. "Any fresh water, no matter how foul. Some survive. That doesn't look all that bad all things considered. So . . . lots of water, lots of zombies."

"I understand, ma'am," Barnard said.

"Which means this island is *crawling* with them," Faith said. "Intel had that marked as a *field* so I didn't expect this many to have survived. Without that there's not enough water on this island. And with all the terrain stuff, hills, fences, stuff, they didn't all make it to the beach."

"I see, ma'am," Barnard said. "It hasn't been . . . bad so far."

"They're scattered," Faith said, shrugging. "They do that. So we're hitting minor leakers and pockets like this one," she added as there was another burst of fire. There was also a yell. "That didn't sound good."

"Marine team leader, Squad Two," Hooch radioed.

"Go," Faith replied.

"We've got a casualty . . ."

"There goes *my* fitrep," Faith said. "How bad?" she asked.

"Bad," Hooch replied. *"Need evac."*

"Move the casualty back to the trucks," Faith said, switching frequencies again. "Force Ops, we have a casualty. We are moving casualty back to the pier at this time. Will require medical support."

"Roger," Force Ops replied.

"Oh, shit," Faith said as the squad came back. Haugen had Goodwin over his back in a fireman's carry and Goodwin was dripping blood from *somewhere*. "Get him in the five-ton. Where's he hit?"

"In the back," Hooch said, jumping into the five-ton to pull the lance corporal up.

"Get his gear off," Faith said, jumping up as well. "Staff Sergeant, recover the rest of the teams and then head back to the pier. Hooch, up front and make sure we don't get lost on the way back."

"Aye, aye, ma'am," Hooch said.

As the armor came off a small hole was revealed in his back with a larger one on the front. The bullet was lodged in his frontal armor.

"We were sweeping and Curran..." Haugen said, shaking his head.

"I really don't care," Faith said as Hocieniec jumped out of the back and ran to the front of the vehicle. "Roll this vehicle, Barnard!"

She dove into her assault ruck and started pulling out medical supplies.

"Ma'am," Barnard said.

"I am also the closest thing we've got to a *corpsman*, Staff Sergeant," Faith snarled. "What part of my orders did you not understand *this* time, Staff Sergeant? Hooch! ROLL OUT! Force Ops, we have one GSW to the abdomen, rear entry. We'll need at least one unit of...AB negative... Hey, Goodwin, this isn't bad, okay? Seriously, this is a fucking flea bite, dude..."

"Colonel," Walker said. "I'll go prep the sick bay. Sophia can do the sweep for materials."

"Agreed," Hamilton said.

CHAPTER 16

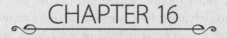

Here's health to you and to our Corps
Which we are proud to serve;
In many a strife we've fought for life
And never lost our nerve.

—Marine Corps Hymn

"You all right, Lieutenant?" Hamilton asked. The lieutenant had taken a position well outside the perimeter around the base of the dock and was squatting in the light waves to wash the blood off her hands.

"Just fine, sir," Faith barked.

"Seriously," Hamilton said. "Are you good to continue the mission? Especially tonight?"

"I am just fine, sir," Faith said. "We'll get it done one way or another. I'd say never better but that would be a lie. I've had better days and worse days, sir."

"What happened?" Hamilton asked.

"What happened was that we put a mix of trained and untrained personnel into a cluster of people who knew each other and had worked together, with people they didn't know and hadn't worked together, sir," Faith said. "And in many cases, the untrained people were *in charge*. Then we sent them out with a bunch of ammunition and guns into conditions that

261

in the case of the untrained personnel were unfamiliar and nervous-making. When you couple that with an absolutely untrained senior NCO who can't find her ass with both hands, and conflicts in the chain of command, what we had, sir, was a shit sandwich, sir."

"I take it you're still having problems with Staff Sergeant Barnard," Hamilton said, his face blank.

"The staff sergeant shouldn't be a lance corporal, much less a staff sergeant, sir," Faith said. "And that is documentable, sir. On four occasions so far she has failed to perform to anything like minimum standards, sir. And she can't seem to just take a God-damned order, sir, which I thought was, word... Inigo Montoya... inconceivable in a Marine senior NCO. I recognize that she is working in ways that she is not prepared for by training, sir. And the whole thing about... ice water, sir. But if I am ever given the choice, sir, I'd make her your administrative assistant and have Sergeant Hocieniec run the platoon, sir. Or Sergeant Smith who has more time in grade, sir. Sergeants Hoag and Weisskopf are equally untrained for this form of operation, sir. I haven't decided if they're fundamentally ill-suited or just having a hard time adjusting, sir. Having Sergeant Smith, a trained infantryman with not only pre-Plague combat experience and training but significant combat experience post-Plague, as a gun bunny is not, in my opinion, the way to have the TOE laid out."

"I see," Hamilton said. "I will take that under advisement, Lieutenant."

"I'm not sure you see the full point, sir," Faith said, straightening up and dropping out of command voice. "There really is a point, sir. The *Iwo* Marines, as they're called, most of them were various other MOS than infantry, sir. Goodwin is a 3381. But they were all in combat *units*, sir. They had all had more recent combat training, sir. They'd trained up for deployment into hot zones before the Plague busted out. Plus we trained them on shipboard clearance *before* we threw them out in teams. And they've got *lots* of down-range time at this point, sir. Hundreds and thousands of hours, sir. They have had time to adjust and adapt, sir. *Your* Marines, sir, were all various support MOS which were *far* less likely to encounter enemy fire. 0100s. 0300s. 27s. Okay, the 27s like Corporal Rock have spent some serious time in the Sandbox. But they were always surrounded by security teams. They weren't the security.

"That doesn't make the Marines from Gitmo bad or even bad *Marines*, sir. That makes them utterly *unprepared*, sir. And it shows, sir. Specifically, sir, what happened was that Curran swept across Goodwin's back 'cause they thought they had movement and jerked the trigger. Because he, Curran, hadn't been dropped and yelled at, repeatedly, by Gunny Sands and Staff Sergeant Januscheitis, about sweeping his fellow Marines and because he was nervous about sweeping a building that had live infected, sir. Especially since they were coming from *everywhere*, sir. Not enough to overrun us, but enough to make everybody jumpy."

"I understand," Hamilton said. "We'll cover it in the after action report."

"Roger, sir," Faith said. "In the meantime, sir, as soon as Staff Sergeant Barnard returns with the other five-ton and the rest of the platoon, we will continue the mission, sir. By your leave."

"Carry on, Lieutenant," Hamilton said.

⚬◠⊝◠⚬

"You okay, Sis?" Sophia asked as they were boarding the five-tons.

"Had better days," Faith said. "Had worse. At least I'm not having to put up with you all the time on the *Mile Seven*," she added with a grin.

"I sort of miss those days," Sophia said.

"Days like this so do I," Faith admitted. "I just hope Goodwin survives. I really need him." She stopped and grimaced, then put her game face back on.

"Be advised, Sis, there's no such thing as 'clear' on this island. We found what I thought was a field on the overhead and it turned out to be a pond."

"Aggh," Sophia said. "I was figuring a lot of them would have died of dehydration."

"Nope," Faith said. "So they just pop up. Tell your teams to keep their heads up. And for God's sake, don't sweep each other. We're going to have to sweep the shit out of this island tonight to have it clear enough for... You know."

"Will do," Sophia said. "Looks like we're loaded."

"What's that thing about 'actions of a tiger'?" Faith said.

"Once more into the breach?" Sophia said, rolling her eyes.

"It's 'unto,'" Faith said, grinning. "Unto the breach. Thought you were the *smart* one?"

"I hate you."

Colonel Hamilton was waiting when they arrived back at the pier.

"Bust, sir," Sophia said, waving an extended hand in front of her throat. "We even checked the little drugstore. The hospital and drug store had been ransacked, actually ransacked, before the Fall from the looks of it. The medical school had some textbooks and disks we grabbed but it was pretty much a bust. No real labs at all."

"Permission to ask how Goodwin is, sir," Faith said, her face tight.

"Mr. Walker is a much better doctor than he lets on," Hamilton said. "He was able to patch everything up. It just missed the kidneys and passed through, hitting only intestines. If infection doesn't get him, he should be fine. He's already out of recovery and conscious."

"Oh, thank God," Faith said, turning away and putting her hand over her face.

"I'll call it in," Hamilton said. "Time to start the real mission."

"Aye, aye, sir," Faith said. "Staff Sergeant Barnard! Set out security . . . !"

"We're going *back*, ma'am," Staff Sergeant Barnard said, neutrally.

"Roger," Faith said. "Commander's intent is to *thoroughly* sweep the island and ensure that all remaining infected are drawn to lights and sound, by *making* that light and sound and drawing them to ourselves. Where we will then give those poor infected all the courtesy and friendliness for which the United States Marine Corps is known. Due to the potential, given limited visibility, of actions getting to close quarters, we will rerig in full contained-space combat equipment. After clearance, Marines will remain in combat gear pending further orders.

"The exception in the sweep are Staff Sergeant Decker and PFC Condrey," Faith said, looking at

Decker, "who will direct Naval Landing Force personnel on the proper manner and method of detail cleaning the back of one of the five-tons. They will, for the period, be under the command of my sister, Ensign Smith, oorah, and they will follow her orders and give her all the professional courtesy they give any officer, oorah? Further, after the five-ton is fully detail cleaned they will assist in sealing it against environmental factors in a manner consistent with Nuclear, Biological and Chemical procedures to ensure no trace of exterior infection can enter the five-ton while in movement. Any further questions on that will be directed to the ensign, Staff Sergeant Decker. No questions from any personnel as to the precise nature of this mission will be entertained. Is that all clear, Staff Sergeant Barnard?"

"Yes, ma'am," Barnard said. She had her professional mien on but she was clearly curious.

"Staff Sergeant Decker?"

"Yes, ma'am," Decker said, his face wooden.

"Ah," Faith said. "Staff Sergeant Decker, anybody can sweep an island for infected. Both the colonel and I, independently, chose you for the mission of making sure that there is not one single influenza virus on the interior of that five-ton. You were not, in other words, left out of the fun of continuing to kill zombies. You were the only one trusted enough to be sure that the job was done right. I am aware that you've been counseled that at a certain point things are as good as they are going to get. In this case, that does not hold, Staff Sergeant. There is no such thing as 'too clean' for the interior of that vehicle. Are we clear, Staff Sergeant?"

"Aye, aye, ma'am," Decker said, relaxing ever so slightly. It was clear that he really didn't care why he was being given an order to GI a five-ton as long as it wasn't because he was considered incompetent to lead troops in combat in the dark.

"In that case, Staff Sergeant Barnard, it is time for you to go round up my devil dogs and *git it on*," Faith said, grinning ferally. "We shall have the joy of glorious battle upon this glorious night. Ain't nothin' better than fighting zombies on an island in the dark. Yuh git in *scrums* that way."

"Ahayt!" Faith bellowed as she approached the Marines assembled on the back deck of the *Grace Tan*. She had her full "liner" clearance gear on, her helmet under her arm and her gas mask pushed back on her head. It was hot as shit. And she'd worn it so much in so many hot spots she'd almost started to not notice. "Listen up, Devil Dogs! We are going to have a party tooo-night! Commander's intent. We *shall* attract and eliminate every *motherfucking* zombie on this *motherfucking* island. We shall do that by using *light* and *sound* to draw them to *our* position and then shooting them repeatedly until they are *good* infected and lie down.

"Method: The Platoon, led by their *fearless* leader, shall proceed by five-ton and local vehicles, previously acquired, to the Quarter. There they will disperse. Bravo Team, squad two, led by Sergeant Hoag, *shall* remain with the five-ton aaand their fearless leader in the Quarter as a rapid response team.

"Squad One, under Staff Sergeant Barnard, and Alpha Team, Squad Two, under Sergeant Hocieniec, *shall* break down into three-man teams. They shall use local vehicles to drive *slowly* around and about the island, each team having a designated zone, with the lights on and honking the horn, until they observe approaching infected. They shall then engage such infected with small arms fire and convince them to lie down and be good.

"We shall continue that exercise until *zero one hundred hours* at which point you *shall* turn your happy asses around and head back to rendezvous at the Quarter. We are to be *off* the island by *zero two hundred.*

"When, not if, you get your silly asses lost you *shall* continue to drive on, on foot if needs be, to make it back to the Quarter or this location, whichever is directed, based upon time and location. We will use the usual frequencies but we have increasing numbers of subs moving into the area and they have frequency scanners. If you lose contact, just start calling on the emergency frequency for the subs. Each of you Marines *should* be carrying a radio and backup batteries. Team leaders *shall* ensure that such is the case. If *one* don't work, use the *others.*

"If you get into *close* contact with the infected, don't you worry none. You're in this gear for a reason, not *just* 'cause I like it hot. Just scrum 'em. If you hit a big pocket of infected and get stuck somewhere, like up a tree, just git on the radio and call for your fearless leader and I *shall* come and pull you out of the dunny. The reason I'm staying back ain't that I want to miss the party, it's 'cause I'm figurin' the reaction team's gonna get called on at *least* once and I want the opportunity of *glorious* battle upon this glorious tropical night. My kukri ain't et in weeks and we're *hungry*! I am offering a nice bottle of hooch for whichever team finds a really *good* pocket of infected so I can get in the scrum.

"Do *not* take off one single item of gear! Do *not* fail to make it back *here* by zero two hundred! Run the whole damned way if you must. You do not, trust me, want to be left on this island. Do *not* shoot each other! If the infected surprise you, let them come to you and go to hand-to-hand. That's the *fun* way to kill them! *Do* hydrate! *Do* kill infected! *Do* find my rugged Nepalese beauty something to *eat*! Go be my fine and beautiful devil dogs! Oorah?"

"*OORAH!*" the platoon boomed, grinning. Miss Faith was back.

"Right, team leaders, gather round for your assigned sectors..."

"Nothin' can be finer than clearin' out a liner in the, mooornin'," Lance Corporal Richard "Dutch" Van Dijk sang softly as the Zodiac neared the beach. "Nothing can be sweeter than sendin' Zs to Peter in the, mooornin'..."

"At ease, Lance Corporal," Sergeant Weisskopf snapped. "We are aware that you have a 'senior boarder's badge,' whatever that is. But this is a *tactical* landing."

"Aye, aye, Sergeant," Dutch said. "Just happy to be able to take my shades off."

"Don't tell me you can *see* in this?" Weisskopf said sharply. The approach to the beach was being done on Zodiacs and the orders were do not fire until landing and "tactical" approach—basically they were sneaking in. The point being that they were going to need to be on the land to effectively engage the enemy. Firing from a Zodiac, especially at night, was a fairly precision skill.

"Not like day, Sergeant," Dutch said. "But some, yes. And we have company on the beach. Infected feeding at two o'clock."

Ignoring his whole "tactical landing" speech, Weisskopf switched on his weapon's light and shone it to the right. Sure enough, there was an infected gnawing one of the bloating corpses on the beach.

"Ow," Dutch said, shielding his eyes.

The infected looked up at the light and snarled, then went back to feeding.

"Engaging," Weisskopf shouted. He fired twice to no effect as the boat was rocking on the light waves. "Damnit."

There were two rapid shots and the infected dropped.

"What was it about 'tactical landing' that you did not understand, Sergeant Weisskopf?" Faith radioed. *"All teams. White light now that we are definitely not tactical. Boats, screw the noise, get us on land, fast."*

The line of Zodiacs powered up, heading into the beach at nearly fifteen miles an hour. Not their top speed but they were within fifty meters of the beach when they got the order.

"Brace, brace, brace," Faith called just as the Zodiacs slid up onto the white sand of the beach. Then: "HIT THE BEACH MARINES!" she screamed at the top of her lungs.

There were customers. There had been leakers all day but apparently there were some that only came out at night. And they were feeding in singles and doubles all along the strand on the bodies left by the morning's serenade.

Faith cleared the bow of the Zodiac in a hurdle and fired as soon as she hit the ground, dropping the only infected in her sector. There were more closing and some of the Marines were, clearly, panic firing. Her ear was attuned to the rapid and uneven *bang-bang—bangbang—bang* and she could tell by the way the gun-lights were jerking around everywhere.

"Calm it down, folks," Faith radioed on the command frequency. There were two frequencies the radios could pick up, one was the local "team" frequency and one was the "command" frequency. When the command frequency was running, it stepped on the local. She was also careful to use her best "golf announcer" impression. "Shooo, soooft, soooft. Squad leaders, team leaders, let's get this fire under control. We're Marines. Marines don't panic. We *aim*. Div One, could we get some support fire on the flanks, if you please. *Careful* support fire."

"Freeman, Twitchell," Sergeant Smith snapped. "Check fire! Check fire!"

"They're all around us, Sergeant!" Twitchell yelled. He was pulling on an empty trigger.

"I said Check Fire, Marine!" Smith shouted. "What is it about 'check fire' you do not understand?"

"That *I'm* in charge, Sergeant!" Sergeant Hoag said, firing repeatedly at an infected in among the trees. It just wouldn't *fall*. She fumbled her reload and started clawing for another magazine until her hand fell on a grenade...

"That's a BUSH!" Smith screamed. "You can't kill a BUSH, Sergeant! Check fire! There are *no* moving infected in our sector!"

"You are *not* the team leader, Sergeant Smith!"

Hoag shouted, then took a deep breath as the firing died down. "Fuck. That looks just *like* a guy. That looks just *like* a fucking guy."

"A guy with *clothes*," Smith said. "It's trash bags on a bush. Even if it *was* a guy, it would be a survivor. Has clothes. Check fire, okay?"

"Roger," Hoag said, breathing heavily. "Team, check fire. Check fire."

"And, Sergeant, could you *very calmly* let go of the pin on the grenade and put it *back* in its pouch?"

"Freeze," Faith said on the command frequency. She was scanning the entire line and couldn't see any infected. "I can see lights still twitching. Who doesn't understand the command 'freeze'?"

"Fucking *freeze*, Saul!" Sergeant Weisskopf snapped.

She waited until every gun light was still. Still no infected.

"On my command," Faith said. "Non-NCOs only, even if you have a full mag, will reload. NCOs only, cover if you have rounds, if not, just stay still. When you are reloaded, and take your time, put your light back on your sector and freeze. Execute."

There was a *budda-budda-budda* from one of the gunboats that had spotted what it thought was an infected on the flank. Some of the lights started shifting that way.

"Back on your sectors and freeze if you're reloaded," Faith said calmly. "If you are *not* reloaded, your NCOs are going to have you drilling every free moment the rest of the cruise…"

❧⊖☙

"We need to put your sister in a glass case like Snow White," Colonel Hamilton said, his arms crossed. He was monitoring the radio chatter from the deck of a gunboat. "With a sign on it that says 'Break in the event of a zombie apocalypse.'"

"That's Faith, sir," Sophia said, also watching the action. "Got it in one." In the darkness she gave a very slight smile.

"On my command," Faith said. "*One* junior enlisted in each team, as designated by team leader, will cover the team. NCOs will reload. Team leaders, designate a shooter..."

Hoag opened her mouth for a moment, then said: "Kirby."

"Aye, aye, Sergeant," Kirby said, not moving a muscle. He let his eyes do the searching for targets. "*Aaaand... Execute...*"

"At my command, all personnel will move slowly and carefully *backwards* until both boots are *in* the water at *ankle* depth," Faith said. "Execute."

She moved back to the water. The Zodiacs had powered off the beach so there was plenty of room.

"Take a knee, take your sectors and hold that," Faith said. "Team leaders and team leaders only may engage if there are targets. All others will direct their attention to the center of the formation. All lights but mine shall remain *still* absent approaching infected and then only team leader lights may move. Lights are used for signaling at night. Notably, a light going like this..." she moved her light rapidly back in forth, "is a signal of distress. If for no other reason than anyone moving their light like *this*," again rapid back and forth, "is having *some* trouble. This," she continued, moving it around in a circle, "is saying that you're okay. When you are checking a broad sector, you move your light in calm, regular, sweeps," she said, continuing to demonstrate. "Staff Sergeant Barnard, you have an approaching tango... Take your time... The staff sergeant will now demonstrate the proper method of engaging targets using tactical lighting."

Barnard took a couple of deep breaths and realized that it was causing her light to shake. Which she knew made her look weak, something that was just absolutely *idiotic* in a Marine Senior NCO! She just felt totally out of her depth. She hadn't done any "infantry" shit since Basic. She could *shoot*, she was a God-damned *expert* marksman, she was a Marine Senior NCO! But this wasn't just about shooting. And that little bitch was so Fucking Calm about it. She didn't have any *business* being in the Marine Corps, she didn't have any *business* being an officer, she didn't have any *business* telling a Marine staff sergeant what to do, much less making her look like a *fool* in front of her Marines. And no thirteen-year-old girl had any business being so God-damned CALM!

The entire thought was a single instant that took no time at all. But it was enough time for the loping infected to close twenty meters. Barnard decided that she was *not* going to let the little bitch rattle her. The staff sergeant put the aimpoint on its chest and squeezed.

The round hit on the upper right chest and she

put a second into the chest area, more centered, then a third. The infected finally fell.

"*Standard for killing an infected is five rounds of five-five-six,*" the lieutenant radioed, still in that golf commentator voice. "*Note that the Staff Sergeant took a bare three which is not surprising. She is a Marine Senior NCO and we should all aspire to her marksmanship. That is how Marines shoot. The Army sprays and prays. Marines choose their targets and kill them efficiently, as the Staff Sergeant just demonstrated. At my command, all personnel are authorized free fire on their sector. If I hear anyone panic firing this time, you will return to the ship until such a time as you can be retrained for night combat. Execute. We will hold what we have for a few minutes to let the teams engage approaching infected and get comfortable with the night.*"

"*Marine ground commander, switch to channel seven.*"

"*Roger,*" the lieutenant replied. "*Squad leaders, maintain control of your teams.*"

"*How comfortable are you with continuing the mission, Shewolf?*" Hamilton radioed.

Faith gave a slight dimple before returning the call. It was the first time that the colonel had used her handle.

"It's all good, sir," Faith replied. She'd waded out into the water knee deep. The wind was coming from the land and it carried her voice away so the conversation wouldn't be overheard. Of course, there was blood in the water which meant sharks. She didn't want to stand here all night.

"I probably pumped 'em up too much before we landed. They'll get it together. We're good to continue the mission. I'd like fifteen minutes..." There were some shots from down the line and she didn't even turn around. They were calm. It was clear that the shooter was having trouble getting the zombie to be good but that was just Barbie guns. She did wait until the firing stopped to continue. "Then I'll secure the perimeter for the arrival of the Navy. Over."

"Concur. Kodiak, out."

"Yo, Cindy, 'sup?" Faith said, walking along a bit more than ankle deep behind the line of Marines. There were occasional shots but no panic firing. She held her hand up for a fist bump. "Sweet shot, Staff."

"Thank you, ma'am," Barnard said, standing up and fist bumping. "Pleasure to be of service."

"So, we'll give it ten more minutes for everybody to realize that we're not going to be eaten by hordes of the walking dead," Faith said. "Then we'll continue the evolution. Actually. Funk!"

"Ma'am?" the PFC said.

"Front and center! Staff Sergeant, do you think you can manage to get them to totally check fire on a sector?" Faith asked.

The staff sergeant paused in answering.

"Yeah, me neither," Faith said. "Listen up, Marines," she radioed. "I want a one hundred percent check fire on the road leading from the pier. *I* am going to be moving up it."

"Ma'am," Barnard said.

"Gaaawd *damnit*, Staff Sergeant," Faith said, shaking her head. "I did not ask for your *opinion*! I do not *want* your opinion. And I swear to *God* if you inject one more time like some untrained fucking *recruit* I am going to request you be boarded, do you understand me, Staff Sergeant?"

"Yes, ma'am," Barnard said tightly.

"Marines, if you fire on 'movement' on that road, you are going to be shooting *me*," Faith continued. "And since you will not *kill* me, because apparently *nothing* can kill me, the penalty *will* be *severe* when I come walking *back* down that road."

"Is she *nuts*?" PFC Haroldson asked.

"At ease, Marine," Weisskopf snarled.

"The purpose of this is to demonstrate that infected are not the problem you're all thinking they are," Faith radioed. *"I will proceed up the road with Funk to the edge of the light. There we will probably be able to attract some zombies and have some fun. Check fire. Check fire. Let us handle them."*

CHAPTER 17

If the Army and the Navy
Ever look on Heaven's scenes,
They will find the streets are guarded
By United States Marines.

—Marine Corps Hymn

"You ready to go, Funk?" Faith asked, stepping up onto the pier.

"Yes, ma'am," Funk said tightly.

"Staff Sergeant," Faith said. "Just this once, *please* do your job and ensure that my Marines do not frag me."

"Aye, aye, ma'am," Barnard said.

"Funk, unload your weapon," Faith said.

"Aye, aye, ma'am," Funk said. He jacked the round out of his weapon.

"You have to *drop your magazine first*, Marine," Faith said. "Drop your magazine."

"Confirmed infected in west sector," Sergeant Hocieniec radioed.

"Roger, Hooch," Faith said. "Scrum it, over."

"Scrum it, aye," Hocieniec replied.

"Second Squad, check fire," Hocieniec said. "Check fire, check fire. Smitty, scrum that motherfucker."

278

"Scrum that motherfucker, aye," Sergeant Chris Smith said, standing up and drawing a tactical knife. "If any of you fuckers shoot me in the back I will shoot you in the *head*."

The infected had closed to the edge of the light and was now dodging through the shadows, apparently unsure what was going on at the beach. Without a pack of its fellow zombies, some shred of self-preservation had kicked in.

Smith walked up to the edge of the beach and took a crouch.

"Come on, zombie," Smith said, waving to it. "Come to papa."

The zombie, driven by hunger, charged and Smith caught it with a hip roll, throwing it over his hip and onto the sand of the beach. He followed it down with his full weight and drove the Gerber into its eye.

"The problem with that technique is getting your knife out," Smith said, putting his foot on the zombie's head and wrenching at the bloody knife.

"Hey, Smitty, you got more incoming," Hooch said, grinning.

Faith had, meanwhile, strolled up the road with PFC Funk.

"Zombies cannot even begin to harm you until they are at arm's length, PFC," Faith said. She had her radio "open" deliberately this time. "Which was why you wait until they're close, generally, to fire. You hit them that way and you can be sure that they are zombies and not survivors or fellow Marines."

"Yes, ma'am," the Marine said nervously.

"And in this gear, they can't get to you at *all*," Faith

said. "Last but not least, they are *not* the walking dead. Are they Corporal Douglas?"

"No, ma'am," Derk yelled.

"So they can be killed in various ways that don't require shooting them in the head," Faith said. "Unless you're using a fucking Barbie gun. In which case... well... check fire, check fire, check fire," she shouted just to be sure.

She'd heard the zombie closing in the darkness. She let it charge and slam into her from behind. She flipped it across her shoulder and onto the ground, then let it have her left arm to bite.

"Notice that he's not gaining an inch," Faith said, drawing her kukri. "Human teeth cannot penetrate this bunker gear. And..." she reached across his arms and chopped downward. There was a spray of arterial blood. "They are *not* hard to kill.

"All Marine personnel will now *unload* their weapons," Faith said, flicking the kukri to clear it of blood and pushing herself to her feet. "Squad and team leaders will assure that they are *unloaded*. Not just on safe. And that goes for all Squad and team leaders. Then the Marines who are from Gitmo will move up to the tree line and engage infected in hand-to-hand while the *Iwo* Marines conduct the class. We will continue this evolution until I call it. Staff Sergeant that includes you."

"Permission to..." Staff Sergeant Barnard said and paused. She'd finally realized that the infected on top of her wasn't going to kill her. But he was massive and incredibly strong. "Okay, what the hell do I do *now*, ma'am?"

"The mistake was letting him get on *top* of you, Staff Sergeant," Faith said. "*And* you're only carrying one knife *and* you let him pin you in such a way as your Ka-Bar is inaccessible. I would suggest using your forty-five. Just put it into his stomach and pull the trigger. Bet you're glad you're wearing a gas mask, huh? That guy's got a heck of a schlong..."

"Discontinue exercise," Faith said. "Any remaining wrestlers, *Iwo* Marines take out the infected. Then everybody *keep* your guns unloaded and huddle up at the base of the pier..."

"The purpose of this exercise was to show you that it really doesn't *matter* how many infected pile up on you," Faith said. She had the *Iwo* Marines out on security while she talked to the "Gitmo" Marines. "The most dangerous thing out here in the dark is us. Yea, though we pretty much literally are going to be walking through the valley of the shadow of death, fear no evil. Because we are the most dangerous motherfuckers in this valley.

"If you're nervous about getting hit by these infected, you're going to make the mistake that Curran made and we will have more wounded. So don't be nervous. We are God-damned *Marines* and we are *covered* in fucking gear and the only thing that can hurt us *is* us. That and heat stroke so drink! Pay attention to where you're pointing those weapons, keep them unloaded unless we really *need* to fire. I am making an on-the-fly change to the current manning table. We'll do it like choosing teams at dodge ball. Gitmo Marines line up behind the *Iwo* Marines. Except you,

Staff Sergeant. You stay with me. And we'll need...
Edwards. Can you drive a truck, Edwards?"

"That's my MOS, ma'am," PFC Robert Lee Edwards
said.

"Perfect," Faith said. "But before you do that. I'm
aware that rank is, like, everything in the Marine
Corps. But for the rest of this exercise, Gitmo Marines
follow the orders of the *Iwo* Marines, even if the
person is lower rank. *Iwo* Marines should try to use
proper military courtesy. But... Corporal Rock, you're
with Hocieniec. He's in charge, got it? You obey his
orders even though you outrank him. Sergeant Hoag,
you're with Dutch. Sergeant Weisskopf... Randolph.
Now let's sort the rest of it out..."

"Oorah," Faith said. "Now the Navy left us some
functional vehicles. I bet they don't have gas, though.
So we need to find... seven vehicles and make sure
they're full. Otherwise you guys are going to be walking
back. We can't 'establish a perimeter' while doing so.
And we're going to be muttering around in something
of a cluster fuck getting it done. So the only ones
who can fire are *Iwo* Marines and by God if you fire
without my okay I will make you sorry and sore. So
let's go find the cars and get 'em filled up..."

Filling the vehicles, in the dark, was a nightmare.
It was a bit that had been overlooked in the planning. There were ten cars in all in the area. The Navy
personnel had used five of them. The teams needed
two more started. They found two more that would
start. Then there was the matter of gas. They had to
siphon fuel from the remaining three and spread it

around. None of the cars ended up with a full tank of gas. And as they'd found throughout the operations, the gas was usually contaminated.

And they *were* getting hit. The zombies kept trickling in in ones and twos. Which wasn't a huge problem and gave everyone some more training in that fact. However, it sometimes was a bit of an issue. Say, when Lance Corporal Ferguson was siphoning out a car's gas tank and got hit from behind by an infected.

"The good news is, you're in bunker gear," Faith said, chopping the infected on the back of the neck. "But since your ammo would probably cook off if that gas catches, the smoking lamp is *out.*"

"Okay, so we also got to reformat the patrol areas," Faith said. "Hooch, take your teams up to the east end of the island past the town. Dutch, you and Sergeant Hoag have between here and the town. Smitty, your teams have from here to the west end of the island. Got it?"

"Aye, aye, ma'am," Sergeant Smith said.

"Okay," Faith said, sorting through the maps. "So here's your maps and assigned sectors. Dutch, you can probably just drive around the airport real slow, that will give you some range. The rest of you, just drive up and down slow and bring them in, then kill them. I mean, you've seen that it's easy if they ain't swarming. If you shoot, *aimed fire*, people. We're going to be often moving close to each other. We *have* to get every last infected on this island. Every last one. Blow your horns. Play your music loud. Bring them *in*! Understood?"

"Aye, aye, ma'am," Hooch said.

"Staff Sergeant and I will take the town with the five-ton," Faith said. "If you get in the busy and feel like you can't handle it, call us. Make sure you don't run out of gas. Load up and move out."

"Permission to speak, ma'am," Staff Sergeant Barnard said as they were cruising down Valley Road.

"Speak, Staff Sergeant," Faith said. She was up on the .50 in the lead of the convoy and triggered a burst into an infected in the road. "Go around that so the cars can see it, Roberts. I don't want them getting stuck on a body."

"Aye, aye, ma'am," Roberts said.

"A Marine obeys orders, ma'am," Barnard said tightly. "But . . . why the *hell* are we doing this? It's unsafe, as you've said, and it's—"

"Not in your . . ." Faith said. "Crap, cannot think of the word. Bucket? You don't get to know. Not now. If something happens, it'll all make sense. If it doesn't . . . It will hopefully never make sense. Think of it as a training exercise. Which we by God *need*. Any other questions? I've killed a few infected tonight. With a kukri. I'm in a good mood."

"No, ma'am."

"Roberts, this one's too close. Just run her over. Following teams, body in the road. Don't get stuck . . ."

"Let's just park out here," Lance Corporal "Dutch" Van Rijk said, pulling the car to a stop on the runway of the airport. "We'll crank up the music and climb up on the car in a triangle. That way we can see them coming."

"Roger," Sergeant Hoag said, her jaw clenched. She

did not like being under the authority of a fucking lance corporal.

"In deference to your rank, Sergeant, if you've got an iPod you can pick the tunes..."

"Got one," Fumitaka said. "Closing."

"Wait for it to get close," Dutch said, looking over his shoulder. "You don't want the round hitting somebody in the distance."

"Aye, aye," Fumitaka said. He waited until the infected was twenty meters away and fired. And fired again. "It ain't stopping."

"Fucking Barbie guns," Van Dijk said. "Keep shooting."

Fumitaka put seven rounds into the infected, which stopped nearly at his feet.

"Shit," Fumitaka said. "Shit, shit, shit... That *sucked*."

"Try putting five rounds into their chest, fast," Dutch said. "That usually stops them. Or double tap, one to the chest one to the head. If the first one slows them down. Stand by, got one." He waited until the infected, a rather small woman, had closed. He put one round into her chest and another in the head. "That usually gets 'em."

"Usually?" Hoag said. "Shooting them in the *head* doesn't always work?"

"Eventually," Dutch said. "I've seen 'em keep coming even after they've been shot in the head."

"Firing," Hoag said. She put five rounds into the chest in rapid fire and was rewarded with an infected that *wasn't* at her feet. "Yeah, that worked."

"Good training, huh?" Dutch said.

"Good training."

"By the way, Sergeant," Van Dijk said. "With due respect, I like your taste in music."

"Thanks."

"I think we got one chasing us, Sergeant," PFC Jesse Summers said.

"Okay," Hocieniec said, slowing to a stop. "Get out and kill it."

Summers opened the back door of the 1980s Malibu and stepped out into the darkness.

"I swear it was right..." she said as the infected popped up around the back of the car. "Shit!"

She fired two rounds and the infected grabbed her, biting at her neck and shoulders.

"Pistol," Hocieniec said watching from the other side of the car. "Or knife."

The infected suddenly slumped to the ground as "I'm shot in the heart" finally got through to the brain.

"Or you can wait for it to die," Hooch said, shrugging. "That works, too."

He slammed into the car as a big infected hit him from behind.

"Fucker," Hocieniec said, pulling his pistol. He put it into the hip of the infected and pulled the trigger. The zombie let out a howl and fell on the ground, writhing. Two more rounds put it out of its misery. "Okay, everybody pick a sector and let's just see how many come to us..."

"*Shewolf, Hocieniec, over.*"

"Go, Hooch," Faith said. They'd stopped the truck and had Barnard and Edwards out as security.

"We got stuck on a dirt road and sort of got swarmed, over."

"Define swarmed, over."

"Uh... You remember Tenerife?"

"Hot diggity dog," Faith said. "HEY, LOAD UP! On our way, Hooch. I don't suppose you know where you are?"

"Sort of..."

"Shewolf, Annapolis, over."

"Hear you, *Annapolis*," Faith said as the staff sergeant loaded into the vehicle.

"Our intercept gear says they're up Albert Lake Drive near Long Pond, over."

"Staff Sergeant," Faith said. "Find that. Thanks for the steer, *Annapolis*."

"Good entertainment as always, Shewolf. Sorry to hear about your casualty."

"He'll make it," Faith said. "Somebody told me one time this wasn't a safe job. Pretty sure Goodwin knew that, too."

"Head up to the medical school," Staff Sergeant Barnard said. "That way..."

"Oh, holy shit," Edwards said.

"Now that's what *I* call a concentration," Faith said, gleefully.

The Kia sedan the three Marines had squeezed into was covered in infected. The miracle was that the windows hadn't broken under the weight.

"Hocieniec wins the bottle of good hooch!" Faith caroled on the general circuit. "None of you bastards better get in here and ruin my fun. Stay on your sectors. We got this."

"Ma'am, with due respect..." Barnard said.

"I'm not going to use the God-damned machine gun, Staff Sergeant," Faith snarled. But she wasn't sure *what* to do. With the infected literally covering the vehicle, a fifty-caliber round would go through an infected, the occupants and the engine block. The question was how to use *any* weapon against them without hitting the occupants. "Oh, fu—fornicate it."

Faith jumped out of the gunner's ring, slid down the windshield of the truck, then onto the ground.

"Do *not* run me over, Edwards," Faith radioed. "HEY! FRESH MEAT!" she screamed, waving her hands over her head.

"Fuck," Barnard said, rolling out of the truck.

Faith had drawn her .45 and was servicing targets as the infected, blinded by the truck's lights, turned from the unavailable meat and headed to apparently easier pickings. She dropped the pistol and clawed another out of her chest holster as the infecteds closed.

Barnard had barely gotten out of the truck when the lieutenant was swarmed.

"...sometimes I get overcome thinkin' 'bout..." Faith sang, slamming a trench knife into an infected's face. "...makin' love in the green grass..." The trench knife sunk into a throat as she fired her .45 single-handed into a stomach. "...behind the stadium..." Another pistol hit the ground and her third and last came out. "...with you, my brown-eyed girl... Wait. Does singing this make me gay?"

"Fuck, fuck, fuck," Barnard said, wading in with her Ka-Bar.

She found it surprisingly hard to kill this infected with a knife. She couldn't seem to get it to stop struggling and it was a woman, not even her size. She suddenly realized that the little bitch really was unbelievably deadly, since in the time it took her to finally stab the infected to death the lieutenant had killed three.

"Stab *up*, Staff Sergeant," Faith panted, firing into a belly. "And you might want to use the pistol in contact instead."

The Ka-Bar slid out of Barnard's blood-covered rubber gloves and she scrabbled for her pistol as an infected tackled her.

"How can you stay on your *feet*?" Barnard snarled as she fired the 1911 into the infected's chest.

"The same way you get to Carnegie Hall, Staff Sergeant," Faith said. "I also play a fair trombone."

The three-man team had finally bailed out of their vehicle and with them wading in they made quick work of the remaining infected.

"Tha' was a fair dinkum scrum, mates!" Faith caroled as she helped the staff sergeant to her feet. "Fair dinkum an ah! So far you win the prize."

"Can we get it *tonight*, ma'am?" Hocieniec asked. "I couldn't figure out how to kill them from inside the car."

"Shoot through the window next time," Faith said. "O— oorah. Staff Sergeant?"

"Ma'am," Barnard said, bent over and panting.

"This vehicle needs extracting," Faith said. "Put out security and handle it. I'm going for a walk. Oh, zombies! Zombies, zombies, zombies? There's a poor little girl all alone and lost in the woods..." She wandered back down the road continuing to call. "Ooo! Ow! I think I twisted my aaankle..."

"Lance Corporal," Barnard said, still bent over. She straightened up and twisted her neck. "You and Rock take security. Haugen, there should be a tow strap in the back of the five-ton. Hook it up to the car."

"Aye, aye, Staff Sergeant," Haugen said.

"Lance Corporal," Barnard said.

"Staff Sergeant?"

"I'm going to need a shot of that hooch."

"Aye, aye, Staff Sergeant! Miss Faith is a tad nuts, Staff Sergeant. But you get used to it. Have you met Trixie, yet?"

"Okay," Sophia said through her mask. They were working in Tyvek suits and air masks to avoid contaminating the interior. "Seal it up. Put fricking rigger tape *everywhere* and seal it tight..."

Cleaning and securing the five-ton had been a bitch and a half even with the powerful spots of the *Grace Tan* illuminating the scene. For one thing, the flies that always hovered around fresh kills were all over the place and with all the light they were active. For another there was the wind, which was from the land so it was carrying dust and potentially flu. They had finally just turned the five-ton around so the back was pointed at the *Grace Tan* and away from the land.

"Staff Sergeant Decker," Sophia said. "Thank you for your assistance in this."

The staff sergeant and his sidekick Condrey had, in fact, been of assistance. A pain in the ass but a necessary one. He had insisted on going over every inch with a toothbrush. At one point there had been seven people in the back of the vehicle scrubbing every square centimeter to the staff sergeant's painfully precise direction. But if it wasn't perfectly antiseptic, it wasn't for lack of trying.

"Staff Sergeant, moment of your time," Sophia said, walking away from the five-ton.

"Aye, aye, ma'am," Staff Sergeant Decker said, following her over at a slow march.

"This is not for dissemination," Sophia said. "We are going to have to get seven people from a vehicle into the five-ton without contaminating them or the interior of the five-ton. We then are going to have to drive it back, back it onto the *Grace Tan* and get them into the container that the *Grace Tan* is preparing. I'm going to leave that last up to Mr. Walker and the *Grace Tan* crew. Getting them out of the vehicle, which will be somewhere on the island, and into the five-ton, without contaminating the interior, concerns me."

"Yes, ma'am," Decker said, frowning. "What type of vehicle, ma'am?"

"Think an Apollo moon lander," Sophia said.

"Ma'am . . ." Decker said, then froze.

"No ideas?" Sophia asked.

"No, ma'am," Decker said. "No ideas, ma'am."

"We'll figure it out when we get there, then," Sophia said with a sigh. "I'm going to need you and Condrey to accompany me. And we're going to need lots of plastic and tape I guess. We'll need to decontaminate the suits again but we're going to be going onto the *Grace Tan* in a bit. We'll get out of them and then suit back up later."

"Aye, aye, ma'am," Decker said.

"I'm calling this exercise complete," Sophia said, pulling off her mask. "Fall into the *Tan* with Condrey and unrig."

"Yes, ma'am," Decker said.

"Soph?" Olga said as the staff sergeant marched back to the *Grace Tan*.

"Yeah, Olga?" Sophia said. It would be a nice night if it wasn't for the smell of iron and shit and the occasional burst of fire in the distance. Okay, the fire wasn't so bad. She *really* didn't want to try to extract the ISS crew with infected swarming. On the other hand, she didn't want Faith getting shot by her undertrained Marines.

"What the hell is going on?" Olga asked. She'd pulled off her mask as well.

"Thanks for waiting till now to ask," Sophia said with a sigh. "I appreciate you just going along with the madness. The answer is, I can't tell you."

"Oh, come on," Olga said. "What the hell could be that important?"

"Olga, you're smart," Sophia said. "Why in the hell would we be *thoroughly* clearing an *entire* island while simultaneously preparing a germ-free transport vehicle? Why did we carry a container that was just as thoroughly decontaminated and has an air lock? And when you figure that out, ask yourself why in the hell we're keeping the reason secret. And until you can answer *that* one, don't talk about it, okay? If by tomorrow at noon there's no apparent reason for all this . . . Then if you think you've figured it out you'll also understand why we're just calling it a training exercise."

"None of that makes any sense," Olga said darkly.

"Like I said, you're smart, you'll figure it out," Sophia said. "There is a reason. Now keep an eye out for the returning Marines. We can't fall back onto the ship till my sister gets here . . ."

CHAPTER 18

So you must carry this light into the darkness
You shall be a star unto the night
You will find hope alive among the hopeless
That is your purpose to this life

—"Sophia"
Crüxshadows

"Do not, say again, do *not*, contaminate my truck," Sophia said, standing at the base of the pier with her hand out. "We're bringing in Zods to clear you off."

"Do we have something set up to *clean* us off?" Faith asked, holding her arms out for a hug. "I sort of got covered in blood again."

"This was not the night to be scrumming, Sis, you know that," Sophia said, shaking her head. "Stay away from me."

"Feel the love," Faith said as the Zodiacs came into the beach. "You getting while the getting's good?"

"All your people here?" Sophia asked. "*Tan*, we'll need wash-down for the Marines. They've been scrumming."

"We found the lost ones courtesy of sub intercept systems," Faith said. "Who knew they were so accurate?"

"Omaha, radar locked on predicted track..."

Commander Isaac Luallin, skipper of the SSBN USS *Tennessee*, wasn't having the best week. Or month. Or for that matter year.

Ballistic nuclear submarines are all about risk aversion. Not for them the chasing other boats, doing hull shots, sneaking into the back yard of other powers. No, SSBNs were all about finding a big, empty, deep patch of water and disappearing. For months. Drive slow, stay deep and pray that you never have to actually do your job.

They had in fact been doing pretty much that since the Plague was announced. Even after the SSNs started "assisting" Wolf Squadron, the SSBNs had pretty much stayed in their patches except for the occasional, necessary, fishing expeditions. At one point they got an alert to stop even that when the Soviet general in charge had gotten frisky and ordered some of his remaining SSNs to hunt U.S. subs. According to the Hole that had come to nothing when the subs mutinied and the general had "retired." Apparently he'd committed suicide by shooting himself in the back.

They were finally going to get to help out and... now all they could do was radar support. So they'd surfaced and put up the radar mast.

"Roger *Tennessee*," the "controller" in Omaha replied. "Incoming ballistic track predicted for five minutes. Stand by..."

Luallin locked the periscope on the predicted track and connected it to the crew monitors. No reason not to. Unless it failed, which would be icing on the damned cake.

∽⊖∾

"When do we bring it up openly, sir?" Faith asked. She was freshly showered and back in MarPat. By the end of the sweep they were finding zero customers so the plan was for them to land in standard "light fighter" gear, not bunker gear.

"When we have to," Hamilton said. "Stand by . . . Roger. So the answer is: Now. Listen up, people!" he bellowed. "Look to the west and up at sixty degrees." He pointed and raised a pair of binoculars. "Anybody see anything different?"

"I've got an inbound ballistic track on projected heading," the *Tennessee*'s radar tech said. "Forty-five thousand feet. Seven point five six kilometers per second. Decelerating . . ."

"There it is," Commander Luallin breathed, watching the monitors. "Son of a bitch. It's past the plasma zone."

"Go baby go," the chief of boat said.

"I've got radar lock by six boats," the digital compliance technician said. "Track is as predicted to ninety-eight percent."

"Let's hope ninety-eight is good enough," Brice said, grimacing. "At that range, ninety eight is *miles*. Miles as in in the drink."

"Is that it?" Faith said, pointing up. "By that red star?"

"That's Mars," Sophia said, scanning the sky. "And . . . yeah. That's it. Look for the two red stars people. One of them is an inbound space ship!"

"It's lit up," Faith said. "Fire?"

"They're well past the plasma stage," said Colonel Hamilton. "It's reflected sunlight. Red because the sun's about to come up. It will disappear in a minute. That's when it gets tricky."

"Okay, now it's making sense," Sergeant Smith said.

"They're trying to land on the island," Sergeant Hoag said. "Son of a bitch. So why couldn't they tell us?"

"'Cause if it didn't work, it'd be another morale blow," Faith said from behind them. "But that's why we had to land at night and thoroughly clear the island. And now we're going to be providing security for an extraction team. Assuming it lands on the island."

"When will we know, ma'am?" Sergeant Smith asked.

"The subs are surfaced," Faith said, pointing out into the channel. "They're following it on radar. Since they could find you to the meter, I figure they can probably find where it landed."

"Ma'am," Sergeant Smith said thoughtfully. "If they are coming down by parachute, they'll need winds aloft."

"I understand that Mr. Walker figured that out, Sergeant," Faith said drily. "Believe it or not, some of your superiors do have a clue, Sergeant."

"Yes, ma'am," Smitty said. "Understood."

"Shit, it *missed*!" Lance Corporal Ferguson snarled as the capsule passed overhead. It was clearly headed for the channel on the far side of the island. A moment later it winked from view as it dropped out of the sunlight.

"Winds," Sergeant Smith said, scanning to the southeast. "It's going to drift with these winds..."

"There," Faith said, spotting it again. "You can see the chutes..."

ॐ ⊖ ॐ

"Drift is in predicted track," the compliance tech said. "I think. Sorry, General, not precisely my area of expertise."

"At this point we just have to wait and hope," Brice said. "The reentry worked and the parachutes worked. That's better than we had any reason to expect."

Commander Luallin had slaved the camera to the radar track and now widened the field of view, trying to get some perspective. He looked at the radar track and frowned.

"I think it's going to miss," he said. "Certainly the primary LZ."

"It's going to be close, sir," the COB said.

"In this case, a miss is truly as good as a mile," Luallin said.

"Oh, shit," Faith muttered. "Oh, shit. Oh, shit. Oh, shit..."

The main chutes had deployed at four thousand feet with the capsule well over the island. But the strong tropical wind had it moving northwest at a high rate of speed.

Straight at the flotilla.

"That thing's got rockets on it," Faith said. "If they fire over *us*..."

"Won't, ma'am," Smitty said as the capsule continued to descend rapidly. "Where was the LZ?"

"By that pond in The Valley," Faith said.

"Not going there, ma'am," Smitty said. "I think it's going to hit by the airport..."

The dimly perceived capsule dropped from view

and there was a massive fire signature as yellow-orange flames and smoke poured into the predawn darkness.

"Rockets fired," Smitty said. "That's a good sign."

"I think the Dragon has landed," Colonel Hamilton said.

"*All personnel,*" the tannoy boomed. "*Stand by . . .*" There was a crackle of static.

"*Hello?*" an unfamiliar voice said. "*Anyone listening? We're down in one piece . . .*"

"*Dragon, this is Omaha. Good to hear your voices again. We're sending in a rescue party as soon as we're sure the fires are under control.*"

"*Roger, Omaha. We'll just lie here, then. Gravity is taking a little getting used to.*"

"*Subs, go to closed frequency. Omaha, out.*"

"And that is that," Hamilton said, looking into the darkness. "I don't even see any fires, yet." He touched his radio key. "Omaha, this is Kodiak Force Commander. Request direct contact, Dragon crew. We need to touch base . . ."

"*This platform is pretty bare bones,*" Mission Commander Ollie Daniels said. "*Not that I'm complaining or anything. But we've only got walking around bottles. We'll need air in about forty minutes or have to pop the hatch. According to Doc Gordie and Doc Riz, while we're immune compromised, very slight contamination shouldn't harm us. And the blast zone should have cleared contaminants from this immediate AO.*"

He sounded remarkably calm for a guy who was depending on people he didn't know to save him from a plague in a zombie apocalypse.

"We're doing all we can to make 'slight' contamination

equal zero," Colonel Hamilton said. "But roger on the air situation. We'll go ahead and punch our force now rather than waiting for daylight."

"Suit up," Hamilton said, looking at Walker. "You're going to have to figure out a procedure when you get there."

"We've got spare plastic, tape and tubing in the second five-ton," Walker said. "We'll kludge something up. I'm putting the ensign, Decker and Condrey in the sterile five-ton. Decker and Condrey are . . . used to handling human bodies even if the conditions are difficult. I'll remain on the outside to handle setting up the transfer system."

"That makes a tremendous amount of sense," Hamilton said. "But why am I not surprised? Good luck."

"Holy crap," Faith said. "There it is."

The capsule had clearly once been bright white. It was now mildly fire scorched. But the Space X logo was brightly noticeable on the side. It also was bigger than she'd expected. It was nearly three stories tall or so it seemed. The hatch was more than a tall man's height off the ground. And there was no convenient ladder.

The capsule was canted at a slight angle on a hill near the airport. The scrub around it was on fire but the fire seemed to be burning out by itself.

"Stop here," Walker said as they approached the spacecraft. "Marine units, deploy and get those fires out. Navy decon teams, stand by."

"Grab the fire extinguishers," Faith yelled, bailing out of the front of the five-ton. The back was packed with Marines and the Navy away team. "We need to get these fires out. But I think the fire truck was overkill..."

The sea grape and tantan in the area had apparently had some recent watering as the fires were only smoldering. The Marines spread out with heavy-duty extinguishers and had the ones that threatened the approach out in minutes.

"Sir, we have the approach fires out but the ground is still hot," Faith said. "Not sure what to do about that unless we go try to find the fire truck."

"Keep putting fires out, Shewolf," Walker said, clambering out of the front of the five-ton. He was wearing a moon suit and had a hard time watching his step. "Don't worry about the hot ground. Ensure that we've got security. These fires are sure to draw any remaining infected, and I don't want blood contaminating this environment."

"Aye, aye, sir," Faith replied.

"Decon teams," Walker continued. "Set up east of the septic five-ton. Sterile five-ton will remain in place until we've got the situation under control."

"Roger, sir," Sophia replied.

"I'll just sit here in the darkness, then," Sophia added sotto voce.

Decker, Condrey and she were in the back of the "sterile" five-ton. Five-tons have a canvas top and "rear closure" system with a drop tailgate. The tailgate was up and the canvas "rear closure system" was in place, making the interior dark as a cave. In addition, the entire interior had been covered in plastic and sealed to a fare-thee-well. If they hadn't had air bottles they would have used up the oxygen in the interior.

"What was that, ma'am?" Decker asked, sitting on the personnel bench at the position of attention. Which was tough with a fire fighter's silver suit.

"Just proud to be here, Staff Sergeant," Sophia said loudly.

"Put it right there," Sergeant Major Barney said, pointing to a spot next to the "septic" five-ton.

"Roger, Sergeant Major," Hadley said, laying down the child's tub.

"Wait," Barney said. "Hold it up. Get the water into it while it's off the ground at first. The ground is hot. If it burns through the tub, you are all in the shitter."

"Aye, aye, Sergeant Major!" Seaman Apprentice Yu, said, pouring a five-gallon can of water into the tub. Olga walked up with a bleach bottle in either hand and added to it. She, too, was wearing a moon suit. When there was water on the bottom, Hadley set it down.

"Take off the bloody *caps*," Sergeant Major Barney said. "You're not filling canteens..."

"That's enough," Walker said as Yu poured another five gallon bucket of bleach water over his suit. "All septic personnel back away. Sterile five-ton."

"*Sir?*" Sophia replied as there was a shot in the darkness.

"Stand by, security team?"

"One infected," Faith said. "Down. Well away from the capsule. Situation still clear, sir."

"Roger. Sterile five-ton will back up to the capsule

taking my hand and arm signals. That's not you, Ensign, that's Lance Corporal Edwards."

"*Aye, aye, sir,*" Edwards said.

"Stand by, Edwards, and listen. I want you to get lined straight up to the hatch on the capsule. Do you even know where that's at?"

"No, sir."

"Unass from the vehicle and come out here," Walker radioed.

Edwards jumped out of the vehicle and at Walker's direction walked around the capsule, keeping a distance, and found the hatch, which was at two o'clock from their approach.

"Can you back up to that?" Walker shouted.

"Aye, aye, sir!" Edwards said. "I can put it right up to it."

The back of the five-ton was, conveniently, about the same height as the hatch. In fact, with the tailgate up, the top of the tailgate would just about be at the level of the bottom of the hatch.

"I will ground guide," Walker shouted. "Watch my hand and arm signals."

"Aye, aye, sir!" Edwards said.

"Let's get a move on," Walker said, then changed frequencies. "Any sub retrans to the Dragon capsule. Do *not* pass this message to *any* squadron personnel..."

"*Dragon, incoming call from Thomas Walker for Mission Specialist Troy Lyons, over.*"

"Uh, Roger that," Commander Daniels said, puzzled. "You're up, Troy."

The mission commander was a forty-five-year-old Canadian, six two and formerly a hundred ninety pounds, with sandy blond hair and blue eyes. A former Canadian Air Force fighter pilot, he had a master's degree in mechanical and aviation engineering.

"Thomas Walker?" Lyons said. The mission engineer was American, stocky with dark, nearly black, brown hair and equally blue eyes. A former SEAL, he had degrees in mechanical and oceanic engineering and had been on his second trip to the ISS as one of the onboard mechanical systems engineers when the world came apart. There went his shot at being mission commander.

"*Trojan, it's Skaeling,*" Walker radioed. "*Night Walker. Do not reply with my name. I'm using a cover for various reasons. Short explanation: While I obviously outrank Captain Smith, Wolf Squadron is a cult of personality. People know Captain Wolf. I've been careful to ensure that nobody knows who I am other than, well, upper echelon. Taking over would not work and I'm frankly enjoying just helping out. So when you see me, do not react. Understood?*"

"Roger, sir," Troy replied. "Is it okay to say I'm glad to hear you made it, sir?"

"*Glad you made it too, Troias. This world was made for people like us. Walker out.*"

"Walker?" Colonel Kuznetsov asked.

"All I think I should say is he was involved with U.S. Special Operations," Troy replied. "I met him when I was with Joint Special Operations Command."

"Sounds like just the man for a zombie apocalypse," Dr. "Doc Gordie" Price said. The mission medic was an MD with specialties in diving and astronautic medicine and a Ph.D. in astrophysiology. "Any notable negative symptoms, yet?"

"I am rather missing microgravity," Dr. Rizwana "Doc Riz" Shelley said. The Pakistani born physicist, a naturalized British citizen, was five foot four with black hair and light brown eyes. She had taken a sabbatical from her position with Reading University for the mission. She had Ph.D.s in astronomy, astrophysics, physics, nuclear physics, chemistry, biology, biochemistry and, notably, microbiology. She'd been a researcher in microbiology at Reading as well as a tenured professor. Besides assisting her husband, Thomas Shelley, on his experiments on the mission, she had been managing ongoing microbiology experiments on the ISS. "On the other hand, it has been some time since I've had a tropical vacation."

"Be a while till we can get out and enjoy the breeze," Dr. Price said.

"After six months, ten to fourteen more days I can do," Varfolomei Matveev said. The mission engineer was five foot six with black hair and blue eyes. He was a former fighter pilot with the Russian Air Force as well as a rotary wing pilot with a degree in mechanical engineering. "Is it reasonable to be worried about the vaccine we've been promised?"

"Very," Dr. Price said. "All we can hope is that there will be sufficient information to make a rational decision. Not that we have many choices in the matter."

There was a bang on the capsule and it rocked slightly. The light from the hatch porthole cut off with finality. Fortunately, there were two more portholes. The interior lights had been shut off on landing to conserve batteries but there was plenty of reflected light. It was apparent that there was a truck or car shining its lights on the capsule.

"And I think the five-ton has landed," Troy said. "Whatever happens, we're definitely entering a brave new world."

"I'm hoping for some news of home," Rizwana said.

"From what little we were getting from Omaha, that is unlikely," Commander Daniels said. "I'm sure we'll get more information soon."

"I'm just hoping for a cheeseburger," Troy said. "I'd even take an MRE at this point."

"That sounded like another shot," Tom said.

"The island was certainly inhabited by infected," Commander Daniels said. "We have to hope that a person with experience in special operations would have cleared it as thoroughly as possible."

"Tape two PVC tubes running from the capsule to the top of the five-ton," Walker said. "Then we'll drape the sheets. Shewolf?"

"Still all good, sir," Faith replied. "That was a dog. I authorized it to keep the area from getting messed up."

"Good call, Shewolf," Walker said. "Okay, let's get the plastic up ..."

CHAPTER 19

Do not injustice to another
Defend the weak and innocent
Let truth and honor always guide you
Let courage find the light within

—"Sophia"
Crüxshadows

"Ensign Smith, time to open the plastic . . ."

They'd pulled the contaminated canvas cover off, first, leaving only the plastic covering the back in place. They'd also laid plastic over the tailgate to keep contamination from entering the vehicle.

Decker carefully removed the plastic from the back of the five-ton and Sophia leaned over and looked in the hatch. There was barely any light in the interior but she could see some couches and figures.

"Sir," she radioed. "Do they have lights in there? We can't see a thing."

"Stand by, Seawolf," a voice said, breaking into the circuit. *"Retrans to the Dragon capsule coming up."*

"Hello. I'm the person knocking on your window. Ensign Sophia Smith, United States Navy. You guys ready to get out?"

"Take me to your leader," Commander Daniels radioed, jokingly. *"Yes, we are prepared to exit. We can get the hatch open but we will need assistance exiting the capsule."*

"The United States Naval services have got you covered," Sophia said. "I've got two hulking Marines ready to carry you out. Carefully. You guys got interior lights?"

"Coming on," Daniels said, turning on the lights.

"Ouch," Sophia said, blinking. The lights were bright to her dark-adjusted eyes. "Open the hatch. We've got plastic up to prevent contamination."

There was another shot in the distance.

"What is the security situation?" Daniels asked.

"Don't worry," Sophia said. "My sister's got that covered."

"Sister?" Daniels said as the hatch popped open.

"It's a long story," Sophia said, sticking her head in the hatch. "Youngest Marine lieutenant in history and a pain in the ass. But she's got killing infected down."

There were seven cuplike blue couches arranged in two layers with aluminum foot rests at the end of each.

"Do these footrests fold down?" Sophia asked, clambering into the chamber.

One of the space-suited figures waved, then tapped his helmet.

"What?" Sophia asked, raising her hands, then realized that the previous conversation had been bounced from one of the subs. The crew could, presumably, retrans through a radio on the capsule. But when she entered, *her* radio was cut off. "Son of a bitch. Decker, can you hear me?"

"Yes, ma'am," Decker replied.

"You will repeat my words to the subs," Sophia said. "Repeat this exactly. Retrans sub. This is Seawolf. My commo is cut off in here."

"Retrans sub, this is Seawolf, my commo is cut off in here," Decker parroted.

"Staff Sergeant Decker will repeat."

"Staff Sergeant Decker will repeat."

She waited a moment for the process to be figured out.

"Is there a way to drop these footrests, over?"

"Roger. There is a latch. Slide the latch upwards while pushing upwards on the footrest," Decker said after a moment.

She picked one of the lower couches and dropped the footrest. Then she leaned over and undid the straps.

"Decker, repeat: You can all undo your own straps... I'm going to exit the vessel and let Staff Sergeant Decker and PFC Condrey take over. Decker: Do not repeat. Get in here so I can show you how this works..."

They barely had enough room for all the stretchers. And the threesome had to more or less balance *over* the crew. But they finally had all of them out.

Sophia shut the hatch on the capsule and then she and Decker got the plastic back in place.

"Mr. Walker, we've got the plastic up and taped on this side," Sophia said. "Need you to handle the rest."

"Roger," Walker said. *"Check to see how much air they have left. And check the connections on their air bottles. See if ours will work."*

"I'm not sure how to even talk to them," Sophia said. "Their radio was in the capsule."

"Put the face of your silver suit against their visor and shout," Walker said.

"Roger," Sophia replied.

She bent down over one of the figures, she wasn't sure which was who, and placed her visor on theirs.

"HOW MUCH AIR DO YOU HAVE?"

"TEN MINUTES!" the man replied. It was faint but he had a Slavic accent.

"Ten minutes, sir," Sophia radioed.

"Roger," Walker replied. *"Since when do you call me 'sir,' Seawolf?"*

"Since you're in charge, *sir*," Sophia said.

"Roger."

"WILL OUR AIR BOTTLES WORK?" Sophia asked.

"NO!"

"Might as well open up, then," Sophia shouted. "We're as sterile as we're going to get."

"Talk to him," the man said, pointing to one of the other suits.

"Hey," Sophia shouted to the second suit. "We decontaminated the hell out of this and were careful to keep it sterile. It's not a hospital room but it's as good as you're going to get. And we can't supply oxygen. So you're going to have to take your chances. We need you closed for the final transfer."

"Roger," the man said, opening his face plate and leaning over. It was apparent he couldn't sit up. "Time to crack."

The group tapped each other and slowly each of them opened their face plates.

"Welcome back," Sophia shouted through her silver suit. "I know you've all got questions but if you could hold them until we get you to your temporary home.

We fixed up a decontaminated container with as many decontaminated materials as we could find in the time we had. As soon as the canvas cover is back on we're going to drive there. We'll be backing onto a ship off a dock. Then you'll need to close your suits again. We'll get each of you out and decontaminate the outside of your suits, then get you into the container. Then you can get out of your suits. I don't know, nobody knows, if it's going to keep the flu out. All I can say is we're doing our best and we had the CDC and the Hole looking in on it. We didn't get much warning about this but, honestly, even if we had we couldn't have done much more than this."

The truck started and a moment later lurched into motion.

"Can you tell us what is going on?" the woman said. "How bad is it?"

"Generally people get how bad it is by my telling them I'm a fifteen-year-old ensign," Sophia said. "My sister is thirteen and she's a lieutenant in the Marines."

"A *lieutenant*?" one of the men said with a Slavic accent. "You are joking?"

"Faith's a bit of a badass," Sophia said. "But it's that bad. This is one of the few land areas that you can walk around with nothing but light arms. During the day. And we've been clearing it for about twenty-four hours straight. Total surface mobile manning of the U.S. Navy is less than a thousand. Total Marine Corps is fifty-three. Total known survivors, that is people that we're actually looking at, is right at six thousand. But several thousand of those are in subs and they're only survivors 'cause they're uncontaminated. There are no major land areas that are infected-free. And the 'Navy' and 'Marines' and all the rest is mostly former civilians or former military who have bootstrapped. I'm an ensign and my sister's a lieutenant 'cause we've been doing this right from the start. My specialty is small boat operations and rescue. Recently I've moved to trying to find the materials to make vaccine 'cause . . . I've got some background in bio. I hear one of you is microbiologist?"

"Yes," the woman said. "I am. Dr. Rizwana Shelley."

"Glad to meet you," Sophia said. "I thought I was going to have to do it on my own."

"You?" the guy who had ordered them to crack their suits said.

"Might as well know now," Sophia said, grimacing. "Just before the Fall I worked in an illegal corporate lab making attenuated vaccine. In fact, that's what you're getting. It's the same stuff I and my family used. Same lot even. It works. As long as it hasn't gone bad in six months. And it was stabilized. It was made by a professional. Overseen, anyway. I did most of the work."

"From what source?" Dr. Shelley asked carefully.

"Human," Sophia said.

"What a terrible business," Dr. Shelley said, shaking her head.

"Which is what we're going to have to produce to save the subs," Sophia said, shrugging. "If you've got qualms about that, well . . . I guess I'm going to have to do it, still."

"We're still adjusting to . . . reality," one of the Russians said. "Although, watching every light on the planet go out was . . ."

"Terrible enough," one of the men said. He had an English accent. "Truly horrible."

"Try fighting your way out of New York *when* those

lights went out," Sophia said. "My family is one of the few that is intact in the world that we know of. That makes us fairly unique. You're the only people in the world that haven't really *been* here for what happened. That makes *you* unique. Even the sub crews had a closer look at what went down. You don't wanna know horrible. There's a video. Watch that and then decide how you're going to help. Or not. Whatever. I've pulled over two thousand survivors over a transom or from the land. It was nearly three months after the Fall that I set foot on land and ninety percent of that time I was in command of a small boat. Which is one of the reasons they made me an ensign. I'm in command of *three* boats now.

"My sister has cleared ten liners, which is about the most horrible thing you can imagine. The first one, the second largest in the world, was with my da, a Marine that was barely out of a lifeboat, and an SF sergeant. They'd come out day after day covered in blood, get washed down, eat, sleep, go back in the next day. When I was working in the lab in New York, I couldn't do the first step which was, sorry, grinding the spines in a blender. At this point, it's not even in the top ten of the horrible stuff I've seen. Not sure if it's in the top twenty. Come to think of it, no, not in the top twenty. Probably not the top hundred."

"Okay," one of the men said after a moment.

"This is the tricky bit," Sophia said. "We're backing down this pier, which is almost exactly the width of the five-ton. So far we've done it a few times and not gone in the drink. If we fall over the side, just put your face plates back up. We'll figure it out. We always do."

∽⊖∾

"I'm trying to imagine what is more horrible than grinding up human spinal cords to make vaccine," Rizwana said. "I'm not sure I want to."

The container was, well, a container. It wasn't horrible but it wasn't great. The cushions they were lying on, still in their suits, were clearly salvaged from a boat. But there was a large plasma screen and someone had gone to the trouble of putting in two plexiglass windows. The large pile of MREs meant that clearly Troy wasn't going to get his beloved cheeseburger any time soon. There was a distinct odor of bleach, which was comforting, all things considered.

"And she's fifteen," Dr. Price said. "She has to have horrible PTSD."

"I think that pretty much everyone on the planet has to have PTSD," Troy said.

A silver suit came through the airlock bearing a large plastic box.

"Tomato soup," Ensign Smith said, setting it down. "Pretty much the most common first food we give survivors. These are microwave containers. They've been decontaminated and the box was sterilized. We're going to try to prop you up so you can drink it..."

"Sorry about my... discomfort with the vaccine concept," Dr. Shelley said. Decker and Condrey had gotten the astronauts propped up so they could drink, then left. "It must have truly been terrible."

"Was," Sophia said simply. "Is. World's a pretty messed up place right now. I'm sorry I reacted the way that I did. It has been a *very* long day. And we usually don't clear at night. That was fairly tense. We also had a friendly-fire incident today and I was worried that Faith was going to get hit by some of her Marines. All in all . . . I've had better days. But at least we got you guys back."

"When do you get off shift?" Troy asked.

"God knows," Sophia said tiredly. "Walker, Decker, Condrey and I are the only ones who are supposed to have contact right now. Walker and I 'cause we understand the protocols. Walker won't talk about his exact background but he was an SF medic. He's good. Very good. I think he was actually a colonel or something. Decker and Condrey because, well, the only thing they can really do anymore is very precise protocols."

"Why?" Commander Daniels asked.

"There are *so* many stories," Sophia said, shaking her head. "Short answer. Just before they evacced the *Iwo Jima,* Decker was ordered by his gunny to 'take care of the lieutenant.' He was a newbie LT. And he had the virus and he turned. So Decker and Condrey took care of him. Kept him alive. As a zombie. On a rubber life raft."

"Holy hell," Troy said. "Are they *nuts?*"

"They're Marines, sir," Sophia said. "They are sort of looked at as the epitome of Marines these days. But they're so totally inflexible at this point, they're only good for stuff that is very simple, very strict, protocols. Like, say, cleaning out the five-ton and sterilizing it thoroughly. So, yes, they're nuts. Sir, we're all nuts. I'm nuts. My sister is nuts. Every single survivor, pretty much, is nutty as a fruitcake. But we're getting the job done."

"Evacced the *Iwo Jima?*" Troy said. "The assault carrier?"

"Yes, sir," Sophia said. "Which we cleared right after the *Voyage Under Stars*. That's where we got about half our Marines."

"What about the other carriers?" Troy asked.

"They're scattered," Sophia said, shrugging. "Maybe the Hole knows where they are. But we're on a priority mission right now. You guys and trying to find materials to make more vaccine. And...when you can sit up you can see a wreck out the window, on the point. That's just one of...thousands. And more ships floating. Talk about oil slicks? Every tanker on Earth, pretty much, has gone aground or sunk. Seen some bad-ass oil slicks. And there's about four thousand of us, total. Only about three thousand are helping or any real help. Or sane enough to help. We got plenty of people in rubber rooms. So the rest of the world is going to have to wait. We just do what's in front of us and push the plan."

"What *is* the plan?" one of the Russians asked. "Is there one?"

"Clear the planet," Sophia said, shrugging. "Find survivors and convince them to help and just keep building until we're old and gray or we're done. Da says there's a plan, sort of. Won't get into it. Says he needs the sub crews to be able to get to the next step. So we're sweeping the Caribbean for medical supplies and stuff to make the vaccine. Notably polyacrylamide gel."

"That will be difficult to find, I would think," Rizwana said, sipping soup. "There was a great deal of research going on at the end and it was being used widely."

"A lot of it was going into vaccine production as

well," Sophia said. "Speaking of which, when Walker gets here we'll give you your primer shot. You can turn it down, given that it's from human spinal cords and has all sorts of other negatives. Various possible side effects include causing the disease, auto-immune reaction against your own nervous system and standard allergic reactions. In which case, we'll move you to a cabin to see if you turn. Which with your immune systems, you will."

"That's cold," Dr. Price said.

"There used to be seven billion people on this planet," Sophia said wearily. "Right now we know the condition of about six, seven *thousand*. Every coast is littered with wrecks. Some of them probably have trapped survivors in them who are running out of food and water and air and time. Every shore is patrolled by infected. Every town we've cleared has had about one percent survivors.

"You're astronauts. That's cool. You're all really smart and really capable with lots of degrees and stuff. That's cooler. God knows we need people like you and don't want you to turn or die. We can't keep you in a bubble until hell freezes over. We're holding here, instead of continuing the mission, to give you time to get vaccinated and have it take hold. Or turn. Which is a possibility. We don't want that. We need your skills, and who wants more zombies? But we haven't got all the time in the world."

"Understood," Commander Daniels said.

"So if you don't want the vaccine, the cabins are more comfortable anyway," Sophia said, shrugging again.

"And we'll get H7D3 and go insane," Tom said.

"Probably," Sophia said. "And we'll put a bullet in

you and in your case probably give you a nice funeral like we did for Anarchy instead of just letting your body be picked by the seagulls. Which is what we've done with several thousand other humans who turned. Probably tens of thousands, come to think of it. Beside the wreck, when you can stand up, you can see the pile of bodies my gunboat division created on this pretty beach. The more infected we kill, the more people we can save and maybe save civilization. That's how we roll. Welcome to Wolf Squadron."

"That is the most world-weary fifteen-year-old I have ever met," Tom Shelley said as Walker gave him the vaccine.

Doing so had required getting them out of their suits. All of the astronauts, besides being physically weak as kittens, were skeletally thin. But that was common with survivors. One wag had called the apocalypse "the best diet plan in history."

"More just weary," Walker said. "Seawolf is also one of the brightest young ensigns I've ever met. Her entire family is quite extraordinary."

"Is there some more detailed information we can get than 'it's really bad'?" Colonel Kuznetsov asked. "For example, is there any continuing Russian government?"

"Fourth Strategic Rocket Command," Walker said. "Although General Kazimov apparently committed suicide by shooting himself repeatedly in the back when he tried to order a nuclear strike on Washington."

"The world has gone utterly mad," Tom said.

"By definition," Walker said, straightening up after his last shot. "If you define sanity as what is normal for the standard human, then sanity is being an aggressive animal with no higher brain function, Doctor. I was in a pitch-black stores compartment for five months passing the time doing knot work. Besides the three people who succumbed to the virus in the compartment, I had to kill an additional member of the party when he went stark mad and began attacking people at random.

"There was some issue with hooking up the TV. On the outside of the container; they don't have to come in. When it's working, we'll run the basic brochure then the video they show new arrivals. It's rather good propaganda but it is also truth, which is odd for propaganda. When you view it you will get a new appreciation for that world-weary young lady. . . ."

CHAPTER 20

Stand up when no one else is willing
Act not in hatred or in spite
Be to this world as a perfect knight
Even if it means your life

—"Sophia"
Crüxshadows

"You guys okay?" Sophia asked as she entered the container.

"They finally got the TV working," Troy answered. "They just ran the Welcome to Wolf Squadron video." It was possible the former SEAL was the only one able to talk.

"Your family started this," Tom said.

"Yes, sir," Sophia said. "That shot of me in a suit was where I was working in New York producing vaccine. Like I said, I've pulled half the squadron over a transom. We'd get you all the other briefing stuff but it's paper and there's no good way to decontaminate it and ditto with moving a computer in here. I'm not sure what they'll be playing, next, but I hope you can hang in there with it. We're going to have to crash. After that, we'll be going to four-hour shifts until you guys are recovered and we see if the

319

vaccine holds. Shortest period for turning we've seen is three hours. So we're going to have to secure you while we pass out. Light restraints; you can get out of them if you're sane. Then Mr. Walker will be back in about four hours."

"We'll be fine till then," Dr. Price said. "One question. How many MDs have you found?"

"One," Sophia said. "You. Our other doctors are Lieutenant Fontana and Mr. Walker, who are both SF medic trained. There's one in the CDC who can talk us through stuff. Oh, and we've got seventeen hundred women who are pregnant and about to give birth."

"I'm not sure how many more shocks like that I can handle," Rizwana said.

"Here's another then," Sophia said. "We *had* eighteen hundred. We've lost about a hundred babies or their mothers to complications or miscarriages already. And when Walker isn't in here, he's running around the flotilla checking on the mothers. Including both of my subordinate skippers and six members of our boat crews. Last bit of news. We're moving, so you're going to have to put up with some motion. This beach is getting rather nasty so we're moving to a harbor that hasn't been shot up. Should take about an hour. Since I have to move *my* boat as well..."

She hung her head.

"See y'all tomorrow," she said, exiting the container.

"Sir, I've been looking at the map..." Faith said, her mouth half full of sushi.

The Marines had cleaned up after extracting the astronauts, eaten breakfast, then crashed. It was dinner time and Faith was still barely recovered.

In the interim the task force had moved to Rendezvous Bay. It was on the far side of the island from Road Salt Pond Bay and thus nicely away from the smell and sight of piles of dead bodies. Unfortunately, it was close to Blowing Point, which had been another clearance point. But even though the wind was from that direction, there was no real effect.

The bay was better in lots of ways. It had fewer wrecks and less mess than Road Salt Pond and there was, apparently, no fire damage. There were a couple of resorts in sight that looked almost as if nothing had happened.

"Remember those sayings, Lieutenant?" Hamilton said. "That sounds very much like 'I have an idea...'"

"I'm a second lieutenant not a first lieutenant, sir," Faith said. "But about the map, sir. This beach has another one of those salt ponds behind it. It's just a little strip of sand, sir. It's even narrower than that other anchorage was."

"I noticed that, Lieutenant," Hamilton said.

"Thing is, sir, we put out a couple of security points and infected can't really *get* to it, sir," Faith said.

"Thinking of hitting the beach for a tan, Lieutenant?" Hamilton asked.

"Thinking that most of us haven't had anything like a break in a long time, sir," Faith said. "So, yes, sir, that was sort of asking if the men could have some shore leave, sir. Since we're stuck here till the astronauts recover, sir. I was thinking about Christmas day, sir."

"How would you do it?" Hamilton asked, interested.

"One squad should be able to cover it, sir," Faith said. "One team at each end with the squad leader doing interior patrol as sergeant of the guard, sir. If we're here for a few days we could have them rotate one day on one off, sir."

"Why not Navy away teams?" Hamilton asked.

"I . . . don't run them, sir?" Faith said.

"The force has about the same number of Naval ground combat team members as Marines," Hamilton said. "How would you do it if you had them as well?"

"Not much different, sir," Faith said after a moment's thought. "Possibly have two shifts each day. I'd suggest that all armed personnel who go ashore, go ashore armed. But other than that . . . Just more free time, sir."

"How do you integrate the fact that people who go on liberty tend to drink?" Hamilton asked. "What about a reaction team?"

"I'm getting out of my depth, sir," Faith said.

"There's an outline for a standard liberty schedule in your inbox, Lieutenant," Hamilton said. "Along with our current TOE. I need the details filled in by zero eight hundred tomorrow. That way, people can have liberty on Christmas Day."

"You'd already thought of it, sir," Faith said.

"The definition of intelligence is generally said to be when someone has the same idea you have," Hamilton said. "I've found it to be when someone has a better idea. But you're getting there. . . ."

"Hi, folks," Hamilton said, looking through the plexiglass. There was an intercom with a hand mike set up. "I'm Colonel Hamilton, commander of Kodiak Force. Sorry I haven't made it down here before now. You all nominal?"

"Nominal, Colonel," Commander Daniels said, sticking up a thumb.

"Now that we've got the plasma running, we're working on getting you up on video with the Hole and suchlike," Hamilton said. "We also took the time to extract the seats from the capsule. Doctor, do you think those would be preferable if we can decontaminate them?"

"How contaminated are they?" Dr. Price asked.

"We used the same protocols to recover them that we used to extract you," Hamilton said. "They're in the five-ton, which you can't see is still parked right behind the container. We're just not sure if it's worth the risk. On the other hand, the bedding you are on just came off the cleanest boats we could find that didn't appear to have been opened since the plague broke out. We cleaned the hell out of them, obviously, but . . . *Those* have a higher likelihood of contagion than your capsule seats."

"More wonderful news," Dr. Price said. "The seats would be preferable. They're conformal and we actually need to be somewhat vertical to get our bodies adjusted to gravity."

"I'll have them moved in next shift," Hamilton said. "For general information on the progress of any potential contagion, our experience is that most people who turn start to do so in the first several weeks after exposure. According to Dr. Dobson at the CDC, with your reduced immune systems, that's more like three to five days. So if you're going to turn we should know in a week or so. I'm not trying to be depressing with that. Simply the realities of current existence."

"Understood," Dr. Price said. "We'd discussed on the station what was likely when we landed."

"We'd discussed simply reentering more or less at random," Commander Daniels said. "But the Hole assured us that all we'd find is infected."

"It really is all gone?" Rizwana said.

"It is," Hamilton said, simply. "This is the first place we've cleared that you reasonably can walk around with minimal arms and security. And it took a heck of a lot to make it that way."

"Even looking at the view at night," Tom said, shaking his head. "It's hard to believe."

"It's like that for people who were in enclosed spaces, even lifeboats," Hamilton said. "Cognitive dissonance and denial are fairly normal responses in the current environment. I was in a warehouse. When you can go out at night and there is not a light to be seen and no humans but infected...it's easier to believe and understand."

"Do you have family, Colonel?" Rizwana asked. "We have a daughter in England."

"Point of protocol is that that's generally not a subject of discussion," Hamilton said. "But since you did ask, I had to kill my wife and son, ma'am."

"Oh, my Lord, Colonel," the physicist said, her hand over her mouth. "I am sorry for..." she shook her head again.

"And that is why the subject of family *is* generally off-limits, Doctor," Hamilton said.

"What is the plan for us when we're recovered?" Matveev asked.

"You're probably all headed back to Gitmo," Hamilton said. "If you wish to help out, that's where you're most likely to be of help. We're on a rather specific mission. But back to Gitmo is the plan."

"What is going on there?" Tom Shelley asked. "I assume that the detainees have been released?"

"None of the detainees made it," Hamilton said. "At

the point that we were trying to manage their extraction, things pretty much fell apart. I'm assuming the few who were resistant were eaten by the rest or died in their cells of dehydration or starvation. It was not intentional, there was more effort put into securing the detainees than other, arguably more vital, issues. Like a lot of things, it just didn't work out. At the time I was handling other issues. Family among others. Guantanamo Bay is currently our only land base and it's not even fully secure, from what I've been getting. They're trying to get helos operational as well as building zombie traps. That's where all the building is happening and with the exception of Mr. Lyons, it's assumed that you all would prefer to be builders rather than this rather nasty but necessary destruction."

"Am I being reactivated, sir?" Troy asked, his eyes narrowing.

"Not if you are resistant, Mr. Lyons," Hamilton said. "Your mechanical expertise would be quite useful on the civilian side. But I've got a thirteen-year-old running my Marines and a fifteen-year-old running my Naval Landing Parties. Competently or they wouldn't be doing so. But you'll understand that I'm not going to turn down the help of a former Naval Special Warfare officer if it's offered."

"I'm not exactly in shape at the moment," Lyons said, raising his arm with some difficulty.

"That is what food and exercise are for, Mr. Lyons," Hamilton said. "My only gunnery sergeant, who is not here unfortunately, had to be carried off the *Iwo Jima*. He is currently again leading PT at Gitmo. Although they go running in combat gear since they occasionally run into infected who have penetrated the fences."

"You have helos," Kuznetsov said. "Do you have other aircraft?"

"The helos are yet to be certified for flight," Hamilton said. "That is where a good bit of my Marines are, working on them. As to other aircraft, there are no current plans to get airplanes working. The only strip we could use is Gitmo and possibly here. And we have virtually no mechanics qualified to work on most of them. Obviously, if we're talking about a Cessna, any of the Marine mechanics could fix one up."

"Any of us could fix one up," Commander Daniels said. "Well, most of us. *And* drive them."

"Captain Smith is concentrated on helos," Hamilton said thoughtfully. "There are planes at this airstrip. The ones at Gitmo are either too large to be viable—there's a Hercules there—or too complex. Most of the rest are corporate jets. But I suspect there are some smaller ones here. Probably not worth the effort, though. We don't do much in the way of reconnaissance and that would be about their only real utility."

"Critical parts and supplies?" Commander Daniels said.

"Scavenge and kludge," Hamilton replied.

"Seriously?" Lyons said.

"Pretty much what we do," Hamilton said. "Captain Smith noted to me that his master's thesis was on the Siege of Malta and the many work-arounds that were used to keep their aircraft flying. He holds the opinion that letting people scrounge in a situation like this, if not at will then widely, is more effective than trying to do everything by the book. So far it's working, so I suppose my boss has a point. It's a decidedly eccentric one, however."

"What about medical evacuation?" Dr. Price said.

"The most serious issue we've had on this float was an AD," Hamilton said. "Which was an abdominal through and through."

"Ouch," Troy said. "What happened?"

"As Lieutenant Smith said when I asked, we're taking undertrained Marines mixed with trained ones, few of them infantry MOS, and throwing them out into a chaotic environment," Hamilton said. "The short answer is one of them swept his buddy and jerked the trigger in panic. Mr. Walker—whose medical training was an intense but brief course thirty-some-odd years ago and about three years experience putting bandages on pimples—then opened him up like a trout and stitched everything back together as best he could remember. I'm given to understand he had someone hold open a copy of *Gray's Anatomy* while he was working."

"Jesus," Dr. Price said.

"The Marine is currently recovering in sickbay," Hamilton said. "So far the infection is under control. He has some rather spectacular scars but it appears he will live. And that more or less defines current reality. Dr. Price, ever delivered a baby?"

"I heard," Price said, sighing. "I'm hoping there are some obstetrics texts."

"We just raided the medical school on this island," Hamilton said. "They had some. Now we do."

"Any surviving faculty?" Tom asked.

"This is the first island where we have yet to find a single survivor," Hamilton said. "And we'd have found them by now what with one thing and another. We're not sure why this one had zero. We'd expected, statistically, to find twenty. But there were none."

"That is so sad," Rizwana said, shaking her head. "What London must be like."

"The ocean is made of tears, Dr. Shelley," Hamilton said. "The only thing we can do is keep lighting candles, one by one, and try to bring back the light. And with that, I really must bid you adieu. I have to go see a subordinate about a liberty schedule. The one benefit to being forced to stay in place is I can spend the free time giving my people some time off on Christmas Day before we institute a rather strict training schedule..."

"That is gonna cause one hell of an interesting set of tan lines," Sergeant Smith said, making sure his shades were in place so it wasn't obvious he was watching his jailbait boss.

Faith had just run down the beach to dive into the water wearing a blue bikini top, pink shorts, a trench knife and dual .45s in tactical thigh holsters.

"It's like Zombie Raider," Hooch said, shaking his head.

"But with a better butt," Smith said, then grimaced. "I'm going to hell for that, aren't I?"

"Yes, you are, Sergeant, yes, you are," Hooch said. "You're going to the *special* hell." He looked at his watch and lurched up. "Gotta go get it on."

"I'm not even sure the security is worth it," Smith said. "We haven't had a single incident all day."

"We were still shooting them last night," Hooch said, then shook his head. "Two nights ago."

"Hey, guys, why aren't you swimming?" Faith asked, walking out of the water and wringing out her hair.

"Uh, sharks, ma'am?" Sergeant Smith said.

"So far so good," Faith said, shrugging. "I think they're all over at Blowing Point getting stuffed. The water's great."

"Okay, ma'am," Smith said, getting up. He wasn't going to get out-oorahed by a thirteen-year-old even if it *was* Miss Faith. "I'm not sure about my M4, ma'am."

"Sling it over your back," Faith said. "We're going to have to clean the shit out of our weapons, anyway. And that way if there *is* a shark you can shoot it."

The water was gin clear and smooth as a mill pond. Smith was pretty sure that they'd see any approaching sharks.

He was also pretty sure he was going to the special hell.

"Can't catch me!" Faith said, splashing him, then diving away.

Smith stayed where he was.

"I'm trying for friendly uncle, here, ma'am," Smith said, wiping salt water off his face. "I'm not sure that fits in with playing chase games."

"If you're an uncle, you must be from West Virginia," Faith said, grinning. "At least from the look of your bathing suit."

"Crap," Smith said, turning around.

"Sorry, Smitty," Faith said. "That was sort of pushing the limit, wasn't it?"

"A bit, ma'am," Sergeant Smith said.

"It's like the only guys I meet are my subordinates," Faith said, frowning. "Not to dump on you, but it's sort of getting weird. I'm not, you know, gay. But there aren't any guys I meet who I like and I'm *not* the boss. Sorry to, you know...bitch I guess."

"Not a problem, ma'am," Smith said, frowning. "I guess it's kind of tough on you that way."

"I think Da did this on purpose," Faith said, darkly. "He *knew* I was going to go for the Marines so he put them all off-limits!"

"That, yeah, sort of sounds like a dad, ma'am," Smitty said, grinning.

"Not that I'm like super attracted to you or anything, Smitty," Faith said. "More like a brother kind of thing."

"That's cool, ma'am," Smitty said. "I can handle brother. Better than most of the alternatives."

"Hey, it's getting crowded." Faith's entry to the water had broken the ice, sort of. Plenty of people were still on the beach but there were more people getting in the water. "Let's go check out the resort."

"Ma'am, with due respect, are you nuts?" Smitty said. "It's outside the perimeter."

"This island is as clear as a liner after we're done," Faith said. "We've got guns."

"And no reloads," Smitty pointed out.

"Spare mags," Faith said, pointing to her pistols. Each holster had two integrated magazine pouches.

"One mag," Sergeant Smith said, tapping his slung weapon.

"There may be booze," Faith responded.

"With your permission, ma'am," Sergeant Smith said, "I'm going to go ensure that that largish resort is clear, ma'am. Prevent infiltration and all that."

"Well, you shouldn't go by yourself, Sergeant," Faith said, nodding. "I'll be your backup. Or maybe vice versa."

∽⊖∾

"Hey, Rusty," Faith said. "'Sup?"

"Hot as hell in all this gear, Faith," Seaman Apprentice Robert "Rusty" Fulmer Bennett III said, shaking his head. "Can't wait to get off."

"Have to talk to somebody older than me, Rusty," Faith said, grinning.

"Uh . . ." the seaman apprentice said, his mouth hanging open.

"Close your mouth, you're attracting flies," Faith said. "We're gonna go check out these buildings outside the perimeter. Don't shoot us."

"Uh, okay, Faith," Rusty said. "Is that safe?"

"No," Faith said. "But I figure somebody else is going to wander over there, and better me and Smitty than some civilian."

"Okay, ma'am," Rusty said.

"Hey, Rusty," Smitty said. "Check the time and pass this on to the Marines when they take over. If we're not back in an hour, send the reaction team."

"Okay, Sergeant," Rusty said.

"Jesus, Navy," Smitty muttered as soon as they were out of earshot. "And it's *worse* these days."

"The lack of 'aye, aye' you mean?" Faith said. "They're civilians that just raised their right hand. But they *did* raise their right hand, if you know what I mean."

"Hope he passes on the message," Smitty said. He had his M4 in a tactical carry position and was scanning the surroundings. "Should we be making noise, ma'am?"

"This one I'm not so sure," Faith admitted. She still hadn't drawn her side arm. "I wonder what's in here?" she said as they came to a container that had floated ashore.

"Please God, it's not illegal immigrants," Smitty said as Faith used her trench knife to pop the seal on the container.

The interior was filled with large plastic cases.

"Running shoes," Faith said, looking at the manifest. "Explains why it floated. This is useful. Maybe Rusty can find a pair in his size. Keep going?"

"Sounds good to me, ma'am," Smitty said. He'd turned to cover the lieutenant while she explored. "There's a small hotel up the beach."

"Trying to get me into a bedroom, Sergeant?" Faith asked.

"Now why would a brother do that, ma'am?" the sergeant asked.

The one-story hotel had a small pool half filled with green-tinged, debris-filled water. The rooms were mostly open and had been ransacked. Ditto the tiny bar and kitchen.

"What is this?" Faith asked, looking behind the bar. There was a cluster of . . . junk. Some blankets, children's toys, remains of what looked to be fish and maybe rats. Human bones. "Phew. Stinks."

"Looks like some sort of nest, ma'am," Smitty said.

"A survivor?" Faith asked. "No."

"Probably a zombie, ma'am," Sergeant Smith said. "Too nasty even for a kid."

"That's new," Faith said.

"We didn't really clear many houses in the Canaries, ma'am," Smitty said, shrugging. "Maybe that's how they live when they've got the materials."

"Point," Faith said, walking out of the open bar. "I

want to go check out the big resort before our hour's up. How come you said an hour, anyway?"

"Because that's about as much time as we should take, ma'am," Sergeant Smith said. "And if you're going off exploring, you make sure people know where you're going, ma'am."

"Point, again, Sergeant," Faith said.

"God," Faith said, looking down the long wading pool at the Cuisinart Caribbean Resort. "Why didn't I get to go places like this *before* the zombie apocalypse?"

The resort centered around a three-story building with a vaguely rococo style. A series of villas in the same style lined the beach. A large zero-edge pool led from the main building to the wading pool which continued nearly to the beach. On the west side of the pool were additional support buildings. The pool was flanked by a line of palm trees waving in the trade winds. At the beach, at the base of the wading pool, was a circular "beach bar" with a folding canvas cover. Prior to the apocalypse it had been a rather idyllic spot with a wonderful view of St. Martin in the distance.

The pool was again half filled with green-tinged water. The wading pool held barely a skim of water so foul she was pretty sure even the zombies wouldn't drink it. The lawns were covered in blown debris, mostly limbs and leaves, and a tropical storm had thrown the chairs and patio tables around in a helter-skelter mess. The canvas cover, despite having been folded down, was torn by the winds.

There was a small skull, some fine blonde hair still attached to it by a scrap of skin.

The one thing going for it was that there didn't appear to be any infected.

"I dunno," Smitty said. "A little paint, a little police call..."

"Let's see about the villas, first," Faith said. "I'd like some idea if we've got infected behind us."

The villas, however, were inaccessible. All of the windows and doors were covered with solid steel shutters that were locked on the inside. Even after circling one of them, they couldn't find an entrance that wouldn't require entry tools.

"Somebody was careful to prep this place," Faith said, standing by the westernmost villa's private pool with her hands resting on her hips.

"Yes, ma'am," Sergeant Smith said.

"Okay, main building it is," Faith said.

The main building was also covered in steel shutters but at some point someone had already broken in. The shutter on the main ocean-side doors had been forced open.

"Oh, not without a flashlight," Faith said, poking her head up to see through the opening. "No light. Well, not much."

"How's it look?" Sergeant Smith said.

"Zombies have been in there," Faith said, sniffing. "But...not a bunch or not real recently. Sort of trashed out but not bad...Sergeant, I think...we might have found a land base."

"I don't think we can secure it, ma'am," Smitty said.

"I'd want to have another night sweep," Faith said, musingly. She turned and headed back down the pool towards the beach. "But I'm not sure it's an issue anymore. I mean, by the end of the sweep, we were having almost *no* contact. The only leakers we had were two at the landing site and a *dog* for God's sake. I mean, face it, we need a secure land base, Smitty. Hell, think of this as a hospital for all the pregnant ladies."

"That . . . is an interesting point, ma'am," Sergeant Smith said.

"Be nice to fence it," Faith said, kicking a palm frond. "But that would take one hell of a lot of work." She stopped, bent over and pulled a brochure out from under the frond she'd just kicked.

Sergeant Smith quickly turned around to check six. Security and all that.

"Sweet," Faith said, continuing to walk as she perused the brochure.

"Ma'am, I think we're being followed," Smitty said quietly.

"From the Force?" Faith asked, looking towards the beach and the boats.

"No, ma'am," Smitty said. "I just saw movement by the main buildings. Too tall to be a dog, ma'am."

"So you're saying it's *not* clear?" Faith asked, not turning around.

"It's gone whatever it was," Smitty said. "But I'll back out if you don't mind, ma'am."

"SEAL spin," Faith said, drawing a pistol. "Rotate."

"Rotating," Sergeant Smith said.

They did a rotational movement, covering each other, until they reached the beach.

"Let's try to keep an eye on our back trail as we head back," Faith said.

They walked down the beach for a bit, passing the villas and Faith casually turned and picked up a shoe that was part of the debris.

"Saw it," Faith said. "Out of the corner of my eye. Darted into cover. Can still see it, though."

"Infected?" Sergeant Smith asked.

"Human, anyway," Faith said. She straightened up and tossed the shoe into the bushes. "Why can I never find a *pair*? Not to mention in my size. Yeah, I know, I've got big paws like a Labrador puppy. Let's go swimming."

"Ma'am?" Sergeant Smith said.

"Sling your weapon," the lieutenant said, holstering her pistol. "If we're playing in the water, maybe it will come down where we can get a better look."

"Yes, ma'am," Smitty said, slinging his weapon. "Uh, first one in the water is a rotten..."

Faith was already running.

"There it is again," Faith said as she came up out of the water.

"I am just not catching what you're seeing, ma'am," Sergeant Smith admitted.

"Young female," Faith said. She was apparently looking down the beach. "Black. I'm pretty sure it's an infected. Just not very aggressive."

"That would be a change," Smitty said.

"Let's head back to the official beach," Faith said. "I need to check in with Hooch. Oh, and I need some more sunscreen..."

"You want to do another night sweep?" Colonel Hamilton said.

"I want to get some training in, first, sir," Faith said, trying not to squirm. Sophia may have spent half the last six months developing her tan but Faith had spent most of it in uniform. A point she'd forgotten, along with regular application of sunscreen. She, fortunately, had fairly dark skin naturally despite being blond. She'd still picked up one heck of a sunburn. "Notably Close Quarters Battle training onboard the *Tan*, sir. Then some live fire, possibly on one of the nearby desert islands, sir. Then another sweep of the island, sir."

"To clear it," Hamilton said. "I'm not sure that's possible, Lieutenant. Not thoroughly."

"Not sure myself, sir," Faith said. "Not entirely. But it may be clearable enough to secure a land base. Somewhere for a ground hospital even, sir. It's in better shape, and more securable, than Gitmo, sir. It's an island, sir. Zombies aren't going to swim the channel, sir."

"Have anything to do with that world-class resort you and Sergeant Smith did an unauthorized reconnaissance of?" Colonel Hamilton asked.

"It wasn't unauthorized, sir," Faith said.

"*I* didn't authorize it," Hamilton said.

"Your Marine force ground commander authorized it, sir," Faith said.

"So, better to beg forgiveness than ask permission, Lieutenant?" Hamilton said.

"I'm not begging forgiveness, sir," Faith replied. "The orders for the landing party did not define that all personnel *must* remain within the confines of the secured zone, sir. During the landing, your ground force commander made the determination, based upon experience and the perceived threat level, that a low-support reconnaissance of nearby buildings was a low-risk mission, sir. And, sir, your ground force commander was correct, sir. Should I be begging forgiveness, sir?"

"I would not have authorized it, Lieutenant," Hamilton said.

"I understand that, sir," Faith said. "In the future I will keep that in mind, sir."

"And you really think it was a good idea?" Hamilton said.

"I'm sure you don't think so, sir," Faith said. "However, sir, having very briefly swept the two resorts, the smaller one by the main beach and the big one, I'm of the opinion that I could walk from one end of the island stark naked with maybe one pistol and not have a problem. Except I don't go around stark naked, sir. Obviously. Sir, I think this island is *clear*, sir. I mean, pretty much deserted. No real threats left. Or so close that I'm not sure we'd pull up leakers with one more sweep. We did detect one possible infected, sir. But it was . . . shy. It was following us but it was staying away."

"Really," Hamilton said, leaning back. "A shy infected doesn't seem . . ." He paused and frowned.

"My da ran into something similar one time, sir," Faith said. "Early on he made a covert landing on one of the small Bermuda islands. It's where he picked up his little helpers, sir. And he ran into a female that just ran away when he . . . sort of did like a chimp. Oook! Oook!" she finished, bowing up.

"So some of them are beta?" Hamilton said.

"Yes, sir," Faith replied. "Still not . . . word . . . sounds like sentence . . ."

"Sentient?" Hamilton said.

"Yes, sir," Faith said. "They're still not sentient, sir. But they're also nonaggressive. Or at least less aggressive. I'm not sure I'd want to try to catch one, sir. On the other hand... I had a clear shot at this one and didn't take it, sir. She didn't seem to be a threat, sir."

"Plausible," Hamilton said. "The human brain is a tricky thing. But that means the island is not clear."

"You saw how the zombies act, sir," Faith said. "Your pe—The personnel from Gitmo had more time watching zombies than any of the rest of us. They are territorial and only... swarm when there's an apparent food source, sir. Sort of like piranha. The... beta ones that are... smarter have probably learned to not even turn up for the feeding frenzies. Which means they avoid the normal attractors like light and sound, sir. On the other hand, based on this one and the one in Bermuda, they also are low-threat. Sir... we need a secure ground base, sir. I think we have one. Low yellow to... lightish green, sir. Yellowish green."

"Chartreuse?" Hamilton said.

"Excuse me, sir?" Faith said.

"Yellow with a touch of green, Lieutenant," Hamilton said drily. "Slightly more yellow and less green than lime or spring-bud. And, no, despite the recall of Don't ask, don't tell, I am not gay. Just into information."

"I would say more lime, sir," Faith replied. "More green than yellow."

"Perhaps spring bud, then," Hamilton said.

"Are we actually having this conversation, sir?" Faith asked.

"Not anymore," Hamilton said. "More important item. I've convinced Squadron that Gunnery Sergeant Sands is more valuable to us than to Guantanamo."

"Oorah, sir," Faith said.

"Oorah, indeed, Lieutenant," Hamilton said. "So he and the captain are on their way down. The captain wishes to talk directly to our astral visitors, and the gunnery sergeant will take over as platoon sergeant as well as running training. Issues?"

"No, sir," Faith said, a slight tone of surprise in her voice. "Looking forward to it, sir. NCOs handle training, sir. That's how it's supposed to be as I understand things, sir."

"I understand that you ran the training of the *Iwo* Marines, Lieutenant," Hamilton said.

"That was before the gunny was back on his feet, sir," Faith said. "And I wasn't an officer then, sir. And it was showing them the difference between regular clearance and zombie clearance, sir. NCOs handle training, sir."

"Very well," Hamilton said, ticking off an item on his checklist. "When the gunnery sergeant gets here he will coordinate training for all Marine personnel as well as Navy Landing forces with the appropriate senior NCOs on the Navy side. Once training is complete, or as complete as we can make it given time constraints, we will consider doing a night sweep as further supplemental training."

"If I may add, sir?" Faith said.

"Yes?"

"There are sure to be some liners tied up over in St. Martin, sir," Faith said. "No training like crawling around in the bowels of a ship, sir."

"They also take a good bit of time to clear, Lieutenant," Hamilton said. "And we are already well over our planned time for this sweep."

"Yes, sir," Faith said. "Permission to ask when the gunnery sergeant will arrive, sir?"

"They're supposed to be arriving this evening," Hamilton said. "Apparently they left Gitmo in your father's fast boat, then sent the message. If I'd had more warning I'd have had everyone do a nice GI party."

"Yes, sir," Faith said.

"As it is, we *will* have a greeting party," Hamilton said. "Go get with Staff Sergeant Barnard and have her ensure the greeting party is prepared. I'll have Sergeant Major Barney do the same on the Navy side."

"Yes, sir," Faith said.

"And that's it," Hamilton said. "We're on short time. Roll it, Lieutenant."

"Yes, sir," Faith said.

"Welcome aboard, sir!" Hamilton boomed, saluting Captain Smith.

"Thank you, Colonel," Smith said, returning the salute, then saluting the colors. "Very nice turn-out."

There was a line of sailors and Marines in surprisingly neat uniforms lined up to greet the arriving Commander Atlantic Fleet.

"Thank you, sir," Hamilton said, returning the gunnery sergeant's salute. "Pleasure to have you aboard, Gunnery Sergeant Sands."

"Thank you, sir," Sands said, running a gimlet eye over the Marine guard. He didn't look all that pleased. "Looking forward to joining your force, sir."

"Shall we repair below, sir?" Hamilton asked.

"Of course," Smith said. "Though, you'll need to get a working party together. We didn't just bring ourselves. One of the containers we opened was destined for a hospital in Ghana. It didn't have much in the way of materials to produce the vaccine but it did have useful medical supplies. So we arrive bearing gifts. What we could fit in the *Achille*. There's more on the way via the *Pit Stop*, which is following us."

"Yes, sir," Hamilton said. "Sergeant Major Barney. Manage that."

"Aye, aye, sir," the British sergeant major said.

"Get those to Mr. Walker, Sergeant Major," Smith said. "Now let's repair below. You lead, Colonel."

CHAPTER 21

Here I am
Alive among the injured and the dead
Here I am
Thy will be done
Santa Sophia (here I am)
Pieces borne to your victory
Athena Sophia (here I am)
Thy will be done

How can I hope to live
What I cannot dream?
You cannot map the ways of divinity
This much is known only unto God

—"Sophia"
Crüxshadows

"The materials on the *Achille* are mostly what Fontana thought Walker would need for a recovering gunshot wound," Captain Smith said as soon as they were seated in the colonel's office. "Notably, Keflex. I'm not putting that on you, by the way, Colonel. I didn't give you time to get trained before you went on the float and the short time your units had together was doing police call. In retrospect, I should have had the gunny run them through combat action training. My mistake. One I'm not prone to repeat."

"Yes, sir," Hamilton said. "My man, my failure, sir."

"Not if you were under other orders, Colonel," Smith said. "And it touches on one of the main issues I have, both upward and downward, with the current situation."

"Sir?" Hamilton said.

"In the pre-Plague military, that sort of thing could have been a career killer," Smith said, taking a sip of the scotch Hamilton had produced. "Just as this might be. It would depend mostly on politics, I suppose. But as with my decision to essentially not give out awards like so many Christmas presents, I'm trying to get both the newly inducted civilians *and* the professionals to grasp that this is *not* pre-Plague. The military culture can't be, exactly, pre-Vietnam in nature. We don't have the sort of personnel numbers to afford that degree of fatalism. We cannot *afford* a Somme or a Hamburger Hill. On the other hand, we also do not have an infinite supply of even *vaguely* trained officers and NCOs, so we can't kill any career over any fault without it affecting our overall efficiency. That, as much as any reason, is why I'm here. I have already pointed out to the Joint Chiefs that the blue-on-blue was as much my fault as anyone's and offered to retire in favor of Mr. Walker, whatever or whoever he is."

"I...don't see that working, sir," Hamilton said, frowning. "There are cultural psychology issues..."

"Which is sort of the point, Colonel," Smith said. "They said the same thing. Nor can I kill your career over it, demote you or something. It wouldn't be honest and I need *you* just as the Joint Chiefs need *me*. In fact, we can't even get all that down on PFC Curran. We're that short on Marines. And it was a training failure which falls on us, not the PFC. Now, if he can't seem to control his fire in the future..."

"He won't stay a Marine, sir," the gunnery sergeant growled.

"And where are we to get a replacement, Gunny?" Smith asked. "But that is probably the way to go. I leave it up to you two. The subject is closed except to say that you don't continue the mission until the gunnery sergeant is satisfied with the small unit tactical training of the Marine Force. We're going to have to be a bit more lenient with the Naval Landing Forces."

"They are...honestly about as good as could be expected, sir," Hamilton said. "Sergeant Major Barney has been taking their training in hand very well. And they're not used for missions that are..."

"Difficult?" Smith said. "I think you and I both realize that daytime clearance of one of these islands is not difficult by pre-Plague standards, Colonel. Which is another philosophical issue I brought up with the JCS."

"Sir?" Hamilton said.

"Does your career stretch back to Grenada, Colonel?" Smith said. "No, it wouldn't, would it?"

"No, sir," the colonel said. "Shortly before my time."

"It was, from all reports, an absolute cluster fuck," Smith said. "But the U.S. military learned from it. So was much of the Aussie response to the Indonesian quake, which I was in on. But we learned from it. The point is that the U.S. military got so good that it was expected to be able to perform any mission, anywhere, under any circumstances, and get it right, first time, every time. Which, surprisingly enough it was able to for some values of 'right.' An example is the essentially 'green' units in the first *and* second invasions of Iraq who *performed* like *veterans*. Do you know how historically insane that is, Colonel?"

"Yes, sir, I do," Colonel Hamilton said. "I read a paper on it from CGSC and had to agree with the conclusions."

"Which was the amount and reality of training," Smith said. "I think we read the same paper. The problem being, we no longer have the luxury that the DOD did to do that amount and reality of training. We don't even have *blanks* much less MILES gear, Simunitions, AirSoft, entire bases like Polk devoted solely to as realistic training as possible, et cetera. And we don't have the months that it takes or the people to do the training. We may occasionally get the false impression that things are going well. One look at a satellite map tells a different story. The *entire world* is bleeding every moment of every day. We have word that there are some other groups, similar if less orga-nized and still out of contact, doing something similar in other areas. But they are smaller and, as noted, disorganized and not in contact. They also don't have our resources and aren't close enough—they're in the Pacific—to get to them to help. We cannot afford six months of training to get your Marines to the elite level of pre-Plague Marine infantry. Even if we *could* do so with a group that is mostly composed of 'fobbit' MOS's. I don't think anyone questions the ability, in this world and our missions, of my daughter in terms of lethality and ability..."

"No, sir," Hamilton said.

"But she wouldn't have stood a *chance* in Marine Infantry Officer Course," Steve said. "I take it you agree with that as well?"

"Yes, sir," Hamilton said, shrugging. "Sorry, sir, but as good as Lieutenant Smith is—"

"She is both thirteen and female," Smith said. "She might have made it through entry qual, with some training and if she was fully grown. I doubt she'd make it all the way through the course. No woman *had* prior to the Plague. I *know* how tough it was. Nonetheless, she has shown her ability to lead and fight in *this* environment."

"Agreed, sir," Hamilton said. "She is even...flexible, sir. She reacted extremely well to the change of mission to a night attack and sweep. Her...methods raised some question of favoritism towards the Marines who were from the *Iwo Jima* ..."

"Official questions?" Smith asked.

"Unofficial, sir," Hamilton said. "And I stomped on them. The lieutenant's methods were mostly proven by the results, sir. The Marines from Guantanamo were under-trained for this mission and it showed. I'm considering a change to the TOE based upon it."

"If I may, sir," Gunny Sands said. "Let me have them for a week and then we'll look at it, sir."

"Agreed, Gunny," Hamilton said. "A Marine officer should not show any weakness, but I can honestly say I'm glad you're here."

"I'll get 'em dialed in, sir," Sands said.

"I needed him to organize the helo unit," Smith said, shrugging. "It was necessary, then. But Januscheitis has it well in hand at this point. Another example of critical personnel. At this point the gunny would have to be caught with a dead *boy* in his bed."

"That *ain't* gonna be an issue, sir," Gunny Sands said, grinning. "I'll get 'em dialed in," he repeated.

"The point to this discussion is that, much as with the vaccine production and beginning clearance of the continents, we simply have to do the best with what we have," Steve said. "And we have to accept that perfection is simply going to be unobtainable. So we maximize what we *have*, both in terms of materials and personnel. Which means that the competent people we have are always going to find themselves having to do more and more. And one aspect of that is, sometimes, *selection*.

"Gunny, this is not disrespect to the Marine Corps. In any group of people there are those who are better at some jobs and less so at others. I threw every Marine I had into the breach from the time we found Hooch to now because I *had* to. I still would prefer to. Clearance is the number one issue after finding the materials for a vaccine. But if any of them are determined to be either truly incompetent at clearance or just too difficult to get trained to do it . . . we'll find somewhere they can help. And I'm not just discussing Decker and Condrey. If they cannot be trusted to keep their damned finger off the trigger, after reasonably sufficient training, I do not want them trying to clear liners. In the distant past the infantry was the place you put your incompetents. That is *not* the case in Wolf Squadron's Marines. The clearance personnel *will* be our *best*. That's an order."

"Aye, aye, sir," Gunny Sands said.

"That goes for NCOs as well," Steve said. "I can't

imagine a Marine NCO who is truly incompetent at battle, but if any of them cannot handle battle management...we'll find somewhere for them. That *does* include Staff Sergeant Decker."

"We've been...managing the staff sergeant, sir," Hamilton said. "For example, he's excellent at ensuring all sterile protocols are followed with the astronauts."

"Do you have to keep to this harbor while the astronauts recover?"

"Not really, sir," Hamilton said. "We can float with them as cargo."

"We just added an island to your operation," Steve said.

"Which one, sir?" Hamilton asked.

"Sint Eustatius," Smith said. "It's on the list after you check Saba. And we'll need Sint Eustatius as clear as this one."

"The oil storage point," Hamilton said.

"You noticed," Steve said. "Yes. When you're approaching it, we'll send down a POL and security team to secure it and get it into operation. Probably permanently, or at least as long as the materials hold out."

"It's primarily unprocessed crude, though," Hamilton said. "Isn't it, sir?"

"No," Steve said. "Yes, by volume. But there are also supplies of diesel, aviation, gas and even bunker C. Assuming the stuff hasn't leaked or something. And large stores, larger than Gitmo. At last report, which was pre-Plague. There are two other facilities like it in the Caribbean but that is the only one in the Leeward Islands and the largest on the smallest island. So securing it is important. It's going to be a long time before we're pumping crude again, much less refining it."

"Yes, sir," Hamilton said, making a note.

"We'll punch the team down on the *Pit Stop* when you get to Saba," Steve said. "And that covers all the major issues. I suppose I should go talk to our visitors..."

"Hello," Steve said, looking through the plexiglass and using the external mike. "I'm Captain Smith, U.S. Navy and acting Atlantic Fleet Commander. Hope my people are treating you folks well?"

"Just fine, sir," Commander Daniels said, sitting up in his chair. "Better than we'd had any reason to expect, sir. Really appreciate the hospitality."

"Out of four thousand plus survivors we have one guy with a masters in mechanical engineering," Steve said. "Zero MDs, zero SEALs and, really importantly, *zero* microbiologists. To say that I was surprised when I was informed of this mission is an understatement. I'll add when I was told who we were rescuing, I was *overjoyed*. I'm obviously hoping that you're all interested in helping out."

"We are," Commander Daniels said. "We've been having some difficulty adjusting to current realities. Even seeing all the lights turning off couldn't quite prepare us for *how* bad it is."

"I fully recognize, and even understand, Dr. Shelley's reported discomfort with the vaccine program," Steve said. "I don't even have an issue with it. Given her many areas of training and education, there are other areas where she can contribute tremendously. I've given the order that it's simply not a subject for discussion.

She should make her own decisions on it. And until we can secure the rest of the production materials, the question is moot. Not why I'm here to talk with you. I'm not even really here to see you, particularly. Could have done that over the video screen. There were some issues to address with the Marines having to do with clearance ops and some other conversations I'd like to have. Dr. Price, I understand you've been reviewing the obstetrics issues."

"I have," Dr. Price said, smiling wryly. "OB was one field I'd never even considered as an MD. But... guess it's time to be a baby doctor."

"I'd like you to discuss with Dr. Chen at the CDC and Mr. Walker the viability of setting up an...assembly line, if you will, for C-sections on mothers who are likely to have complications or are already experiencing complications," Steve said. "Among a thousand things we haven't found and need is countercontraction medication. But it seems likely that going ahead and pulling the kids would make more sense than waiting until we've got complications in childbirth. We're going to have enough of those as it is. We'll probably need the assembly line prepared when the tidal wave hits to handle the complications, then."

"I'd...have to review what literature there is available," Dr. Price said. "And discuss it with Dr. Chen."

"Of course," Steve said. "It's something that I'm leaving up entirely to the medical team. My knowledge of obstetrics begins and ends with standing by my wife going 'Breathe, honey, breathe,'" he added with a grin. "Twice."

"That certainly seemed to have turned out well enough, sir," Commander Daniels said.

"Indeed," Steve said, sighing slightly. "Mr. Lyons."

"Sir?" Lyons said.

"I can always use a mechanical engineer," Steve said. "I'm honestly not sure whether I need a mechanical engineer or a SEAL more. We're going to crack the boats at some point and many of their engineering officers can at least hum the tune. So I suppose the answer is 'a SEAL.'"

"If you're asking would I prefer to shoot zombies or run a CAD program, sir, the answer is 'kill zombies,' sir," Lyons said, smiling. "Take me a while to get back in shape, but I'm your man, sir."

"Take a reactivation?" Steve asked.

"Absolutely, sir," Lyons said.

"Consider yourself reactivated as of now, Lieutenant," Steve said. "As to getting back in shape... Really think that's an issue?"

"No, sir," Lyons said. "Looking forward to it."

"Biggest problem will be time," Steve said, shaking his head. "As in: There is never enough. You may have to just hit the gun rack when you're marginally cleared and get back to SEAL shape as time permits. Colonel Kuznetsov."

"Sir?" the assistant commander said.

"Had my first face to face talk with Colonel Ushakov about you and Mr. Matveev," Steve said. "We're trying to get him up on the video conference here. There is an issue with it since it has to go through the Hole and there are incompatibility issues. His take is what you want to do is up to you given that, like the Hole, he's trapped for the time being. I understand you are a rotary wing pilot as well as fixed."

"Yes, sir," Kuznetsov said.

"I have a crying need for rotary wing pilots," Steve said. "You have the usual problem of being a foreign national, but I'd be more than happy to give you the functional position of, say, captain as opposed to colonel if you'd take it. The problem with colonel is that your pilot in command, at least initially, would be a Marine captain. However, I'd have you as an instructor pilot rather rapidly. I need *a lot* of helos and a lot of helo pilots for land clearance eventually. The plan is to set up a helo training site in the Keys when we've cleared them. The focus would be on cargo and heavy utility helos."

"I would be comfortable with that, sir," Kuznetsov said, frowning. "The situation would be . . . strange, but I am sure I can work with your Marines. If they are willing to work with me."

"Colonel, without any sarcasm whatsoever, this is a zombie apocalypse," Steve said, smiling. "You're simply suffering a bit of cognitive dissonance. I was a digger in the Australian paras and now am a U.S. Navy captain and Commander Atlantic Fleet. Which is composed of a group of civilian boats and not one single pre-Plague Navy platform with the exception of the subs. Asking a Russian colonel and cosmonaut to take a dip in position to Navy lieutenant, which is what the position would be, and then not even having it be an *actual* rank since I still cannot so appoint a foreign national, is not even in the *top ten* weird items in my last *week*. Part of why I *can* do this job so effectively is that I just ignore the cognitive dissonance and look at the situation as it actually is.

"For example: I know that if you're put in a position and given *any* rank, no matter how odd it might be legally, the people you'll be working with are so untrained on military basics that they'll salute, or more often not, and just follow the orders as long as they make any sense whatsoever. When they don't is when it gets to be a problem," he added with a sigh.

"I've got a person who is technically a civilian, given that he's a retired *British* sergeant major, as my official NCOIC of my *U.S. Navy* landing parties. And his people call him 'Sergeant Major' without even realizing that sergeant major is not a *Navy* NCO position. They assume it's what you call a chief that is a master-at-arms. Sometimes they still refer to him as 'sir' and he's pretty much given up telling them not to. Because in the game 'Halo,' the master chief is referred to as 'sir' and that's as much training as most of them *have* in military protocol," he added with a grin.

"Cognitive dissonance is a common feature of this universe," he continued. "The meme is a Zombie Apocalypse Moment, a ZAM or zammie. The ability to rapidly overcome the cognitive dissonance is sort of the definition of competence in this universe. Those people who can, and are otherwise fairly competent, are gems. Those who are stuck in pre-Plague mind-sets and have an impossible time getting their brains around zammies, no matter how competent, are only barely useful.

"I'm hoping that all of you will be gems," Captain Smith concluded. "But if you're simply good, that is fine as well. Heck, if you decide you want *nothing* to do with us ... This island is functionally cleared and we'll be glad to give you some guns for self-protection. If you can keep the ISS going for six months without any support I'm sure you can survive, and it's a nice little place. Up to you each individually. And with that I bid you adieu."

"That was not...the pep talk I was expecting," Dr. Price said after a moment.

"I am glad he did not press me to be part of the vaccine production group," Rizwana said.

"Have you made up your mind?" Commander Daniels asked.

"I have not," Rizwana said. "It is a very difficult decision. But that is why I am glad he said that."

"We'll leave you to consider it," Commander Daniels said. "If you wish to talk, feel free. But I think we should respect the captain's wishes in this. Change of topic."

"Thank you," Rizwana said.

"I am wondering why he wants a fleet of helicopters," Mr. Matveev said. "And we did not take the opportunity to ask about planes."

"I have been thinking about that," Commander Daniels said. "It is probably something to raise, again, with the local chain of command. What they could probably use is a small float plane. And we have, between us, more than enough technical expertise to both get one into operation and use it."

"We have enough expertise between us to make one," Lyons said, grinning. "Although, I'm almost regretting taking the recall. I can sort of see just retiring to Anguilla. Nah. I'm going to have too much fun killing zombies."

"I never really saw that side of you on the mission, Troy," Rizwana said.

"That is because I didn't pull it out, Doctor," Lyons said. "The International Space Station is about peace and international brotherhood. But once a SEAL, always a SEAL, Doc. You don't go to BUD/S, much less pass it, if part of you doesn't long for combat. It was part of my frustration and stress being up there. That I couldn't be down *here* in a very target-rich environment. Admittedly, like the majority of my SEAL buddies I would now be dead or infected. That does not reduce my desire to engage in the fight. Dr. Price, permission to attempt, again, to stand?"

"Wait for the aides to return," Price said. "If you break a bone it will hold you back even longer. Symptoms check."

"Continuing fever," Commander Daniels said. "Still moderate. Malaise."

"The same," Kuznetsov said.

"So far so good," Price said since nobody had any indications of negative effects.

"Now if we could just *do* something," Troy said, sighing hard. "I am more than ready for my next therapy session."

"Follow the program, Troy," Price said. "You'll get there."

"*Astro unit,*" the intercom squawked. "*Be advised. Flag has left. We are undocking to move to our next objective.*"

"They don't sit around much, do they?" Commander Daniels said.

"Sort of my point," Lyons replied. "They seem to know what they're doing and I'd sure like to help..."

CHAPTER 22

I am done pretending
You have failed to find what's left
I will suck you dry again
Some are not worth saving
You are such a pretty mess
I will choke the life within

—"Lights Out"
Breaking Benjamin

"I'm not sure about this," Anna said. "Why should *we* get special treatment?"

Anna Holmes, child star of the Wizard Wars movies, had been in St. Barts as a contestant in *Celebrity Survivor: St. Barts*. Decried as the most blatantly racist TV show since, well, *ever*, the show mixed a group of skinny white female celebrities with a group of hulking male celebrities, mostly drawn from MMA and WWE, and all "of color."

If Anna had paid more attention to the line-up, she would have passed on the opportunity. She probably should have, anyway. It wasn't like she was one of the "reality TV" stars that made up most of the female side. She was just filling time between two A movies. And many of the "challenges" came down to an

357

opportunity for the women to flirt to get the guys to do the work. "Build a rock wall for defense against zombies" was, ironically, one of the challenges. Anna had managed to lift about six of the massive rocks provided for the wall before she gave out entirely. But she at least *tried*!

All that being said, she'd actually been enjoying it. She hated the majority of the other women. But most of the guys were very down to earth and grounded. She'd teamed with most of them at one point or another, throwing in with a will that was virtually unheard of among the rest of the "celebutantes."

Then the Plague had been announced. Their challenge coach, famous survivalist Tiger Dour, had just returned from New York and, as it turned out, brought along a hitchhiker called H7D3. So, naturally, the first person to go down from the disease was the one person you'd *want* in a survival situation.

Air traffic was cut off as soon as Tiger was confirmed as a positive case but by then it was too late. Yachts started punching out in every direction but Anna and most of the cast and crew stayed. For one thing, it was hurricane season. Being in a yacht, even one of the megayachts, in a hurricane didn't sound like a very good idea. And she, frankly, didn't know most of the people well enough to trust them.

Then events began to turn for the worst. Tiger was only the first to "turn." He was quarantined but he wasn't the only carrier. Others turned. The on-site producer. Crew. Her favorite cameraman. People throughout the island were turning to the point that the police couldn't control it. Nobody could, judging from the news reports which became more and more sporadic as satellite up- and downlink began to fail. When one of the MMA fighters turned and the police wouldn't even *respond*, everyone knew it was out of control.

When the local police finally did respond it was in force and with an edict. The shoot was already shut down and they had their own ideas of how to handle things. The celebrities had been rounded up and marched to the police station for "protective custody." Apparently that was going on with all the "names" on the island, as in Gustavia they had been herded in with another group.

They were climbing the steep hill to the gray concrete building that housed the local gendarmerie and where they would, presumably, be safe until rescue could be arranged. But she had to wonder what was going to happen to the crew, not to mention most of the rest of the people on the island.

"Because the worst possible thing that could happen to them is to have a bunch of celebrities bitching about how they were treated when this blows over," Athena Perez said, shrugging. "Rich people will continue to have a lot of power but it's not the same thing as having, well, *you* on Letterman or Leno, if they survive, talking about how poorly the St. Barts police handled the crisis. People will want to know about *Celebrity Survivor: Zombie Apocalypse*. They're covering their asses."

Athena was, surprisingly, one of the women Anna *did* get along with. The heir to the Vinyards Inn fortune was a well known diva and had been among the most manipulative at getting the "guys" to do all the work. But she was also grounded and professional as long as a camera *wasn't* on her. It was only when she knew she was being publicly observed that the "little princess" came to the fore.

"Do you know what this place is?" Anna asked. Anna had quickly realized that the "photog whore" was the smartest and most knowledgeable woman in the group by far. "It looks like a fortress."

"Former DGSE electronic listening post," Athena said. "This isn't my first visit to St. Barts. I managed to wheedle my way in when it was still in use. I felt like a Russian spy or something. But the commander was a fan and I totally banged him for the tour."

Although, she *was* an unabashed slut. She hadn't just been batting her eyes at the guys to get them to bow to her every command.

"They turned it over to the local gendarmerie when it was deactivated," Athena continued. "So it is, yeah, a fortress."

"How much farther do we have to walk?" Christy Southard whined.

"Probably to the great big building, Christy," Athena said, slowly and carefully. "Maybe if you had worn *real* shoes it wouldn't seem so far."

The "singer" and reality TV star, mostly known for enormous boobs and being one of several live-in girl-friends of an eighty-year-old producer, had worn her de rigueur stiletto stripper heels for the walk across the island from Anse Grand Saline to the police head-quarters. She'd worn them the whole shoot except for her occasional ventures into the water. Give her credit, she was actually good at underwater foraging. Athena had pointed out, on camera no less, that Christy had the benefit of a built in flotation system.

"I'll be happy to help you up the hill, miss," an older English gentleman said, holding out his arm.

"Do I know you?" Christy asked, warily.

"Let me handle the introductions," Athena said airily. "Jerome Arthurson, *Top Speed* announcer, Christy Southard, professional slut. Christy, Jerry, Jerry, Christy."

"Hello, Athena," Jerome said, smiling broadly. "I see you've been enjoying the sunshine."

"Better than your show," Athena said. "Does it ever *not* rain in Sheffield? And I swear I could still smell Michael Moore on the seats. It's a distinct smell. Don't you fumigate it? Ever?"

"Positive and encouraging as always," Jerome said. "Miss Southard, please let me take this opportunity to invite you on my show as soon as this unpleasantness is passed."

"What show?" Christy asked.

"*Top Speed*?" Jerome said, sounding somewhat miffed. "Number one show on the Beeb?"

"What's the Beeb?" Christy asked, confused. "Is that like Bravo? I've got my own show on Bravo! It's called *Christy Says!*"

"Jerry," Athena said. "You learn to dial it back a bit with Christy. Speak slowly and use words of no more than two syllables."

"It is a car show on the BBC," Jerome said slowly.

"They put a star in a cheap ass car," Athena said. "And then you race around a track like a crazed squirrel."

"Oh, like NASCAR?" Christy said. "I just *love* NASCAR!"

"How...unsurprising," Jerome said. "Yes, somewhat like... NASCAR," he finished with a wince.

"What are you doing on Sunny St. Barts?" Athena asked.

"Vacation, oddly enough," Jerome said. "Quite ruined at this point."

"Unaccompanied?" Athena said.

"My wife and I are having some complications," Jerome said. "Nothing serious. Just time for a short change of scenery."

"Wasn't what I asked," Athena said archly. "That would be wife four, right? Interviewing for five were we?"

"If I were I assure you I'd have a beautiful lady on *both* arms," Jerome said. "And, no, just some time off. As it is . . ."

"Worried about your family?" Anna asked.

"Very," Jerome said. "Friends, family. Family."

"We all are," Athena said seriously. She patted him on the shoulder. "They're not going to let anything happen to Jerome Arthurson's family, Jerry."

"I think my educational background might have prepared me more for the eventuality that nothing 'they' can do may matter," Jerome said. "I understand the Black Death is rather scarcely covered in American schools."

"I didn't go to most schools," Athena said. "Although I think Poe covered it best. It won't get that bad, Jerry. She'll be there when you get home."

"I'm worried about Steve," Christy said. "The last time I got through to his cell all I got was voicemail. And that was two weeks ago."

"We're all worried, Christy," Anna said. "We all have people we're worried about—"

"*Attencion!*" a man with a bullhorn said. "We will use

English, then I will translate to French and German. There are two storehouses for disaster materials in the building. You will be segregated by sex so as to avoid any... problems during the period of your, hopefully short, stay. It is hoped it shall be *very* short as there are minimal facilities of all types in this building. But it is the most secure building on the island and here we, the gendarmerie, can deal with any problems that arise much more swiftly and surely. Now, English speakers please wait while I translate..."

"Well, it appears I must bid you adieu, fair lady," Jerome said, kissing Christy's hand. "I hope that you enjoy your 'hopefully short' stay in the castle."

"I'm already hoping for Prince Charming," Athena said, looking up at the gray, three-story, precast concrete building. "Or princess. I'm easy."

"That you are, dear lady," Jerome said. "That you are." He winked at the group and headed over to the "male" side.

The room was, as promised, a storehouse. More like a warehouse. There were industrial shelves holding boxes, as well as pallets with more boxes and stacked five gallon cans. There were three windows but they were covered by roll-down hurricane shutters. If the lights went out, the room was going to be quite dim.

What was entirely missing were cots, mattresses, blankets, sheets or, perhaps most importantly, a loo. Nor were there any apparent bottles of water. All of which was causing the various women who had been led to the room to have conniption fits.

"I can *only* drink Holister Springs..."

"Are there vegan meals...?"

"Where are we supposed to *sleep* . . . ?"

"Where's the bathroom . . . ?"

"HEY!" Athena suddenly bellowed like a drill sergeant. "Shut up all you bitches or I swear to *God* I will *cunt* punt you. Next bitch says a word I will slap you silly. *Monsieur,*" she said, changing to a purr. *"De la plus grande importance est la question d'une toilette? Et de l'eau?"*

"Mademoiselle," the harried gendarme said, nodding in thanks. "We will take individuals to the toilet in the main police area. As to water, those boxes have emergency water bottles in them," he added, pointing. "For the rest . . . there are currently no good answers and with that I must leave."

He quickly shut the door and was gone.

"There is no way I'm—" Brenda McCartney started to say.

Athena took two steps and hit the larger girl with a roundhouse slap so hard it knocked her off her feet.

"We are in a fucking *disaster*!" Athena shouted, striding to each woman and looking them in the eye. "Not a fucking *movie*. Not a fucking *reality* show. Real reality. A fucking disaster! Who knows how much *worse* it's going to get? Which of you are going to turn, huh? Am I? You feel sick? How's that head? Huh? Spinny? Got a fever? Huh? We've all SEEN IT.

"So forget the *bullshit*! We are fucked. Screwed. Blued and tattooed. There is no Evian! There are no special meals! There are no PAs with fruit baskets. There is no kosher if that's your bitch. There is pure and simple really real *survival*. Not the fucking show. So start acting like it! All a human needs is a little nutrition and some water that's hopefully not *too* fucked up. Or you can sit in the corner and starve, which in your case, Brenda, wouldn't be a bad idea. But you *will* die in three days without water and I *guarantee* you you would drink *piss* long before that.

"The real question is not whether there's what you'd *like*. There are three big questions: How long are we going to be here? How long will the supplies hold out for all of us? How are we going to keep from killing each other when we turn? Anybody got any *helpful* suggestions?"

"We've got one thing going for us," Anna said.

"*What?*" Athena said, spinning on her.

"We're all used to dieting."

There was a moment of silence, then a giggle. In a few seconds the whole group was laughing hysterically. Christy looked as if she couldn't decide whether to laugh or cry and had settled on both.

"So short rations won't be a problem," Athena said, nodding. "Good point."

"I've got a question besides those," Brenda McCartney said, still holding her cheek. "Who put *you* in charge?"

"I did," Athena said. "Because I know *all* of you and you're mostly airheaded *idiots*. And you fucking well *know* it. Any other stupid questions?"

"Not a question," Anna said, raising her hand. "But I second her self-nomination. Athena's capable and you know it."

"There aren't any guys in here to get to do all the work," Brenda said, crossing her arms. "*I'm* not going to do it, that's for sure."

"You know she's come up with half the good ideas on the challenges," Anna said. "And she is organized. You most certainly are *not*."

"*You're* a leader," Christy said quietly. "Why not you?"

"Age," Anna said, ticking off the reasons on her finger. "With it experience. Athena *runs* her businesses, she doesn't just let others manage things. And force of personality. While I could and would...ahem... 'cunt punt' any of you if it were necessary, you're rather less in fear of it than Athena's threat. She has more force of personality. I do, however, back her one hundred percent. And as to that specific threat, I have played football since I was four. It would be a quite righteous cunt punting, I assure you."

"Any other takers?" Athena said. "And, Brenda, if you raise your hand I swear I will break it off at the wrist."

There weren't.

"Fine," Athena said. "And, yes, I get the guys to do all the work. It's called 'delegation,' Brenda. And if I delegate something to you, you're *going* to do it. In fact... You wanted to know what kind of water. Fine. He said those boxes had water," she said, pointing. "Find out what kind and how much. Take Sarah..."

"Wait," Sarah Cassill said, raising her hand. "I've got a question."

"What now?" Athena said, tiredly.

"Um...What's Brandon doing in here?"

The crowd parted to reveal Brandon Jeeter, vocalist and every teen girl's heartthrob.

"Good question," Athena said, her hands on her hips. "What *are* you doing in here?"

"I *wanted* to go with the guys," Brandon said, holding up his hands helplessly. "This cop just kept pushing me into the girl group."

"Figures," Sarah said, laughing. "*Nobody* believes you're a guy. Even French cops can figure out the truth."

"I am totally a dude," Brandon said shrilly. "And, by the way, got *nothing* for any of you. That's why I wanted to be with the *guys*. I told him, 'Do you know who I am?' and he, like, said 'Nun' or something. I am *not* a *nun*! I'm not even a *chick*!"

Athena, Anna and at least three of the other women dropped their heads into their hands. Athena got enough of a look to know which had at least *some* clue.

"The word is 'non,'" Athena said. "French for 'no.' Meaning that he didn't know who you were and could care less. Sarah and Janet help Brenda get an inventory of the water. Anna and... Oh, hello, Your Highness."

"Hello again, Athena," Princess Julianna Gustavason said. "Nice of you to finally notice."

"I'm surprised you didn't raise your hand is all," Athena said sweetly.

"Like I *wish* to be in charge of this?" Princess Julianna said. "Why don't Anna and I take the food stores?"

"Thank you," Athena said. "But hold off for a second. Any thoughts on how we're going to keep from biting each other when one of us turns? Seeing Hector go all Hulk was really fucking unpleasant. It took half the crew to subdue him and he bit Terry and Phillip in the process. *And* it could happen any second."

There were a series of prettily furrowed brows, then Christy tentatively raised her hand.

"Yes," Athena said, pointing. "Christy."

"We could tie each other up?" Christy said tentatively.

"This isn't a porn flick, Christy," Athena said with a sigh.

"No..." Anna said. "She has a point. If we're secured, the... afflicted is easier to subdue. Or she should be."

"I'm not going to be tied up when one of you goes nuts," Sarah Cassill said. "Not going to happen. And besides who is the last to get tied? Leaves one untied, right?"

"Possibly light restraints?" Princess Julianna said. "Easily removed on the wrists. When we're not moving around, tight on the feet. Possibly some sort of hobble when we are forced to move. That way, at least, the afflicted isn't free to move around. When one of us turns, we can pile on?"

"What's this *we* shit?" Sarah said. "*I'm* not getting bit."

"It's a thought," Athena said. "I'm just having a hard time with it being *Christy's* good idea. No offense, Christy."

"It's okay," Christy said.

"Is there any rope? Yes . . . Christy," she said, pointing as the girl raised her hand again.

"I gotta pee," Christy said.

"Why didn't you go before we left?" Athena said angrily.

"It was a long walk," Christy said, hanging her head.

"Fine," Athena said. "Somebody bang on the door for our friendly—"

She paused as there was a clearly heard shot in the corridor beyond the door. Then screaming.

"Or . . . perhaps not," Athena said, running over to one of the partially empty shelves. "Julianna, Anna, Sarah, Christy! Help me push!"

There was a loud bang against the door followed by a series of irregular thumps and a keening howl.

"PUSH DAMNIT!" Athena yelled.

The shelving section tipped over and effectively barricaded the door. Whatever was on the other side just kept banging, though. And now there were ration boxes all over the floor.

"Now I *really* gotta pee," Christy whimpered. She had her hands over her crotch.

"I think we all do," Athena said. She walked over to a pallet of five gallon buckets and read the labels. "Sarah, Brenda, new job. Get into this pallet and get out a bucket. It's semolina, basically cream of wheat. Dump it on the floor. Keep some in the bottom for absorption. Christy, use that. Everybody else, start looking for anything that resembles rope before one of us turns..."

"Fuck you, you pampered bitch!" Snoopi Lucessa suddenly screamed.

"What did you say?" Athena said, raising one eyebrow.

"I said fuck you!" Snoopi screamed. "I don't take orders from some...what the fuck is on me? WHAT THE *FUCK* IS ON ME...?"

"TURNING!" Princess Julianna yelled.

Most of the women scattered, screaming, but Julianna, who was slightly behind the smaller woman, height-wise anyway, hit her with an expert rugby tackle and drove the New Jersey native facedown to the floor.

"Rope! String! Anything!" Athena yelled, grabbing Snoopi by the hair and holding her gnashing teeth away from the princess.

Christy, who hadn't run but only because she was standing dumbstruck, reached under her blouse and whipped out a Texas-small bikini top at the speed of light. There was a tidal-wave of objects. Cash, change, lipstick and make-up, a tiny Bible, a micro bottle of Hennessy brandy, four packages of peanut M&Ms, a bottle of mouthwash, a package of nylons and three Trojan "SuperMax" unlubricated condoms all tumbled out. After a moment a small gold bar clinked to the floor.

"Yeah," Athena said, taking a moment to boggle. "That works."

It eventually took six women to subdue the "afflicted" but with various bits of underwear, bathing suits and strips of cloth ripped from blouses and sundresses, they finally had her hogtied. Christy also turned out to be surprisingly good at knots.

"That caught me off guard," Athena admitted. She was sitting on the struggling *Jersey City* star since it was the only pillow around. "I'm still not sure she's actually turned. Is there a *difference* between this and her regular personality...?"

"God, Athena, you are such a bitch," Brenda McCartney said.

"Takes one to know one," Athena said. "And, yeah, I am. I'm *such* a bitch I've already thought about what happens *next*. Like, what the fuck do we do with her, now?"

"Wait till the guy outside seems to be gone and throw her out the door?" Sarah Cassill said after a long moment of contemplative silence.

"Do we untie her first?" Athens said. "No? Think that's a bad idea? Me too. So we turn her into zombie chow? That's the same as killing her. Worse, really. Not saying no, but be clear about it. That's killing her. *And* letting her be eaten. Votes on throwing Snoopi off the island?"

"We have to take care of her," Brenda McCartney said definitely. "She's sick. We have to take care of her."

"That's so... *paladin* of you, Brenda," Athena said.

"Fine. You do it. How are you going to keep her from getting free and biting the rest of us? In *here*. We don't even have a fucking mattress. You going to feed her? Clean up when she craps and pisses? You want the Snoopi puppy, you have to take care of it. Speaking of which: What do I smell?"

"I don't have to pee anymore," Christy said, wiping her eyes. Her makeup was smeared all over her face.

"Do we have anything to clean it up?" Julianna said. "Don't worry about it, Christy. I think I peed myself, too."

"Snoopi's clothes?" Anna said. "And you obviously know what to do, Athena. You're using Socratic Dialectic to lead us to your conclusion."

"I don't have a good answer," Athena said, frowning prettily. "I have an answer but it's not a *good* answer. I don't think there *is* a good answer. The best is probably Sarah's in some ways. *If* we could safely open the door. I don't think we can. Can we get those shutters off the window?"

Ten minutes of fruitless searching for a control or release yielded the answer: No. The shutters were immovable. And when they tried the door, even moved the shelf blocking it, there was an immediate response from the other side.

"So what is the bad answer?" Julianna said.

"She's already gagged," Athena said. "Hold her nose till she stops struggling."

"Mercy, Athena," Julianna said. "Even for you that is cold."

"That's murder," Brenda McCartney said. "You'll go to jail for the rest of your life. At least *you'll* deserve it!"

"That is what well-paid lawyers are for," Athena said. "'Oh, it was so terrible in the storeroom!'" she said in a little girl voice, looking pitiful. "'The claustrophobia! Boo hoo! I don't know what came over me! It was just like Patty Hearst. And it was Brenda's idea!' But there are still more physical, non-social, problems. The body will...decompose. It will get much nastier than a puppy puddle on the floor in here. It's going to, anyway. But a decomposing body is a whole other order of nasty. And I'm not sure I can do it. I mean, I've *thought* about holding her head under water until she stops struggling since her show started, not to mention the whole damned *shoot*. But actually doing it is another thing. So I'm open to suggestions."

"Table it," Anna said. "She is not going anywhere. We still need to find something besides Christy's reducing remnants of clothing to secure ourselves. And in the meantime, we can build...facilities and possibly find some answer to the dilemma."

"I don't think there is an answer to the Plague in here, Anna," Athena said, standing up. "But I take your point. Let's go shopping!"

There was more than food and water in the room: The storehouse had been set up to respond to a variety of disasters. St. Barts was subject to both hurricanes and earthquakes, as were surrounding islands. Besides food and water there was a supply of blue tarps, three boxes of "thermal" blankets, rope, rigger tape and other materials of the disaster response trade. There were even boxes of baby wipes. What there was not came down to medical supplies, a knife to *cut* the rope—couldn't they have included some box cutters?—toilet paper, so much as *one* chemical toilet, damnit, or a cure for H7D3. Or some toilet paper for God's sake? And, oh, yeah, some *tampons* maybe?

"What are these?" Anna said, holding up what looked like an American MRE package except for being an odd pink.

"Emergency meals," Athena said. "Hey, Sarah, good news! There's vegetarian! It's even halal."

"What's halal?" Sarah said warily.

"Kosher for Islamics," Athena said. "Just one case of toilet paper is too much to ask?"

"Baby wipes," Anna said.

"We only have two cases of those," Athena said. "These bitches will go through them in a day. Baby wipes are only for personal body cleaning. You can use one to clean your ass when you're done with the rest of your body. Open up one of the halal meals and see if it's got toilet paper in it."

"How do I get it open?" Anna said. The package was strong plastic and had no convenient opening tabs.

"A knife," Athena said. "Your teeth?"

"I'll get it," Christy said. She tore into the package with her teeth.

"God, I hope you don't turn," Athena said, wincing as the girl chewed through the heavy plastic. "If this was being recorded, no guy would ever again accept a blowjob from you."

"She's not going to be able to bite through this rope," Julianna said, holding up a coil of line.

"Speaking of Brenda..." Athena said. "Sorry, I meant Snoopi..."

"Very funny, Athena," Brenda snarled.

"How you feeling, Bren?" Athena said with mock sympathy. "Wishing you had some *vaccine*?"

"Just shut the fuck up, Athena," Brenda said.

"Prisoners figure out how to create knives out of nothing," Athena said. "Now if we only had Linsey in here with us..."

"You take a piece of metal and grind it on the concrete till it's sharp," Sarah said.

"Sounds about right," Athena said. "Where'd you pick that up?"

"Hello?" Sarah said. "*Jailhouse Island*?"

"Ah, yes," Athena said. "Academy material at its finest. Right up there with *Casablanca* in the annals of American cinematography. I was surprised you didn't win the Oscar for that one. Especially given your nickname in the Academy."

"And what do you call this?" Julianna said, amused. "A group of female celebrities trapped in a storehouse during a plague. What madman would try to submit *that* script?"

"A total pervert," Athena said. "That's for sure. And the answer is: '*Celebrity Survivor, Zombie Apocalypse: The shit just got real.*' Still not getting the rope cut. We need sections of rope to play bondage-girl-party. We can't just keep tearing up Christy's clothes. I mean, well, we c— *Just try to find something with an edge!* I can't believe none of you have so much as a nail file."

"Like this?" Christy said, pulling one out of her hair.

"In your *hair*?" Athena said, clearly trying not to scream. "Your *hair*, for God's sake? Do I even *want* to ask what a full body cavity search would turn up? Do you happen to be carrying a *helicopter* somewhere?"

She looked at the girl's face and sighed. "I'm sorry, Christy," she said, hugging her. "I'm scared, too. And it's great you were carrying so much useful stuff. I wish I had your..." She looked down, then back up. "Foresight."

As she spoke the lights went out.

"Joy," Athena said, with a sigh. "In seriousness, I don't suppose you have a flashlight...somewhere...?"

"No," Christy said. "Sorry."

"I'm not sure if I'm disappointed or relieved," Princess Julianna said, chuckling.

Fortunately, there were enough gaps around the edges of the hurricane shutters that after their eyes adjusted they could see. Sawing through the ropes with one small nail file took time However, they had nothing but. And, even more fortunately, the gagged Snoopi was so far the only one to turn. And gagged.

There was, surprising Athena not at all, a massive collective knowledge of various ways to tie someone up.

"Or we could tie our wrists to our knees, like this..." Sarah said, using Christy as a model.

"We need to be able to get out of them," Julianna said.

"Tighter," Christy said huskily.

"Not the *point*, Christy," Anna said, hands on her hips.

"Wanna make out?" Christy asked, her eyes lighting.

"LATER!" Athena bellowed. "Just concentrate to the extent you can."

"Getting harder," Sarah said.

"I always wondered if you had those parts, Sarah," Athena said.

"Why is everyone in my industry *insane*?" Anna said, holding up her hands. "Can we get serious for a moment? I am going to kill my agent for talking me into this. 'It's in St. Barts, for God's sake. You'll have fun!'"

"Honestly," Athena said, "I'd rather be *here* than L.A. And if there is a God, all agents are going to be eaten. Not getting the problem solved..."

Best ways to secure themselves were eventually determined and Sarah and Christy got some, more or less, alone time at the back of the compartment. Although it was pointed out that either one could turn at any moment.

"I just wish they would keep it down," Anna said, hopping over to sit next to Athena. She leaned up against the shelving and sighed.

"Oh, I don't know," Athena said, shrugging. "If I didn't have a strong sense of self-preservation, I'd think about joining in."

"Don't look at me," Anna said. "Go see Rebekah if you want someone's neck to bite."

"But it's a very nibblable neck, Anna," Athena said, smiling.

"Not funny in the circumstances, Athena," Anna said. She gestured with her chin to Snoopi. "And that problem still remains. The answer to your earlier dilemma is the tarps and tape in case you hadn't noticed."

"I did," Athena said. "But...I can't do it. I just can't."

"Fine," Anna said, standing up and hobbling over to Snoopi. She dropped her light wrist restraints, turned the struggling girl over facedown and sat on her back, pinning her to the ground. Then she reached around and pinched the former reality star's nose closed.

"What do you think you're doing?" Brenda said angrily.

"What does it *look* like I am doing?" Anna said. She had her head turned away and her eyes closed. But she was still holding the girl down with almost no expression on her face.

"You can't do that," Brenda protested weakly.

"Just bloody well shut up, Brenda," Anna said. "If I face the High Court I'll simply plead guilty."

Finally, Snoopi stopped struggling. Anna checked for a carotid pulse, then stood up with the back of her hand over her mouth.

"Brenda, go get a tarp and a roll of gaffer tape," she said, her voice muffled. "Julianna, Athena, strip her. We need the rags and ties. Now, I'm going to go throw up. And don't *anyone* make a joke about the world 'becoming a better place.'"

"How are you doing?" Athena said, sitting down next to Anna.

Brandon Jeeter, a "male" teen heart throb of such questionable sexuality *French* police categorized him as a woman, had just been added to the growing pile at the back of the storehouse. One by one over the last week members of the group had turned. First Snoopi, then Brenda McCartney, who before her death confessed she would have "cracked her own mother's skull" for access to a vaccine despite her long-running opposition to the entire concept of vaccination. Rebekah Villon, famous mostly for her role as insipid character Berra from the *Midnight* movies and amazingly useless douchebag. Ines Moretti, has-been *Beverly Hills Teen Force* star, PETA activist, aggressive sponsor of all things vegan, peace activist and flaming bitch, frankly. Heather Marks, overendowed blonde-bombshell super-model, virtually an Untouchable in Hollywood since coming out of the closet in opposition to abortion and as a concealed carry proponent. Also one of the small group Athena had come to depend upon to get things done. Last, prior to Brandon, was Michelle Bazuin, just about the most cold-hearted bitch in a land of cold-hearted bitches, whose transformation was particularly ironic, in Athena's opinion, given her one big movie was *Zombiehood*.

And Anna, quiet, composed, caring Anna, had strangled every single one to death with that same quiet, composed, cold expression.

"Strange," Anna said, rubbing her hands. "Feeling very much like Macbeth. The king, not the lady. Out, out, damned rope burns. And conflicted. I feel immense loss when someone as wonderful as Heather turns. We needed her."

"Agreed," Athena said. "I miss her."

"And I feel even more guilt with those who..." Anna said, her face working. "I hate that... It was *Brandon*. The only guy, sort of, in the compartment and he could barely be forced to lift a box of rations much less be any *real* help. The world truly *is* a better place. God help me for thinking it much less saying it no matter how true. Conflicted."

"New rule," Athena said, slipping out of her restraints and putting her arm around the girl. "Only you get to. And I think you switched a u for an a in that sentence. But you're right. *This* is certainly a better place with him gone. Now if I could suggest Sarah?"

"Don't, please, Athena," Anna said.

"I'm scared," Athena said. "I'm also...I've had a fever the whole time we've been in here. It won't go away. I know what that means and it scares me. I get...bitchy, sarcastic and have a bad sense of humor when I'm scared. We all are. Christy just wants to fool around as much as possible before she goes. I don't know why that girl never did porn."

"She told me nobody would take her seriously as an actress," Anna said, holding up her hand as if swearing. "Honestly. That's what she said when I asked."

"Well, she had good advice in that," Athena said, boggling slightly.

"If I turn..." Anna said, frowning. "If you're going to keep any credence as our leader, you will have to do it. And simply do it, Athena. Do not hesitate."

"I know," Athena said, her face working. "And I don't know...I don't..." She twitched and grabbed her left arm with her right hand, trying to quell a sudden muscle spasm. "I don't... NO! No...*Please*..."

"Sweet merciful..." Anna said, backing away fast. "ATHENA'S TURNING!"

When they had the group's leader pinned down, Anna slipped a rope around her friend's neck and gave herself more rope burns.

"Julianna, you're in charge, now," Anna said when Athena's body had been added to the pile. Even through double tarps the pile stunk and was covered in flies.

"I think you're in charge, kid," Sarah said sarcastically.

"I have *one* job in this room, Sarah," Anna said, turning to the starlet and staring at her with blank, dead, eyes. "Do not require my services."

CHAPTER 23

"Saint Barthélemy," Faith said, pointing to the satellite image. It was hazy due to cloud cover and thus there was a secondary map up. "It is generally called St. Barts. Main town and capital is Gustavia. French island, sort of. Usual history, got passed around in wars, in this case for a while to Sweden . . ."

The gunny had already taken training in hand and things were starting to shake down. She still wasn't happy with so many of the Gitmo Marines in squad leader positions but she was going to let the gunny and the colonel argue over that.

"That's why the capital has a Swedish name, oorah? Pre-Plague population estimate was seventy-three hundred but it had a lot of tourists. Those were mostly in the winter so we don't know how many, exactly, were on the island when the Plague hit. Harbor is a really nice U shape in Gustavia. Town sort of hooks around it. If it was bigger it would be an awesome harbor for big boats but only the yachts are going to be able to fit into it. Cargo pier is over here..." she said, pointing to the north of the main harbor.

"If we hook off the *Grace* that will be the landing point. This peninsula..." she continued, pointing to the west side of the main harbor, "has a military base for the local police. But it's occasionally used by visiting French forces. Satellite imagery has detected possible survivors here, here, here and at the military base. Recommend gunboats here, at this unnamed beach north, at this beach by the cargo pier, Shell Beach, south of Gustavia, *Anse du Governeur*, which is 'Governor's Cove.' Last division here, in the harbor, firing up this boat launch.

"After clearance fire, have the division by the boat launch, whichever is chosen, move over to support landing here on the tip of the peninsula. We can sweep the town and the military base on foot, then link up with the *Grace* to off-load the five-tons, if we choose to do so. This town doesn't have a medical school, there's no really big hospital and the only reason we're really clearing it is it's on the way to the other objectives. Up to command if you want to do a thorough clear. Those are my recommendations, sir."

"Why the peninsula?" Hamilton asked. "Rather than the cargo pier?"

"If we don't get a really good clearance, the infected are going to have a hard time figuring out how to get over to the peninsula, sir," Faith said. "Sort of narrows their approach, sir. We can pull out any time pretty easy. And it's close to the military base, which seems to have some survivors, sir. From the looks of the pier we may be able to offload from the *Grace* there. It may be tight, though, but it's possibly doable. Worse comes to worst, we pull the survivors at the police station and shift by boat to the cargo pier."

"Concur," Hamilton said. "Lieutenant Commander Chen, Navy side."

"Ensign?" Chen replied.

"The main issue with the approach is reefs and shoals, sir," Sophia said. "Also wrecks. We've dealt with those before but this place is a whole 'nother order of crazy. The approach to the harbor has several small islands in the way and their reefs and shoals are very extensive. Then on the satellite it appears there's a large vessel, possibly an island support ship or a megayacht, overturned in the harbor entrance. It's hard to tell on the satellite but it looks as if the harbor is littered with sunk boats. We'll need to be very careful with navigation on the approach and we should make that very clear, and why, to all captains. The other firing points are actually clearer than the harbor approach. Stay away from the capes and you're good."

"Gunnery Sergeant Sands," Hamilton said. "Status of the Marine landing party?"

"They're still not up to the standards I'd prefer, sir," Sands said. "But they should be able to handle a simple vehicle level sweep, especially from open five-tons. I'm mostly uncomfortable with the lieutenant's choice to go ground mount and sweep for the initial landing. They're getting less skittish about infected, but it's still a toss-up if they will maintain fire discipline. I will be accompanying the landing, sir."

"Are you recommending against the peninsula landing?" Hamilton asked.

"No, sir," Gunny Sands said. "I'm going to be all over them the whole time we're on the ground, sir.

We won't have a repeat of the incident at the medical school, sir."

"Lieutenant," Hamilton said. "I want you and the gunny to coordinate closely on how far you're going to do the ground sweep. Recover the survivors from the police base, then determine if you're going to sweep to the pier or shift. But I want you to discuss it. Issues?"

"No, sir," Faith barked.

"I want the full operations order on my desk by thirteen hundred," Hamilton said. "Good brief."

"Mission...blow the fuck out of a bunch of infected and rescue survivors...No, won't fly..." Faith said, biting her lip as she slowly typed with two fingers. "E... Expectations? No, Environment? C-O-M-E...? No, shit, it's...P-O-M-E? Why the fuck does the U.S. Marine Corps use Aussie slang...?"

"Pretty," Sophia said as they approached the island.

Saint Barthélemy was a volcanic island with lush vegetation. The main town, Gustavia, and the surrounding hills were packed with houses of all sizes, most sporting red-tile roofs. Once a destination for the "rich and famous" of Europe, it had obviously suffered from the secondary effects of the Plague. Many of the houses were burned out and the numerous cliffs and reefs that surrounded it were littered with boats of every size. And it wasn't just the shore. There were sunk boats *all over the place*. The "rich and famous" had had a lot of boats.

Sophia had the *Bella* anchored with the rest of the force well off-shore to the west of Les Gros Islets. She was making her way in in a Zodiac piloted by Olga and carefully checking the soundings.

"Nope," she said, looking back over the side into the clear water. There was a wooden sailboat, about sixty feet, sunk and turned on its side in the channel. Partially unfurled sails were flapping in the light tide. There was a school of medium sized fish using the boat for cover. "I'm not sure we *can* get the *Grace* in here without doing actual salvage and raising some of this."

"So what are we going to do?" Olga asked.

"Change the plan, I guess," Sophia said. "We've got to find a way to get the gunboats in at least. And we'll have to check *each* of the approaches. This is going to take time."

"Now is when we could use a helicopter, sir," Lieutenant Commander Chen said. "Much of this wasn't apparent on the satellite due to cloud cover."

"What's your plan, Commander?" Hamilton asked.

"Getting the *Grace* in is out of the question," Chen said, looking up at the police station. There were survivors. They were up on the roof waving a French flag at the moment. He wasn't sure if that was an order to stay away or what. Usually people had the sense to wave the American flag when they turned up. The odd part was that they all seemed to be women. "We'll find channels to get the gunboats in and just continue the plan, if that meets with your approval, sir."

"Any thoughts on the sweep?" Hamilton asked.

"We've swept towns this size in the Canaries just using locally acquired vehicles, sir," Chen said, shrugging. "This has more people, which *may* mean more infected. But we should be able to clear it without the five-tons, sir. The other issue is the gunship placement.

Governor's Cove looks like a nonstarter. There isn't easy enough egress to attract many infected."

"Recommendations?" Hamilton said.

"We need to look at Baie de Saint Jean," Chen said. "We'd ignored it since it was on the windward side. And it's rocky. And even in the satellite you can see submerged wrecks. And their guns will be pointed at, well, us. And there's almost no channel. But it looks to be the only viable alternative."

"We need someone competent and responsible with that division," Hamilton said.

"I'll attach Chief Schmidt, sir," Chen said. "He'll make sure they're in their fire zones. And there are hills in the way. And I'll send Div Five. Bowman's a pretty good boat driver, sir."

"We're going to have to take another day," Hamilton said, looking up at the buildings on the peninsula. "I'm not going to pull up and then sail away. But we need to figure out these channels and pick our way in. That's a daylight operation. We'll pick our way in tomorrow, then do the usual zombie pre-wake. Without the party, of course."

"Of course, sir," Chen said.

"Get that spread and have Div Five move out as soon as the chief can get aboard," Hamilton said, watching an infected moving along the wharfs.

"Aye, aye, sir," Chen said.

"Bonus is it gives the gunny another day to rehearse the landing action," Hamilton said.

"That would be useful, sir," Chen agreed.

"What part of 'keep your barrel pointed at the deck' was unclear, PFC?" Gunnery Sergeant Sands growled.

"No excuse, Gunnery Sergeant!" Summers said, gulping.

"Why are you still standing, then?" Gunny Sands asked. "FRONT LEANING REST POSITION, MOVE! WHAT? YOU CAN'T COUNT...? THAT GOES FOR THE REST OF THE SQUAD! MOVE IT!"

"How's it going, Gunny?" Faith said, poking her head in the compartment.

The Marines had been training in the lower deck areas of the *Grace Tan*. Being a good little lieutenant she had stayed out of it and spent her time continually updating the operations plan when yet another snag was discovered.

"Just fine, ma'am," Gunny Sands said. "Coming right along."

"Passing the word that the operation has been put off for a day," Faith said. "All the harbors and other firing points are choked with wrecks. And we won't have the five-tons."

"Aye, aye, ma'am," Gunny Sands said. "Hear that, Marines? Good news! You get another full day of training! The more you sweat, the less you bleed!"

"I won't interfere with your fun, Gunny," Faith said, grinning. "But I'd like them to be able to walk and, you know, hold their arms up, when we hit the beach."

"They'll be dialed in, ma'am," Sands said. "We'll get it done. RECOVER! Now, try it again, this time WITH FEELING...!"

"I said to *port*, helmsman!" Chief Schmidt said, pointing. "That's *left*, you frigging yardbird!"

Trying to find a way into Baie de Saint Jean was bad enough. There was only one, narrow and twisty, channel

deep enough to get the yachts and gunboats into the bay.
And it was partially blocked by a powered catamaran
that was upside down on the bottom. The "edges" of
the channel weren't just shoals, either. They were nasty,
jagged rocks that were slightly below the low tide line.

Dealing with another undertrained, moronic *child*
driving a Zodiac was simply icing on the cake.

"Yes, sir," the Zodiac driver said nervously.

The nearly sixty-year-old formerly retired chief petty
officer ground his teeth. *Damn that stupid game!*

"I am not a 'sir,'" he retorted angrily. "And do not
quote Halo or I swear to God I will throw you to the
sharks and drive this boat myself!"

"Yes, si . . . Okay?" the driver said. "Hey, Chief?"

"What?" Schmidt growled.

"There's a boat coming this way."

"What?" Schmidt said. Sure enough, there was a sea
kayak headed their way. It was only then that he noticed
there were people, survivors, up on the big rock situated
by the beach. The "rock" reared ten to twenty feet out
of the water and had a cluster of buildings on it. Now
there were people up on a balcony waving. About five.

*"Away team, be advised, you're about to have
company."*

Schmidt straightened up and went back to the radio.

"Roger, Div Five, got that," he radioed. "Are we
following the Prime Directive, over?"

"Bonjour! Bonjour!" the very tanned man in the
kayak said, pulling alongside the Zodiac and grabbing
the sponson.

"Hey," Schmidt said. "Hope like hell you speak
English."

"*Mai oui*," the man said. "Yes, of course! Serge Laurent Lamar, *monsieur*. We are pleased to finally see the U.S. Navy. We had given up hope. You are the U.S. Navy, yes?"

"We are the U.S. Navy, yes. Chief Petty Officer Kent Schmidt with Division Five, Kodiak Force."

"We are prepared to leave at any time," Lamar said. "St. Barts is beautiful but it palls after this long."

"Might want to hold off on that, sir," Schmidt said. "Although, probably gonna need to evacuate your group. We're going to be making a mess sometime in the next couple of days. This won't be someplace you want to stay for a while. But right now, I'm trying to figure out how to get into the bay. You got any clues about a better channel, sir?"

"No," Lamar said. "This is the best entry. *Pourquoi* do you want to bring your boats in? There is a harbor in Gustavia."

"There are other boats over there, sir," Schmidt said. "See the fishing trawlers? They're gunboats. We've got the mission of killing off the infected in this area. Which we do with machine guns. The boats over on the other side of the island will do the same. Then Marines land and sweep the island. Then we leave and you can have it back."

"Will all the infected be . . . dead?" Lamar asked.

"As many as we can get in a day or so, sir," Schmidt said. "After that, up to you. We brought some guns along and there are some survivors at the police station. Presumably some of them are police."

"*Certainement*," Lamar said thoughtfully. "And for us? Our party?"

"When we do this we end up leaving behind a big

pile of bodies, sir," Schmidt said. "You'll want to be elsewhere since it will have to be on that beach," he added, pointing to the smaller beach south of the rock. "You won't want to be around them as they decompose. Even if we can't get the boats in, we can pull you all out by Zodiac. If you're ready to go, they can all fit on this one. No luggage, though."

"*Je comprends,*" Lamar said, nodding. "Can I ask... How bad is the rest of the world? Have you heard news of France?"

"Gone, sir," Schmidt said. "What you see here is everywhere. And the U.S. Navy is about a hundred small boats like this. Most of them aren't even Navy, sir. Gone pretty much covers it, sir. Believe it or not, you're not in bad shape here. You're out in the fresh air and sunshine but not on a lifeboat. Most of us were either trapped in compartments on ships, like myself, or on disabled boats or lifeboats. This isn't actually that bad compared to most of the world."

"*Je comprends,*" Lamar repeated, sighing. "We had hoped... But as the time passed."

"*Oui, monsieur,*" Schmidt said. "*Mes condoléances.*"

"*Vous parlez francais?*" Lamar said.

"*Oui, monsieur,*" Schmidt said. "*Parfait.*"

"Then why did you ask if I spoke English?" Lamar asked.

"*Je parlais Francaise, monsieur,*" Schmidt replied. "*Ce n'est pas ma préférence.*"

"And that's the skinny, sir," Chief Schmidt said. After the day he'd had he dearly wanted a drink. But he'd given that up years before and knew that one was too many. He took a sip of *un*reinforced coffee instead. "We *might* be able to get in at high tide."

The survivors had been evacuated and spread out in the boats. There were only five of them and they were grateful for some real food. They'd been surviving on raw fish and rainwater.

"And high tide tomorrow is seventeen thirty-seven," Lieutenant Bowman said, letting out a breath of air. "What's your take on getting this cluster of . . . Should we call it? Tell Force this isn't possible?"

"Pilots," Schmidt said. "My recommendation is that we bring all the captains forward tomorrow and have them get a good look at the problem. Then I'll take the helm of the boats, sir. Bring them in one by one. That way, if one of them gets grounded it's on me. We can get them in. It's just going to be tricky. And we don't, technically, have to bring in the yachts. Just the two gunboats. The rest will stay moored out here. If that meets with your approval, sir."

"Good plan, Chief," Bowman said. "Make it so."

"Aye, aye, sir," Schmidt replied. "*You* might want to explain it to the captains, though."

"That wasn't a bad set-up," Bowman said, circling in close to the rock.

The buildings were part of a resort perched on a prominence called "Eden Rock." The nearly circular rock, essentially a mini-island, reared up out of the shallow water surrounding it between ten and fifteen feet on the water side, then sloped down to a short stretch of sand and rock at near water line that connected it to the rest of the island. At that point, the survivors had cobbled together a series of wood and chain-link barriers. The water spouts of the buildings were connected to jury-rigged cisterns for water. Fish and even lobster had been available by fishing off the rock or venturing out in one of the kayaks.

"From what your crews say, one of the better," Serge Lamar said.

The former chef had worked at the Eden Rock Hotel and had, like most survivors, fallen back on food stores immediately. There hadn't, apparently, been many visitors at the resort when the Plague broke out or they had gone home while air-travel was available. All the survivors had been workers at the hotel.

"Did you have many turn?" Bowman asked. "Although if you don't want to talk about it I understand. What happened in the compartment, stays in the compartment."

"We had some," Lamar said, shrugging. "We had to put them outside. Most . . . did not survive long. We tried not to joke about 'throwing them off the island' but just before the plague they were filming a *Survivor* episode here. The joke was too obvious however black, no?"

"I suppose it's better than most alternatives," Bowman said. "I was the compartment's official strangler."

"Oh," Lamar said. "I believe the term for that in English is the same as French. A non sequitur."

"It's become sort of a . . . mixed blessing," Bowman said, turning the Zodiac back out to the channel. "Someone in each compartment or lifeboat had to do it. While nobody *liked* it . . . The people who were able tended to also be the ones who ended up running the compartment. Which means most of the captains of these boats were the official stranglers. Because the sort of person who *could* do that, even if they hated it, are the sort of people who *can* run a boat. If for no other reason than at a certain point everyone is fully aware that you're not going to take any more shit."

"I'll keep that in mind," Lamar said. "Would it be giving you shit to ask if we could pick up one of the lobster traps?"

"Not at all," Bowman said. "I could do with some lobster for supper. Where?"

"You *sure* you can get this in there, Chief?" Ensign Gary Poole asked as the chief carefully negotiated the *Noby Dick* through the channel.

"She's a tight one, that's for sure, sir," Chief Schmidt said. "That's why I chose *your* boat to go *first*, sir. Get ready, we're probably going to grind on the catamaran."

"Oh, joy," Poole said as there was a scraping sound from underneath the boat. "You're going to get me the same reputation as Buckley, Chief!"

"Think of it as a quicky way to clean off your hull, sir," Chief Schmidt said as they cleared the worst part of the channel. "Your boat, sir. I need to go get the *Guppy* . . ."

"Permission to speak, ma'am?" PFC Jesse Summers said as the platoon awaited the go order. There were seven Zodiacs filled with heavily armed Marines idling just off the point of Gustavia peninsula.

Faith was sitting in the front of the lead Zodiac in a full lotus position despite her gear, her eyes closed, and appeared to be meditating. The iPod buds in her ears were emitting a pulsing beat that could be heard over the putter of the idling motor.

"Speak," Faith said, loudly.

It was finally done. All the op orders had been written, issued, re-written, re-issued, lather, rinse, repeat. The platoon had gone over a map table of the upcoming landing. Everybody had been shown the primary and secondary routes to the objectives. Probable infected routes of attack had been analyzed, spun, folded and mutilated. Fire objectives and primary defense points had been defined, designated and resignated.

Now all that was left was killing zombies. But the final, final, really final, no, seriously, this is the absolutely last, frago had just taken it out of her. She could not even muster interest in rescuing people. They were probably French, after all. And her dad was already having a hard time with the French collective in the squadron. And all the people at the police station looked to be girls. There was no fun to rescuing girls. Cute guys, maybe. Girls not so much.

"May I ask what you're doing, ma'am?" Summers said.

"Centering my aggression," Faith said.

The song changed and she glanced at her watch. A few seconds later, the gunboats opened fire. She could hear it even over the pounding music in her earbuds.

"That's our cue," she said, holding her finger over her head. She made a circling motion then pointed at the shore. The Zodiac started moving forward, gaining speed quickly. *Once upon a night we'll wake to the carnival of life* . . . LOCK AND LOAD!"

She slid out her left earbud and slid in her radio bud, seating it hard to ensure it stayed. She knew she should use cans, full headphones that slid under her helmet. But the hell if she was going into battle without her tunes.

"And you keep your muzzle *up* in a boat, PFC," Faith said, pointing Summers's muzzle skywards. "That way you don't shoot a hooole in the bot-tom."

"Aye, aye, ma'am," Summers said.

"First Platoon, do you require fire support, over?"

"Better over than on," Faith muttered, then keyed the radio. "Negative. Position is currently clear."

"Ish," she added as an infected loped into sight from around the corner. She switched frequencies without thinking about it. "Gunny, can you bag that one?"

There was a shot from the gunny's boat and the infected dropped from a headshot.

"Show-off," she said as they arrived at the jetty. She stepped off the Zodiac and waved for the rest of the team to pass her. God knew she didn't want most of them *behind* her.

She and the gunny were in the lead and center boats. But one of the "revisions" to the op-order had subtly moved the teams that were "*Iwo* heavy" to the outside of the formation. The flanks were where infected were most likely to leak through and the reality was that the *Iwo* Marines were just steadier.

Colonel Hamilton had finally come to the conclusion that was the case when the gunny asked him to review comparative combat times. Which Faith should have thought of given her discussion with Staff Sergeant Barnard. When Colonel Hamilton realized that despite his eight tours in the Sandbox, three in "combat leadership" positions, and nearly twenty years in the Corps, Sergeant Smith's combat time had surpassed his own in a matter of months, he accepted the disparity.

Of course, their own combat time started from when the unit's boots hit the ground here in Gustavia.

Which wasn't real combat time in Faith's opinion. It should start from the first shot at confirmed infected.

'Course, the gunny had shot one on the way in. She wasn't sure if that counted or not.

"First Squad, get started on finding useable vehicles," Faith radioed. "Second Squad, let's roll."

The gunny was going to stay behind with First Squad, squad leader still Staff Sergeant "I'm so Salty I squeak" Barnard while Faith took Second Squad, led by Hooch and with Smitty as his Bravo Team leader, up to the police barracks.

They had landed right in front of the *L'Hotel De Colectivite,* which sounded like something commie to Faith. Probably not, since nothing commie ever looked that good. At least before it burned.

There was a narrow dirt path between the north-west side of *"L'Hotel"* and the bay which the squad followed. Hooch had put Lance Corporal Quade on point, then Hooch to make sure he could figure out the way. Faith was between the two teams. She'd quietly moved Kirby to the lead position in the rear team since the alternative was Sergeant Hoag and she didn't want Sheila behind her with a loaded weapon. Smitty was following at the rear and keeping an eye on his team's movement and weapons control while she was doing the same with Alpha Team.

"Curran, your sector is *right,*" Faith said. "Keep an eye on *your* sector. Filipowicz, you're up, not left. They do occasionally get on balconies..."

The area behind the burned building was cluttered with equally burned vehicles and the usual materials, dumpsters, carts, you found behind commercial build-ings. It looked as if somebody had tried to barricade the road at one point. And it looked as if it had flooded for some reason. What it didn't have was infected.

The drive behind *L'Hotel* connected directly to Rue Shkelcher. She'd wondered about that name, it didn't sound French, until she recalled her own briefing on the Swedish heritage of the town. The fort was right above them and they could just climb the steep ass hill through the thick ass jungle foliage. Which was the "by the book" route the staff sergeant pointed out since it "avoided paths and potential ambushes or IEDs."

The staff sergeant had been reading the Marine Infantry manual. "With supplements." Unfortunately, everybody in the current Marine Corps had been too busy to write many supplements on zombie fighting. They had some for clearance operations on ships. Ground was still come-as-you-are without the "assistance" of properly written manuals. Faith pointing out that zombies don't prepare L-shaped ambushes—they just hit you randomly no matter where you moved, and getting hit in constricting foliage, where they could come to grips, negated the effect, such as it was, of their Barbie guns—didn't seem to faze the experienced USMC Staff NCO.

Honest to God, Faith was starting to get the thing about second lieutenants. Every time Staff Sergeant Barnard said "In my experience" Faith wanted to laugh out loud. Thank God her first Staff had been Januscheitis. Otherwise she'd have assumed all Marine staff sergeants were given a lobotomy along with their certificate as a Staff NCO in the United States Marine Corps. Fontana had been a *Special Forces* staff sergeant and he didn't make any big deal about it.

Barnard's attitude seemed to imply that Staff NCOs in the United States Marine Corps automatically shit gold bricks.

Faith realized she needed to center her aggression again. Not to mention keep an eye on the fire team, which was technically an NCO's job.

"Curran, I am going to fucking shoot you if you don't keep an eye on your sect—"

She fired five times in rapid succession. At an infected. That burst out of cover in Curran's sector. Headed for Curran.

"Clear!" she yelled. "Keep moving. Haugen, cover Curran's sector. Curran, you swept the *fuck* out of Randolph. Again. Drop your mag and jack out your round. You are limited to support for the rest of the mission."

"Aye, aye, ma'am," Curran said, unloading his weapon.

"Cover your own damned sectors, people!"

CHAPTER 24

"... can still see zombies moving on the Grapevine.
It's like they're never going to end!
Where the hell is the government...?"

From: *Collected Radio Transmissions of The Fall*
University of the South Press 2053

"Holy crap," Smitty said, looking through the binos. "I would swear that's Christy Fucking Southard!"

The group of women on top of the police station were still up there and didn't seem in a mood to get down. Most of them were throwing kisses to the Marines. Faith had put the unit in a circular perimeter while she and the NCOs considered the situation from the road a couple hundred meters away.

"Really?" Curran said, turning to look.

"Your fucking *sector*, Curran!" Faith barked. She didn't see him turn, she just knew he would. She knew most of the Marines were going to be looking around. "Keep on your fucking sectors, oorah? Yes, that looks like Anna Holmes as well..."

"Holy shit," Hooch said. "That's Sarah Cassill! I'm sure it is."

"Dibs on inviting a star to the Marine Corps Ball," Kirby said.

Faith didn't bother to check. She knew Kirby was still covering his sector.

"Sector, Lance Corporal, with respect," Kirby continued. Freeman clearly wasn't.

"So why aren't they coming down?" Faith said. "Rapunzel, Rapunzel, let down your hair. People, keep a very sharp lookout for not just infected, oorah?"

"You thinking a *Money for Nothing* thing, ma'am?" Smitty asked.

"Possibly," Faith said, referring to the Russian oligarch who had tried to hijack her sister's boat. They'd ended up with his megayacht instead, which was now the support yacht for this mission. "Or they're just too God-damned dumb to be able to figure out how to open their own doors. So much for being belle of the damned Ball."

"You'll always be the Belle of the Ball, ma'am," Smitty said. "You're Shewolf, ma'am."

"Thank you, Smitty," Faith said, lowering the binoculars. "You're just bucking for a promotion to Staff, right? Don't worry, it worked. Why aren't they coming down? Who has a good throwing arm?"

"I used to play baseball, ma'am," Hooch said. "Semi-pro on the Marine team."

"How long have we known each other and I didn't know that?" Faith asked, pulling off her ruck. "Take one of the Coastie radios and toss it to them. It's shock resistant so it should handle landing on the roof."

"Aye, aye, ma'am," Hooch said, taking one of the radios.

"Better turn it on in advance," Faith said. "They probably can't operate it with their fingernails and all."

The first toss by Sergeant Hocieniec was a perfect

parabola that would have landed on the roof. Had not Christy Southard done a flailing attempt at a catch that batted it out into thin air.

Fortunately Hooch was as good a fielder as a thrower and caught it. Despite being shock resistant the three-story fall probably would have broken the radio.

He waved for the women to clear a path, then threw again, this time getting it onto the roof.

Faith waited until one of the women came into view with the radio in hand.

"Listen carefully," Faith said. "The way that a radio works is there is a button on the side that's red. You press that and speak into it. But when you press it, you can't hear me so you have to let up. Press it, say something, say 'over' to tell me you're done, then let up on the button, over."

"*I am familiar with the operation of a radio,*" the woman said. She had a cultured accent that was a mixture of English and something Germanic. "*I am Princess Julianna Gustavason, Baroness Chelm. Princess of Bad-Werschtein und der Uld. To whom am I speaking, over?*"

"Jesus," Smitty said. "A for *real* princess?"

"Dibs on being Prince Charming," Quade said.

"Can it!" Faith barked. "Second Lieutenant Faith Marie Smith, United States Marine Corps. Are you trapped on the roof, Rapunzel, or just enjoying the sunshine? Over."

"Oh, *snap*," Sergeant Hoag said, trying not to laugh.

"*Many of the interior doors are sealed and there are shutters on the windows which have been resistant to our efforts to open them. There is only a small area we can access. We can access the roof and a*"

*few interior areas but have thus far found no means
of egress. Over.*"

"Egress?" Smitty said.

"Exit," Faith said. "Stand by." She switched radios.
"Hooch, is that front door as solid as it looks?"

"*Yes,*" Hooch radioed. "*Solid steel construction and a
keypad entry. We're gonna need a cutting torch, over.*"

"Roger," Faith said, then switched back to the
handheld. "Can you get to one of the windows, over?"

"*Yes, over.*"

"Put one or more persons on the roof, oorah, over
where that is, oorah? Then somebody go down to the
window and bang on it. We will move to that window
and see if we can get in that way. Over."

"*I understand, over.*"

"Go," Faith said, waving a hand. "Which side of
the building, over?"

"*The seaward side, over.*"

"Hooch, we're moving seaside," Faith radioed. "On
your feet, Marines. Swing this caravan to the sea-side
of the building..."

"Ma'am," Hooch said. "Please don't say 'Get this
window open, Sergeant.' 'Cause I am clueless, ma'am."

The hurricane-shuttered window was nearly a story
off the ground at its base and the shutter was made
of heavy steel construction.

"What the fuck was this place?" Faith said. "This
is like no police station I've ever seen."

"Don't know, ma'am," Hooch said.

"That was a reticle question, Sergeant," Faith said.
"Form a human pyramid up to the mechanism," she
said, pointing to the metal-box-covered lifting system.

"Then we'll get that open and break it if necessary. If that don't work, we'll go get a cutting torch from the *Grace*. Oorah?"

"Oorah, ma'am," Hooch said. "Quade, Randall, Curran, Haugen, get lined up side by side, palms against the wall, shoulder to shoulder..."

"Sandman, Shewolf," Faith radioed.

"Sandman, over," the gunny replied.

"Status on wheels, over."

"Negative item. All vehicles surveyed so far are suffering from water or fire damage or both. Over."

"Roger," Faith said, watching the squad build the pyramid. "Move your unit up to this location. We will extract ground mount. Over."

"Roger."

"Be advised, group is...persons of interest. Female celebrities. Discipline issues are cropping up. Request movement this AO soonest."

"Wilco."

"Shewolf out."

"Look out below," Faith said as she prized the cover off of the mechanism. It sprung loose under the leverage of the Halligan tool and hit Sergeant Hoag in the helmet.

"Thank you, ma'am!" Hoag said. "Can I have another?"

"Oh...crap," Faith said, trying to balance on the sergeant's shoulders. "This is when we need Janu or somebody." She had no clue how the mechanism of the door worked. It was just gears and stuff to her. "Well, I think there's no such thing as too fucked up..."

She stuck the Halligan tool into the mechanism

and prized until something sprung loose, almost overbalancing her. But a push on the roll-top shutter showed it was loose.

"Hey, Rapunzel," Faith said. "You still there? Over."

"This is Princess Julianna, over." The voice seemed a tad chilly.

"Get your people to see if they can get the shutter to lift, now, oorah?"

"Oo—What?"

"See if you can lift the shutter, over. Ok... Oorah, let's break this down. Carefully."

"I never thought I'd be glad to see Marines," Sarah Cassill said as she was helped off the shoulders of PFC Randall.

"We get that a lot," Faith said. "We're always so *glad* to hear it. Why don't you go over there," she continued, pointing to where the group of survivors was gathering. "And keep your idiotic mouth *shut*."

"Oh, thank you, thank you!" Christy said, throwing her arms around Faith. "Are you gay? Aren't most girl Marines gay?"

"No!" Faith said, prizing the woman's arms off.

"Oh, too bad," Christy said. "I just want to kiss you all *over!*"

"Ick!" Faith said, pushing her back. "I've got a whole platoon of Marines ready to take you up on that."

"At the same time..." Randall muttered.

"What was that PFC?" Faith snarled. "Why don't you just go over there with the rest of the...with *them!*"

"Everything under control, ma'am?" the gunny asked, striding over to the window.

"Get Barnard's squad securing the survivors," Faith

said. "And tell them to wait on introductions, kisses or promises of massage with happy ending until we've actually got them *off the fucking island!*"

"Aye, aye, ma'am," the gunny said. "Barnard . . . !"

"Thank you," Anna said as she was helped down. "I truly appreciate this."

"Disobeying my own order," Faith said nervously. "Hi . . . I . . . Sort of always wanted to meet you . . ." She stuck out her hand.

"It is a pleasure to make your acquaintance," Anna said, graciously shaking hands, then ducked her head. "I . . . I should go join the others."

"Wow," Faith said. "She's really shy for an actress."

"I guess, ma'am," Hooch said.

"I am the last of this group," the woman said, holding out the radio as she reached the ground. "Lieutenant Faith Marie Smith I presume?"

"Sorry about the Rapunzel thing, ma'am," Faith said. "We generally don't use rank or names on the radio. We need to move your group to the boats. . . ."

"If we could speak for a moment, Lieutenant?" Julianna said. "It is important, I assure you."

"Sure," Faith said, waving for them to step aside.

"Is it . . . safe?" Julianna said, looking around nervously.

"No," Faith said after a short pause. "But I usually nail them before they nail me. You seemed like you wanted to talk in private."

"There was another group of survivors," Julianna said. "We . . . haven't seen or heard anything from them since we forced our way out of the storeroom. But . . . they should be somewhere in the building. I know it is an imposition . . ."

"We can deal with that later, ma'am," Faith said, pulling out her notebook and making a note. "Any idea where?"

"No," Julianna said. "They segregated us into gender-based groups when they brought us here. The male celebrities were in the other section."

"That would be..." Faith said, perking up. "I don't suppose one of them was Brandon Jeeters?"

"He was accidentally put in with us," Julianna said after a pregnant pause. "And I regret to inform you he did not survive."

"Damn!" Faith said. "I was hoping to get his autograph. But I guess I shouldn't be surprised. I mean, the only previous celebrity I ever met was Mike Mickerberg and that was for just long enough to blow him all over his yacht."

"Excuse me?" Julianna said, her eyes wide.

"He'd zombied," Faith said. "Long very ugly story. Join the Marines, travel to exotic foreign lands, meet interesting people and kill them. Oorah, then, let's move out. We'll come back later and see if we can find the guys."

"There is one other thing," Julianna said.

"There's not a lot of infected left on the island," Faith said. "But there are some. We should be inside the perimeter. Quick."

"The situation in the storeroom..." Julianna said. "We...Some of us had to...Deal with..."

"You figured out quick you couldn't keep them alive?" Faith said. "No harm, no foul. What happens in the compartment, stays in the compartment. That all?"

"Yes?" Julianna said, clearly surprised.

"Long story again," Faith said. "We're getting ready to make them into vaccine. Strangling infected is sort of the story of the day for survivors. Oorah, if that is absolutely all, Rapunzel, let's roll."

"Holy cow, Sis, is that who I think it is?" Sophia asked. She and the Naval Landing personnel were securing the landing point.

"The boss is..." She pulled out her notebook and frowned. "Princess Julianne Gusterston or something. And, yeah, it's all celebutantes and stuff. I didn't get the whole story. I was too busy wading through the drool from my Marines. And Miss Boob of the Month tried to molest me she was so excited."

"SERGEANT MAJOR!" Sophia bellowed. Her Landing Force personnel were starting to cluster up on the starlets and debutantes.

"Hadley, what the bloody hell are you doing off your post?" Sergeant Major Barney bellowed. "Eyes had better bloody well stay *out* and on your *sectors*!"

"Get the evacuees moved off to the boats, Sergeant Major!" Sophia ordered.

"You heard the ensign!" Barney bellowed. "Help the ladies to the Zodiacs you sods!"

"Gunny, pin the perimeter," Faith said. "I need to talk to higher."

"Aye, aye, ma'am," Gunny Sands said. "First Squad right, second left, spread it out and take fixed position..."

"Kodiak Ops, Kodiak Ops, Shewolf, over."

"Go, Shewolf," the colonel replied.

"Survivors from the fort recovered," Faith said. "Report additional possible survivors interior. Break.

No functioning vehicles found in immediate AO. Request additional frago, over."

"What is your evaluation of the security situation, over?"

"My opinion is that we can ground pound this island," Faith said. "But I may be wrong. There could be clusters, and vehicles make them easier to break contact. My suggestion is that we move out in a group and try to find functional vehicles, then sweep for additional survivors, over."

"Confirm," Hamilton said. *"Use caution. Over."*

"Wilco," Faith said. "Be advised, group is celebrities. Have been some discipline issues. Over."

"Any major incidents, over?"

"Negative," Faith replied as Anna Holmes walked over. "I've waded knee deep through dead bodies. I can wade though ankle deep drool easy enough. Over."

"Will keep issues in mind. Kodiak, out."

"May I help you, ma'am?" Faith asked.

"I . . . One of the men told me you two are in charge?" Anna said firmly.

"Yes, ma'am," Sophia said. "It's a real pleasure to meet you, Miss Holmes. I'm a big fan."

"You may not be for long," Anna said, lifting her chin. "I need to turn myself in on the charge of murder in the first degree."

"Oh," Sophia said, blinking. "Seriously? *You* were the strangler?"

"Yes," Anna said after a puzzled moment.

"I'm sorry for that," Sophia said. "That's hard. I've never had to do it but . . . Plenty of people have. Our chief had to strangle his wife."

"Colonel had to kill his wife and kids," Faith said,

shrugging. "I was wondering why you sort of ran off. But I told Rapunzel: What happens in the compartment, stays in the compartment. We were talking about whether that's different 'cause we're on land instead of a boat. But . . . we're not going to bring charges or anything. Hell, I'd be up for so many murder charges at this point you'd have to have a really big computer to figure them all out."

"I'm credited with saving over two thousand people at sea," Sophia said. "My thuggish sister here is credited with probably two or three times that number of kills."

"Never strangled one, though," Faith said, shrugging. "I've always got knives and guns to go around."

"Halligan tool," Sophia said.

"Machete."

"Axe."

"Crow bar."

"So . . . what do I do now?" Anna said. She seemed deflated.

"Three days grace, then you see if there's anything you're good at," Sophia said softly. "Clean compartments if that's all you can do. Or go in with the sick, lame and lazy who aren't willing to help. And we need all the help we can get. But . . . you're famous and everything. I mean, I'm a really big fan. But . . . that was then. It's about what you do now that counts. Now."

"Okay," Anna said.

"And right now what you need to do is get on the Zodiac, ma'am," Sophia said, shaking her hand again. "Keep the faith. You survived. That's important. There still aren't many of us."

They waved as the boat left, then Faith turned to Sophia.

"Thuggish?" she said.

"It means a person who is a brute," Sophia said. "A murderer..."

"I know what it *means*!" Faith said. "Thuggish? Seriously? You think I'm *thuggish*? *Thank* you! You've never said anything so *nice*..." She sniffed theatrically. "Gunnery Sergeant!"

"Ma'am?" Gunny Sands said.

"I need *wheels*, Gunnery Sergeant," Faith bellowed. "Your boss has a delicate figure that is disinclined to walking. Think of me as a tottering little celebrity in high heels. You *will* find me a working vehicle on this island. Oorah?"

"Oorah, ma'am!"

"In the meantime, it is...what's that thing about personal carriers?"

"Leather personnel carriers, ma'am?"

"Leather personnel carriers it is, Gunny. Oorah?"

"Oorah, ma'am."

"Move out."

"I have never hated a fucking island more," Faith said as a tall, distinguished and very thin man walked up with an angry expression on his face. Before he could even open his mouth, Faith made a lightning draw and put the barrel in the man's face.

"If you say 'Do you know who I am?' I swear I will pull the trigger," she said, then holstered the weapon. "No, I *don't* know who you are. No, I don't *care* who you are. I wouldn't care if you were the God-damned *President of the United States*. We have *one* car, it is purely for people who are too far gone to walk and you are *not* in that category. *I* am walking. *You* are walking. Gunny! Get this idiot out of my face...!"

"Before you *even* start," Sergeant Major Barney bellowed. "No, we do *not* know who you are! No, we do not bloody well *care*. Unless you're a prince of the blood royal, of Britain mind you, *I* really do not care. Follow bloody damned directions, even if it's from the snotty driving the bloody Zodiac, and you'll all come out right and tight. If you would prefer, and *we* certainly do, we will issue you a weapon and a magazine of ammunition and you can take your chances with the bloody infected on the island. Takers? No? Then line the fuck up and shut your stupid mouths!"

"Oh, my God," Faith said, almost squealing. "I know who *he* is!"

"Is that...?" Sergeant Smith said.

"I have always appreciated the brave men and women who protect our nation," Harold Chrysler said, shaking Faith's hand. "But never has my heart been more filled with the pride of being an American than today. It is an honor to shake your hand, Lieutenant." He'd played a president in more than one film and had the presence to pull the line off.

"It's...uh...Oorah, sir," Faith said. She realized she was getting ready to babble and cleared her throat. "It's an honor as well, sir. Big fan, big fan."

"I'm honored," Chrysler said. "Is there anything I can do to help?"

"Uh...oorah?" Faith said. "Sir?"

"Try to help herd the cats, sir?" Sergeant Smith said, thumbing towards the civilians. "We have *got* to keep them in the perimeter and not straggling or scattering..." There was a shot from the rear and the gunny bellowed: "STAY ON SECTOR."

"'Cause of, well, *that*, sir," Faith said, regaining her composure. "They keep...not staying in the perimeter. Which means if they get too far out, they're in the target zones. And they keep bugging the Marines who need to stay on alert and not answering questions. I swear, they've got no more sense of survival than a baby duck."

"The wealthy and powerful, even after all they have been through, tend to believe that they are invincible because of 'who they are,'" Chrysler said. "I have no such illusions, but I grew up a working stiff." He leaned forward to whisper in Faith's ear. "I don't suppose I could borrow a pistol?"

"Round in the chamber, sir," Faith said, ripping one of her chest carries out.

"In the chamber?" Chrysler said, pulling back the slide just far enough to check. He carefully slipped the safety on as well.

"It's a zombie apocalypse, sir," Faith said. "I'd appreciate it if you don't use it to herd the cats, though, sir. I've had to draw more than once but that's me, sir. I can get away with it."

"I'll keep that in mind, Lieutenant," Harold said, slipping the H&K into the waistband of his jeans. "Is there any news from the States?"

"I'll put it in perspective, sir," Sergeant Smith said. "You're looking at sixty percent of the total manning of the United States Marine Corps, sir. The LT is

number six in line of succession from the commandant.
And she's thirteen."

"Almost fourteen!" Faith snapped.

"Oh, God," Chrysler said, breathing deeply. "I
thought...I thought maybe this was just what was
available for such a minor... This is *all*?"

"Yes, sir," Smitty said softly. "I was on the *Iwo
Jima*, sir. We lost it to the infected till the LT and
her dad came in and pulled us out."

"Sir, we need to get going," Faith said. "You'll get
some time off at the boats. We'll have to cover the
questions there."

"I understand," Harold said, shaking her hand
again. "Again, thank you for your service. And you
as well, Sergeant. I'll go do what I can about the
baby ducks..."

"Why can't they all be that way?" Faith asked.

"Like he said, ma'am," Smitty said. "Born a working stiff."

"I guess," Faith said. "Gunnery Sergeant! Get this
wagon train a-movin'!"

"Aye, aye, ma'am. YOU HEARD THE SKIPPER!
MOVE OUT...!"

CHAPTER 25

"...cleared a big grocery warehouse in Mandan. The zombies are still hanging in there in downtown Bismarck somehow. Go around if you're coming in from the east. And bring all the ammo and guns..."

From: *Collected Radio Transmissions of The Fall*
University of the South Press 2053

"How is the clearance going, Colonel?" Steve asked.

He generally touched base with the Kodiak Force once a day in the evening to keep abreast of progress.

"In action terms, just fine, sir," Colonel Hamilton said. "That being said, I'm starting to regret not skipping to primary targets."

"Problems?" Steve said.

"No casualties or injuries, sir, thank God," Hamilton said, knocking the surface of his desk. "And we're about to suspend operations. Island has been pretty much swept for survivors. Still a fair infected presence but just the usual. All that is fine, sir. The survivors, however..."

"Pregnant pause there, Colonel," Steve said. "Not the usual odds and sods?"

"About half are, call it 'labor,'" Hamilton said. "Island residents. Hotel staff. One facilities engineer

413

which is pretty much the cream of the crop. The rest are...If I hear the words 'Do you know who I am' one more time, sir, I swear I am going to kill that person."

"Oh," Steve said, putting his hand over his mouth to cover a smile.

"I had to station Decker and Condrey outside the door to keep them from interrupting this meeting, sir," Hamilton said. "With orders to be as polite as possible and as violent as necessary. I suspect you are going to get a fair number of complaints, sir."

"No, I'm not," Steve said. "I have people. But I understand your problems, Colonel. I even have a potential solution."

"Other than slapping the hell out of them, sir?" Hamilton asked. "One of the complaints I fielded was on the subject of your daughter using very nearly deadly force in one case."

"Why am I not surprised?" Steve said. "She had, it seems prehistory now, experience dealing with the same sort of folk during the Fall and used much the same approach. Do you have an issue with that?"

"I told the complainant that based upon their attitude and tone that I was equally unsurprised, sir," Hamilton said. "Then I told them I used to be an interrogator at Guantanamo and asked them if they really wanted to get on my bad side. I apologize, sir. It just slipped out; I was that frustrated."

"How'd that work?" Steve asked.

"They shut right the hell up and walked away, sir," Hamilton said.

"Dare I hope we got more than the usual one to two percent?" Steve asked. "Even if they are a handful?"

"No, sir," Hamilton said, shaking his head. "Just short of eighty so far. Bit over one percent."

"Christ," Steve said, shaking his head. "If you had asked me, Colonel, pre-Plague, if it was possible to essentially wipe out the human race I'd have laughed at you. And this hasn't but . . . Christ almighty."

"Yes, sir," Hamilton said.

"I don't suppose any of them preferred to stay?" Steve asked.

"None apparently, sir," Hamilton said. "There is a real dearth of what you might call survivalist types. Despite the fact that the first group rescued were the *female* survivors from *Celebrity Survivor: St. Barts*. We have determined that the males all succumbed to the virus."

"That is so . . . wrong," Steve said.

"There isn't a single person with anything resembling military training, LEO or even paramilitary, sir," Hamilton said. "There are only a few with the vaguest familiarity with firearms. And as I noted, there is still a noticeable infected presence, sir. They have one and all declined to stay on the island. The only one who might have been willing to fight it out is both . . . elderly and an American citizen who has requested repatriation. Most of them don't think much of the boats, either, sir."

"Sounds like you're having boatloads of fun," Steve said. "Pardon the pun. I will dispatch a potential solution to your locale tonight, Colonel. I have a specific cat herder for this sort of thing. In the meantime, move on to the next objective as soon as you're ready."

"Yes, sir," Hamilton said.

"Squadron out," Steve said, closing the circuit.

∽⊖∾

Steve leaned back in his chair and chuckled for a moment.

"'I was an interrogator at Guantanamo Bay,'" he said, imitating Hamilton's Northeastern accent. "'You sure you want to take this up with me? I've still got my waterboard.'" He chuckled again, then bellowed: "ISHAM!"

"You can use the intercom, you know," Isham said over the intercom a second later.

"There are times I just prefer to yell," Steve said. "Got to get *some* fun out of this job. Speaking of which... Tell Ernie he has ten minutes to pack. He's going on a tropical island cruise..."

Faith set her tray down across the mess table from Sophia and leaned on the table with hands spread.

"'Do you know who I am?'" Faith said, looking her sister in the eye angrily.

"Oh!" Sophia said, holding her hands up as if to strangle someone. "Do NOT get me started!"

"But I met Harold Chrysler!" Faith squealed. Quietly.

"Me too!" Sophia said, bouncing in her seat. "And he was so—"

"COOL!" they both squealed.

"Most of the rest sucked ass, though," Faith said, sitting down.

"Oh, God, yeah," Sophia said, taking a bite of mashed potatoes. "You might want to check on your troops, though. Christy Southard was last seen trying to find out where the Marine barracks were at."

"I think I'm going to consider that an NCO issue," Faith said, tasting a bite of dolphin. Which was not bad. "Although I'm not sure how the gunny will react.

I'd say 'Let 'em at it.' They deserve some pussy after this mission."

"Good God, Sis," Sophia said, chuckling. "Being a Marine just so suits you. At least tell 'em to use a condom—" She stopped and gulped down her food. "Oh, hi . . ."

"Am I interrupting?" Anna Holmes asked.

"I didn't think this was mess time for the civilians," Faith said. "But grab a chair."

"That means no, you're not," Sophia said. "How *did* you get in?"

"The guard on the door was a fan," Anna said, shrugging and smiling. "And I told him I knew you and you wouldn't mind."

"Technically, I should ream his ass," Faith said, taking another bite of dolphin. "But again, I'm gonna let it slide. I don't mind and it has been one bitch of a day."

"Fighting your way across the island must have been tough," Anna said worriedly.

"Oh, *that* was a picnic," Faith said, shrugging. "I'm starting to think I prefer liners to the land, though. Fricking infected come out of *nowhere* on the land. But it wasn't like there was a heavy concentration . . ."

"You're welcome," Sophia said.

"Yeah, Sis," Faith said. "Thanks. Go Navy. But it was the *un*infected who were the pain."

"'I'm the Chairman of the Board of . . .' some company I've never heard of," Sophia said. "'I'm the mother of . . .'"

"Rapunzel had it together compared to most of them," Faith said.

"I have to keep stopping myself from calling Julianna

Rapunzel," Anna said, snorting in a ladylike fashion. "It shouldn't be so funny."

"Well, she's a princess," Faith said, ticking points off on her fingers. "And she was trapped on top of a building..."

"Oh, I got the reference," Anna said, laughing. "We all did. Except Christy but it was a bit complicated for her. She'll probably start laughing anywhere from a day to a week from now. May I bring up a delicate subject?"

"Go," Faith said.

"If it's the thing about..." Sophia said. "The compartment..."

"I read the brochure," Anna said. "I am still... troubled."

"Try seeing bleeding bodies in your sleep every night," Faith said. "Although, I suspect you've got your own nightmares."

"Yes," Anna said quietly. "I do."

"When you want to talk about it, come see me," Faith said, taking another bite. "And, yes, there's a reason. My da actually covered the omerta with us before we ever got into this."

"The omerta?" Anna asked. "Like a Mafia secret?"

"There is a secret known only to people who have taken lives in violence," Sophia said. "And if you're not part of that group, you're not let in on the omerta. Unless your da happens to be one of them and wants you prepared as you can be in case you have to. And even then he approaches it delicately. Short version: Know all those feelings you've got? To say 'you're not alone' is an understatement."

"Tell me about it," Faith said. "There's a reason I

do what I do, Anna. Lots of reasons. And you know most of them, now. You wouldn't have, literally *couldn't* have, understood them back when you were a nice little famous actress from a liberal background. If I'd talked about them to you, you'd have called the cops. Now . . . you're already in the omerta. Honestly, I like you better now that you're part of the sisterhood. What you don't know is how to cope with them. So . . . when you're ready, we'll talk. Or Soph, if you feel more comfortable."

"Okay," Anna said, still unsure. "When I'm ready I will. But I don't think you really know what I'm thinking."

"Bet you a dollar," Sophia said, leaning over and whispering in her ear.

"I wish you hadn't said that," Anna said, grimacing.

"There's ways to handle it, Anna," Sophia said. "There are ways to deal with it. And the payment is when it's your time to talk to somebody about the omerta, you bring them in on it."

"Make it soon," Faith said. "Otherwise it gets to be an issue. And you don't want it to get to be an issue. 'Cause you may feel pretty billy badass from your experiences but you're not. The good news is there are three billion zeds on this planet. And even if we can clear all the zeds, then we get brigands and pirates and raiders. War red war is the future of this world for a long time. You ain't done by a long shot."

"What's the other delicate subject?" Sophia asked.

"I *asked* about enlisting," Anna said. "And I was told that as a British subject, I couldn't."

"There, right there," Faith said, grinning and knife-handing her. "That is the omerta. Reenlistment rates in Iraq were sometimes one hundred percent. And now you know *why*. Like I said, welcome to the sisterhood."

"I hope it's not that," Anna said. "Really?"

"Don't listen to her," Sophia said, shaking her head. "My sister has her uses..."

"Opening jars for you..." Faith said.

"But she is fucking nuts," Sophia said. "You're not her. I'm not her. Take those feelings, add in a barely controlled vicious streak and then pump up the bass."

"Oh, yeah," Faith said, grinning ferally. "This is the only world where I really fit."

"I'll talk to the chain of command about it," Sophia said. "There are waivers for everything. And you can work my boat until we get some determination. Which means you'll be around two almost sane members of the sisterhood."

"Wait," Faith said. "You think I'm less sane than Olga?"

"Faith, I think you're less sane than *Charles Manson*..."

CHAPTER 26

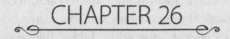

*"The Trans-Canada highway is clear of infected from Wawa
to Thunder Bay. Long ride on a snowmobile, ey? But at
least the Mounties weren't on me for speeding..."*

From: *Collected Radio Transmissions of The Fall*
University of the South Press 2053

"That's no space station," Faith said, looking up at
the island of Saba. "That's a moon!"

Saba was quite simply a currently inactive volcano
rising up out of the Caribbean Sea. It looked like a
shorter version of Mount Rainier with fewer trees.
There was a small "harbor" big enough to get a few
yachts in and cliffs with straggling bright green vegetation trying to keep hold.

From the satellites and the limited intel on the
island, the main town, "The Bottom," was at the top
of the mountain in the caldera of the extinct volcano.
The entire area had been cloudy during the one
direct overhead pass and images were blurred. They,
thus, had no intel on survivors or probable infected
numbers. From her own experience, right at eight
hundred infected would be about right.

"Now fill it with twenty-eight thousand heavily
armed, fanatical, Japanese soldiers in bunkers and

421

you've got some idea what taking Iwo Jima was like, Lieutenant," Gunnery Sergeant Sands said. "It's even got a sulfur mine."

Faith thought about it for a few seconds, took another look through the binoculars and shook her head.

"There's no way," she said. "Taking this place against an armed force would be impossible."

"Not for the United States Marine Corps, Lieutenant," Gunny Sands said proudly.

"That climb is going to be a bitch," Faith said, looking up at what could be seen of the road. Seeing the island on the satellite overhead had not prepared her for the reality.

"No, Lieutenant," Sands said, pointing at the vertical cliffs. "Climbing *that* would be a bitch, ma'am. And if that was what it took to complete the mission, that is what we would do, ma'am. Climbing the road will be a minor hump. Especially compared to some of the stuff we've done in Afghanistan."

"Point," Faith said, nodding. "Very valid point, Gunnery Sergeant. Never thought of Marines as mountain climbers but... Well, time to get it on and go for a little stroll. And we'd better make sure everybody drinks!"

It was ninety degrees and despite the trade winds the conditions were sweltering.

"Aye, aye, ma'am," Gunny Sands said, smiling slightly.

"I think we need to stay frosty on this one, Gunny," Faith said as they landed on the small breakwater. She had gotten a pretty good feel for how many infected to expect the Navy to chew up compared to the population density. Total pre-plague population of Saba in the off-season was about 1800. From that and given only two "clearance" points, the other on the far side of the island, there should have been about three hundred infected chewed up on the beach. There were barely twenty.

"Not enough carrion, ma'am?" Gunny Sands said.

"Not nearly enough," Faith replied. "I want us to proceed with caution on this one. There's going to be a concentration, somewhere. In The Bottom would be the most obvious choice. We're going to do a hold for more two-forty ammo and I'm going to go 'coordinate' with the Navy landing force."

"That's not enough bodies, Sis," Sophia said, gesturing with her chin to the small pile.

"Noticed that," Faith said. "My guess is most of the rest are going to be in the Bottom. From there they just wouldn't have noticed the lights and sound. And even if they did they might not have been able to *find* this place. I'm bringing up more two-forty ammo. My intent is to move up to the pass, then recon the objective. We may need resupply runs and, as usual in the fricking Caribbean, there aren't any cars."

There were a few cars. Tidal surge had pushed most of them off into the harbor or the surrounding waters. The few on land were on their sides or, in one case, high-sided on a wall. It must have been one hell of a storm.

"You think your people can hump the ammo or do we need to come back for it?"

"We can do that," Sophia said, nodding. "I mean, if you've got the people free . . . But if you need it we're there."

"I'm going to commo up with higher," Faith said.

"Get approvals on that. But I'm pretty sure we're going to need the support at some point. . . ."

"That's the sitrep, Force. Hotwash is majority threat not say again not eliminated by Naval fire. Request on-call materials support from NavLand if necessary, over."

"Understood," Hamilton said, nodding. "Concur. Note: Personnel not materially prepared for scrum. Avoid physical engagement."

"Concur, Force. Not interested in scrumming in regular uniform. Any further, over?"

"Negative," Hamilton said, looking at the narrow road up to the main town. "Use caution and in this case will remind you of Maxim Thirty-Seven."

"Maxim Thirty-Seven, aye, Force. That's why we're calling for more ammo. First Platoon, out."

"Maxim Thirty-Seven?" Ernest Zumwald asked curiously. The former Hollywood executive had rendezvoused with the Force at sea during the crossing and had been designated to "handle" the refugees from St. Barts who couldn't figure out that a zombie apocalypse trumped "do you know who I am?" He was getting ready for the first meeting on the subject and "touching base" with the colonel on what he'd like covered.

"There is no overkill," Colonel Hamilton said. "There is only 'Open Fire' and 'Cover me while I reload!'"

"Cover me while I reload!" Sergeant Smith shouted, ripping out another magazine.

The road up from the harbor to the pass had been nearly straight uphill, twisting back and forth through a narrow gorge but only hairpinning once. The road was broken concrete with a small "curb" less than knee height on the sweating Marines marching up it. The sides were nearly vertical walls of rough pumice with viney vegetation and straggling grasses covering the black earth and rock. The vegetation hadn't been enough to keep the material together in one or more tropical storms: there were several washouts and landslides, one of them completely covering the road in dirt and rock.

But there had also been zero infected. Apparently all the ones with territories on the seaward side had turned up for the party.

The road *down* from the pass hairpinned several times. At one point there was a small turnaround or water run-off point, Faith wasn't sure which. But it was a large enough, fairly open area that was protected on most sides by vertical rock walls or the road cuts of the road itself with a good overlook of the terrain. She had had the platoon hold there while they evaluated the situation.

Barely had the Marines dropped their rucks when the first infected came into view. Smitty had, on orders, taken it out with a single aimed shot. Even with a stock M4, a Marine Scout Sniper does that sort of thing. Then the birds had descended. Then more infected had showed up to see what the birds were eating. Then more. And more. And then they realized the Marines on the overlook were fresh meat.

There was a trail of bodies from the hairpin where the first infected had been killed. And it was getting inexorably closer to the Marines as more and more and MORE infected turned up for the feast. The only good part was, the terrain was so steep they were channeled into the road.

"Grenades!" Faith yelled as the lead group of infected got within thirty meters.

NCOs stopped firing and pulled out grenades instead.

"On my command!" Faith said, pulling the pin on an M87. "All ready? Good... Throw! TAKE COVER!"

The Marines ducked down behind the low wall as the grenades went off in a series of loud "pops" followed by howling. Faith counted the grenades and waited until all five had gone off.

"UP AND AT 'EM!"

"This is where dialing in the long-range accuracy would have helped, ma'am," Gunny Sands said, taking another head shot.

"*You* get my dad to schedule the range time, Gunny, and I'll *get* the ammo," Faith said. "Where the *fuck* is Sophia with the damn Singer ammo?"

"You rang?" Sophia said as Yu dumped a pile of .308 ammo by the machine gun team. He went ahead and started opening boxes since it looked as if Edwards was out. She looked at the pile at the switchback and the trail up the road. "Oh, my, that *is* a lot isn't it?"

"A few," Faith said, bagging another one with a double tap. "A few." There were several hundred bodies on the narrow road. And the infected seemed at this point to be ignoring them in favor of trying to close with the Marines.

"Want some help?" Sophia asked.

"*Your* accuracy would be a benefit," Faith said, missing her next shot. "I'm not so sure about the rest of your team, no offense. So, no, we've got this. We just needed the ammo. Thanks. I don't think we needed it so much for *here* as this probably isn't all of them."

The flood of infected was clearly starting to fall off.

"I'm going to go back up to the pass and see about holding this point," Sophia said. "We can use it for hand-off and get LandTwo to hold the harbor up to the pass. Nothing's getting past this to the harbor."

"Roger," Faith said, standing up. There was still a trickle of infected coming up the road but as they came to points that the 240 could spot them they were being engaged and made good zombies. Sergeant Hoag had been essentially useless as a squad leader. She was fairly good as a machine gun team leader. As long as somebody else carried it.

And Condrey turned out to be a damned *artist* with the 240. Unfortunately, he was still so... rigid, and he had to have each target pointed out to him. If Sheila didn't designate the target, he'd just sit there on one azimuth until an infected ate him. On the gripping hand, point out a target and it was toast.

"Gunny, we're going to move forward," Faith said. "I'm not going to sit here all day waiting for them to come to us. Put out a point that's got good snap-shot ability and let's take this slow. But we're going to take it."

"Aye, aye, ma'am," Sands said. "ON YOUR FEET, MARINES. WHAT, YOU THINK THIS IS A VACATION...?"

"You okay, Sergeant Smith?" Faith asked. The squad leader had stopped to readjust his ruck and wasn't looking all that hot. Well, he was looking hot, he was sweating up a storm. And not looking so hot.

The town of The Bottom was composed of mostly two- and three-story white buildings with red tile roofs. The foundations were generally tufa volcanic rock blocks; upper stories were wooden. It also was simply crawling with remaining infected. They were hitting the platoon in ones and twos in a continuous trickle. Fortunately, the Marines had settled down since Anguilla and were handling that.

"Legs are just feeling a little rubbery after the climb, ma'am," Smitty said. "All gung ho, ma'am."

"Wouldn't have anything to do with a certain reality star spending the whole night in the Marine quarters, would it?" Faith asked, innocently. "I'm sure everyone was having great conversation and party games. Right?"

"Not at all ma'—two steps left, ma'am."

Faith took two steps left and Smitty fired past her to take out an infected.

"I'm sure it had nothing to do with that," Faith said, grinning. She didn't even look around to see if he got it. "If it did, the next time I'd have to bring it to the gunny's attention. For now, drink water."

"Of course, ma'am," Smitty said, getting his assault ruck adjusted and stepping away from the rock retaining wall. "We were just playing cards and having a tea—"

The infected came out of nowhere, diving out of the bushes above the road and pile-driving the sergeant into the road.

Faith didn't even hesitate. Before it could get past the high neck of the sergeant's body armor, her kukri had cut into its upper neck, severing the cervical vertebrae and killing it instantly.

"Did it bite me?" Sergeant Smith screamed.

"No," Faith said, grabbing the infected by its long, greasy, hair and pulling it off the sergeant. "Close but I don't think so."

"I think I'd rather be clearing liners, ma'am," Smitty said, pushing himself to his feet. His nose was bleeding and his chin was scraped. "Damn," he said, slowly moving his head from side to side. "Thanks, ma'am."

"You're slurring," Faith said. "You going to be okay?"

"Gung ho, ma'am," Smitty said. "Just took a hit on the chin. Just got to shake it off."

"*TARGET!*" There was another flurry of shots.

"I'd definitely rather be clearing liners," Faith said.

"*I have seen Him in the watch-fires of a hundred circling camps,*" Faith caroled in high, perfect, soprano as the platoon marched up the steep road to the medical school. "*They have builded Him an altar in the evening dews and damps;/ I can read His righteous sentence by the dim and flaring lamps:/His day is marching on . . .*"

"*Glory, glory hallelujah!*" the platoon chorused. "*Glory, glory, hallelujah!/Glory, glory, hallelujah!/His day is marching onnn.*"

"FORRRM *PERIMETER!*" Faith bellowed.

"Gotta love a lieutenant that knows *all* the words to 'Battle Hymn of the Republic,'" PFC Funk said as the unit spread into a perimeter on the lawn of the medical school. The "school" consisted of a few small two-story buildings and had been swept by fire. They probably weren't getting much out of it.

"All six verses of the 'Star Spangled Banner' is the part that gets me," Sergeant Weisskopf said. "I'd never even *heard* the sixth verse. 'Then conquer we must, when our cause it is just, And this be our motto: "In God is our trust."'" Why don't they sing *that* one at games?"

"Maybe they will, Sergeant," Funk said. "TARGET!" He fired five times in quick succession and the charging infected dropped. For a change it was a white female. Most of the infected so far had been black males. "New day and all that..."

"By teams," Gunny Sands said. "Prepare for sweep. And so help me God if you can't keep from shooting each other this time, I will transfer you to the fucking Navy as no use to our Blessed Corps..."

Faith kicked a pile of burned textbooks and shook her head.

"I am not sure this island is worth the price of the ammo, Gunny," the lieutenant said.

"Think there are survivors, ma'am," Gunny Sands said. "That's worth something."

"Hopefully these won't expect me to know who they are..."

"Jesus, mon," the haggard man said, staring at Sergeant Smith with wide eyes. "Oh...God mon..."

"No, sir," Smitty said. "United States Marines, sir. But people do get confused..."

"We've found about twenty survivors so far, break," Faith radioed. The intervening mountains had required climbing up a hill to get a shot at the ocean. She could see a sub surfaced in the distance and, beyond it, another island that was probably Sint Eustatius, the next objective. "That is in clearance up to the edge of The Bottom and the medical school. School burned, no faculty or students found. Also found functioning vehicles. Query is multiple. Continue clearance, yes or no. Break down force to cover more ground, yes or no? Over."

"Security condition, over."

"Mixed," Faith replied, frowning thoughtfully. "Since the encounter at the road in, it's died down. Frequent close-quarters attacks with low numbers. Probability of...break...Probability of incidental infection reduced with vehicles. Given current time, recommend rapid sweep of additional...stand by."

She drew her .45 and fired twice, dropping the infected that had tried to sneak up on Sergeant Weisskopf. "Recommend rapid sweep by small teams using vehicles of additional heavily inhabited areas, then fall back to pick-up, over."

"How close is the contact, over?"

"Running out of Marinespeak, break," Faith said. "There's just a *lot* of these buggers and there's lots of concealment. They keep popping up like jack-in-the-boxes at really short ranges. That was the 'stand by.' One popped up ten meters away. I think we can maybe sweep the other areas with vehicles. Good news is more survivors than normal. Bad news is more leakers than normal. Over."

There was a long pause.

"Two vehicles together at all times. If the road is blocked, they do not proceed. Keep back a reaction force. Repeat back."

"Two vehicles together, aye. Blocked road, do not proceed, aye. Reaction force, aye. Over."

"We are doing a thorough clear on Sint Eustatius, break. Recommend to the locals a change of scenery. Over."

"Haven't gotten to discussing that," Faith said. "Was next on my list, over."

"Roger. Keep me apprised. Kodiak, out."

∽ ⊖ ∾

"I know how to use a gun," Jennifer Toplitz said, raising her hand. "I don't really like them, but I know how to use one."

After their first visit to Saba, Jennifer and her husband Tom had given up the life of corporate ladder climbing managers, bought a small bungalow and moved there to live out the rest of their lives.

The bungalow had, fortunately, been walled. And she had managed to push Tom off a balcony when he turned. Between a small garden, a mango tree and hurricane supplies, she had survived. Stay? That was another matter. A zombie apocalypse had caused the allure of unspoiled Saba to pall.

"Why?" Faith said. "I mean, if you don't like them..."

"I'm from Texas," Jennifer said. "Not particularly proud of it, but I am. I grew up with guns and hunting. My dad made me. I've never shot a machine gun before, though."

"This isn't a machine gun," Faith said, unclipping her M4, dropping the mag and jacking out the round in the chamber. "It's an assault carbine. Here's the mag. Think you can load it?"

"Like I said, I don't know these," Jennifer said, looking at the magazine. Faith had deliberately handed it to her upside down and backwards. Toplitz managed to turn it right way around and even could figure out how to jack the bolt. "At that point, there's a safety and a trigger, right?"

"Right," Faith said, holding out her hand for the weapon. "We've got some more of these on the ship. We're doing a strong clearance on Sint Eustatius and leaving a security detachment to secure the oil point. Think you could train a local militia for defense?"

"No," Jennifer said. "I really don't."

"I was in the Dutch Army for a while," a heavyset man said. "I think between us we could organize something. I *do* know machine guns. I did not use the M4, though."

"We're already crowded with refugees from St. Barts," Faith said. "And we don't really want to pick up everybody from all the islands. If someone *doesn't* want to go to Sint Eustatius and can handle the fact that there may still be a few infected, we sort of need them to stay. And pretty much everybody is getting off at Sint Eustatius. This isn't a pleasure cruise."

There was a flurry of shots from outside the emergency center and the crowd stirred.

"Is it safe, mon?" one of the men asked.

"Takes at least five rounds from one of these to put down an infected," Faith said, touching the M4. "Generally. We train that everyone who has an infected in their sector opens fire and fires at least three rounds. That was three Marines firing five rounds each. Tango down. That, in fact, is how you're supposed to do it. Trust me, you'll fire a lot more. Only Imperial Storm Troopers are that precise."

"How many infected are there left on this island?" Toplitz asked.

"We really don't know," Faith said. "We've got about five hundred stepped on, most of them up the road to the harbor. You really can't know how many you've got but I'd say at least two hundred more scattered around the island. And if you get generators going and put on lights, especially at night, they'll cluster down to wherever you're gathered. Good news is you can whack them easier. Bad news is, if you're staying you'll need to do something with the bodies. We generally just make them and go."

"Oh, great," Jennifer said. "Is it going to be like that in Sint Eustatius as well?"

"Probably."

"So now we're supposed to clean up the bodies, too?"

"No," Faith said, slowly. "You clean up the ones near where you're at and let the bugs, birds, dogs and pigs do the rest. These kind of temps, they'll be down to bones in a week or so. Cluster up somewhere with supplies, keep the windows closed for a week or two and you're good. We're looking at an estimate of one percent total survival, world-wide, ma'am. That is the *definition* of 'not enough left to bury the dead.' Then clean up the bones if it matters to you. If you've got a backhoe and someone who knows how to use it it helps."

"How old are you, Lieutenant?" Toplitz said, frowning. She clearly didn't think much of those suggestions.

"Thirteen, ma'am," Faith said.

"Th-th-th—"

"I'd just finished seventh grade if that's what you're asking, ma'am," Faith said evenly. "Since the Fall, I don't know how many infected I've killed but this is pushing my twelve hundredth hour in combat conditions. Thousands is the easiest way to say it, ma'am. I've cleared ten liners and fought my way out of Washington Square Park. I'm starting to get carpal tunnel in my trigger finger. And *I'd* be *very* proud to have been raised in the great state of Texas, ma'am. *I* had to settle for *Virginia*."

"When do we leave?" Toplitz asked.

CHAPTER 27

"Stockholm har fortfarande många smittade men områdena utanför tullarna verkar rensade. Vi samlas på Tranholmen. Isen håller för överfart från Stocksund. Lidingö är också rensat och en grupp ansamlas där. Om ni finner någon mat, ammunition eller vapen, var vänlig ta med...."

From: *Collected Radio Transmissions of The Fall*
University of the South Press 2053

"Well, as I live and breathe," Sergeant Major Barney said. "It's bloody Cloggies."

Some of Sint Eustatius' history had been well known to Colonel Hamilton. During the American Revolutionary War it was held by the Dutch, who were generally contemptuous of Continental customs enforcement. So it was the primary weapons supply point of the American Revolution. A certain British lord had claimed in Parliament that if Sint Eustatius had only sunk into the waves, "George Washington would have been dealt with years ago." It was also the place that American forces were awarded their first recognition as a new country when Fort Oranje rendered a salute to an American man-o-war.

This laissez faire approach to business had resulted in a booming economy during the late 1700s. Warehouses lined Oranjestad Bay, sugar and rum flowed like honey and the island was referred to as "The Golden Rock" for the immense wealth made from the trade transfers.

However, the support of the Colonial Rebellion resulted in a great deal of ire on the part of the British and it was subsequently conquered by the British and then the French after the revolution. The traders, mostly Jewish, were deported, the economy more or less collapsed and the island was at one point virtually depopulated. It was eventually returned to the Dutch and again, for a while, became a linchpin of trade in the Netherland Antilles. Eventually that faded to generalized farming and tourism. Just prior to the Apocalypse it had been selected as the perfect site for an oil transfer station. The deep waters and sharp shoaling in humorously named "Tumble-Down-Dick Bay" meant that tankers could, carefully, come close in shore to hook up to an off-shore oil-transfer pier that led to a series of large containers on the hills overlooking the bay. It was upgraded to provide refined products as well and smaller support tankers and even large freighters were stacked up nose to nose waiting to either off-load or onload various forms of liquid gold. So, once again, Sint Eustatius was in trade and the economy was booming...

And now it was depopulated again. There were all the signs of the Apocalypse—the burned houses, the infected picking the beach and fighting seagulls for scraps. But there were two good signs. The oil transfer point appeared to be intact. There were, or had been, two high volcanic hills with a narrow valley, more of a gorge, between. The northern hill had clearly been flattened and now held several dozen oil tanks ranging from multimillion gallon to a few tens of thousands of gallons. None of those appeared to be damaged nor had the area been swept by fire: the area had been thoroughly brushed to prevent just that. The oil pier appeared to be in good shape from the close pass they had made. Although they were going to have to raise a tug that was sunk nearby. There were some support buildings and large generators that were near the waterline which might have taken damage but even those seemed to have survived whatever tropical storms came through with minimal damage. The numerous tugs that supported the pier were, unfortunately, missing, other than the one upended by the pier. But the squadron had tugs. Now they might have fuel for them.

The second good sign was revealed as they came in sight of the town of Oranjestad. Fort Oranje, the antique defense of the town, was occupied. There was an untorn Flag of Orange flying from the mast, indicating it had been taken in in bad weather, and people were gathered on the ramparts watching the approaching Force.

"Cloggies?" Colonel Hamilton said.

"There appear to be persons in the uniform of the Dutch Marines on the ramparts, sir," Barney replied. "We refer to them as cloggies, sir. Sorry."

"I see," Hamilton said. "I see who you're talking about. Signaller, send a standard code signal and see what we get. In this case, we sort of need permission to perform an assault."

"Aye, aye, sir," Petty Officer Simms said. He began flashing the Aldis lamp at the fort.

"Very good," Sergeant Pier Niels Roosevelt said, reading the transmission. Americans frequently asked

Sergeant Roosevelt about his name, given that he was both black and Dutch. He would calmly tell them that Roosevelt was originally a Dutch name and that, in addition, his great-grandparents had changed their name to Roosevelt in honor of Theodore Roosevelt, whom they much admired.

One company of Netherland Marines was stationed on Curacao, which was where Sergeant Roosevelt was born. He'd joined the Marines when he was eighteen and managed to wangle a transfer from MARSOF, the Marine Commandoes, back to the "regular" Marines in Curacao just in time for a zombie apocalypse. As soon as the situation was clearly getting out of control, the company commander had dispatched one platoon to "maintain security" in Sint Eustatius. Given the strategically critical oil terminal, it was a no-brainer decision.

Unfortunately, what he hadn't sent along was vaccine. Two-thirds of the platoon had succumbed to either the direct flu-based plague or bites from infected before the sergeant, a remnant equaling about a squad, and a handful of locals fell back on the fort.

They'd been holed up there ever since. Fortunately, his platoon leader had immediately recognized its utility and laid in food stores. Water had been a potential problem but simply fixing up the original cisterns, which had taken some work, and waiting for the inevitable rainfall in the summer had taken care of that problem. There were thirty-three survivors in the fort and he had calculated that they could hold out for another six months. After that, they'd starve.

"What are they saying?" Counselor Michel Roelof Van Der Beek asked.

"They are asking permission to perform a dawn assault," Sergeant Roosevelt said.

"Why are they here?" Counselor Van Der Beek asked.

The relationship was touchy. Counselor Van Der Beek was, as far as anyone was aware, the senior remaining member of the Island Council, the local governing body. From his point of view, that put him in charge.

Martial law had been declared before everything fell completely apart. So that put the military in charge. And Sergeant Roosevelt only took orders from his chain of command. He'd accept orders from, say, a civilian member of the Ministry of Defense or the Prime Minister's office. A local official could not give him orders, legally. And Counselor Van Der Beek could not seem to get his head around that fact.

"It really doesn't matter," Sergeant Roosevelt replied. The fort was in view of Saba and they had seen the dawn attack the previous day. They couldn't make out much more than that but he was prepared to let them have the whole island if they wanted. "We can't break out on our own and we have only three months' supplies left. Would you prefer I told them to go away?"

"Are they here to take the oil is the question?" Counselor Van Der Beek asked.

"If they were simply here to take the oil, they would not have cleared Saba," Sergeant Roosevelt replied. "None of which matters. This is clearly a military decision."

"Concur ground assault. Thirty-three survivors this location. Ten Marine, rest civilian. Intentions?"

"Send this:" Colonel Hamilton said. "Aggressive day and night clearance purpose establish green zone Statia AO. Reestablish oil point to support ongoing military operations. Drop civilian refugees, Saba, St. Barts for recolonization. Link up by zero eight hundred hours tomorrow to discuss ongoing operations."

"So they are really here for the oil," Counselor Van Der Beek said triumphantly. "I told you."

"Which they obviously need to continue their operations, Counselor," Sergeant Roosevelt said. "I'll remind you that both the Netherlands and the United States are members of NATO and required to give assistance in times of need. This, Counselor, is very much a time of need. Their assistance is obviously clearing the island. We will discuss it with them tomorrow. At least now we know there will *be* a tomorrow." He began to signal the cluster of ships, wondering if they were really who they said they were.

"Good morning, Marines!" Faith said, standing on the body of a good infected and looking up at the Marines on the guardhouse of Fort Oranje. "Are you going to open the door? Or do you want us to just take the ammo boxes back to the ship...?"

"This is all?" Counselor Van Der Beek asked, stunned.

"You're looking at about half the remaining USMC, sir," Faith said. "Colonel Hamilton is on his way up. I'll let him handle the rest of the negotiations, if you don't mind, sir. My men and I have some more zombie hunting to do...."

∽ ⊖ ∾

"Colonel, I understand your concerns," Counselor Van Der Beek said. "And I fully support your mission. However, we are Dutch, Colonel. We trade. You could say it is in our blood."

Colonel Hamilton forebore to comment on the fact that Counselor Van Der Beek was blacker than Sergeant Roosevelt. He had enough history to know that the Netherlands, like the United States, had always been a nation of immigrants.

"What are you looking for in terms of trade, Counselor?" Hamilton asked.

"The island is somewhat poor for farming, and the refugees you want to land are going to need to be fed," Van Der Beek pointed out. "We would like a weight for weight measure of materials for oil products from the supply point. And before the point is accessed, we are going to need some boats. The storms destroyed all of ours."

"We cleared your island and intend to put the supply point back into operation, Counselor," Colonel Hamilton said. "Which will take some doing. Not to say that your points don't have merit, but I'd have to put a value on those items as well. If we calculated the costs based upon pre-Plague numbers, we could more or less pump everything out of the oil point for the cost of that operation alone."

"This is not pre-Plague," Van Der Beek pointed out. "Do you know of another point with similar quantities of material?"

"Not available," Hamilton admitted. "But that one wasn't available until we cleared the island. Our current standard on salvage of ships is that survivors retain fifty percent of material onboard. That would seem to be equitable. U.S. military, in return for clearing the island and getting the oil point back in operation, retains fifty percent of the material at the oil point with the Dutch local government retaining the other fifty percent. When or if we burn through the first fifty percent, we'll negotiate what we pay for additional material. Or you can finish clearing the island with your Marines and try to get the oil point back in operation yourself."

"I'll accept on the condition that you throw in thirty days' supplies for the refugees."

"I'll see what I can do on that," Hamilton said. "I'll need to get it from Gitmo. We should have the materials available, but I'm not sure what Squadron's needs are. I'll also see what I can do on the boats. They're scarce throughout this area due to the storms. But both points obviously have merit and I fully support them."

"You drive a hard bargain, Colonel," Counselor Van Der Beek said, smiling and standing up with his hand out. "We look forward to becoming the grand refuge of the Caribbean . . ."

"We can run the *Eric Shivak* down with a general load of supplies," Steve said, frowning. "And we'll see what we can figure out on boats. Last year's storms must have been doozies; all the satellite images show pretty much nothing but wrecks from Puerto Rico down to the Windward Islands. Any luck with your primary mission?"

"No, sir," Hamilton said. "Dry hole again. More medical texts but we've got about every standard and nonstandard text you could want at this point."

"Finish clearance, then hold in place," Steve said. "There's another possibility in the wind I'm discussing with the Joint Chiefs. If the local authorities are comfortable with it, have your platoon engage in training local militia. Eventually other groups will start clearing and moving around and at a certain point we probably have to worry about raiding. So it's for more than zombie clearance. I'm going to do some consulting to higher about what better potential targets are."

"Roger, sir," Hamilton said.

"What's the status of our astronauts?" Steve asked.

"They're all still with us, sir," Hamilton said. "About to get their booster shots, which is the trickier injection but . . . still with us, sir. Lieutenant Lyons is chomping at the bit, I'll tell you that."

"I can imagine," Steve said. "Clear the island, get started on the oil point, train the locals. And I'll look at a new mission."

"Aye, aye, sir."

"Mission," Faith said, pointing to the sand table scale model of the island. "First Platoon, USMC, reinforced by Dutch Marine personnel, will perform night clearance of the island of Statia with purpose of reducing infected presence to the level of lightish green, sort of an aquamarine would be nice but we'll settle for chartreuse . . ."

"Rigged up like this, the infected can't get to you," Sergeant Smith said, his voice muffled by the gas mask. "But we only use it at night on land. It's hot as hell any time and fucking *horrible* in the daytime."

The Dutch Marines had chosen to "augment" the U.S. Marines clearing the island by night. They had been detailed, one to each clearance team, to get some training on night clearance. Fortunately, they all spoke English.

Smitty thus had Sergeant Roosevelt, who seemed like a steady guy, and PFC Haroldson in the car, cruising down a darkened street called "Kapelweg" with the windows down and the tunes going full blast.

"So if we have to, we'll go to scrum," Smith continued. "That's hand-to-hand. With this stuff they can bite all they want and they're not getting anywhere. Target." He was driving so he just lifted his M4 one-handed and fired three rounds into the infected stumbling out of the darkness. "Biggest concern is not getting stuck, obviously."

"Obviously," Sergeant Roosevelt said.

"Questions, comments, concerns?" Smitty asked as Haroldson called "Target" and took a shot out of the back.

"Not really," Sergeant Roosevelt said, firing into the darkness at another infected. It dropped like a stone. "It is . . . odd. I was MARSOF, our version of your Recon Marines. The technique is to be as invisible as possible. This is . . . strange."

"Tell me about it," Smitty said as Haroldson took another shot. "I was a scout-sniper. Making noise is against my religion. But you want to draw them to you . . ."

"Missed that one, Sergeant," Haroldson said. "Could you stop to wait for it to . . . Never mind. Damn Barbie guns . . ."

"One question," Roosevelt said. "Is your lieutenant as young as she appears?"

"Younger," Smitty said. "But let me tell you about Shewolf, brother . . ."

∽⊖∾

"Target, two thirty," Sergeant Hoag said, tapping Condrey on the shoulder and pointing.

The road past the airport ran through a low cut that led to the oil point. Since firing up the oil point was, obviously, out of the question, Sergeant Hoag's machine gun team had been augmented with two Dutch Marines for security and placed on the edge of one of the hills that made the cut. With three cars shining their lights onto the road, they were drawing a trickle of infected. Which Condrey was studiously mowing down.

"Target two thirty, aye," Condrey said, targeting the infected.

"Fire."

"Firing, aye."

The latest infected tumbled to the ground, scythed by three 7.62x51 rounds. Hoag had carefully waited until it was clear of the road. There were a few bodies blocking it but just below them was a gravel pit with some front-end loaders. They'd be easy enough to clear come daylight.

"So, you guys are just called 'Marines First Class' and stuff?" PFC Edwards asked. They had one of the cars turned away from the machine gun team and beaming its lights up the hill.

"Yes," Marine First Class Henk Geert Cloet said. "Makes it easier."

"Makes sense to me," Edwards said. "We've got most of the same ranks as Army and people ask me what I do in the Army sometimes. Pisses me off. Well, it used to. I think we've only got one Army guy and he was SF and now he's one of the doctors."

"Do you always talk this much?" M1C Adam Vogels asked.

"Got anything better to do?" Edwards said as the machine gun barked again.

"No, not really," Vogels replied. They were spread out and keeping an eye on their sectors but nothing seemed to be moving in the brush. "What is the American expression? This is shooting fish in a barrel."

"Better than clearing liners, that's for sure... Speaking of which, you guys better get the skinny on Shewolf..."

"Attention on deck!" Sergeant Roosevelt boomed, snapping a parade ground salute as Faith dropped out of the five-ton. "Good morning, ma'am!"

It was just past dawn and the island was "as clear as it's gonna fucking get for now." The Marines had assembled in front of an old church near Fort Oranje. The cars they'd been using were lined up with military precision.

"Good morning, Sergeant," Faith barked, returning the salute. "You guys all straight?"

"Yes, ma'am," Sergeant Roosevelt said.

"Listen up, Marines," Faith said. "Refugees start landing at twelve hundred hours. Between now and then, I want you to do a rotating stand-down, thirty percent on security, thirty percent getting your shit cleaned and chow and thirty percent getting a doze. We've got to keep going all day. We'll get refugees into secure points for overnight, then start training local militia tomorrow. Just hang in there and remember that sleep is for the weak. Oorah?"

"Oorah," the U.S. Marines responded.

"Status, Lieutenant?" Hamilton said, returning her salute.

The Dutch Marines were tearing into the first hot meal they'd had in months. The rotation was by squads and Second Squad was cleaning weapons and gear, having taken a "whore's bath" with baby wipes while First Squad had the unspeakably hard job of keeping awake while manning the walls of a fort.

"All good, sir," Faith replied. "Island's pretty clear. After we get through the training period, I'd like to do some foot patrolling of the outer areas, that volcano..." she said, pointing to the Quill, "and over past the oil point. Probably some betas hiding out, still, but getting all of those is pretty tough, sir. And they're not an excessive threat, sir."

"Sounds good," Hamilton said. "Lieutenant, I got sleep last night. I want you to stand down until tomorrow morning. I've got this."

"I can keep going, sir," Faith protested. "I just told my Marines that sleep is for the weak, sir! Mission, men, me, sir!"

"This is physiology, Lieutenant," Hamilton said. "A thirteen-year-old cannot keep going the way that someone nineteen can. And dealing with the refugees is going to require a certain amount of tact. When you are tired and frustrated, tact is not your strong suit. You're off until tomorrow at zero five. The gunny and I can handle this. You've done your usual excellent job at killing infected and breaking things. Now go get some sleep."

"Aye, aye, sir," Faith said.

"Oooh..." Master Sergeant John Doehler said, holding his head.

The senior imagery analyst in the Hole could blame

many things. He could blame the fact that he only had one other analyst, and the kid, while pretty experienced at this point, was still a kid. He could blame the fact that there was an entire world to sweep and only two people to do it. He could blame the fact that, since the remaining birds were the only ones that would ever be up there in anyone's lifetime they could no longer retarget for things they might be interested in. Once their onboard fuel was used up they'd eventually start to degrade orbits and then, well, he'd be out of a job. Most of the world was empty and only occasionally did the spysats on ball-of-twine orbits cross something that they were really interested in. He could blame generally crappy weather in the target area as well as frequent mass-fires that often obscured the rare city shots.

However, he knew that one reason was that nobody thought there would be any critical survivors in London. So he just basically hadn't looked closely enough.

He really, really, should have spotted this months ago. Especially since the imagery had been sitting on the drive for, well, months. He'd just checked two previous passes and each clear pass had the same image.

He looked at the image again and checked it against the file photo. There was no real question. The facial recognition software was just a cross-check and it was saying eighty-seven percent accuracy. The low value was due to the angle and the weight loss, probably.

He looked at the images, especially the placards held overhead, one more time and picked up the phone.

"Sir . . . We may have a priority target for Wolf Squadron . . ."

CHAPTER 28

*"... sad duty to report that the Queen is dead. We have two
survivors of her SAS bodyguards and they confirm that the
Queen contracted a non-H7 influenza and died of pneumonia
last month shortly after her compound was compromised.
The location of the remaining members of the Royal Family is
unclear. Prince William and his wife were in the Seychelles on
vacation while Prince Harry was on duty with his Army unit ..."*

From: *Collected Radio Transmissions of The Fall*
University of the South Press 2053

"I shouldn't state the obvious at this juncture, General," Steve said, looking at the image. "But it would have been nice to have this a month ago. We couldn't have extracted them a month ago but some planning time would have been nice."

"Can you now?" Brice asked, seriously. There was no joking around about the general on this call.

"We have one CH-53 certified," Steve said. "It has been test-flown and is good to go. We've got a Seahawk almost ready to go. I was going over what it would take to insert on USAMRIID yesterday with Captain Wilkes. We're not finding what we need in the Caribbean so going for one of the major research centers that is coastal seems to be the only option.

"The problem is time of float and, well, details. Nobody is trained in air insertion being the top detail. Most of which can get worked out on the float. And the whole weather issue, North Atlantic in winter, but using solely the *Grace Tan* cuts down on that. Lots of dangers, of course. We'll be putting our primary platform way out on the end of the line. There are wrecks everywhere and if it hits one... None of which matters. I'll recall Kodiak Force immediately. They'll train up on the way."

"Understood, Captain," Brice said. "Good luck."

"We'll need it, ma'am," Steve said. "Good news. We needed another helo pilot and should get some first class soldiers out of it..."

"Oorah, Marines!" Faith said, setting her tray down at the table. "It's a beautiful day to be in the United States Marine Corps!"

"You look better, ma'am," Sergeant Weisskopf said. "You were looking pretty gray, yesterday."

"I was feeling pretty gray," Faith said. "I was upset with the colonel pulling me off duty. It felt and still feels wrong. But I'd have probably killed some stupid refugee the way I was feeling. How'd it go?"

"Easier than we expected, ma'am," Weisskopf said. "Mr. Zumwald apparently got through to them. Some of 'em, anyway. Lot less 'do you know who I am?'"

"Lot more 'I've got a better plan, get out of the way...' Sergeant," Lance Corporal Saul said.

"There was that," Weisskopf admitted. "But some of them had their act together. Some of it was actually helpful. A lot, really. Face it, a CEO is sort of a civilian general and sometimes you need that."

"Some of them were just people who were rich," Faith said, shrugging. "Some of them were people who got that way through being smart. Even retired CEOs tend to know how to get shit done. Probably a situation of too many cooks but that's a problem for the Dutch authorities on the island."

"I guess I need to go check in with the colonel," Faith said, finishing off her light meal. "Training day is gonna be—"

"Ma'am," Corporal Douglas said. He'd entered the mess compartment, looked around and made a bee line to her table. "Colonel would like to see you at your convenience."

"I was just headed that way, Derk," Faith said, standing up. "Gonna be another oorah day in the Marine Corps, Marines."

"Oorah, ma'am," Sergeant Weisskopf said, grinning.

"I'll get your tray, ma'am," Derek said. "I'm pretty sure from his tone 'at your convenience' meant 'double time.' And he sent word for the gunny, your sister and that Dutch Marine sergeant. It's a general 'right now' call."

"I'll let you take it, then," Faith said, frowning. That list made sense for the training day but the urgency didn't.

"Go right in," Sandra said. The refugee had taken over as the colonel's administrative assistant. "Something's up."

"Reporting as ordered, sir," Faith said.

The *Grace Tan* was big but it was also crowded and not really set up as a command and control ship. The colonel's office wasn't much bigger than her closet. If the people on the plasma had been in it, her da, General Brice and the NCCC, there wouldn't have been room for Faith. And that meant something was up. It was zero four hundred Omaha time. They weren't there to kibitz on the training of the locals.

"Think you're standing, Faith," Colonel Hamilton said. "We won't be long. Captain?"

"We just got a priority extraction," Steve said. "Doehler, show them the image."

The faces were replaced by a satellite image of a burned-out city. It was big and had a river running through it was all Faith could tell. It looked familiar but she couldn't place it. The image zoomed down and held on some sort of fort or castle by the river. In the middle of the courtyard—there was some other word for it but Faith couldn't dredge it up from memory—was a sign picked out in white rocks that read: "HRH." A group of men were standing by the sign. Two of them were holding up a white cardboard sign with more writing.

The view zoomed again and it was clearer.

The sign said "Remaining rations: ____ days." There was a "60" crossed out, then a "30" and now a "7."

And the person standing by the sign, his face up and pointed at the passing satellite, was very recognizable. Also very thin. But Prince Harry of Wales, just possibly King of England, was alive.

"How old is this?" Colonel Hamilton asked.

"The pass was yesterday," General Brice replied. "And for those who don't recognize it, that is the Tower of London. The following is not for discussion. Task Force Kodiak will halt all sweeps in the Caribbean, proceed immediately to Guantanamo to pick up Marine and Navy helo forces, then proceed directly to London to effect extraction of His Royal Highness and his bodyguards."

"What kind of helos do we have?" Colonel Hamilton asked.

"We've got a CH-53 up and running," Steve replied. "We'll put a Seahawk aboard as deck cargo. It's ninety percent there and Lieutenant Szafranski assures me they can get it up by the time you get there. We'll have the *Shivak* accompany you in case something happens to the *Grace*. If worse comes to worst, you can all pack into the *Shivak*. The *Grace*'s helipad is rated for a bird the size of a 53. The only pause will be ensuring that it's up to its rating and to take on fuel and supplies. You'll take onboard all the helo support people and then steam out. Can you refuel there?"

"Not yet," Colonel Hamilton said.

"Well, we've got the fueling dock up and running," Steve said. "Sergeant Roosevelt."

"Sir?" Sergeant Roosevelt said.

"You were Dutch commando trained, is that correct?" Steve said.

"Yes, sir," Roosevelt replied. "I was in MARSOF for eight years, sir. MARSOF is what it was called these days, sir."

"That includes significant air-assault training?" Steve asked.

"Yes, sir."

"All of the infantry Marines have air-assault training but it is limited," Steve said. "I cannot order you and your men to accompany this mission but there is a second one that is almost as high priority and will need significant air-assault training in the run-up. We need your expertise, badly."

"That will leave this island with a group of . . . untrained refugees of questionable nature to defend it, sir," Roosevelt said, frowning.

"We'll leave a Navy security team to defend it as well as the POL people who are also combat trained," Steve said. "And we really need your expertise. For that matter, the secondary mission could use your people's help as well."

"What is the secondary mission, sir?" Colonel Hamilton asked.

"Doehler, research institute," General Brice said.

The image swerved to a building in London. Although much of the city had burned, that portion was still intact. The fires had just missed it by a couple of streets.

"This is the London Research Institute," General Brice said. "It was primarily a cancer research facility but it also did other biological research. And cancer research uses the same materials you need for vaccine production. We had been looking at an insertion into USAMRIID, Bethesda or Johns Hopkins, all of which might have gel and all of which are near the ocean. However, since you're going to London *anyway* . . .

"Marine forces with supplementary materials experts will be performing an air assault on this facility with the primary purpose of extracting vaccine production materials as well as the usual 'get anything that's useful medically' out of it. That is *after* you have rescued the prince. And that, Sergeant, is why we need you *and* your people. That's a big damned building in the middle of a city and we can *see* some of the doors are still opened. It's liable to be crawling with infected and will have to be extensively searched for materials."

"Yes, ma'am," the sergeant said, clearly less than

thrilled to have to tell a general no. "I can see the importance of both missions, General. However, the problem of the security of . . . General, this is *all that remains* of the Dutch holdings, ma'am. Leaving it unsecured . . ."

"Sergeant Major Barney will absolutely flip being left behind on this one," Steve said. "But he's getting left behind. Sergeant, we will leave two Naval security teams *and* the sergeant major to ensure the security of your island and train the local militia. I would leave either Faith or Sophia so you could have some personal assurances that I'm not going to let pirates or infected take it over. But one is our 'materials expert' and the other is our Marine Platoon Leader. They both have to go. And, Sergeant, I'm sending my daughters out across a massive and very violent, wreck-filled, ocean, in winter, to perform this mission. *That* is how important we all gauge it. Nothing is going to happen, further, to Sint Eustatius. Not on my watch. If for no other reason than we're going to need that POL."

"Yes, sir," Roosevelt said, clearly unhappy.

"Do you agree to support the mission?" Steve asked.

"Yes, sir," Roosevelt said, after a brief pause. "I agree to support the mission, sir. Both missions, sir."

"Oorah," Steve said. "Colonel, promulgate the change of mission and I want anchors aweigh by dawn."

"Yes, sir," Hamilton said.

"Good luck, Kodiak," Brice said. "Shut it down."

"I'm going to send a task force of subs with you," Steve said. "Usual commo support and they are going to plow the road with active to make sure you're not going to hit anything. I am seriously worried about wrecks and oceanic debris."

"Thank you, sir," Hamilton said.

"Land the Navy people and go ahead and push over as much ammo as you can to Sint Eustatius," Steve said. "I'll punch down some more security as it becomes available. Right now, Statia and Gitmo are our linchpins. When you get here, we'll be prepared to top up the *Grace* with POL and av gas. You're going to need a lot of both for this mission. But that's all the time we have for planning right now. Get a move on."

"Aye, aye, sir," Hamilton said.

"Gitmo out."

"Ensign Smith," Hamilton said.

"Sir?"

"You're going to need to turn over your division," the colonel said. "We obviously are not going to be taking yachts on the crossing."

"Aye, aye, sir," Sophia said after a brief pause.

"The *Bella* will be there when you get back," Hamilton said. "Right now, get a working party together. All the Marines and Navy personnel as well as any of the refugees we can get up and moving. We need to cross-load all of the ground combat ammo onboard to Sint Eustatius before dawn. As well as all of the weapons that were designated for local militias. Lieutenant Commander Chen."

"Sir?"

"Designate two of the divisions that are *not* Div One to stay behind, vessels and crew, to secure Sint Eustatius as well as Sergeant Major Barney."

"Aye, aye, sir. Divisions Five and Three, sir. With reluctance, I'm going to leave the chief behind as well, sir. I'll put Lieutenant Bowman in charge."

"Take the fifties from all three divisions *not* being left behind as well," Hamilton said. "We'll mount some on Fort Oranje as well as set up a defense point to secure the POL point. That can wait until after we've left. After they've offloaded the guns, the remaining divisions can follow us to Gitmo and get rearmed and ammoed there."

"Permission to speak, sir," Sophia said.

"Go."

"I would like to take a few of my NavGround people with me, sir," Sophia said. "If there is material in the research institute, I'll need porters. And they've gotten . . . okay with being around infected, sir."

"Agreed," Hamilton said. "You choose any Nav-Ground personnel you prefer. Any significant questions otherwise?"

There weren't any.

"Let's roll."

"So you're going to England?" Anna said. She wasn't great at passing massive ammo boxes but she was turning in with a will.

The problem of landing the ammo was that they, as usual, could not just pull the *Grace Tan* up to the dock. There were too many wrecks and it wasn't a big dock. So the ammo had to be cross-loaded to small boats and then carried to the dock, or the beach, and unloaded. The term was "lightering."

Sophia was in charge of supervising the Zodiacs unloading on the beach and providing security. The actual security of the island was demonstrated by the fact that they were unloading predawn and an infected had so far failed to show up for the buffet.

A few of the refugees and locals had agreed to get out of bed and help out. Anna was, unsurprisingly, one of them.

"Looks that way," Sophia said. She felt kind of like

a schmo not helping unload the ammo. But she was busy as a one armed paper-hanger.

"Can I go?" Anna asked, sadly. "It's . . . my home."

"London is a burned-out shell," Sophia said, signing another damned sheet of paper. The ammo couldn't just be handed over, willy-nilly. It had to be signed for. She had Olga making sure the numbers were right. "There's not really anything to see. We're not taking anybody who's not critical to the operation and I'm not taking my boat so I can't smuggle you along. So . . . I don't see a way."

"Are the astronauts going?" Anna asked.

"Oh . . . crap," Sophia said. "That question never even came up. Since I handed off quarantine duty . . . I had completely forgotten about them. I mean, not *completely*, but . . . Crap. I need to go. I'll see if I can get a slot for you on the float, but . . . I need to go."

"Go," Anna said, hefting a case of 5.56. "I can handle hanging out on Statia. But I'd like to at least see England."

"It's covered, Ensign," Hamilton said. He, too, was on the beach supervising the off-load.

"Aye, aye, sir," Sophia said. "I was just wondering."

"Occasionally, people do think of things before you, Ensign," Hamilton said. "It's covered."

"Yes, sir," Sophia said. "I'll get back to counting ammo boxes."

"Sir," Lieutenant Bowman said, pen poised over the sheet of paper. "Please tell me that if this is off by, say, a couple thousand rounds it is not going to come back and bite me in the ass."

Ammo and supplies were piled higgledy-piggledy all over the beaches and piers of Sint Eustatius. There was no way in hell the inventory was accurate.

"Do a recount after we're gone," Hamilton said, looking at his watch, then up to the sky which was clearly starting to lighten. "I'll recertify it. And, no, it's not going to bite you in the ass, Lieutenant. Holding me up will bite you in the ass."

"Yes, sir," Bowman said, taking a deep breath and signing for more ammo than any one newbie straight-from-civilian lieutenant should be responsible for.

"*Grace*, up anchor," Hamilton said, keying his mike. "Get moving. I'll catch up in a Zod."

"Roger."

"Thank you, Lieutenant," Hamilton said, taking his copy of the receipt. "Good luck."

"Thank you, sir," Bowman said. He stepped back, came to the best position of attention he could muster and saluted. "I'll make sure the island doesn't go anywhere while you're gone."

"Oorah," Hamilton said, returning the salute. He stepped into the waiting Zodiac and keyed his mike again. "Gunny, tell me that we've got everyone we need off this beach."

"*We are all feet wet except for yourself, sir,*" Gunny Sands replied. "*So, with due respect, if you would kindly get your ass moving, sir.*"

"Aye, aye, Gunny," Colonel Hamilton said, making sure the mike wasn't open. He grinned. "I was getting tired of this island, anyway..."

Councilor Van Der Beek stepped out onto the ramparts of Fort Oranje, scratching his bare and very hairy stomach. It had become his custom to step out each morning and urinate over the wall, hopefully on one of the damned zombies.

He idly looked out into the harbor, then stopped. He looked north. He looked south. He looked down at the beach where some remaining Navy personnel were apparently counting the piles of boxes that had mysteriously appeared overnight. What he did not see—

"Waarom zijn alle boten verdwenen?" he asked. "En waar zijn mijn mariniers? WAAR ZIJN MIJN MARINIERS?"

CHAPTER 29

I have seen Him in the watch-fires of a hundred circling camps,
They have builded Him an altar in the evening dews and damps;
I can read His righteous sentence by the dim and flaring lamps:
His day is marching on.

(CHORUS)

—"The Battle Hymn of the Republic"

"Ah, beautiful Guantanamo Bay," Sophia said as the *Grace* rounded Corinaso Point. "Again."

It had been a forty-hour run back to Gitmo with the *Grace Tan* more or less "hauling ass" at its flank speed of 25 knots. Which was not exactly smoking for most combat ships but truly was hauling ass for a support and supply ship.

It was the middle of the night but the dockyard areas were bright as day and tugs were already prepared to take the big support ship alongside.

"That's got to be attracting some infected," Faith said, leaning on the railing.

"I heard that every now and again there's a boom from over at the fence line," Sophia said. "When they hit the minefield."

"That's one way to get rid of them," Faith said.

"You don't sound your usual chipper self, Sis," Sophia said. "This is me being supportive."

"You heard the colonel, Soph," Faith said. "Two words: Air Assault."

"Oh..." Sophia said, trying not to laugh. "Seriously? I'm looking forward to it!"

"*You* like *roller coasters*," Faith growled. "And I thought you were being supportive?"

"The heroic, the indomitable, Lieutenant Faith Smith, darling of the Marine Corps!" Sophia said.

"Terrified of heights," they both said in unison.

"Bite me, Sophia," Faith said.

"Whatever you do, don't let them see you sweat," Sophia said seriously. "You can do it. 'Cause you have to. You know that."

"I know I *can* do it," Faith said. "I know. Doesn't mean I *want* to. I'd almost rather fight my way in on foot if that made any sense at all."

"I asked Colonel Hamilton about the astronauts," Sophia said, changing the subject. "He told me it was covered. Do you know what the plan is?"

"Nope," Faith said. "But it's above my pay grade. I need to go get ready to take aboard all the gear and ammo we need for this. I don't know who is signing for all the helo parts but I know it's not me. Or, at least, it better not be. I don't know for helo parts."

"My question is, where the hell are we putting it all?" Sophia said.

"So, basically, we're going to have to break down your quarantine," Walker said, shrugging. "You're eight days into the cycle. If you have an immune system at all, it's either working or it's not. And we need to get this container off the ship."

"Doctor, do you concur?" Commander Daniels asked.

"We're probably going to get sick," Dr. Price said. "But we're going to get sick, anyway. Breaks of the job. You always do. We should be sufficiently resistant to the neurological packet we should not 'turn' at this point if that is what you are asking. Even assuming some reservoir of H7D3. Most of which should have burned out at this point. We should be fine."

"Dr. Shelley," Walker said. "Mrs. Doctor, that is. The powers-that-be have asked if you'd be willing to accompany the mission. Not to do insertions, you understand. But we can take helmet cams along and your expertise could be crucial. Also, are either of you familiar with the London Research Institute?"

"We've both been there many times," Tom Shelley replied. "Is that your target?"

"For the vaccine materials, yes," Walker said. "It's a big building. We can use any intel on where materials might be stored."

"Am I invited as well?" Tom asked.

"That would be a natural assumption, Doctor," Walker said. "I did not mean to leave you out."

"I understand. My wife has more experience in this matter," Tom said. "Rizwana? Are you willing to take an ocean voyage in winter?"

"I will accompany you, of course," Rizwana said unhappily. "Would there be any possibility of making a slight detour?"

"How slight and to where?" Walker asked.

"Our daughter lives in Clapham," Tom said quietly. "It's a borough of South London."

"Oh," Walker said. "We'll have to see what the situation is when we arrive but... should be doable. Don't get your hopes up. The overheads are... Don't get your hopes up. Two last questions for the group. Well, passing an order and one question. Lieutenant Lyons, you are included on the mission. You may not be up to clearing buildings by then but we can use you for an air assault instructor."

"Got it," Lyons said.

"Oddly enough, no one has asked me to help on that one," Walker said. "Air assault, that is. But I'm a bit tied up being a baby doctor at the moment. Last, Colonel Kuznetsov. Captain Wilkes has asked if you would agree to be his copilot?"

"Absolutely," the mission's assistant commander said. "I look forward to flying with the captain. I look forward to it so much, I don't even mind being a copilot."

"It may be variable," Walker said. "The captain's previous experience was with SeaCobras, Hueys and CH-46s. The 53 flies more like an upgraded Hip. The size is taking some getting used to, from what I hear."

"It would," Colonel Kuznetsov said. "On the other hand, I've never landed on a moving ship."

"As long as it's not a pitching deck it's easier than it sounds," Walker said. "Again, nobody's asked if I can fly a helo. Much less a 53. All things considered, we should do this with some ceremony, but if you're ready to crack the hatch... We're scheduled to pick this container up in about ten minutes."

"Time to go breathe real air again," Commander Daniels said, pulling himself up. "We're still a bit unsteady. Can we get a hand?"

"Line of people waiting on you," Walker said.

"Colonel," Steve said, saluting the colors and returning Hamilton's salute as he bounded up the gangway of the *Grace Tan*. "Good to have you back, however briefly."

"Good to be back, sir," Hamilton said, looking around. While the piers weren't in quite as good a shape as before the plague, they were in remarkable shape given the time they'd been gone and were a scene of bustling activity. "Hell of a job here, sir."

"Mostly Isham," Steve said. "Guy has a positive fury at messy industrial areas. How'd the astronauts take the news?"

"They're all out of the container, sir," Hamilton said. "I understand we're taking Lieutenant Lyons, Colonel Kuznetsov and the Shelleys, sir? What about Dr. Price?"

"We've got more total bodies here at Gitmo," Steve said. "And a lot more pregnant women. He's more needed here. And I've got plans for the others if they're willing to pitch in. So, yes, just those four. You'll be taking Walker, of course. He'll have to do for a doctor. We've got a container of ammo, including ammo for the door guns on the 53, a container of helo parts and tools, the Seahawk and mixed supplies to load. And the rest of your Marines as well as Lieutenant Szafranski are prepared to board. Last but not least, in the event you find the materials to make the vaccine, since you're taking the experts with you, one container has been made up as a turn-key lab for vaccine production. Hopefully, the glassware will survive the journey. Despite all of that, I want you out of here by zero four hundred."

"Aye, aye, sir," Hamilton said. "We've got the working parties ready to start loading."

"Not sure what we're waiting for, then," Steve said. "Time's a-wastin'."

∽ ⊖ ∽

"I'm aware this is completely inappropriate," Faith said, hugging Staff Sergeant Januscheitis. "And I really don't give a shit."

Faith had taken time she really shouldn't to track Janu down to where he was getting his gear secured in his quarters.

"Good to see you, too, ma'am," Janu said, hugging her back.

"You know, before this last float, losing you was 'well, that's how it goes,'" Faith said, releasing him. "Now, I'm fully prepared to bitch, whine, moan and complain until I get you back. You have no clue. All Marine Staff NCOs turn out to *not* be the same."

"Issues, ma'am?" Januscheitis asked.

"Nothing that I'm prepared to discuss officially, Staff Sergeant," Faith said. "But, yes, issues. Serious issues. Now I really need to go. I'm sure there's something I'm supposed to sign for."

"So do I, ma'am," Januscheitis said. "I need to oversee loading the Seahawk. And Captain Wilkes is flying aboard with the Super Stallion and I'll need to be there to ensure it's secured properly."

"We'll have time to talk on the float," Faith said. "But for now, mission face."

"That is sort of..." Sophia said as the Seahawk was slung aboard from a barge. "It's sort of odd watching a helicopter get *loaded*. *Flown* on, I can see..."

"Yeah, well, this ain't getting signed by itself, Sophia," Olga said, holding out the clipboard.

"Work, work, work," Sophia said, looking at the form. "Wait a second. Why am *I* signing for a helicopter?"

"You're the officer of the deck," Olga said, shrugging. "*I'm* sure as hell not signing for it."

"Is it complete?" Sophia asked. "I mean, are all the parts installed?"

"I don't know!" Olga said. "How the hell would *I* know? It has to be signed for, though."

"Looks like I'm just signing for the airframe," Sophia said dubiously. "And that looks like it's all there... Hey! Staff Sergeant Januscheitis!"

"Yes, ma'am!" Januscheitis shouted.

"When you sign for a helicopter, are you signing for all the parts or what?"

"Just the airframe, ma'am," Januscheitis replied. "And it's got all its parts. It just hasn't been fully certified, yet."

"I'm going to regret this," Sophia said, signing the form. "I know I'm going to regret this. Ah, well, they can take it out of my pay..."

"I don't sign for ammo until the Navy turns it over to us," Faith said, holding her hands up. "And that's on a mission by mission basis. Take it to my sister," she said, pointing.

"You *do* sign for weapons," Walker said, handing her a clipboard. "Spare M4s, two-forties and parts for same. Now you understand why I'm sitting out being an officer at the moment."

"Work, work, work," Faiths said, scribbling her name for what seemed the thousandth time.

"You're supposed to count those, Lieutenant," Walker said.

"Sir, aware that you *are* an actual 'sir,'" Faith said, "and I really should take your advice: One, we're in a hurry. Two, *you're* the one handing it to me. Three, they'd have to actually pay me to take it out of my pay."

"You have a point, Lieutenant," Walker said, grinning.

"Mr. Walker," a seaman said, holding out a clipboard. "Additional medical supplies."

"Hah!" Faith said. "Your avoidance of responsibility will not avail you now, Flame of Udun!"

"If I didn't have a perfectly suitable handle, I'd *take* Balrog," Walker said, looking at the sheet. "Where *are* these supposed medical supplies, seaman? Because I *am* going to count them..."

"How does zero *three* hundred sound, sir?" Hamilton radioed as the *Grace Tan* was pulled away from the fueling dock by two harbor tugs.

"It sounds like Captain Wilkes is taking off," Steve replied. *"Any additional questions?"*

"No, sir," Hamilton said. "Although, I'm going to have everyone go back over the inventory of what was just loaded. I'd like you to keep the *Pit Stop* available to chase us down in case we missed anything critical."

"Will do," Steve said. *"FYI, some fellow named Councilor Van Der Beek has been screaming at everyone who will listen. Something about you shanghaiing his Marines. I have no clue what he's talking about. And apparently you negotiated an oil for food program?"*

"Sor..., si...," Hamilton said. "Skgritch! Sgrrrr! You're break...up... S'...gain...?"

"Have fun in the North Atlantic, Colonel," Steve

said. *"I'll take care of it. Come to think of it, sounds like international relations. I'll get him in touch with the Hole..."*

"Whew," Hamilton said, wiping his brow theatrically. "Missed a bullet, there."

"They'll figure it out," Captain Victor Gilbert said. The captain of the *Grace Tan* was watching the tugs balefully. "At least we left them the *Alan Garcia*."

"Honestly, the *Shivak* and the *Garcia* were what we should have taken to the islands," Hamilton said. "Not that I haven't enjoyed your company. Question: have you coordinated with anyone on landing the Stallion?"

"You're assuming I've never worked with a helo before, Colonel," Gilbert said. "We had to get some new radios installed. I'll talk to the pilot when he's in the air."

"Got some Marine on the air frequency wants to talk to you, Captain," Kolb said.

"Speaking of which..."

"Yeah. I know to come into the wind. And I'm not going to be going fast 'cause 'into the wind' is pointed at the shoals. In fact, I ain't gonna be moving at all if I can help it. Roger?"

"Roger," Captain Milo Wilkes said, banking the Super Stallion around to line up with the M/V *Grace Tan*. "Honestly, just hold it there. The winds are light. I can put it on the pad where you are."

"Going aback. How's that? Wind and tide are drifting us a bit."

"Good," Wilkes said, lowering. "I've got this..."

He followed Staff Sergeant Januscheitis's hand and arm signals and put the bird down on the platform.

He stayed light for a bit, then slowly let off on the collective to test the platform.

"Marine Six has landed at zero three twenty-two hours," Wilkes radioed, going through shut-down procedures.

"*Yeah. We noticed. As soon as your jarheads have it tied down to my satisfaction, we are out of here. Might be a bit since I ain't easily satisfied.*"

"Nice working with a professional," Wilkes muttered, starting his post-flight checklist. "I can tell this is going to be a great float..."

"You have *got* to be kidding me..." Faith said.

The swells off Kings Bay, Georgia weren't bad but there *were* swells. So the fast-rope hanging from a crane was swaying back and forth. And it was *just* in reach. She was going to have to step *all* the way to the edge of the catwalk around the bridge, from which a section of railing had been cut away, and grab it. As it was swaying. And the boat was rocking.

"You're on a secure line, ma'am," Sergeant Roosevelt said. Two American Marines were belaying the line attached to her harness. "Even if you miss the grab you're going to be fine."

"There is nothing fine about this, Sergeant," Faith snapped. She wished she could close her eyes but there was no way she was fumbling in mid-air, on the edge of a catwalk, with nothing below here but...well, air.

She leaned out and snatched the rope. The combination of swells and the weight of the rope more or less dragged her off the catwalk and fortunately she got both hands around the rope as it did.

"AAAAAHHHHH!" she screamed as she slid down the slick rope.

"You were supposed to get your legs around it, too, ma'am," Staff Sergeant Januscheitis said. "And you can let go, now. Ma'am? You can let go . . ."

Faith slowly unclenched her fingers from the rope.

"And that was a really lousy job, with no disrespect, ma'am," Januscheitis said. "Back up and try it again, ma'am."

"I don't wanna be a Marine anymore," Faith muttered, trotting to the ladder. "I don't wanna be a Marine anymore . . ." But she kept it down.

"Wheeee!" Sophia squealed, sliding down the rope. She hit the ground with a spring in her step and bounced back up. "Can I do it again?"

"Go for it, ma'am," Januscheitis said, grinning. "That was fun!"

"Ooooraaaah!" Faith said all the way down.

"That, ma'am, was better, and admittedly it's not the first time I've ever heard someone scream 'Oorah' in *terror*, ma'am," Januscheitis said. "With no disrespect intended, ma'am, it was not exactly motivational. And, again, you need to get your legs around the rope, ma'am."

"But you have to let up enough to slide down," Roosevelt said. "Ma'am? You have to unclench, ma'am. . . ."

"I can and will *do* it," Faith said, picking at her mashed potatoes. "I am a Marine officer. I will not let fear keep me from performing my duty. That does not mean I like it."

"That's sort of the definition of courage, ma'am," Staff Sergeant Januscheitis said. "It's not about being fearless, it's about overcoming your fears, ma'am. But you're going to need to get to the point you can do it without screaming the whole way down. It's unsettling to the troops."

"I'll be all right on the night," Faith said. "And we get to rescue a prince. That's cool."

She looked around the mess hall and then at the cups hanging from racks in the corner.

"Is it just me, or are we bouncing more...?"

"What do you want to do, Colonel?" Gilbert asked.

The weather map was one giant red swirl off the coast of Carolina.

"We *can* weather it, Captain." Colonel Hamilton asked. "Correct?"

"Oh, *we* can plow right through," Gilbert said. "Wouldn't want to be in a small boat but we can do it. Assuming I go out enough from the Outer Banks. Going to get a bit nautical, but we'll be fine. You can't *train*, though. No flying, none of the planned actual air-assault training. And there's another one right behind *that* one. Basically, looks to me like we're going to be hitting one squall after another from here to England except maybe mid-Atlantic and you don't want to do your training in those conditions. And whatever the Marines may think about fast-roping off my bridge in a storm, I'm not going to allow it in this weather. It's flat out unsafe. I could duck into the Chesapeake and take a few days there between squalls..."

"No," Hamilton said, shaking his head. "We're just going to have to go with what we've got. We don't have time to turn aside. Plow on, Mr. Gilbert, plow on. But do, please, try to miss the Outer Banks. Grounding would be decidedly unpleasant to report."

"This is why I loooove being a Marine," Faith said as the ship nosed up and then crashed down again. She was looking fairly green.

"Bah," Sophia said, taking another bite of eggs. "Big boat sailors! This is nothing! Why this one time off of Spain..."

"You've never been to Spain," Faith said, glowering.

"Ma'am," Sergeant Januscheitis said, grinning. "Don't never get in the way of a good sea story, with due respect. Were there mermaids?"

"Let me tell you about mermaids, Staff Sergeant," Sophia said in a gravelly voice, waving her coffee cup.

"We sure she's not bucking for chief?" Derek asked.

"I think I just spent too much time around Chief Schmidt," Sophia said, laughing. "You okay, Sister dear?"

"I hate you..."

CHAPTER 30

I have read a fiery gospel writ in burnished rows of steel:
"As ye deal with my contemners, so with you my grace shall deal";
Let the Hero, born of woman, crush the serpent with his heel,
His God is marching on.

(CHORUS)

—"The Battle Hymn of the Republic"

"HOLY FUCK!" Faith screamed as she stepped out of the hatch.

The storm that had kept them below-decks for two days had finally passed and she could step outside and breathe free air. Which was UNBELIEVABLY FUCKING COLD!

"AAAAAHHHH," she said, thinking her breath would appear as smoke. But, no, it was simply wrenched away by the wind. Or, and this was a distinct possibility, instantly turned to ice. There was ice accumulating on the ammo containers.

"They did not cover this in the recruiting video," she muttered.

She slammed the hatch shut and went below.

"Gunny," she said, sticking her head in his compartment.

"Ma'am?" Gunny Sands replied.

"Tell me we remembered cold weather gear," she said.

"None available, ma'am," the gunny replied. "Not short of going back to the *Iwo* to find it and break it out. We've got wooly pully's for most personnel including yourself. We'll need to start acclimatization training as soon as possible. Other than that, ma'am, it's exigencies of service."

"Roger," Faith said, closing the hatch. "This mission just keeps getting better and better. Five days ago we were sweating like a river on a volcano, now we're going to turn into corpse-sicles." She walked down the corridor and thought about that. "Heh, heh. *Corps*-sicles . . ."

"FEELING LIKE A CORPS-SICLE, PRIVATE?" Faith screamed at the Marine PFC standing at attention on the quarter deck.

Acclimatization training comes down to being put into whatever the climate may be for a period of time and then allowed to "recover" for a short time, lather, rinse, repeat with increasing periods "in climate" until the body is adjusted. In this case, it was standing at attention, with occasional bouts of exercise, in the freezing wind of the North Atlantic in winter. Ice-spray added to the misery. Which was par for the course for any acclimatization training.

Fortunately for Faith, she got to walk around and shout at people. She wasn't sure if she *could* just stand there. It was *much* easier to walk around and be shouty.

"NO, MA'AM!"

"WOULD YOU LIKE ME TO TUCK YOU IN FOR THE NIGHT? ARE YOU *SNIVELING*, PRIVATE? IS THAT A *SNIVEL* I HEAR . . . ?"

∽⊖∾

"Okay, I'm getting impressed again, sir," Gunny Sands said, watching the current evolution from the bridge windows. "That's the third iteration and she's still out there."

"Agreed," Colonel Hamilton said. "I'm wondering if we should check for frost bite. It's like she just doesn't *feel* the cold."

"*Oh*, that was a bad idea," Faith said, shivering under a half dozen blankets and anything else in her room that was insulated. Fortunately, she had a compartment to herself and nobody could see what a *boneheaded* move it had been to stand outside in the *freezing cold* for *hours*. "I am *such* an *idiot*..."

"ARE YOU *COLD*, PRIVATE?"

"I AM FROM THE *NETHERLANDS*, MA'AM!" Marine First Class Vincent Schurink shouted against the wind. "IS THAT A JOKE, MA'AM?"

"Never mind," Faith said after a moment. "Forget I asked..."

"There's no critical need for your involvement, Sis," Faith said, shrugging. "You're just here to pick up some vaccine stuff. Do a little light shopping. I'm here to do all the derring-do. Face it, you're screwed..."

There was no "officers' mess" or wardroom on the *Grace Tan*. So the occasional sisterly wrangle tended to be played out in public.

"What are they arguing about this time?" Januscheitis asked, sitting down next to Olga. Usually Marines and Navy don't mix but Januscheitis was ready to mix with Olga any time.

"Who gets the prince," Olga said, leaning back with her arms folded. "They figure who ever meets him first has a shot..."

"Ten bucks, scrip, on Faith," Januscheitis said.

"Yer on."

"He's a pilot," Sophia said archly.

"What's that got to do with it?" Faith asked.

"You really think he's going to be interested in someone who's afraid of *heights*?" Sophia replied primly.

"Oh..." Faith said, waggling a finger in front of her nose. "If you *tell* him..."

"Like I'll have to," Sophia said, her arms crossed. "Everybody on board knows. Aaaaah!" she said in a high falsetto, clutching her arms to her chest like she was gripping a rope. "It's so HIGH! WAH! WAH! I'M A MARINE AND I'M AFRAID OF HEIGHTS!"

"I am going to *sit* on you!" Faith sputtered. "I'll *do* it!"

"Have either of you considered that you're both still *jailbait*, ladies?" Januscheitis said loudly.

"I. Will. Clear. *Arkansas*." Faith said.

"The good news is we can put in on the Tower Green," Captain Wilkes said, pointing to the overhead. "There used to be trees. Pretty obviously, they've been cutting them up for heat. Gives us enough room, barely, to put in the 53."

"We'll load up the first sortie in with supplies, sir," Hamilton said. "Along with a small Marine security detachment. It's possible that they may want to leave a token force behind. Then pull out all the refugees. We'll have to determine the pattern of extraction on the ground. I'll leave that up to them."

"*Sounds good*," Steve said. "*Any questions?*"

"Comment?" Sophia said. "Navy Security could handle the insertion just fine, sir. It's not like we're going to fast-rope in."

"But it is the correct way to do the operation," Steve said. *"And, daughters of mine, it is time to stop playing around and focus on the mission, not who gets to... meet the prince first."*

"Marines, Ensign," Hamilton said drily. "And as your father said, neither of you get to... Ahem. It will be Marines, Ensign. And, yes, that means sending your sister."

"Yes, sir," Sophia said.

"Oorah, sir," Faith said. "But it's me!"

"Colonel, sir," Faith said, tapping at his door. "Moment of your time?"

The small convoy of ships had passed Margate, England and was picking its way, slowly, through the bay of the Thames. Slowly, because according to the *Louisville*, which was preceding them with active blasting, the area was littered with wrecks. Some of them were ships so large that they were definite hazards to navigation. The Thames itself was simply impenetrable by any ocean-going vessel.

They had one more day to get ready for the mission and the last niggling details were being cleared up.

"Enter," Hamilton said, leaning back in his chair. "Another issue?"

"Possibly, sir," Faith said. "It overlaps personal and professional, sir. I would prefer to handpick my landing team, sir."

"My guess is that would include Staff Sergeant Januscheitis?" Colonel Hamilton asked.

"Yes, sir," Faith said.

"Approved," Hamilton said. "Anything else?"

"No, sir," Faith said, slightly surprised.

"I was going to suggest it," Hamilton said. "And as soon as some Navy personnel get trained in on helo support, he's moving back to the platoon. All of the Marines except air-crew are moving back. I'm sending the gunnery sergeant as well. So it will be you, a gunnery sergeant, the staff sergeant and I'd suggest letting the staff sergeant choose the rest of the team. My suggestion on that is either the Dutch Marines or Second Squad. Second is Iwo-heavy."

"Yes, sir," Faith said, clearly puzzled.

"Is there anything else?" Hamilton asked.

"No, sir," Faith said.

"Dismissed."

"Okay, why doesn't *this* bother me?" Faith shouted.

The tail ramp of the CH-53 Super Stallion was down and she was hanging onto a stanchion while standing on the ramp. She had a safety-strap on but that shouldn't have been much consolation. It was a *long* way down.

The view, though, was spectacular. If Armageddon was your choice of views. *Everything* was burned. Fires had raged through London and its sprawling outskirts. The 53 was following the line of the Thames and the devastation was enormously evident. Ships and boats were sunk all along the river. The houses and wharfs on either side of the river were ruins. There were infected crawling everywhere she looked. It was enough to give her chills. The reason they were following the river was that if they went down, they'd have a better chance in the *water* than on *land*.

"Survivors," Januscheitis shouted, ignoring the question. He was pointing to the north. There were definitely people on a miraculously unburned building, waving at the passing helo.

"We'll determine if we're going to do extraction later," Faith shouted. She looked at her watch and tried to figure out the landmarks. They were passing over a dropped bridge so that meant . . .

"Time to get on game face," Faith shouted as the helo slowed and banked. And banked tighter. *Then* she clutched the stanchion in both hands. "SON OF A BITCH!"

"There it is!" Januscheitis shouted, pointing down.

The outline was engraved on her brain and she even knew most of the portions of the fortress. Develin Tower. The Bloody Tower. The Traitors' Gate. And there *were* survivors. Quite a few. Most were in British camo standing sentry or manning machine guns that tracked the helo suspiciously. A few civilians ran out into the open areas, waving at the 53.

As they passed over the Bailey, Januscheitis tossed out a radio attached to a small parachute. The helo banked away and out, spiraling upwards.

Faith pulled a set of cans off a hook and put them on.

"Hello? Jolly good to see you, Yanks. Captain Carl Whiteshead, First Royal Rifles. Over."

"Lieutenant Faith Smith, United States Marine Corps," Faith replied. "Plan is as follows. We have supplies in case you wish to leave a token force. Land on Tower Green, unload security element, unload supplies, load refugees. Given the numbers we're seeing here, at least two lift sorties. Then the last of the last go out. We cannot guarantee resupply any time in the next six months. So we're bringing in one year's supply for twenty people. All we can loft. You're going to need to figure out if anyone stays and if so who. Is that all clear, over?"

"*Roger. Define security element, over.*"

"One squad of Marines to assist with loading of refugees, over."

"*Understood. Be aware, you will be under guns until we determine you are, in fact, United States Marines. Over.*"

Faith looked at Januscheitis. He nodded and mouthed "Makes sense."

"Understood," Faith replied. "Make sure all your personnel know to stay away from the rotors at the rear. It would be a real bitch to spread some of your people all over the walls if they walk into them. Clear the Green and we're inbound."

"*We're clearing it, now. Come ahead. Out.*"

"Captain Wilkes?" Faith said, switching to intercom.

"Preparing to land," Colonel Kuznetsov said. "Thirty seconds."

"On your feet, Marines," Faith shouted, waving for the Marines to stand up. She took off the cans, put on her helmet, then grinned at Januscheitis. "This is the good part."

"I'm not counting chickens till they're all in the boat, ma'am," Januscheitis said, buckling his own helmet. "Remember to stay away from the rotors yourself, ma'am!"

"Roger," Faith said, holding the stanchion in a

death grip as the helo slowly crested the walls of the Tower. She was fine high for some reason. A thousand feet was just sort of surreal. Fifty feet scared the shit out of her. They were low enough she could see the sentries on the walls clearly and was surprised that they were Oriental. Her innate and highly trained paranoia went off like an alarm bell and she started tapping her pistol.

"Ma'am?" Januscheitis said. He could read her like a book.

"The guards!" Faith shouted, pointing. "They're not English!"

Januscheitis peered at the one guard in sight suspiciously, then grinned.

"Your knife, ma'am!" the Marine shouted as they flared out.

"What?" Faith yelled.

"Gurkhas!" Januscheitis shouted. "They're Gurkhas!" He leaned over and tapped the lieutenant's kukri.

"Oh," Faith said, walking down the ramp.

One thing that her da had told her, years ago, was that Gurkhas did *not* like just *anyone* carrying a kukri. You had to *earn* it. In *their* opinion.

"Oh . . . crap!"

"Lieutenant Faith Smith, United States Marine Corps," Faith said, saluting the captain. He wasn't the prince. From his rank tabs, he was the guard unit commander. "Captain Whiteshead, I guess?"

"Yes, Lieutenant," Whiteshead said, returning the salute. "Although shouldn't it be 'I presume'?"

"I'm not sure, sir," Faith said. "I speak American and Australian, sir, but I'm still working on British.

We ready to get unloaded? And *are* you planning on leaving a contingent?"

"Yes, we are, Lieutenant," Whiteshead said, clearly bemused by the reply. "And we're prepared to unload immediately."

"Gunny!" Faith bellowed, turning around. "Hook in and get those stores moved!"

"Aye, aye, ma'am!" Gunny Sands said. "Start unpacking, Marines!"

A line of civilians and military, mostly the Gurkhas, started unloading the food, a combination of MREs, "humanitarian service packs" and canned rations.

"What's your preference for moving out your personnel, sir?" Faith said, waving to get away from the still cycling helo.

"We'd prefer to load the women and children, first," Whiteshead said. "Along with a small military contingent. Then the rest of the men and the soldiers who are going out."

"Oorah, sir," Faith said. "How many you got? We couldn't get a good count from the satellites. We only have occasional overhead and there's been weather."

"One hundred twenty-three," Whiteshead said. "That are going out."

"Any notable medical conditions other than pregnancy?" Faith said, making a note. "We've got a pretty good medic on the ship."

"We've lost most of those," Whiteshead said, then paused. "Lieutenant, may I inquire . . ."

"In another month I'm legal to marry in Arkansas," Faith said, looking up and grinning. "Thirteen is the answer, sir. Almost fourteen. I always get that question about now."

"Bloody hell," Whiteshead said.

"Tell you how bad it is," Faith said. "I'm number...
six, I think, in the chain of command of the Marine
Corps. Another bad day and I'm the commandant. If
you're going out you'll meet the rest of the Marine
Corps in the ship."

"Did you bring a helo carrier?" Whiteshead asked.

"Civilian oil platform supply ship," Faith said,
making a note and not looking up. "The *Grace Tan*.
And another support ship and a big yacht for the
evacuees. The only LHA we know the location of is
the *Iwo Jima*, and we don't have enough people to
man it. Most of the Marines came from the *Iwo* or
Gitmo. We're holding Gitmo right now. Took it last
month. Stand by, sir.

"Kodiak Ops, Kodiak Ops, Shewolf, over. Okay,
Louisville it is. Count is one twenty-three, say again,
one-two-three, coming out. No major medical. Mal-
nourishment as usual. Three sorties should do it....
Roger. You going to be able to get up on retrans any
time soon? Roger... Shewolf, out.

"Okay, sir, you're good to go. Look like the gunny's
got the bird unloaded. Let's get to loading... Oh,
hello," she finished as the prince walked up.

"Captain Wales," Captain Whiteshead said. "Lieutenant Faith Smith, United States Marine Corps."

"Thank you for coming to our assistance," Harry
said, flashing a smile.

"No problem," Faith said, shaking hands. "So far
I've rescued a princess on a tower and a whole bunch
of people who think they're important. You're my first
prince so I can check that off on my bucket list. I'm
hoping you're going out. We need helo pilots."

"That is the plan," Prince Harry said, looking slightly confused for a moment. The response was, again, not what anyone would anticipate. The gunny had dubbed his reaction FEWSS: First Encounter With Shewolf Syndrome. "Lieutenant, is there any plan to pick up other survivors? We are sure there are some..."

"Right now, no, sir," Faith said. "We've got one other mission planned which is to raid a research center for some vaccine production materials. That's planned for tomorrow. Then, as far as I know, we're going to float back to Gitmo. The priority right now is get the vaccine production up and get the sub crews vaccinated so we can get some trained personnel. You'll have to take up any further rescue ops with the colonel or higher, sir."

"I...understand," Harry said. "Did you happen to see..."

"Saw some on the way in, sir," Faith said. "Could you give me a second? I've got to coordinate with the gunny on the extract, sir."

"Of course," Harry said. "Mission comes first."

"Excuse me, sirs," Faith said, walking back to the bird.

"Is she as young as she appears?" Harry asked as soon as she was out of earshot.

"Thirteen," Whiteshead said. "Month shy of fourteen. And number six in the Marine chain of command. Which sort of covers how bad it is, sir. They're operating off of a civilian boat. No Navy platforms survived."

"Bloody hell," Harry said, shaking his head.

"Gunny," Faith said.

"Ma'am," Gunny Sands said. "Last of this lift is onboard. They even had them chalked for a 53."

"Good to hear," Faith said. "Let's get clear . . . Gunny, moment of your time?" she said, as they cleared the bird to let it lift off.

"Ma'am?"

"Could you please handle interacting with the prince?" Faith asked.

"I . . . *can*, ma'am," Gunny Sands said. "But it would normally be the platoon leader's job."

"I had to go all Marine or I was going to babble," Faith said.

"If you would like the recommendation of your gunnery sergeant, ma'am," Sands said, trying not to smile, "stay all Marine."

"I *wanted* to meet him, now I'm trying not to act like a brain-dead cheerleader," Faith said, grinning tightly. "I don't do this well. Where's some infected to shoot?"

"Tomorrow, ma'am," Gunny Sands said. "All you can wish for, unless I miss my guess."

"Oorah," Faith said, walking back over to the two officers. "Thanks for having them chalked up."

The Gurkha guards were busy getting the rations stored in the White Tower and the Marines were getting names of the evacuees. All was in order so she sort of had to make small talk.

"Not a problem," Captain Whiteshead said. "We assumed it would be Marines or Navy coming in so it would probably be Super Stallions, according to Captain Wales."

"So what's with the Captain Wales, thing?" Faith asked.

"Captain Mountbatten-Windsor sounds sort of pompous, don't you think?" Harry asked, grinning.

"I dunno," Faith said. "Is it your name?"

"Yes?" Harry said.

"Then it's just your name," Faith said.

"May I inquire why you carry a kukri, Lieutenant?" Captain Whiteshead said to fill in the pause.

"'Cause they're good for cutting off the hands of infected that grab me," Faith said. "Good for necks, too. Either direction."

"Have you had much of an . . . opportunity . . . ?" Captain Wales asked.

"There's kind of a video that covers that," Faith said. "Sir. How many people are you holding back? I'm asking for two reasons. One, is it enough to hold the perimeter, and two, we could use more troops. We sort of shanghaied some Dutch Marines from Statia but there's a big fucking world to clear."

"How much of it have you cleared?" Harry asked.

"Ten liners, two super-max, the rest ranging down, one helo carrier, sort-of cleared six towns in the Canary Islands," Faith said, ticking off her fingers. "Bunch of piddly freighters and oil tankers. One oil platform. Gitmo and three . . . no, four islands in the Caribbean. St. Barts and Saba are only half-ass cleared. Anguilla and Statia are sort of chartreuse, maybe lime green. Still some betas running around but all the alphas are seagull bait."

"And how much of that have you been involved in, Lieutenant?" a new officer asked. He had a thick accent and was clearly a Gurkha.

"Captain Dattahadur Thapa, Lieutenant Faith Smith," Captain Whiteshead said.

"Sir," Faith said, nodding. "And pretty much all of it, sir. I've been clearing in the Atlantic since before we hooked up with the Navy, sir. Over twelve hundred hours combat time in the last nine months. Starting in New York, sir. Like I said to these gentlemen, there's a video. So, again, how many troops are we getting? 'Cause we're really bleeding for troops."

"Seventy-two," Captain Thapa replied. "We're leaving twenty-six including myself and the chief warder. Will that do?"

"It'll help," Faith said, making another note. "Hell, we'll be outnumbered. As soon as we get them back in shape. And retrain them on clearance."

"Retrain Gurkhas, Lieutenant?" Captain Whiteshead said, smiling in amusement.

"Fighting infected ain't the same as fighting people, Captain," Faith said, looking him in the eye. "If you use the techniques you use fighting people, you get in the scrum. Which is fun, don't get me wrong; bashing heads with a Halligan tool and chopping necks is what makes the job worth doing. But it ain't getting the mission done. So, yes, sir, retrain Gurkhas, sir. Just like I had to retrain an SF sergeant and all my Marines, sir. Although at least Gurkhas know how to use a knife when they get in the scrum, sir. Which is when you *really* need a kukri. Nothing better for cutting off hands. Except a machete, maybe."

"I . . . see," Whiteshead said.

"May I inquire what the badge is, Lieutenant?" Thapa said after a moment.

"Master Boarder Badge, sir," Faith said. "Struck post-Plague. Nine million feet of belowdecks cleared of infected, sir."

"Nine *million*?" Harry said.

"Estimated, sir," Faith said. "I got it after only

two super-max cruise ships, the *Iwo* and a couple of piddly ones. I'm not sure it was well thought out, sir. Stand by..." She held her earbud and nodded. "Roger. Understood. Bird's on its way back."

"Where is the ship?" Captain Whiteshead asked.

"Mouth of the river, sir," Faith said, thumbing over her shoulder. "It's nothing but wrecks from one end to the other, sir. Couldn't safely get any closer. We talked about doing a water insertion but we had the helo so..."

"Even getting through to the Traitors' Gate would be tough," Harry said.

"I have, trust me, done crazier shit, sir," Faith said. "But we had the helo so we took the easy way. I've got to do a rope insertion tomorrow and I'm still arguing for fighting our way in on foot. Do *not* like rope insertions. Stand by, please, sirs. Gunny! Bird's on the way back! Chalk 'em up!"

"Aye, aye, ma'am," Gunnery Sergeant Sands yelled.

"You guys okay for ammo?" Faith asked. "We've got a bird coming back after this and we use Barbie ammo if you need some."

"Barbie ammo?" Captain Whiteshead said, confused.

"Sorry, sir," Faith said, tapping her M4. "Five-five-six. Also seven-six-two. Barbie ammo for five-five-six 'cause it's a Barbie gun," she said, tapping the weapon again. "And it don't kill infected for shit. I'm carrying my Saiga tomorrow. Stand by... Kodiak, Shewolf, over... Need the ammo drop... Roger... GUNNY!"

"Ma'am?"

"Ammo drop coming in on this bird! Get some bodies!"

"Aye, aye, ma'am!"

"Figures the colonel would anticipate me," Faith said.

"Can you cover some of the conditions outside, Lieutenant?" Harry asked. "Do you know...anything about the rest of the Royal Family?"

"We have a pretty good report, fairly confirmed, that your grandmother passed away, sir," Faith said gently. "Pneumonia from a non H7 influenza. I'm sorry for your loss never cuts it, but...sorry for your loss."

"I see," Harry said, shaking his head.

"Other than that," Faith said, shrugging. "We've got about four thousand or so that we've picked up one place or another. Started with small boats and life rafts, then liners and small towns. If we can get the vaccine produced we can vaccinate the sub crews and that'll be another four thousand or so. We just...find people. And get the ones that want to help helping. We sort of dumped most of the people we found in the Caribbean on Statia. Most. Oh, you may know some princess named...Shit..." She stopped and pawed through her notebook. "I just call her Rapunzel... long story...Julianna Gustavason?"

"Julianna survived," Harry said, nodding. "That is good to hear."

"Also some other actresses and stuff," Faith said. "Found them on St. Barts. Anna Holmes for one. Anna's actually along on the float. But...the world is a very screwed up place. Just got to keep pushing the ball. The more people you have, the more you can do. We couldn't have done this two months ago. Well, we probably would have figured out a way. We do. Okay, I suppose I should start with:

"There are three command posts left, American, Russian and Chinese. American is the Hole in Omaha.

The NCCC is Under Secretary Galloway who was something like a hundred something on the list. Russian and Chinese are similar. You're the most senior people we've found of the Brits. We've got one former... congressman sort of? Like military police?"

"Member of Parliament?" Whiteshead asked. "MP?"

"That's it," Faith said. "One of them. Most of the subs were uncontaminated and they're closed up. They're surviving on fish. No serious land areas cleared. There are some people forming in various places but...you gotta have a lot of ammo to clear much land and even civilians in the U.S. don't have enough. And we got a lot, trust me. We had ten thousand rounds when we started and it burned up fast. My dad is LantFleet which is, yeah, part of the reason I'm an officer. The other reason is I've been doing this since right after the Fall and I'm getting okay at it, I suppose..."

CHAPTER 31

"Permission to poke my head in the cockpit?" Harry asked.

The last lift was going out. Staying behind were twenty Gurkhas and ten Warders. The Warders were all former military, all veterans and all determined that whatever happened, the Tower would remain in British hands.

"Grab the jumpseat," Colonel Kuznetsov said, pointing to it. "Colonel Nikifor Kuznetsov, Your Highness."

"Pleasure to meet you, Colonel," Harry said.

"Captain Milo Wilkes," Wilkes said. He was piloting the bird. "Pleasure to have you aboard, sir."

"Very glad to be out of there, Captain," Harry said. "I shouldn't feel that way but being trapped like that was . . . unsettling."

"You're the first people we've pulled out of a city," Wilkes said. "It's . . . unpleasant. I can't believe the fire damage."

"It is . . . worse than I'd realized," Harry said, looking at the torched landscape. "But there are survivors."

"A few, sir," Wilkes said, pointing to the side with his chin. "We've passed this group three times. I'm sure they're getting annoyed."

"Can we pick them up?" Harry asked.

"I'm going to request we be allowed to as a supplementary mission from the colonel, sir," Wilkes said. "That one, at least. But not right now we can't. From the looks of it, we'd have to winch someone down and then winch them back up. We can do it. We have the equipment. But it's not part of the primary mission."

"With a helo and some support we could pick up pretty much everyone," Harry said. "Most of them had to access rooftops to survive."

"Like Katrina," Wilkes said, nodding. "I didn't work it but I knew people who did. Marine Reserve picked up more people than the Coast Guard. But it would take a lot of support. You'd need somewhere to keep them, food, and . . . Lots of logistics, sir."

"There is that," Harry said, grinding his teeth. "But these are my people, Colonel. In a very real sense. It's possible I'm their sovereign if the reports of Grand-mum's death are accurate. I need to *do* something."

"Take that up with higher, sir," Wilkes said, banking around. "It's possible they'll support it. Or give you support to support it. Until the subs are vaccinated, though, we're sort of focused."

"You cleared in the Caribbean," Harry said.

"We were looking for vaccine materials, sir," Wilkes said. "Give me a moment, would you? Winds are tricky . . ."

"Welcome aboard, Captain," Colonel Hamilton said, shaking the prince's hand. "We're sort of crowded at the moment but we've got a room for you below. Although I'm sure you'd like to get some food in your belly..."

"We can do that," Hamilton said, nodding. "The one group, at least. I'll have Captain Wilkes schedule it for later this afternoon."

"Is there any possibility of staying in the area to do more recovery?" Harry asked. "That's an official question of the British government."

He was sipping soup. They'd been on very short rations for a very long time, and as other survivors had, he needed something light to start.

"Our first and primary mission is recovering some supplies from the London Research Center," Hamilton said carefully. "After that... it would be up to higher. But let me point out that what holds for London holds for every city in the world. There are survivors. There are survivors *everywhere*. With helos you can pick some of them up. But we only have two pilots, three with you, and one fully functioning helo. The other is ready for a test hop but... Logistics. Support. Especially for the helos. Do you have any other pilots?"

"No," Harry said, frowning. "We have one more helo, though. I flew it in on my own. It's tucked up against the wall in the Tower. Getting it fueled and supported, though... And it's not very good for rescue. It's a Lynx. Only a few people at a time."

"That's all you generally get, Captain," Hamilton said. "Hang on. Sergeant."

"Sir?" Sergeant Weisskopf said.

"Tell Captain Wilkes he's authorized to pick up the survivors spotted on the way to the Tower," Hamilton said. "Assuming the bird is still good. And he'll need a detail with it. Take Januscheitis and his team."

"Yes, sir," Weisskopf said, leaving the compartment.

"Thank you, Colonel," Harry said.

"It's not outside our parameters," Hamilton said, frowning. "There should be something we can do . . . I hate to do this. PFC!"

"Sir?"

"Get Shewolf and Seawolf in here," Hamilton said.

"Shewolf was the young lieutenant we met at the Tower, sir?" Captain Whiteshead asked.

"And her sister, Sophia," Hamilton said. "They are . . . green as grass and yet far more experienced at this than I am."

"And . . . cold, sir?" Harry said. "She seemed very . . . flat."

"Faith is . . ." Hamilton said. "You'll have to see the introduction to Wolf Squadron video to even begin to comprehend either one of them. And it really doesn't cover it."

"You sent for me, sir?" Sophia said, sticking her head in the door.

"Grab a seat, Ensign," Hamilton said. "Have you met Captain Whiteshead and Captain . . . Wales . . . ?"

"Can the platform on the *Social Alpha* handle that other chopper?" Faith said as the conversation paused. She'd spent most of the last ten minutes sitting with her mouth shut, leaning on her hand.

"Yes," Prince Harry said. "Probably."

"Whatever," Faith said. "Reinforce it. The *Grace*

has got a machine shop. You can fly the helo off from there or at least support it."

"That is a point," Colonel Hamilton said. "Assuming we're willing to give up the *Social Alpha*."

"Dad will dump that ghost-ridden tug in a heartbeat, sir," Faith said. "Trust me, he likes it about as much as I do. Eventually, you'll need somewhere bigger to put people. And you need to be able to feed them.

"What you need is a cruise ship that's not too wrecked. Bottom line, you want no more than one direction the infected can attack and if you can get out on water you're golden. You're going to need supplies. There are fricking boats alongside, wrecked, drifting, every way from Sunday. Salvage. You got supplies. Not sure about helo supplies. Don't know about that. But you can do it. *We* can't do it. *You* can do it. It's just a matter of doing it.

"If we take a liner, we can show your Gurkhas and the new Dutch Marines the Wolf Way of Clearance Fu and get a liner for you to use at the same time. Of course, they take a bit of clean-up, but that's the breaks. For ammo and even helo parts I'm sure we can get a shipment up to you from time to time. Or you can come back to Gitmo and do pretty much the same on the other side of the Atlantic. Up to you. Sirs."

"Sounds like the first thing we need is a not-too-damaged liner," Whiteshead said after a moment.

"Saw one alongside in some docks just upriver," Faith said. "Of course, it's alongside in a city. A really *big* city. But you can probably use it. You just got to do some serious scrumming to get the main hatches closed," she ended with a feral grin.

"We don't have gunboats to support you this time, Sis," Sophia pointed out.

"Where'd we put them fifties?" Faith said. "We made the other ones right here on the *Grace*."

"You are suggesting clearing a liner which is *alongside*, Lieutenant?" Hamilton asked. "Tied to a dock."

"It'll be easy compared to most of the stuff we've done, sir," Faith said. "Among other things, this time I don't have to climb over the side. We can *slide* down, sir."

"I thought you didn't like air-assault," Sophia said.

"Beats climbing up into a scrum over shark-filled water," Faith said. "Beats it all hollow."

"I'd have to check on changing the mission orders," Hamilton temporized. "And only after the main mission is complete."

"Understood, Colonel," Prince Harry said. "If it is possible... It would be a great aid to the British people."

"We'll look at the feasibility," Hamilton said. "After the main mission is complete. Lieutenant, Ensign, get your final preparations for tomorrow's mission done, then get some rack time. Tomorrow is *not* going to be a walk in the park. Even Washington Square."

"You rang, Colonel?" Steve said. It was earlier in the day in Gitmo and while Hamilton had put off replying on the prince's plan, he was interested in the answer as well.

"His Royal Highness brought up some points in our first meeting I thought you should be aware of, sir," Hamilton said.

"Which are?" Steve asked.

The colonel gave a quick précis of the discussion before asking, "Not do you approve the notional plan or disapprove, sir," Hamilton said. "I'm wondering what you think?"

"With some rather critical bits left out, you just covered Plan Sisyphus," Steve said, leaning back.

"The Greek legend of the man who was condemned to roll a ball up a mountain, sir?" Hamilton said.

"The same," Steve said. "Details you left out, not to mention getting ahead of yourself. Take about ten barges, lash them together. Cover in steel plates. Stick some containers onboard with housing and support. Anchor in the water source of the major city. You now have a helo-port that infected cannot access. Use a liner if you have one available as discussed to house the refugees. Otherwise find some land facility with strong defenses, such as the Tower of London, to do so. I'd suggest using the Tower until you have a liner cleared. But that is the simplest synopsis of Plan Sisyphus."

"That won't clear all the cities in the world, sir," Hamilton said.

"Ninety percent of the major cities in the world are on a navigable waterway, Colonel," Steve said. "Some of them will be difficult to get to, but they're mostly on water. It's practically a requirement to be a major city.

"With enough helos or time, you should be able to rescue ninety percent of the survivors in a major city. Which in the case of, say, London, will require more than one liner. To do it, you'll need some trained personnel. Since you're not focusing on boat crews, as we were at sea, you'll need a core of trained personnel to train the willing. Which is why I need the sub crews.

"No disrespect to people like Staff Sergeant Januscheitis, but what takes six weeks to learn for your average aviation mechanic is a *week's* class for a nuclear machinist's mate. They're simply a different breed of cat. They can absorb the information at phenomenal rates. Their primary purpose won't even be wrench turners. Their primary purpose will be ensuring that newly minted helicopter mechanics are doing the job *right*. There's not enough sub crews in the world to maintain all the helicopters we're going to need. And we need them for other tasks.

"You'll also need more helos and more helo pilots. And a better, more mobile, platform would be useful. I said—Jesus, it seems like years ago but it was in my first serious discussion with the Hole—that I'm going to need the *Iwo Jima* and lots of helicopters. Now you know why. Questions?"

"Am I the only person you've discussed this with, sir?" Hamilton asked curiously.

"You, my wife and Mr. Walker," Steve said. "He was the one who suggested the helo barge. I was still at your plan or using the deck of a ship. He also extensively critiqued my written version. I'm starting to lose patience with 'just leave him alone.' I need his brains and experience, whoever he is or was. *Whatever* he is or was. Anything else?"

"Should I authorize the mission?" Hamilton asked. "Getting ahead of myself, sir."

"As long as the primary one succeeds," Steve said. "With the caveat that until we've built up the right force structure, the prince is going to be more or less on his own. All we'll be able to supply is some parts, not as many as he'll need, and some ammo. Starting an area and then having it bootstrap itself is *part* of the plan. Wolf Squadron, the U.S. Navy, the entire pre-Plague U.S. military were it still extant, cannot make a dent in clearing the world. Every nation will have to bootstrap itself. All we can do is give them the seeds. But we still need the sub crews to have any chance of even that succeeding. So we are back to the primary mission. What are your thoughts?"

"If they can access and close the doors," Hamilton said, "I think they'll be able to clear the building, sir. If they cannot . . . Abort. We also don't know if the materials are available."

"Positive thinking has long been shown to have an effect far beyond the strictly rational," Steve said. "Some quantum physicists argue that sufficiently large belief can move a sufficiently small mountain. In other words: Don't take counsel of your fears. You will succeed. We always do. After which we get a *more* impossible mission," he added with a grin. "Wolf out."

CHAPTER 32

In the beauty of the lilies Christ was born across the sea,
With a glory in His bosom that transfigures you and me:
As He died to make men holy, let us die to make men free,
While God is marching on.

(CHORUS)

—"The Battle Hymn of the Republic"

"Think you have enough weapons, Lieutenant?" Hamilton asked, looking at Faith's rig-out.

Faith was rigged up the way she'd been since the *Voyage Under Stars*, now with more ammo. She had three pistols, twenty magazines for those, Saiga, forty magazines stuck absolutely *everywhere*, grenades in pouches, kukri, trench knife, half a dozen other knives tucked in various places including hanging off of magazines, Halligan tool and machete strapped to her assault ruck, and Trixie staring out of the back of the ruck.

"This is going to take some serious clearance, sir," Faith said, squirting some CLP into the action of her Saiga and cycling it. Then she tucked Trixie into the ruck all the way and zipped the top. "I'm pretty sure this is going to be all hands. If I bring any of the ammo back you can take it out of my pay, sir."

501

"Oorah," Hamilton said. "The real question is can you handle the fast rope with that much weight?"

"Just watch me, sir," Faith said, tapping the helmet cam she was wearing. Due to the questions about what, exactly, they were supposed to be looking for and where it might be, all of the Marine "leadership" down to team leaders were wearing helmet cams.

"I shall be," Hamilton promised. "Let the grunts take the lead, Lieutenant. That is their job."

"There's a time to lead from the back and a time to lead from the front, sir," Faith said. "When I need to lead from the front, sir, I am going to lead from the front, sir. With all due respect, sir."

"Understood," Hamilton said. "But you can't lead from either position if you're dead."

"Zombies don't bother me, sir," Faith said, dimpling cutely. "They're insane, hungry, angry animals. They won't kill me from professional courtesy, sir."

"Mr. Walker," Sophia said uncomfortably, as the "civilian" walked out of *Grace* in full clearance rig. Somewhere, he'd found a complete set of Army combat gear. Instead of bunker gear he was wearing Army camouflage rain gear, Army kevlar helmet and body armor. He had at *least* as many weapons and as much ammo as Faith. And an H&K 416 instead of M4. "I don't remember including you on the mission plan."

"Ensign?" Walker said. "You know that at some level I outrank you, right? And you need the help. Both in looking for the materials and as a shooter. You're not questioning my abilities as a shooter are you, Ensign?"

"No, I'm not," Sophia said. "I'm questioning your age . . . sir."

"I think I've got one last battle in me, Ensign," Walker said, grinning. "Ever heard the line that 'a general should die with the last bullet of the last war'?"

"No . . . sir?" Sophia said.

"Remember it. It is appropriate to the situation."

"This is a big one!" Faith boomed as the chopper cycled up. "As always, when possible, let the zombies come into *your* fire zone, don't *sneak* into theirs. But do not allow that to stop you moving forward. WE NEED TO SECURE THIS BUILDING. Hit them! Hit them hard! Keep hitting them! MARINES ARE THE FINEST SHOCK TROOPS ON EARTH AND TODAY YOU GET TO *PROVE* IT! The Marine battle cry 'Oorah' dates all the way back to when we took the fortress of the Bey of Tripoli. 'Urah' is Turkish for *'Blood!'* And if you don't want to *drink the blood of the infected,* Marines, THEN YOU ARE IN THE WRONG UNIT! IT'S *SCRUMMIN'* TIME!"

"OORAH!"

"OOORAH!" Faith shouted, sliding down the fast-rope. There were infected pouring onto the roof but that was what a Saiga was made for.

She dropped off the rope and went to pistol since it was faster, targeting the infected and backing away from the rope to let Sergeant Weisskopf have room to land.

Fire started to pour in from the door gunner on the Seahawk. They'd gotten the helo into operation overnight and Captain Wilkes and Colonel Kuznetsov had split duties with Harry taking the copilot position on the Super Stallion. The combined fire of the landed Marines and the machine gun quickly had the roof cleared.

She dropped the pistol and went Saiga, pumping out shotgun rounds until the last infected was cleared.

"MOVE!" Faith bellowed while reloading, her voice muffled by the gas mask. "DOOR, DOOR, DOOR!"

Speed was paramount. The door was the choke point and taking that was just about the most important portion of the mission. They had to fight their way down to the bottom floor, find all the doors and get them closed so they could clear the massive research facility. But first they had to take the high ground.

"Weapon, ma'am," Sergeant Weisskopf said, picking up her .45.

"Thanks, Andy," Faith said as the lead squad piled up on the door. They were pouring fire into the interior but clearly not making much headway.

"CLEAR!" Faith yelled, charging the doorway, kukri in one hand and a grenade in the other. "IT'S SCRUMMIN' TIME!"

She hit the infected at the top of the stairs at chest height, knocking him over and riding him down the avalanche of bodies following him. With only her own mass it probably wouldn't have worked. Another hundred plus pounds of ammo and guns did the trick. She took out a throat at the same time as she pulled the pin on the grenade and tossed it over the side of the stairs down to the other landing. The fragments from a grenade in such a confined space should have bounced all over the place. Instead, they were caught by the press of bodies below.

Then she got down to some *serious* scrumming...

∽⊖∾

"Oh, good Lord," Hamilton said, holding his head in his hands. "I knew I should have gone along."

Of course, it was now hard to *see* out of Faith's helmet cam since it had immediately splashed red.

"We are *missing* this!"

Since Faith's exploits tended to be a bit of a morale boost, if not for the squeamish, the helmet cam videos were available for public view. And the Gurkhas had decided to see who this child was who carried a kukri as if she was due and was going to "instruct" them on clearance.

"I can go to war!" Lance Corporal Ombahadur Ghale shouted. "I can fight! Let us go to *war*!"

"There will be war aplenty to come," Sergeant Jitbahadur Rai said. "We must regain our strength to fight these battles. And if this is the way of such war...A great war it shall be! Oooiya Ghorkali! Look at her *go*!"

"Oooh," Lieutenant Commander Tuttle, commander of the *Louisville*, said as Faith swung a Halligan tool into an infected's crotch. "*That* had to hurt...."

The video was sent without sound. Only the leadership was on the broadcast which had been upgraded to continuous two way. So Colonel Hamilton, along with any "higher" who wished to listen in, was getting Faith's usual running commentary. And he was starting to wonder if she really *enjoyed* being an officer...

"You want some? How's this for a mission plan! Action plan my fucking ass, you bastards! Sure, here's

an acronym for you! And you! I'll PowerPoint you, asshole! There, I just transynergized your fucking head! *It's time for BUZZWORD BINGO MOTHER-FUCKERS...!"*

"Your daughter scares me, Captain," Under Secretary Galloway said quietly.

"She scares me, sir," Steve said. "But she is well suited to the present situation."

"Oh, screw this," Januscheitis said. They'd dropped a few grenades over the side but they couldn't fire into the mass swarming the lieutenant. "I'm going in..."

He pulled himself up on the railing and dropped off onto the lower stair. It would have been a bone-headed move dropping nearly a story, sure to bust an ankle if not his neck, but he was cushioned by the tide of infected. Not to mention all the bodies, blood and guts.

"IT'S SCRUMMIN' TIME...!"

"Oh, hell, yeah!" Lance Corporal Freeman said, climbing up after him. "TIME TO HIT THE BEACH, MARINES!"

"Mr. Walker?" Gunnery Sergeant Sands said as the diminutive "technical expert" trotted past him. Most of the Marines were now clogged into the stairs, scrumming the zombies, creating a macroscopic version of antibodies fighting an infection.

"You're seriously going to *miss out* on this, Gunnery Sergeant?" Walker said, pausing to draw a trench knife. "What *has* the Marine Corps come to?"

"Well, when you put it *that* way," the gunny said,

pulling out a Ka-Bar. "Can't let the Army have the glory. After you, sir."

"Once more unto the breach, dear friend," Walker said, breaking into a sprint. "OR CLOSE THE STAIRS WITH OUR AMERICAN *DEAD*...!" Despite being nearly seventy and carrying as much weight as any of the Marines, the "civilian technical expert" cleared the rail in a bound and disappeared into the maelstrom below.

"Civilian, my ass," Gunny Sands growled. "LEAVE SOME FOR ME!"

"In retrospect," Faith said, sharpening her kukri, "we should have let them get up on the roof and machine-gunned them from the choppers."

It had taken nearly thirty minutes of scrumming to clear the top two floors of the stairs. And they were still coming up. While the rest of the Marines got their combat time in, Faith was sitting on a good zombie while ammoing back up and fixing assorted "issues" that had cropped up during the scrum. Like her kukri needing sharpening, and straightening out her machete.

"But sometimes it's just good to get your mad out," Faith added.

"Probably would have worked better, ma'am," Gunny Sands said, pouring some water into one of Faith's magazines to get it half-ass cleaned. "And I'm not sure it was precisely necessary to scrum the stairs, with all due respect, ma'am. Once we had the landing, we could have used firepower."

"Really, Gunnery Sergeant?" Walker said. "It would have been a superior choice to pour fire into a stairwell that is angled so as to bounce at least thirty percent of the fire back at your position? Especially given that five-five-six would pass through the bodies and continue to rebound?" He was honing his own blood-splattered trench knife.

"Which was what I was thinking, believe it or not," Faith said, looking over at him curiously.

"That is a point, sir, ma'am," Gunny Sands said thoughtfully.

"You just did it 'cause you enjoy scrumming, Faith," Sophia said. She'd stayed out.

"Well, that too," Faith said, standing up and putting away her kukri. "But I think I got one of my filters clogged with blood. That's a first."

"And the colonel sent that he'd appreciate it if you could wash off your helmet-cam, Faith," Mr. Walker said.

"Where's my water bottle . . . ?"

Hamilton reran the video from Faith's entry and considered how the rounds would have bounced around in the stairwell. Then he frowned.

"I hate when she's right," he muttered.

Dr. Rizwana Shelley had wanted to see the conditions of London so she had accessed the camera video as soon as the group left the boat. The young lieutenant and one of her sergeants had spent the flight at the back of the helicopter which had given an unfortunately complete view of the conditions. Idly—and if truth be told, somewhat morbidly—curious, she had continued to watch as the assault took place.

So far she had only thrown up once. But she had not stopped watching.

∽ ⊖ ∾

"There's no doors to close, ma'am," Januscheitis radioed.

"Say again, over?" Faith said, holding her earbud to try to hear over the continuous fire. She was firing a pistol one-handed while she held it.

The fricking infected were swarming from EVERY-WHERE. Every corridor was choked with them and the Marines were literally having to wade through the bodies. They also were clocking out on ammo.

The gunny and Walker were back to back pouring fire in both directions. She'd heard her sister talking about the "civilian shooter" who turned out to have been "someone" but even Sophia had never seen him in a *serious* battle. The little shrimp was a fucking *machine*. Every shot was a head shot; he was getting pretty much thirty infected for every magazine. Even the *Gunny* wasn't that good. 'Course, it was good he *was* a machine, since there were *too many* fucking infected. Finally the latest tide receded but they could hear more closing in.

"This building has all glass at the bottom, ma'am," the staff sergeant radioed. You could hear continuous fire from Condrey's Singer in the background. None of this "five-round burst" shit. *"We've gained the lobby. Multiple panes are gone, ma'am. They're pouring in. Estimate over one thousand infected in view, street is choked.... We're only holding this balcony 'cause of the two-forty."*

"Seahawk," Faith said, thinking about the map. "I need fire on all approaching infected on St. John Street. All teams, this is an abort; hold positions, prepare to extract. Anybody stuck?"

"Team six," Hooch called. *"We're on the third floor,*

east. We've got overwhelming force both ways and we're clocking out."

"All teams, move towards third floor, east to extract team six," Faith said.

"Belay that order, Lieutenant," Hamilton said, cutting in on the command channel. *"Pull your teams out and head for the roof."*

"Stand by, all teams. Hold current positions," Faith said, switching frequencies and reloading at the same time.

"Sir," Faith said. "Did you just override your ground commander, sir?"

"You need to extract what you can, Lieutenant," Hamilton said. *"With the entire ground floor open to infiltration there are approximately six million infected heading to your location and you cannot fight that, Lieutenant. When you're down to fifty Marines, total, 'leave no Marine behind' is not the way to handle it. As your father said, we cannot afford an Iwo Jima. You need to extract while you still can."*

"Understood your order, sir," Faith said, scrabbling for a magazine. "Understood the reasoning. Do not concur. We *can* push to Hooch's position. I'm on fourth floor, central. I can make it. So can Janu and the Dutch Marines. We assemble on his position, cross-load ammo and blow our way to the roof. We *can* do this, sir. And, sir, if we lose every last Marine in this building, sir, you just got an infusion of seventy Gurkhas, sir. People *die*, sir. But honor does not. And if we don't have honor, sir, what do we have *left*? A planet of death and misery and blood and shit. That's all we've got, sir. And if that's all we've got, what's the fucking *point*? If you want to throw my HONOR on that pile, sir, I respectfully resign my commission, sir. And I will fucking well fight my way through to Hooch BY MYSELF!"

"Lieutenant, I appreciate your passion. The order stands. Gunnery Sergeant Sands, if the lieutenant does not obey the order, you will remove her from the building by force if necessary."

"Like *hel*—!" Faith started to scream when Walker shut off her radio then caught her arm before she could strike back.

"Belay that," Walker said quietly.

Faith, under the best of circumstances barely capable of discipline, dropped her arm and nodded.

"Yes, sir," Faith said, looking at him curiously.

"Mr. Under Secretary, are you up on this frequency?"

"Yes," Galloway replied.

"Ensign, turn your helmet cam on *me*," Walker said, just as quietly. His demeanor had changed to anything *but* laid-back. Despite wearing Army gear, until that moment he'd still been "Mr. Walker," surprisingly good at all sorts of things, especially combat, but in some fashion easy to overlook. Unless you knew him, you hardly noticed him.

Now, he seemed to fill the corridor. Barely five two, he suddenly seemed taller, broader. Without any discernible change, he was suddenly the center of attention.

He reached into a pouch and started pulling out velcro patches, slapping them rapidly onto spots on his armor and uniform. Pathfinder, Master Parachutist's Badge, Scuba Badge. Combat Infantry Badge, two stars. Joint Special Operations patch, left shoulder. An odd and very rare patch that looked a bit like the SAS badge, right shoulder.

Last, he pulled out two strips of cloth and slapped one on his helmet and one on the front of his body armor.

Each strip bore three black stars.

"Activating at this time, Mr. Under Secretary," the lieutenant general said. "Assuming command of this mission."

"General on deck!" Gunnery Sergeant Sands said.

"As you were," the general replied, potting an infected offhand, left-handed, while returning the salute. "That means cover us while we work this plan, Gunnery Sergeant."

"Do I get to know who this general is who just popped up in my command, ma'am?" Steve said. "You said you were aware of him."

"Lieutenant General Carmen Montana," General Brice said, speaking rapidly. "Handle: Skaeling, Translation: 'He who walks as death in the night.'

"Seventeen years enlisted Army Special Operations, mostly Delta, directly promoted captain from sergeant major after Mogadishu. Actions in Mog still classified, awarded Distinguished Service Cross to be considered for upgrade to Medal of Honor after declassification. Additional twenty years officer. Former commands: Delta Force, Fifth Special Forces Group, Joint Anti-Terrorism Task Force, Army War College, and Joint Special Operations Command. Turned down SOCOM and retired. More medals than Audie Murphy. Speaks something like thirty languages fluently. Parachuted solo into Dagestan under cover on Nine-Twelve. He was sixty-three at the time. The rest would take hours. Questions?"

"No, ma'am," Steve said. "Not even terribly surprised."

"Bottom line: He outranks everyone but Mr. Galloway. Pre-Plague Joint Chiefs and SecDefs stood up when Night Walker entered the room. *I'm* not going to argue with him because I *know* he knows what he's doing."

"You're a *vice admiral?*" Sophia spluttered. "*Sir?* I was thinking chief, maybe colonel!"

"Lieutenant general, Ensign," said "Walker," reloading. "My last name is actually Montana. My *first* name is *General*. Do you *understand* that, Colonel?"

"*Yes, sir,*" Hamilton radioed.

"Primary mission abort," General Montana said. "Do need to extract. *No one* left behind. *Shall* make it out. *All* of us. Time to unpack my adjectives. Lieutenant Smith, call the plan: They know your voice."

"Yes, *sir!*" Faith said, changing back to the platoon frequency. "All teams fifth floor and above, move to the roof and extract by helo. All teams below fifth floor, converge on floor three, east. If you get stuck, don't worry, take open order, lie down and sit tight. We *will* come for you..."

There wasn't a thing that Steve could do to support his children in the maelstrom. Which he had become as comfortable as any father was ever going to get about long ago. So he picked up the phone and dialed a number.

"Medical Wing, Nurse Black speaking."

"Tina, could you please get me Lieutenant Fontana if he's available?"

"Yes, sir. One moment, please."

"Fontana."

"Turns out Walker's a lieutenant general?"

"Guess he decided to break cover, Captain?"

"Yes. You knew?"

"Duh. *Everybody* in SF knew Night Walker. It's like asking a Marine 'have you ever heard of some guy named Chesty Puller?' Or, you know, Audie Murphy, Alvin York, Patton...Except nobody without a TS was supposed to know his name. It's why he turned down SOCOM. It was a publicly posted position. That and it was all politics."

"And you never even *thought* to mention this? I mean, the first time you met him, you didn't even *blink*, Falcon."

"Of course not. It was *Night Walker*, Steve. *And* under cover. Of *course* I didn't blow his cover. He'd have *killed* me. It's an SF thing. You wouldn't understand..."

"This is probably a stupid order, COB," Commander Vancel, skipper of the attack sub *Alexandria* said. "But I don't want book on this one. Not this one."

"The guys already shut it down, sir," the chief of boat said seriously. "And, with respect, sir, until they get out, or don't, pretty much everything's shut down but reactor watch, sir."

"Approved," Vancel said. "Please God, they make it out. I don't know how we'd keep up morale without the Bobbsey twins."

One by one, the helmet cams of the leadership, and then the radios, succumbed to continual scrums with infected. Along the way, however, the viewers got a new appreciation for the word "fury" watching the combination of Night Walker and Shewolf. The helmet cameras of the whole group had to be doused down frequently as the seventy-something general and the "almost fourteen, damnit!" lieutenant cleared corridor after corridor, room after room, again and again.

Night Walker turned out to have a lot of adjectives he hadn't unpacked. No single human could carry the entire battle, but the phrase "freak of nature" was applicable. The general had immense natural talent and nearly forty years experience of bringing death and destruction to America's enemies. Single-handedly, the diminutive septuagenarian added at least the weight of another platoon. And if his age showed at all, no one could tell the difference. Even the gunny couldn't keep up.

If this was to be the last battle of the Night Walker, it was an achievement to equal any in history.

After two hours the last word that higher had was link-up with Sergeant Hocieniec's Team Six. But Sergeant Weisskopf's team in Fourth floor South was cut off by then. When Weisskopf went into a scrum and his radio was ripped off his gear, that was the last transmission.

The helos continued to circle. Infected were being drawn by the sound from all over London and St. James Street and Pentonville Road were piling up with bodies. The Seahawk RTBed once for gas and ammo and to drop the Marines it had picked up, then returned. And still there was no sign of the rest of the party. Just more and more infected crowding in. Many of them were stopping in the street to feast but others seemed drawn to the sound of conflict in the building and were wading through the fire from the helos to close with the embattled unit.

Finally, eight hours after entry and six hours after the last transmission, a sole blood-covered Marine stepped out of the door carrying another Marine on his back.

But he was followed by more.

In ones and twos, bloodied and battered Marines stumbled out onto the roof and took up defensive positions around the door. Most of them didn't have functioning weapons anymore. M4s were bent. Knives were gone. Many of them had pistols in their hands, gripped by the barrels, that had obviously been used as clubs. Some of them were stumbling out and hitting the deck, flaccid in exhaustion. But they were all alive. Helmets were missing. Some of them might have bites. A few were badly wounded. Sophia's team, less General Montana, burst out in a group. Sophia staggered away from the door, took off her respirator and helmet, threw up, then staggered away a few feet and lay flat out on the roof. Olga just hit the deck facedown.

Thirty Marines, four Navy and "The General" had been left below and Hamilton slowly got a head count. There was a steady trickle. Two, ten, twenty, twenty-five . . .

"Seahawk, prepare to give cover fire," Hamilton said as a burst of Marines blew out of the door. "Try to keep the infected from getting on them when they're boarding."

"Roger," Colonel Kuznetsov radioed. "Standing by."

Finally, Gunny Sands, Januscheitis and General Montana exited the door. Januscheitis was missing his helmet and most of one ear. Sands' gear was definitely not parade ground and a Marine gunnery sergeant had done the unthinkable and left his rifle somewhere in the building. The general was covered in blood but other than that seemed to be unaffected. And still fighting.

General Montana hacked expertly at the arms of infected using a machete he hadn't started with while Gunny Sands and Januscheitis dragged the furious lieutenant out of the stairwell by the back of her combat harness. Faith was missing her helmet, too, her gear was torn and ripped by teeth marks and she had a cut on her cheek. But she was still slashing the infected holding onto her with her kukri. As Hamilton watched, she cut off two of the half dozen hands pawing her gear.

She was the last. That was every single person who had entered the building.

There was a distant cheer and he realized the entire boat must be watching the video.

Marines piled into the door with anything they had left: Halligan tools, machetes, bent M4s, prizing the infected off their lieutenant. Then the entire group, directed by General Montana, managed to push the door closed against the mass of zombies, jamming it with anything to hand.

Faith kicked the door several times, then pushed through the Marines until she found one that had a remaining grenade. She walked back to the door, pulled the pin, pushed the grenade through the gap, cut off another hand to get free, then walked away. There was a brief blast of additional blood and tissue out of the gap.

Then she took off her assault ruck and pulled something out. It was a bright blue plastic package. She held it up to the helos and started dancing as the rest of the teams pulled similar packages out and held them up. Everyone had them. With no ammo in their rucks, there had been plenty of room. A quick estimate was that they were carrying a couple of hundred pounds of what had to be polyacrylamide gel powder. More than enough for all the vaccine they needed for the subs.

"I'll be God-damned," Hamilton breathed.

EPILOGUE

"Liiiisten Up, maggots! This is DEVIL DOG RADIO, an official station of the You-nited States government, transmitting from sunny and zombie-free Guantanamo Bay. To catch all you yardbirds up on what's been going on in the world since the Fall . . ."

From: *Collected Radio Transmissions of The Fall*
Last listed transmission of this compilation
University of the South Press 2053

"I hope like hell you can get this stuff started fast," Faith said, stepping out of the decontamination shower on the deck of the *Grace Tan*. She'd carried a couple of the, fortunately waterproof, packages, and Trixie, in with her to get the blood off them. It had soaked right through their assault rucks. "We've got bites. Janu got bit."

Like rabies, the H7D3 infection could be fought off with continuous injections of vaccine. If you had enough vaccine. Most of the Marines had been exposed and were probably immune. But probably wasn't certainly.

"If I can still stand," Sophia said wearily. "Jesus. Sis, I take back any jokes I've made about you and clearance. You can *have* it. And if I can remember the process this tired. *You* need some, obviously."

"H7 doesn't like me, remember?" Faith said. "I'm

519

not so sure about some of the rest of my guys. They might be immune, they might not. And I'm not losing Janu. I'm not, Sophia. I'll help." She wrung Trixie until the water ran red on the deck.

"You may not be able to make it, Ensign," Dr. Rizwana Shelley said, walking up and holding her hand out for a package. "*I* can. And test it. And make sure it's right. I've already started the lab up. All I needed was the gel. And, of course, the biological material."

"I take it you've decided to assist, Doctor?" Sophia said.

"Yes," Dr. Shelley said. "Entirely."

"What changed your mind?" Sophia asked.

"Your sister's helmet camera," Dr. Shelley said. "Not the fight. Or that as well, perhaps. The destruction. The devastation. It is not necessary to have an additional flight to check on my daughter. Her neighborhood is gone. *Everything* is gone. It has all been destroyed. Not, truly, by people, even insane people. By this horrid disease. Which must be ended. Forever. Whatever it takes."

"Good thing we brought back some nice fresh spines," Faith said, pulling a plastic bag out of her soaking assault ruck. "You might want to wear gloves."

"I'll grind them for you," Sophia said, taking the ziplock bag. "I've done worse."

"That, right there, is a beautiful sight," Steve said as the crew of the SSGN USS *Florida* started landing at the pier in Guantanamo. Dr. Shelley had a full lab set up in the *Grace Tan*, still anchored in the Thames, and was cranking out vaccine like there was no tomorrow. Among other things, if the Marines might be a bit squeamish about stripping out the spines of infected, Gurkhas had no problems with it. And there was a copious quantity of available infected in London. As well as survivors.

Subs were proceeding to the Thames to pick up their vaccine and then delivering it wherever it was needed. And at "in excess of 20 knots," attack subs could deliver it all over the world in record time. The crew of the *Florida* had been subsisting on coconut and fish, and not much of either, for most of the last year on a desert island in the Indian Ocean. There was the best meal the cooks in Gitmo could make for them awaiting their arrival. And the *Alexandria* was alongside taking on stores, the crew as thin as death camp survivors but pitching in with a will. They had more missions to accomplish and now at least they had supplies to do it.

General Montana had declined to take command from either General Brice or Steve. He had taken a voluntary demotion to colonel, "'cause colonel's more fun than being a general," and was slated to move to the Pacific as CINCPAC as soon as all the subs were vaccinated. He and his command team were going to take one of the SSGNs for the voyage.

Nobody was arguing.

"Over a thousand survivors from London alone," Stacey said, holding Steve's hand. "Four thousand sub crewmen. And seventy Gurkhas."

"Survivors self-extracting in the sub-arctic," Steve said, looking out at the rising sun. "About to have a baby boom. All the boat corpsmen are about to be very busy. We're pulling out of the dive, finally. Now we can really get started. Now we can fly . . ."

THE BEGINNING

❧━━━━━━━━━━━━━━━━━━━━❧

He is coming like the glory of the morning on the wave,
He is Wisdom to the mighty, He is Succour to the brave,
So the world shall be His footstool, and the soul of Time His slave,
Our God is marching on.

(CHORUS)

Glory, glory, hallelujah!
Glory, glory, hallelujah!
Glory, glory, hallelujah!
Our God is marching on.

—"The Battle Hymn of the Republic"